# THE WICKED DEAD

## THE TOME OF BILL - 7

## RICK GUALTIERI

# COPYRIGHT © 2015 RICK GUALTIERI



Edited by Megan Harris:
**www.mharriseditor.com**

Cover by Damonza at
**www.damonza.com**

Proofread by BZ Hercules:
*www.bzhercules.com*

Published by Freewill Press

# DEDICATION

*For that circle of close friends I keep. You may be small in number, but you mean the world to me. You inspire me, listen to me vent when I have to, and smack me upside the head when I need it.*

# ACKNOWLEDGEMENTS

*Special thanks to my awesome alpha and beta crews – Alissa, Ruby, Solace, Chris, Evgenia, Matt, Adam, Scott, Angela, Don, and Jim. I couldn't have done this without your help. You pimp-slapped this story into line, kept me grounded, and also helped remind me that Wolverine's claws go SNIKT, not SNICKT.*

# PROLOGUE
## DESTINY'S BITCH

How the hell did I end up here?

Not in this actual place, mind you. That one is pretty damn easy. I mean, I live here – not actually in the bathroom, of course. I'm talking *here* in a metaphysical sense anyway.

See, not too long ago, I died and was resurrected as one of the fiendish ... err ... fiends of the night – the nosferatu, which I'm pretty sure is a movie name and not a scientific classification. In laymen's terms, I got bitten and woke up as a vampire.

That was fucking weird enough, but it was only the tip of the iceberg. Things snowballed from there, all the way to a problem that sorta concerns the end of the world. Pretty heady stuff for a guy whose typical weekend used to involve little more than getting shitfaced.

Sadly, there's a supernatural war raging, one fated to lead to an end state not entirely dissimilar to the Biblical Armageddon.

It gets even better. Through actions not entirely my fault,

I am afforded the *privilege* of receiving credit for starting this war. Go me!

But that's not all. According to a bunch of dusty old scrolls – ones that I'm not even allowed to read – I'm supposed to be a major player in its outcome.

All in all, it's a nightmare I can't seem to wake up from.

It wasn't supposed to be like this. I'm no hero. I'm just a...

Wait a second. Was I actually about to go off into a whining bitch-fest about never asking for any of this? Ugh. That's it; I've become a fucking movie cliché. I might as well change my last name to Potter and resign myself to the fact that, no matter what I do, the dumbasses in charge will be too fucking stupid to stop anything without my stepping in and winning the Tri-wizard Tournament or some shit like that.

Any of a dozen movie plotlines run through my head, and they're all more or less the same: reluctant hero must believe in himself because destiny cannot be denied ... blah blah blah. Goddamn, are there no original stories left to tell? Oh well, at least most of them aren't musicals. According to my sixth-grade band teacher, if I was forced to play for my supper, I'd die a slow death by starvation.

Any way you look at it, I've been shoehorned into a role I don't want – especially right now. If anything, I have plenty of other shit to keep my mind occupied, some pretty good stuff at that.

Hell, two blonde goddesses live just one floor below me – either one of which I would be more than happy to call my girlfriend, lover, or chick who occasionally fucks my brains out but otherwise treats me like shit. One of them is a plucky, mind-scrambled vampire who, if attitude were ice cubes, could sink the fucking Titanic. The other is my former co-worker turned ancient enemy that I am destined to one day battle to the death. Shit, entire romance series have been written about crap like that.

Yet, with all that potential, I'm distracted from what should come naturally. I mean, I'm locked in a bathroom. Under normal circumstances, I'd be more than happy to indulge my imagination so as to take care of *business* – if you catch my drift.

Instead, I'm standing here looking at myself in the mirror – glancing fleetingly into my own eyes, knowing there might be something else inside of me staring back ... hell, almost daring it to.

*Almost*, anyway.

I'm still not sure I want to kick that particular nest too hard. It's one thing to be stung by a honeybee. Sure it hurts, but unless you're allergic, it's not the end of the world.

What lurks inside the deep reaches of my mind, though, is more the equivalent of those giant nightmare hornets they have in Japan. Hell, I wouldn't doubt those things are less insect and more a faction in this war. If I ever found myself standing between an angry Sasquatch and a swarm of those fuckers, I'd...

I shake my head to clear it. Distractions aren't particularly helpful when it comes to getting anything done, and I've always been more susceptible to them than most. Almost makes me wonder if my parents should've put my ass on Ritalin back when I was in grade school. Hell, it's not like I've never subscribed to the better living through chemistry trope. Why, I remember this one time Tom and I got so stoned, we...

I'm doing it again, aren't I? Seems to be the story of my life. Anyway, my point had nothing to do with any of that crap.

The truth for me is that it's all about fear. It always has been.

There have been so many things I've wanted in my life – some of those being more people than things – yet I've never wanted them badly enough to actually do anything substantial about it. It's always some excuse: I'm too busy, too shy, too dead ... *too afraid.*

That last one's the real kicker. I might as well throw all the other excuses out the window. No matter how many ass-kickings I got in school, bosses who have bitched me out at work, or horrors I've faced down since becoming one of the undead, there's always been one underlying factor. I've always been too afraid to do anything that could really move the needle.

A part of me wants to argue that's bullshit. Hell, in the past year alone, I've faced down nightmares that would make normal people shit themselves copiously. We're talking master vampires, assassins, rock monsters, Bigfoot, and even Gan. You'd think that would make me pretty darn brave, but I know better. That stuff was little more than a willingness to do whatever was necessary to keep breathing, all so I could eventually return here again and resume a life comfortably stuck in neutral.

I mean, have I taken the time to study vampire history and learn what I can? Aside from the prodding of others, have I taken it upon myself to train so as to best use my supernatural abilities? Hell, despite working with her for three years, dragging her into this war, and now living less than twenty feet above her, did I ever once sit Sheila down and do what should be the easiest thing in the world for a yappy fucker like me – talk?

Deep down, I know the answer to all of that.

I also know it won't get the job done this time.

Again, I stare at my reflection in the mirror, but this time I don't look away. My brain is too busy working overtime to process this little intervention I'm giving myself in my own bathroom – a bathroom that, quite frankly, could use a good bleaching.

Many of the movie plots running through my head share exactly what I'm thinking – heroes who were afraid to face their destinies, yet somehow got sucked into them anyway.

The more they fought against their fate, the stronger fate pulled them in. It's not much different with me, except that most fiction is a pleasant lie meant to make us feel good. In real life, reluctant heroes probably find little more than an early grave waiting for them at the end of their story.

And that's when a revelation hits me.

It's so simple, I'm tempted to slap the shit out of myself for not thinking of it sooner.

I look at myself and say, "Reverse psychology, you stupid motherfucker."

If I keep fighting against what needs to be done, I'll eventually find myself in a final showdown – one I very much doubt I'll win. I mean, destiny seems to love its fucking irony.

But what if I manned up? If that happened, maybe the universe wouldn't find my eventual fate so amusing. Maybe it would decide the Draculas and Sasquatches could clean up their own fucking mess without using me as their personal jizz mopper.

It sounds crazy and, quite frankly, somewhat stupid, but – according to my eleventh-grade economics teacher – the stupidest idea in the world realized will be infinitely more successful than the best idea that gets shelved because someone would prefer to sit on their ass instead.

Even if it doesn't work, it should sure as shit prepare me a whole lot better than just standing here in my bathroom talking to...

A loud knock on the door causes me to almost jump out of my skin.

"You okay in there, Bill?" Tom, one of my human room-mates, asks, a note of concern in his voice.

"Yeah," I reply, forcing myself out of my reverie.

"Good, because some of us need to take a shit, and your desk is starting to look mighty inviting."

Taking the time to wash my hands, I make him wait a few extra seconds as an unspoken "fuck you" of an answer.

I glance in the mirror one last time, my mind made up. There's a lot of work to be done – and some of it goes so far beyond borderline insane that it's gotten a green card and set up residence there.

Nevertheless, it's time I got to it.

# PART I

# BARTENDER IN TRAINING

"Anything?"

"Yeah." Sally held up her glass. "This needs more vodka."

"I'm not talking about the drink."

"Sorry. The only thing I can concentrate on right now is what a shitty bartender you make."

I grabbed the glass from her hand and stormed out of the room, grumbling numerous unkind words as her smirk followed me. Although her memories might still be scrambled, deep down, she was still Sally. That meant she'd quickly made a game out of her sessions with Christy, settling into a routine that was all about her. Christy would do the magical equivalent of entering my partner's head and rearranging the furniture, often exhausting herself in the process. Afterward, Sally would be the one demanding to be pampered for her *suffering* – refusing to cooperate until she was suitably mollified.

And yet, for some reason, I actually wanted her memories back. Hell, I was willing to do whatever it took to restore her.

I must've had rocks in my head.

I slammed the door shut behind me and let out a weary sigh. No, it wasn't rocks. There was something a lot heavier weighing me down.

Some days, I almost envied the older vampires. To them, power and station were everything. Pesky crap like emotions were too petty a thing for them to worry about. A callous, Vulcan-like attitude sure as shit sounded tempting lately. It would have made things a whole lot easier as I fumbled through the days – trying desperately to sort out my feelings for the women in my life.

I walked over to the kitchen nook, amazed at how life could sometimes hand you everything you ever wanted while still flipping you the finger.

Seriously, if you had told me even a few months ago I would live in the same building as Sheila, the girl I'd been pining after for years, I'd have done cartwheels up and down the halls. That was shit straight out of my best fantasies. Sure, her presence was out of necessity as we prepped for battle – one that we had no guarantee of walking away from alive – but those were just the pesky details.

Allowing myself to have feelings for Sally had muddied those waters, though. A small part of me kept screaming that it made no fucking sense. Sure, physically, Sally was a dream girl for most heterosexual males, but her attitude was enough to drive any sane person to drink. She was an alpha dog to the extreme. In many ways, the concept of just working with her was intimidating – much less doing anything of a more *intimate* nature.

In short, she was a threat to the manhood of any meat-eating, tough-guy male – much less me. She was smart enough to give her biting wit razor sharp teeth and tough enough to let her fists do the talking if need be. Hell, she was out of my league on so many levels that I shouldn't have even been allowed to watch her play.

All in all, there were enough red flags to make me run screaming. Yet, all of it had the opposite effect on me. I greatly respected her. She was strong even when she didn't have any reason to be, and she'd stuck by my side during moments when I wouldn't have blamed anyone for running for the hills.

My thoughts trailed off as I looked through the cabinets in the little nook. Where was that bottle of vodka? More importantly, why was I putting even a modicum of effort into finding it? Was I scrambling to top off a concoction of orange juice and blood in the hope that Sally would claim remembrance of something – *anything*?

Of course I was.

For the sake of our friendship alone, I'd have done that and more had it meant she remembered even a second of our past.

"Getting awfully dry in here!"

Bitch! Yeah, I definitely had rocks in my head.

Speaking of crazy concepts, though, I really had more pressing ones to focus on. The truth was, worrying about any potential relationship with either Sheila or Sally was a luxury I really didn't have.

The end of the world was nigh, but there was a good chance we wouldn't even live long enough to see it. We'd been busy planning an assault on the Boston Prefecture – the heavily fortified former nerve center of vampire activity in the Northeastern United States. That by itself would be tough enough, but it just got *better* from there. Assuming we got in, we'd have to battle our way through an unknown number of vampires, zombies, and god-knows-what-else to reach our true target: Vehron the Destroyer – a nickname not earned due to his fondness for naval vessels.

The whole part about him being a badass was right on target, don't get me wrong. The untruth was that my friends had actually been the ones planning things. I'd made myself scarce the past few days. Worry over Sally had been a part of it, but there had also been some planning of my own – considering a desperate course of action that I knew to be batshit crazy.

The others weren't pleased at me, thinking I was blowing them off. I couldn't blame them for that. After all, under any other circumstances, that's exactly what I would've been doing. This time, however, I'd been deep in thought, mulling the possibility of...

"I remember it all!"

Sally's cry caused my thoughts to scatter. Hope instantly filled me and I actually took a step toward the bedroom, bottle of Smirnoff Red in hand, before I stopped myself short. As much as I wanted to race to her side and confirm it to be true, I had to take care of one small bit of business first.

"What the fuck took you so long?" Sally asked, her tone betraying her irritation. "Were you out there playing with yourself? On second thought, don't answer that."

"Sorry." I stepped into her room and closed the door behind me.

"Didn't you hear what I said?"

"Of course I did." I smiled and crossed over to the side of the bed where she sat. "Tell me everything."

"I'd be happy to, but first..." She trailed off and lifted a hand, palm up.

"Yes, Your Highness." I handed her the now-full glass. "Will there be anything else?"

"I'm good, for now, at least."

"Great. So what did you remember?"

A smartass grin lit up her face. "Just that you were taking your sweet fucking time."

"Really?" I asked through gritted teeth. "That's it?"

"Yeah, but you know how these things go. Rome wasn't built in a day. You need to have some patience." She lifted the glass to her lips. "Being a little less gullible wouldn't hurt either."

I stepped back as she took a sip. My timing was impeccable. She immediately drenched the spot where I'd been standing just a moment earlier with the spray from her mouth.

"What the fuck?!" she cried, wiping her lips.

"I'd say I have the less gullible part down just fine, wouldn't you?" I ducked just as her glass sailed at me, missing and shattering against the wall instead. A few drops splattered my shirt, but it was worth it. "Oops, did I accidentally grab the vinegar instead of the vodka? Silly me. I'm always making that mistake."

She was up in a flash, eyes black and fangs descended. Normally, I'd have backed off. This time, though, I stood my ground, looking down at her despite knowing she wasn't even remotely intimidated by my greater height.

"Look at it this way. Obviously, I'm well versed in your shit. If that doesn't prove we know each other, I don't know what does." I'd barely finished the sentence when I instinctively brought my hands down to block the knee that was incoming. "See?"

To my surprise and relief, a ghost of a smile appeared on her face. "I guess I *have* been milking it a bit."

I held up a hand with my thumb and forefinger an inch apart. "Just a little."

All at once, the volume of her voice dropped, along with any attitude that had been in it. "I want to remember. Really I do." She blinked, and her eyes turned back to their normal dazzling green. I looked into them and could sense the confusion, desperation, and false bravery radiating from within her.

"I know, and believe me, I will do whatever I can..."

The door opened and Christy appeared. "Everything okay in here? I thought I heard something breaking."

"Sally just had an accident with her glass."

"Yeah," she replied, turning away from me, her attitude back in force. "I accidentally missed his head with it."

Christy stepped out into the living room where I stood waiting for her. She put her hands on her hips and looked at me disapprovingly. "Really? Do you have to start with her?"

"*Me?*"

"Are you trying to tell me you didn't?"

"Well..."

"I thought so." She turned back toward her bedroom.

"Wait."

"What, Bill? I'm tired." She had dark circles under her eyes. Mucking around in Sally's head, trying to undo the compulsion put there by Alex – quite possibly the strongest vampire on the planet – was difficult enough. That she was doing so while heavily pregnant was obviously adding extra strain.

Sadly, if I had my way, it wasn't going to get any easier for her.

I'd been putting off this talk long enough, busy debating with myself the downsides of my considered endeavor. I knew deep down, though, no matter how long I hemmed and hawed over things, there was only one logical conclusion. It was time to stop pretending I had a choice.

The chances of Sally getting her memories back before we

were forced to act were almost nil. Without her full faculties, she was at a disadvantage, and we'd be heading north with enough of those as it was. It was time to add a few plusses to our column for a change – or so I hoped.

I stepped away from Sally's room and beckoned Christy to follow.

She joined me with a sigh. "Listen, I'm sure this can wait until..."

"How's it going with her?" I asked in a whisper, hopefully low enough so prying ears couldn't hear me.

"You already know how it's going. You were just in there. We're uncovering bits and pieces, but it's one big jigsaw puzzle."

"You are making progress, though, right?"

Seeing that I wasn't backing down, she nodded and lowered her voice to match mine. "Yes. It's slow, but little by little, I'm making headway."

"So you know what you're doing in there?" I raised a finger and pointed it to my temple.

"That vampire did a job on her, but I'm no slouch when it comes to mind magic. But you know this already. I've told you as much."

"You're right. Just double checking."

"Is that why we're whispering?"

"Not quite." I stepped closer to her, my next words barely audible. "Could you do it to me?"

"What?"

"Could you go inside my mind and do the same thing?"

"In theory, but you're not missing any memories, so why would we even bother?"

"You're wrong," I replied, taking a deep breath. Oh well, in for a penny. "I'm missing three months of my life. That doesn't even count a big fight up in Canada and a battle with a bunch of Mongolian assassins, all of which are a blank for me."

For a moment, she looked confused, but then her eyes opened wide with understanding. "What are you asking me to do?"

"We're in a bad spot right now. We have the Draculas threatening us with their bullshit death sentence. We try to run and they'll find us. The way forward might be even worse. There's Vehron, all the vamps he's swayed to his side, the Jahabich, and then there's all that business with the White Mo..."

She grabbed my arm, her grip surprisingly strong. "Don't say it."

"Sorry, but it's another X-factor ... one that I'm willing to bet won't be in our favor."

She nodded, resigning herself to my point.

"We have a lot stacked against us, and the hand we're holding isn't as strong as we're trying to fool ourselves it is."

"So you think you ... *he* could..."

"Let me finish. We both know there's power inside of me, a lot of it. I don't know if it's enough to even the odds, but I'd be willing to bet it would go a long way toward doing so."

"But he's a killer ... a monster."

"I know, and that's why I need you. I want to go deep inside of myself and wake up Dr. Death, but not in the way he wants me to. I need your help to lobotomize the fucker, or whatever is the closest analogy. He's too much of a loose cannon otherwise."

I looked her deep in the eye. She had once been my enemy, but she'd since become my ally – my friend. Now I needed her to go beyond even that. It was asking a lot for something that I wasn't even sure was possible. I had to try, though.

"We need his power, but I want you to ensure that I'm in control this time."

**2**

# WELCOME TO CRAZY TOWN

I half expected Christy to freak out on me – to tell me I was a nutcase, that I was crazy to tempt fate. Hell, if she had fireballed my ass in an attempt to talk some sense into me, I wouldn't have been half surprised.

Instead, she took a deep breath, and asked, "You're serious, aren't you?"

"I'm pretty sure we're in some serious shit right now."

She nodded. "And it's finally time we started shoveling it back in everyone else's face."

For a moment, I stood there blinking stupidly. I had figured something like that would be *my* snarky response. Though no older than her boyfriend or me, oftentimes, Christy acted far more mature. Part of it was no doubt her impending parenthood. However, I suspected it also had to do with her upbringing as a witch.

I got the distinct impression that during the years when I'd been busy learning the fine art of telling online death-match opponents how awesomely I'd fuck their mothers, she'd been immersed in deeper studies – learning the mysteries of the universe or some such bullshit. Sure, her

18

mentor Harry Decker had been a prime filet of asshole mignon, but luckily, his crazy hadn't rubbed off on her. Still, there was no denying that if any member of our group wouldn't normally react to a situation like a foul-mouthed five-year-old, it was her.

"Oh, don't look at me like that. It's true and you know it," she finally replied. "You're not the only one with multiple demons nipping at their heels. And you're definitely not the only one..."

She looked down for a moment, but then met my gaze again. "...facing the endgame. It's close. I can feel it. The time for playing around is over. There are too many moving pieces, too many enemies and, quite frankly, I'm not sure there's any place in this world left where we can afford to play it safe."

"Oh. Well, okay, then. So you'll help me?"

"Yes, but not right now."

I nodded in agreement. The sessions with Sally had exhausted her. At any other given point in time, she should have been worrying about baby names, hoarding diapers, and other such things that I'm sure expecting couples are supposed to do. Despite the dire circumstances, I couldn't begrudge her a chance for something as small as a nap.

"And you need to tell everyone else what you have planned," she said.

"Well..."

"I'm the one who's serious now, Bill. No more stupid secrets made under the guise of protecting someone else. That's not going to help anyone if this goes bad, and we both know it."

I held up a hand. She didn't need to elaborate. That was the very nightmare scenario that had kept me from pursuing this up until now. When Tom and Ed had first learned of my little Jekyll and Hyde issue, they'd been all over that shit –

pestering me to learn how to control it. I hadn't because I had a feeling that if anything went wrong, their blood would pay for it.

Hell, that still might be the case.

"It's about fucking time," Tom said, crossing his arms before turning to Christy. "So what did you say to get him to stop pussing out?"

"She didn't say anything. It was my choice."

As requested, I'd waited for Christy to get some rest, then summoned everyone up to our apartment's living room. If there were any bad reactions to my plan, I could always retreat to the safety of my bedroom.

I let out a heavy sigh. No, the new me would face down my detractors. I'd look them in the eye and...

I glanced up and caught Sheila staring at me pensively, then immediately averted my gaze. Okay, so I still needed a little practice with this new outlook on life.

"Tom's right," Ed said. "If you'd have done this when we said to, then that whole bullshit with you running off and getting kidnapped to Switzerland would have gone down differently."

"That, or we wouldn't be having this conversation because you'd all be dead," Sheila countered from her spot next to Sally on our tattered love seat ... which, admittedly, hadn't seen too much love as of late. "Don't forget, you told me what happened after I got shot."

"I know, but don't forget I heard it secondhand."

Both of them glanced toward Sally, who waved them off. "Don't look at me. I don't remember any of that. Honestly, I'm still having a hard time even believing it happened."

"Well, believe it. You were there." I addressed the group

again. "Sheila has a point. Even though it's all a blank for me, I know in my gut I tore Remington to shreds. That wasn't the worst of it either." I visualized the cell back in Chillon Castle – all the broken bodies scattered about, thralls sacrificed to my darker half.

I willed the images away with some effort. "That part of me is a monster, a rampaging hell-beast that likes nothing better than bathing in buckets of blood."

"How would one bathe in...?"

I held up a hand to Tom. "I'm talking figuratively, numb nuts. I'm sure the *rest* of you get my point. The thing is, Dr. Death isn't as mindless as we all thought."

"And you know this *how?*" Sally asked.

"Because I had a conversation with him."

I took a seat and explained to my suddenly attentive audience the internal dialogue I'd had back when I was Alex's prisoner. It had been pretty weird experiencing it, but it was only slightly less odd telling them all of getting a knock on the door only to find a demonic, and somewhat assholish, version of myself staring back.

When I finished, Ed asked, "And you're sure you didn't dream it?"

"Pretty positive, especially since evil alternate Bill seemed to know the details of what had gone on in my life after I'd passed out. He also knew Alex would be waiting for me naked when I woke up."

Stunned silence met my inadvertent confession for a moment, until Sally commented, "All right, now this is getting good."

"It's not like that."

"So Alexander was dressed?"

"No."

"Why didn't you tell us this part when you got back?" Tom asked, a shit-eating grin upon his face.

"Don't be an ass," Ed said, coming to my rescue. "Obviously, some memories are best cherished in secret between lovers."

Or not.

Tom, Ed, and Sally brayed laughter like a trio of jackasses. Sheila pretended to find something interesting on the wall while failing to suppress a smile. Only Christy kept a straight face, her look more one of exasperation, although whether for me or the peanut gallery, I wasn't sure.

"It's not like that," I said at last, trying to get us back on track. "He just wanted to wrestle."

Sally wiped tears from her eyes. "Oh, I bet he did."

Christy slammed her hand down on the table hard enough to get everyone's attention. "That's enough. We need to be serious about this."

The laughter subsided as all eyes turned to her.

"That's better. I just need to know one thing before you continue, Bill."

"What?"

"Did Alexander caress your cheek and call you King Leonidas?"

And once more, that set them off. Even Sheila didn't bother to hide the laughter at my expense. As for me, all I could do was stare wide-eyed at Christy.

She shrugged and gave me a half-smile. "Sorry. Tom made me watch *300* with him the other night. Guess I've been hanging around you guys a little too much."

As things settled back down, Ed walked into our kitchen nook and grabbed some beers to pass around. Everyone, save Christy, accepted one and, by the look on her face, she was half tempted. Couldn't say I blamed her. With the world on the brink of annihilation and certain doom only a couple of hundred miles north of us, the Surgeon General's warnings could go take a flying fuck off the nearest skyscraper.

Ed placed the extra on the coffee table and took his seat again. "Gotta say, this whole internal debate thing is a bit weird. I never took you for the split personality type."

"It's not all that strange," Tom replied. "Bill plays with himself all the time, so talking isn't too much of a stretch."

I was sorely tempted to chuck my bottle at him, but figured it would be a waste of perfectly good beer. Instead, I just glared at him. "I'm thinking you should be in the room when we wake up Dr. Death."

"No. *I'm* going to be in the room," Sheila said. "For protection." She had the barest of red color on her cheeks despite her serious tone. Maybe it was the beer she was drinking, or more likely Tom's asshole comment.

"He was just kidding about me playing with myself," I stammered, once again unable to shake off old habits.

She held up a hand. "I really didn't need to know either way."

*Slick one, Bill.*

"But I'm serious. I'm really not convinced this is a good idea, but if the group thinks you should go through with it, then we need to make sure precautions are taken."

"No argument there."

Her wish for precautions wasn't surprising. I knew she considered that part of me a threat, a mad dog that might need to be put down. She was right to do so. I just hoped it didn't come down to that – for both our sakes.

"Well, I still think it's shithouse crazy," Sally chimed in, "but I'll admit to being curious. I want to see what this big bad wolf looks like."

"You've already seen it."

"So people keep telling me."

"What do you think?" Sheila asked Christy.

Christy took a moment to gather her thoughts. I saw the conflict in her eyes. Under normal circumstances, I'm fairly certain her answer would have been a definitive "Hell no!" But the stakes had recently been raised. Her entire belief system had come crashing down just days prior. The mentor of her people – the so-called White Mother – was, in actuality, tinged a different color by all the blood on her hands.

Evidence suggested the White Mother was more a motherfucker – the creator of the Jahabich, unholy monsters made of stone and the enslaved souls of their vanquished enemies. Yeah, it had probably been a bit of a stressful week for the poor girl.

When she spoke at last, her voice was steady, even if her haunted eyes betrayed her. "Controlling a mindless monster is a dangerous game. Even with my skills at mind manipulation, relentless rage is nearly impossible to contain, much less master. But if Bill is right, and this other personality..."

"Dr. Death," I added. "At least, that's what I call him."

"Yeah, but didn't James and that little Chinese bitch call you that too?" Sally asked.

"Her name is Gan."

"Whatever. Bottom line is that's gonna get confusing."

"Well," I said slowly, "since neither of them is here right now, who gives a flying fuck?"

Tom opened his mouth, probably to chuckle, but then closed it again quickly. Sally hadn't been big on him when she had her memories. Now? Well, who knew how she might react?

"Okay, it sounds like we're all in," Ed said, stepping in

before someone got decked. "So when do we unleash the beast?"

I winced at his use of words, but replied, "That's easy. Right before we leave."

Though it didn't need to be said, I had a feeling everyone in the room knew it might be for the last time.

**3**

## BUSY LITTLE BEES
## BUZZING AROUND

"**S**o when are we going?" Tom asked as if we were discussing running out for coffee.

"I need about three days to get myself ready," Christy said, putting a timetable to our plans, which up until then had been nebulous. She turned to Sally. "Sorry, but I'm going to have to suspend our sessions until then. I have a feeling I'm going to need all my strength for this."

"That's okay. I'm sure everyone here will be more than happy to keep reminding me of random shit that might or might not be true."

"Hey," Tom protested. "I was serious when I said we were like *this* before you got mind zapped." He held up two fingers intertwined. "BFFs until the end of time."

"Somehow, I'm having a bit of trouble buying that," she said.

Tom opened his mouth to print some more invitations to the pummeling party he was organizing for himself, but Sally continued. "I need to check out the scene in Manhattan anyway."

That one caught my attention. She hadn't ventured out

since we'd arrived. It may have been because she knew we might be forced to leave at any time, but I had a slight suspicion it had also been partially out of fear. Facing the world with big chunks of your life missing struck me as particularly daunting.

"I can come..."

"In your pants? Yeah, I kind of figured that." Suddenly, her tone softened as she became serious. "Relax, Bill. I may not remember much of you, but I still remember Village Coven, and I remember coming back to pick through the ruins of the Office."

"Then you have to know there's nothing left."

"No vampires, maybe, but that doesn't mean there isn't anything we could use. There's a lot of buildings we had space in. There's gotta be something salvageable in all of it."

"I'll go with you," Sheila said.

Sally nodded, which I found a bit odd. I didn't expect her to want to go traipsing through coven properties, including safe houses, with the Icon in tow. It just didn't seem a very vampiric thing to do – especially with her scrambled memory.

They must have sensed me staring, because Sheila added, "I kept up the rent at my old apartment just in case. Assuming the building hasn't burnt to the ground, I wouldn't mind grabbing a few extra changes of clothes. I'm getting tired of stealing whatever your neighbors left behind."

I was tempted to remark that she looked kinda cute in Mrs. Mahoney's afghan sweater, but now was not the time. Likewise, there probably wasn't much I could do to dissuade them. From what I'd heard, Manhattan was a mess – probably already halfway devolved to making *The Warriors* seem like a Nostradamus prophecy. It certainly wasn't a place for two attractive women to be wandering alone after dark. Of course, most women didn't come pre-equipped with extra options like superpowers.

As long as they didn't run into anything overly nasty, they'd be fine. Besides, I had been considering a field trip of my own. Now that Christy had laid out her timeline, it seemed a good idea to do so before she started mucking with my head.

"I'm going to scout out the Brooklyn safe house," I said.

"Safe house?" Sheila and Christy both asked.

"Yeah, it's over in the naval yards. Village Coven jointly owns it with the Howard Beach Coven. It's neutral ground between us."

Not too long ago, Sally would have known that was bullshit, but Tom and Ed were both kind enough to scoff in her place.

"Fine, *supposedly* neutral ground," I corrected. "Doesn't always work out that way. Anyway, it's a place where we can fall back during times of emergency. Being that Village Coven is gone and so is most of the HBC ... hopefully ... I..."

"That's where you want to do it. That's where you want Christy to try to coax your powers out, right?" Sheila asked.

I nodded, choosing to ignore the "do it" line. New Bill was cooler than that, mostly. "Yeah. The place is reinforced, there's room to maneuver if something goes wrong, and unlike my living room, I don't care if it gets trashed in the process."

I left out that it also gave me an excuse to leave our apartment building unquestioned, giving me ample time to scout an entirely different location.

First, though, Christy had a whole ton of stuff she wanted me to set up for her. Space needed to be cleared, symbols drawn on the floor, and incense burned. I didn't really mind that last part. Abandoned warehouses tended to smell funky at the best of times. Ones that had been the scene of past slaughters were usually even more ripe – all the worse for those of us with superhuman senses.

Unsurprisingly, Tom and Ed both volunteered to come along. Christy, however, nixed Tom's departure. She wanted him close by to work with her on some enchantments – something about the faith-channeling amulet he owned. It was pretty much a watered-down version of what Sheila could do naturally ... albeit still pretty damned effective against vampires.

I managed to talk Ed down from joining me. Despite being explosively resistant to vampire bites as of late, he was still no match for them in a fight. He offered to bring his shotgun as a precaution, but I declined. We'd need that fire-power later, but it seemed an unnecessary risk for now. Besides, as a vampire, I was a lot faster than him. I could traverse the streets quickly and avoid any trouble. Or at least I hoped that would be the case.

During the day, Brooklyn seemed almost normal – at least, the parts I could see from our windows. Hell, we even got mail sporadically – mostly flyers for home security systems interspersed with bills. Jesus Christ, even in the middle of the apocalypse the fucking phone companies still didn't stop haunting people. *So sorry your husband got eaten by a cave troll, but you still owe us two hundred dollars in data overage charges.*

Anyway, my roommates' brief forays out had confirmed how routine life appeared to be out there. Heck, many of the businesses on 86th street were still open, even if the bars on their windows were now thicker than before.

Once darkness came, though, odd shrieks could be heard in the night ... even odder than the usual New York fare. Sometimes, bizarre arcs of energy flashed in the sky. I hadn't taken too many strolls since our return – I may have some semblance of superpowers, but I'm not fucking insane – but I had little doubt that dark alleyways, tunnels, and other such nooks held strange alien things mortal man was not meant to behold. Bottom line: if one felt the need to go jogging past sundown, it might have been best to notify one's next of kin first as a precautionary measure.

Of course, it's possible some of that was just my imagination running wild. I managed to make it to the Brooklyn safe house with no real issues to report. The streets were mostly dark – courtesy of the fluctuating power grid – as well as pretty empty. That was a small blessing – it allowed me to utilize the unnatural speed afforded to me as one of the undead.

Sure, every so often I could have sworn I heard something. Once or twice, I even looked up to the rooftops, certain something was about to descend upon me, but I chalked it up to basic paranoia. Besides, I had only adopted my newfound lease on life in the past twenty-four hours. One doesn't shake off a lifetime of acting like a victim all in one fell swoop, y'know.

Even so, I was kind of proud of myself. My immediate instinct was to pour every bit of speed into my legs and run from the invisible boogeymen. Instead, I forced myself to maintain pace – continually asking myself what Chuck Norris, Duke Nukem, and Mr. T would do in this situation. Would they run? Well, okay, they – or at least their memes – would probably level the block just to be safe. I decided to opt for a slightly less aggressive stance and just kept on my merry way.

Pardon the undead pun, but the safe house was quiet as a tomb. Of everything that had freaked me out on the journey over, that was perhaps the most unsettling. Perhaps, I considered, it had to do with the fact that every single time I'd visited this place, something had tried to smash my face in.

The anticipation put me on edge, followed by the certainty that an ambush lurked around every corner – despite my nose telling me otherwise. But no. It was empty. Judging by the distressed state of the rooms I passed, it hadn't seen much, if any, occupation since the last time I'd visited.

Both James and Calibra – current prefect of the Northeast – had been present that day and it had still almost turned into a total clusterfuck. Four angry and afraid – but mostly angry – members of the HBC had been waiting for us. Following a brief scuffle, Calibra had stayed behind to take stock of their situation. I spared a brief thought, wondering what she'd told them and what had become of them afterwards. Whatever the case, they weren't here now and hadn't been in some time. It didn't mean they wouldn't return, but it seemed safe enough for the time being.

I unshouldered the supplies I'd brought along and then pulled out a detailed printout of instructions from Christy. Screwing this up wasn't a particularly smart option, so I'd had her work with Ed to Photoshop everything in as much detail as they could. A fucked-up "Klaatu, Barada, Nikto" was pretty damn funny in a movie, but I had a feeling it would be slightly less amusing in real life.

Before getting to work, I sucked down a blood pack I'd

snatched from our rapidly dwindling supply – trying to steel myself for what might need to happen once we ran out. I had to force myself to face that reality despite every fiber of my being trying to distract me with more pleasant thoughts, like Sally and Sheila confessing that it was perfectly cool to share me, followed by a sweaty honey-soaked threesome. I let that play out in my head for several minutes longer than I should have.

Yeah, like I said, distractions were my Kryptonite.

**4**

# THE MEAN STREETS

To say the safe house wasn't the tidiest place I'd ever seen was an understatement. For the most part, Village Coven's other properties had been kept in good order. Hell, the last place Sally had set up before everything went to shit was pretty goddamned swank. However, given two rival covens jointly maintained this building, it meant neither gave much of a shit about it. After all, why clean when a bunch of assholes you don't like are just gonna pop in and mess it up again?

Alas, it was also the perfect place for Christy to perform whatever skull-fuckery she needed to do with me. I found a room deep within the structure, with thick concrete walls and only one exit, likewise reinforced, that would serve us nicely. Sadly, it was also a fucking mess. Had I been human, it would have taken me half a day just to clear it out, even after bribing my friends with beer to help. For a vampire, though, it was the work of maybe an hour. – helped by the fact that I wasn't overly concerned about breaking anything.

Another hour found the place prepped and smelling a bit nicer thanks to the burning incense and an economy-sized

33

can of Lysol I'd brought along. I'd breathed in far more than my share of rancid odors in the past. I sure as hell wasn't going to tolerate it in situations under my control. Needless to say, I'd developed a newfound respect for the concept of lemony fresh.

By the time I finished, the night was still young and I had plenty of time to head to my next stop – one I hadn't bothered to list on my official itinerary. There was a good chance it was all for naught, but if my friends asked, I could always say it had taken me longer than expected to prep for Christy ... or maybe that I got jumped by rabid hobos along the way.

It was probably dumb to go it alone, but the last time I'd made this trip, it hadn't worked out so well for everyone else. I didn't care to tempt fate before we headed north to our near-certain deaths. What I had in mind probably wouldn't bear fruit anyway. Who was to say Dave was even there?

Regardless, I had to try. He was my friend and, considering I'd set in motion the events that led to his current condition, also my responsibility.

He'd gone missing right around the time I'd ended up in Vegas for what turned out to be a short-lived tenure as Sally's bitch-boy in Pandora Coven. He hadn't made contact since, which was worrisome on several fronts. Dave was my friend and I didn't want to see any harm ... correction, *any more* harm come to him.

Conversely, he was also an ethically deprived dick when he wanted to be. Hell, I used to joke to my gaming group that if I ever found myself in a hospital under his care, I'd sign a DNR form and then hold my breath until I passed out.

In life, that had translated into him being an angry god of a dungeon master, happily raining spite down upon his players whenever we pissed him off. In death, well, I knew how tempting blood could be for a vamp.

This was something I should have done months ago. As a friend, he deserved better. Instead, I'd been all too content to lick my wounds following Sheila's rejection of me and too caught up in my own rapidly growing interest in Sally.

Bros before hoes be damned.

The problem was that Dave had been AWOL now for three months. The trail was pretty cold if he'd decided to skip town. That being said, in my former life as a programmer, we always kept this saying in mind: KISS – keep it simple, stupid. Always try the easy shit first because oftentimes therein lay the solution.

In this case, that low hanging fruit was called Newark, New Jersey.

Going from one place in Brooklyn to another was a relatively simple matter. Getting from Brooklyn to Jersey was a pain in the ass under even good circumstances. These days, public transportation was iffy at best during the day. The subways and buses ran sporadically – sometimes on, sometimes not, and that was before the sun set every night. I'd likewise been told the ferries were down, a few quite literally at the bottom of the Hudson thanks to a series of unfortunate *accidents*.

I didn't own a car. Running through the subway tunnels at top speed was an option, but a potentially risky one. Considering what had happened in Vegas and then in the bunkers of NORAD, I'd become a little leery of being underground. It was one thing to try and adopt a new persona of bravery, but there was a thin line between heroic and being a fucking idiot.

Thus, I relied on the one trait of humanity that was

simultaneously its failing and savior – greed. Where the public transportation system had failed, intrepid souls had stepped in to fill the void with independent car service. Cabs, both licensed and not, could be found fairly easily – at least in the relatively good neighborhoods.

Don't get me wrong. I'm normally not a fan of any sort of racial profiling, for humans anyway – most supernatural entities were dicks. However, I won't lie. For once, I was glad to be a harmless-looking, nerdy white guy.

Roughly two hours later, I stepped out of the cab onto one of Newark's main drags. The streetlights were still lit, which told me this place probably was hanging on pretty well. The ride hadn't been too bad either – a little slow, and we'd had to take the long way as the bridges from Staten Island to Jersey were closed off. Fortunately, the roads were otherwise mostly clear. The world might be going to shit, but it was still in its early stages. We hadn't yet reached a point where the highways were littered with cars full of people who'd decided to just pull over and die right there.

Don't ask how much the whole thing cost. Let's just say I was glad nobody was stopping by these days to ask for a rent check. Thankfully, I had planned the trip in advance and had left home with a pocket full of bills – albeit probably not enough to get me home again. Oh well. I'd cross that prover-bial bridge when I came to it.

My plan of action was simple: try Dave's apartment and then, if that didn't pan out, make my way to the hospital where he once worked as a resident. Dave was a smart guy, but a shitty doctor – at least when it came to bedside manner. However, the hospitals were doubtlessly overflowing with patients these days. They were also hopefully home to a generous supply of bagged blood. If so, maybe Dave was still responsible for saving lives and not taking them. It was a long shot, but in these crazy days, hope was the one commodity that was still free.

I hiked several blocks toward my first destination – noting the rapidly deteriorating state of the neighborhood as I went. No wonder my cabbie hadn't wanted to go any further.

Dave's apartment complex wasn't exactly in the upper crust section of the city to begin with, but it had previously been safe enough for a group of guys to gather for a weekly D&D game. Now, though, I could easily envision the rest of the group not so politely bowing out of the game. I passed multiple burnt out buildings. Graffiti proclaiming the end of the world shown on others, and that wasn't even counting the bizarre scratches gouged into the walls of a few. All of it combined into a sense of being watched. If I hadn't been an unholy creature of the night myself, I'd have said fuck it and found myself a nice, well-lit place to loiter until the sun came up.

But I was a vampire. More so, I was a Freewill – a special breed of vamp with powers above and beyond the rest of the rabble. Or at least I kept telling myself that as I struggled to maintain my new outlook on life. Let me just mention, it's one thing to stand in your own bathroom and proclaim you're gonna face your fate head-on. It's quite another when you're walking through what looks to be the set of a fucking John Carpenter movie.

I thought back to my early days as a vampire – remembering how Sally had told me that appearance was ninety-nine percent of everything in the world of the unliving. If you acted like a victim, you'd be torn a new asshole. If you walked in like you owned the place, your chances of seeing the next sunset were much better.

Heh, the Sally living downstairs from me wasn't so different from the one I'd first met, I mused as I turned down the block where Dave's old apartment lay. I mean, weren't they in the same boat, essentially getting to know me from scratch?

No, that wasn't true. Despite Alex mucking with her brain, she was a different person from those days – a lot less likely to cause a bloodbath just because someone was walking too slow in front of her. Well, maybe not *a lot*. Either way, she had definitely changed. In some ways, it was hopeful because...

My stroll down memory lane was cut short as something hit me from behind with the force of a small truck. Before I could open my mouth to cry out, I was airborne – flying across the parking lot leading to Dave's place. The blow and subsequent landing – allowing me to experience the gentle tug of the scarred asphalt against my face as I skidded to a halt – would have been more than enough to stun most humans or worse. Pity for the asshole who blindsided me, I wasn't a...

More like pity I wasn't allowed to finish that thought. A pair of hands abruptly grabbed me by the back of my jacket and hauled me to my feet. I was spun around and shoved into the wall of the building. Just then, the scent of vampire registered in my nostrils, something I should have noticed earlier rather than getting caught up in Sally daydreams.

"You're more than thirty minutes late," my attacker growled. "We get a free pizza and your life."

Huh? The attack had caught me by surprise, but I was otherwise relatively unhurt. Whoever this asshole was, he was either a newb or didn't realize who I was. It was going to cost him.

Make that *them*.

I looked up to see two more figures join the first. Though

the darkness couldn't conceal them from my eyes; they all wore masks.

They rushed forward, and I took a wild swing at the nearest. My fist connected with a solid ***clonk*** of flesh meeting metal as I realized too late this one was actually wearing a medieval-style helmet – a pretty decent replica, if my bruised hand was any indication.

Regardless, the blow got the job done. My attacker went down – a big-ass dent in the middle of his faceplate.

"Motherfucker!" a muffled voice cried from within.

Something about the cadence caught my attention, and I hesitated for a second, which allowed the others to close the distance and attempt to pin me. The one on the right wore a green knit ski-mask with Cthulhu-esque tentacles hanging off the front. The other stared at me through the rubber face of a Cyberman. All the fight went out of me as I recognized their headgear.

No wonder the voice of Sir Dipshit had sounded so familiar.

I was being attacked by my own D&D group. Guess I'd missed more games than I realized.

## 5

## TWENTY SIDES OF TERROR

Before I could say a word, the two attackers on either side of me – Adam and Mike, judging by their respective disguises – both swung fists into my stomach, doubling me over.

Okay, I'd had just about enough of this shit. I was sorely tempted to start swinging back – just enough to teach them who was the big bad wolf in this story, but then I had a better idea. Fuck it; when in undead Rome...

*"YOU LIMP-DICKS THINK YOU'RE TOUGH ENOUGH TO FUCK WITH KELVIN LIGHTBLADE?!"*

Normally, my compulsions aren't much to write home about, at least without the blood of another vampire to juice them up, but they're more than enough to catch the attention of newbs.

My arms were freed as the two who'd been holding me stumbled back.

The one still on the ground managed to pry his smashed helmet off, revealing, as expected, the face of the third member of my group – Carl. Or at least I assumed it was him behind the broken, blood-gushing nose.

"Bill?"

And with that, the encounter was over – all XP in my favor. Yeah, baby!

"Yes, it's me. What the fuck are you assholes doing?" I asked, still rightfully miffed.

Adam stripped off his Cyberman mask. "Sorry, man, we didn't know."

"Yeah," Mike added. "We thought you were the delivery guy."

"You thought I was some guy from Dominos?" I asked incredulously, feeling the bruises I'd incurred already healing. "Do I look like I'm carrying a fucking pizza?"

"Well..."

"Seriously, what the fuck? Did they jerk off on your last pie or something?"

"It's not like that, Bill," Mike said. "We were just hungry."

"I get that, but just because someone is late is no reason to beat the shit out of them."

"We weren't going to beat the shit out of him," Adam corrected. "We were going to eat him."

"And the pizza too," Carl added.

My eyes nearly bugged out of my head as I processed this. What the fuck had happened here?

Just then, the sound of a door opening somewhere behind me registered in my overly sensitive vampire ears. Scratch that question, I knew what – or more precisely *who* – had happened here.

"Oh shit." There came a quick gasp of surprise followed by the squeal of the door reversing course.

"Not so fast, asshole," I snapped. "You have some

explaining to do."

"Wait a second," Adam said, looking me over. "Aren't you hurt?"

"Just my feelings."

"Holy shit. Are you a vampire too?"

"No, I'm the fucking Batman."

He turned toward Dave, who I assumed was still standing behind me with a guilty look upon his face. "You didn't tell us you bit Bill too."

What? Oh Jesus Christ. "Everyone get inside now."

"Who died and made you..."

***"SHUT UP, GET INSIDE, AND CLOSE THE GODDAMNED DOOR!!*** It sounds like you guys have a story to tell, and right now, I'm all ears."

It wasn't until we were all settled in Dave's apartment that I realized that had been the first time I'd tried a mass compulsion. I'd been so annoyed at the whole situation, it had just come out ... barely registering with me until I noticed my gaming buddies standing around with glassy-eyed stares on their faces.

All at once, I sort of got an inkling why the other vamps enjoyed doing this. Goddamn, there was something to be said for telling a group to shut up and them actually doing it.

No, I reminded myself. That was a slippery slope. I might be trying to change my outlook on life, but there were some lines I needed to be mindful of lest I completely bypass tough-guy wannabe and end up as a total asshole-in-training.

I glanced around Dave's apartment. Huh, that was interesting. The gaming table was all set up. Despite the power being out, it looked the same as it always did on game day.

Fuck it. There was no point in wasting the opportunity. I sat myself down in Dave's seat and took a deep breath. Clearing my thoughts, I willed my friends free of my control – hoping that's how it worked. After a moment or two, they all blinked a few times and their eyes cleared. Not bad for a first try.

When that was done, I held up a hand before Dave could say a word and indicated the player chairs around the table. This time, I was the dungeon master, and these fuckers were going to play *my* game.

"You're probably a little angry," Dave began, his usual attitude shelved for the moment.

"Let's say I'm more concerned than angry, shall we?"

"What the hell is going on here?" Mike asked, his gaze alternating between us before settling upon Dave. "I thought you said you were a master vampire, hundreds of years old."

"Is that what you said, buddy?" I leaned forward, making a tent of my hands upon which I rested my chin as if listening intently.

"I may have..."

Adam interrupted him. "Fuck yeah, he did. We were all gathered for the game – sorry about what happened to Kelvin, by the way – when he laid it on us and..."

I spun toward him, my brows furrowed. "Wait a second. What happened to Kelvin?"

"You shouldn't have tried to steal the astral gems from that statue of Morog, the demon god of sodomy while..."

"Why was I stealing gems from a sodomy demon?"

"Why not?"

My fangs descended in annoyance. Another few seconds

of this and I was gonna compel them all to act it out in front of me. "Okay, we can discuss that later." I threw another glare toward Dave. "Let's get back to this master vampire stuff."

"No prob, man," Adam said as if discussing just another in-game adventure. "So we all thought he was full of shit, but then he pulled out a lead pipe and bent the fuck out of it."

Carl tapped him on the shoulder. "Don't forget about the rat."

"Oh yeah. Then he told us to follow him back to his lab, where he pulled this rat out of its cage and ate the fucker right in front of us."

"I drained it," Dave said, almost apologetically. "I didn't eat it."

"Either way, we're talking some sick shit. I, for one, was convinced."

"Me too," Mike added.

"Not me," Carl said. "At least, not until he started cutting himself and healing instantly."

"Quite the floor show." I inclined my head toward my former DM, enjoying watching him squirm for once. "So then how did we end up here, with you guys trying to take a bite out of my ass because you thought I was late with your pizza?"

"We weren't going to bite your ass," Mike replied. "Well, maybe Adam was."

An empty beer can bounced off his head courtesy of my other party-mate.

"Back it up," I clarified. "I mean, how did you guys end up..." I put my index and middle fingers up to my mouth to simulate fangs. Not sure why, since I had them myself, but I was kind of caught up in the moment. "Did he attack you?"

"No, he offered," Carl said, leaning back in his chair. For all the concern he was giving my questioning, you'd have thought he was about to roll initiative against a pair of kobolds. "Said he needed to make a coven or something. I still don't get that shit. I thought they..."

"Were for witches, I know. They stole the idea from us." I turned to Dave and raised an eyebrow, waiting until he got the hint it was his turn to answer my unspoken question.

Finally, he sighed, looking much like a teenager who'd been caught sneaking out of the house after dark. "You said it yourself. Uncovened vampires aren't allowed."

"That didn't mean to make your own! That's ... not how it's done."

"Well, nobody bothered to tell me that," he replied defensively, getting to his feet.

"Maybe if you'd stuck around..."

"And be what? Knocked out by that hot blonde over and over again?"

"She didn't do it that many times."

"Are you kidding me? I couldn't even get up to take a piss without her telling me to go back into the other room and take a long nap. Undead or not, I'm pretty sure that's not healthy for a bladder."

Yeah, I could definitely see Sally doing that. "Listen, Dave, I'm sorry for..."

"Hold on," Carl said. "I want to hear more about this hot blonde."

Adam sniffed dismissively. "Hot blondes are overrated."

"Go fuck yourself. Inquiring minds want to know. Seriously, dude, so did she, y'know, *molest* you in your sleep?"

"Well, I did have a couple of dreams that were pretty realis..."

"No, she didn't," I snapped, perhaps a bit harsher than was warranted by what was obviously a bullshit story. Hell, I'd told probably a thousand of them myself to this very bunch. I needed to chill out a bit before anyone questioned why the lady ... err, me ... doth protest too much. "Let's forget about Sally for the moment and get back to..."

Carl and Mike's heads both whipped toward me fast enough to give an old lady whiplash. "You know her name?"

"Well, yeah. She's my friend."

"Your friend, eh?" Carl turned toward Mike and started moving his fist toward his mouth while jabbing the inside of his cheek with his tongue.

"It's not like that. Well, okay, maybe it's a *little* like that."

Fuck it. I was amongst friends.

High-fives commenced, and then I tried to steer us back on track. "Seriously, guys. What's up with the masks and the pizza guy bullshit?"

Dave held up his hands. "Don't look at me."

I raised one eyebrow to express my dubious belief in his statement.

"Seriously. I've been sneaking blood from the hospital. The place is fucking chaos. They're going through so much these days, they don't even notice a few liters missing here and there. I mean, sure, there's been a couple of terminal patients too, but you can't blame a guy for experimenting a bit."

Now *that* was the Dave I knew. "Keep going. I'm listening."

"After I took over ... I mean, made my coven, I started sneaking things out to them – blood, the occasional fresh corpse, shit like that."

"So then what was the problem?"

"Seriously, man," Adam said, addressing my former DM, "that was weak. I mean, you can't turn us into the unholy fiends of the night and then ask us to gnaw on the equivalent of a dog bone."

"Adam's right," Mike added. "I mean, that's like asking someone who was just bitten by a radioactive spider to not hang from the ceiling."

I really didn't like where this was going. "And?"

"So we acted the part, of course. Was kind of messed up at first, but then Carl said…"

"I can speak for myself, thank you. I was like, we could be the motherfucking Lost Boys. Those fuckers kicked all sorts of ass, got all the chicks, and were badass cool … minus the eighties mullets and that poster of Rob Lowe."

"Yeah, what the fuck was up with that?" Mike asked absently.

"I'm pretty sure that was in Corey Haim's room, not the Lost Boy's lair," I replied before shaking my head in disbelief. Fuck me! They'd all become killers just to emulate some stupid fictional bad guys from an era that almost rivaled the seventies in tackiness? "Forget the fucking movie. You guys are hunting down people. Real, innocent people."

"Innocent is really a subjective concept," he replied. "Besides, we started off with lowlifes and gang members … real Dark Knight shit."

"So what happened?"

"They eventually got the hint and moved out of the neighborhood."

"So, you decided the pizza guy was the next great evil to be purged from this Earth?"

"To paraphrase," Carl said, "'You can either die a hero, or live long enough to become the bad guy.'"

"You've only been vampires for a few months," I pointed out.

"We get bored easily."

"Besides, it's not like you would do any different," Adam

added, scoffing. "Remember when Kelvin found that lightning rapier? That piece of shit was just plus one, yet you started a fight at the first inn we came across because you couldn't wait to try it out. Killed the damned pub owner's wife with a crit."

"Yeah, but..."

"And then fucked her corpse."

"Yes, thank you. I remember, but that's not the point!" My fangs descended and my eyes blackened in annoyance.

"Whoa," Mike said. "Easy there, buddy."

I rounded on him with a snarl, my temper fraying, but then stopped myself. They were all in serious need of a good beat-down. Hell, they were all deserving of jail time, really, but I didn't see that in the cards. Even so, I couldn't be blamed for kicking the shit out of them. Fuck, they probably deserved to be dusted because they'd turned out to be such monsters, unlike...

Actually, they weren't all that different from me, were they? Hadn't I considered doing similar stuff when I was first turned? Maybe not the mass murder part, but I'd definitely wanted to try out my abilities. Hell, the motto of any gamer worth his salt when it came to newfound powers was "use it and abuse it."

In my case, though, I'd chosen a different path. It probably didn't hurt that I also had Tom and Ed around. As fucked-up as those two could be, I'm sure they'd have said something if I'd shown an inclination toward depopulating our neighborhood.

"And what did *you* do while this was going down?" I asked Dave, my eyes still soulless orbs of black vengeance.

"What? Between my job and research..." He hesitated when I bared my teeth. "I was the one who suggested the masks and keeping things low key ... you know, maybe a delivery person a week, the occasional crackhead, stuff like that. I also suggested they keep in character."

"In character?"

"Yeah," Carl said, a hint of pride in his voice. "You have to admit that hitting you from behind was definitely worth some sneak attack damage."

"What? You don't even play a thief."

"I know, but we switch off character classes every now and then. Hell, you should have seen it a few weeks back when I pulled out the Barbarian Rage. It took three showers before..."

"I get the hint," I snapped. It was true too. Hell, Village Coven's properties were purposely stocked with the facilities and extra attire needed to clean up after a particularly *fun-filled* evening. But those hadn't been my idea. Those were all in place prior to my taking over, back when Jeff had been boss.

Under my charge, I'd tried to curb things, but it had been an uphill battle. Hell, even the new recruits I'd met recently – their early days as vampires spent under the rule of Starlight – had been bloodthirsty assholes. And she'd been the farthest vamp I knew from being a coldblooded killer.

A thought began to form in my head, maybe more of a revelation. "Why?" I asked, hoping that they didn't give me the answer I knew they probably would.

"Why what?" Adam asked.

"Why the killing? I know you guys. None of you have ever so much as jay-walked."

"I shoplifted a candy bar when I was seven," Mike said.

"And I see how it set you off down the path toward Guantanamo Bay," I scoffed. Mike was, or had been, a middle manager at a large health food conglomerate, about as harmless a job as one could find. "What changed?"

"We did," Adam replied. "Look at us. We're all so much

more than we were. Fuck, I can put my fist through the drywall here without so much as feeling it."

"Please don't," Dave added.

"We're beyond laws, beyond humanity. I mean, jeez, Bill, read a book or something. This is the way we're supposed to act."

Carl nodded. "And it is pure awesome to have absolutely no fucks left to give."

6

# THE DOUCHETASTIC FOUR

I'd been afraid of an answer like that. It amounted to "because we can," which seemed to mirror the attitudes of most other vamps I'd met.

Why? Was it an "absolute power corrupts absolutely" thing? If so, that pointed to some extremely shallow personalities. A newborn vamp got some nifty abilities, but it's not like they woke up as Superman. I remembered my first few weeks as a vampire distinctly, especially a little episode in which I got my ass handed to me by some guy in a club. The freshly risen were tough, but by no means unbeatable. Our powers grow as we age, but that takes several years. I mean, I was the strongest vampire in the room, but it was only by a marginal amount. If the rest decided to gang up on me, they'd potentially fuck up my shit.

Was it maybe because of something deeper? Was there something about waking up as a monster of the night that actually gave you a proclivity toward becoming one? Hell, my turning was anything but normal – even among vamps. I hadn't been given much time to acclimate before I was diving out a window in order to save my own ass.

But then I remembered the first bit of typical vampire business I'd been exposed to – being given a fat, naked dude to drink from ... well, it was the drinking that was typical, hopefully not the fat, naked part. It had almost sucked me in, pun intended. My fangs had descended, and I'd started chewing a hole in the guy's neck before I even knew what I was doing. It was only by force of will that I'd managed to resist.

It hadn't seemed like a big deal at the time. Now, I had to wonder if that had actually been my defining moment. Had I not stopped myself, would it have proven to be a slippery slope? I was sitting here, ready to judge my friends for turning into monsters, but maybe they were just darker reflections of who I was – who I could have been with only the slightest extra nudge that night.

Wow. That could explain why there were so many Jeffs and Colins in the vampire world and so few Starlights and Jameses.

Sadly, we were probably a little late in the game for me to spend time philosophizing about this shit. I didn't have hundreds of years to meditate on the nature of the beast or sit in a cave full of funky vapors, waiting for visions while I poked my eyes out of my head every hour. The end of the world was looming, and I had a sinking sensation a group hug and some understanding wouldn't halt it.

That still left the problem of my gaming group. It seemed Dave had his shit under control. That wasn't surprising. Waking up with a burning desire to cause harm to the human race was probably a slow Tuesday as far as he was concerned. Guess being a dick in life sort of insulated you from it. My other friends, though, had become killers and seemed happy as pigs in shit about it. Something needed to be done.

Sure, I had much bigger fish to fry. What were a few

people compared to the entire world being royally fucked by whichever side won the war? Would saving a few Newark residents from the dork knights mean much if humanity was enslaved by either Alex or the Sasquatches?

Hell, I'm not even sure my roommates would argue with those odds. Still, I had a conscience, a grasp on my humanity – however tenuous at times – and it probably didn't hurt that one of the two women I had feelings for was the foretold last defender of humanity. Purposely leaving a major city at the mercy of a bunch of ... err, deadly nerds ... would probably not score me any points in her book.

I considered my options while they continued bantering among themselves – each one telling tales of their supernatural prowess: who had killed the most people, who'd spilled the most blood, who'd picked up the most one-night-stands via his vampiric charisma – in short, all bullshit, at least that last part.

Dave was alone in keeping his mouth shut. Though his tenure as a vampire was short, he was a smart guy – smart enough to put two and two together and know I was currently the big dog in the room. It felt good for a change.

Still, I hadn't made a trip out here to gloat. I'd come with a very specific purpose in mind. It was time to get to it.

"Can I have a word with you? Alone, in your lab?" That was a bit of a joke, trying to get some privacy from vampires by stepping into another room not ten feet away. Still, I knew my friends – a self-absorbed bunch once they got to bullshitting if ever there was.

Dave arched an eyebrow, probably certain he was about to get a new asshole chewed, but simply replied, "Sure, Bill."

I followed him toward the small extra bedroom that he'd converted into a poor man's Dr. Frankenstein lab. Before closing the door behind me, I addressed the rest of the party.

"If the real pizza guy gets here, pay him, tip well, and

don't fucking kill him. I mean it. Oh, and save me a slice while you're at it."

"I know what you're gonna say."

"How has your research been coming along?"

"Okay," he replied, blinking stupidly. "Maybe I don't know what you're gonna say. Come again?"

"This ain't your personal porno. I need to know if you've been keeping up with your experiments." It was a rhetorical question. A quick glance around confirmed that. Also, I knew Dave. He was the type to plan for the world normalizing again – probably in a way that would ensure he'd make a few bucks in the process. Screw bettering humanity when there was cold, hard cash at stake.

"How could I not?" he asked simply enough. "Especially now that I have an endless supply of samples to draw from. Let me tell you, spontaneous tissue regeneration is fucking awesome."

"Can't argue with that, but the hurting kinda sucks."

"Which is precisely what they make local anesthesia for."

"You never used a local on me."

"You never asked."

Same old Dave. Still my buddy, but a world-class prick. I decided to let that pass for now. He'd never meant to get turned into a vampire, and it was pretty much one-hundred percent my fault that he had. I could cut him a little bit of slack from that perspective. "Fine, I need to know..."

"I wouldn't mind a few more samples from you, of course."

"Why? You just said..."

"I know, but you're different. Yes, you already told me as much, but it turns out that physically that might be the case too. I was comparing my blood to yours via some prepared slides I had made months ago. Hard to get a full readout with this crap here, but your samples seem to have a few extra protein strands that I can't quite identify. It might be contamination, but I'd love to get some fresh blood so maybe I can sneak into the Microscopy unit over at Saint Jerome's and find out for sure."

"I think I'm gonna have to take a rain check on that one."

He opened his mouth, but I held up a hand and then gave him a very brief overview of what had gone down since he'd gone AWOL. Needless to say, I made it a point to drive home the urgency of the situation.

I needn't have bothered.

"So, you're telling me that not only do you have a girl living with you that can heal others with her touch, but your roommate has a condition that's never been seen before?" His eyes lit up as he spoke, the sound of gears turning in his head practically audible.

"As far as I can tell anyway. He's an anomaly ... although this Vehron guy seems to prefer the term 'abomination.' Whatever the case, the main thing is I need to..."

"Yeah, yeah, go on a suicide mission to kill the big scary guy whose head you gave me as a present. I got all that. Let's get back to this whole anomaly thing."

I'd been prepared to use the stick to get Dave's help, but now it seemed I had a big fat carrot dangling in front of him too.

"Here's the deal. I need to know if you've come up with something ... anything at all that could help me with this fucker. Hell, even if it just gives me a smidgeon more than I have now."

He hesitated for a moment. "Maybe."

"And in return for coming along with me to kill..."

"Wait, you want me to come with you?"

"This isn't a field trip to the blood bank. We're leaving ASAP. You want some new toys to play with, you come with me and you stay with me. No more of this running off shit. You're still uncovened as far as vampire rules go. They aren't going to tolerate that shit. You do this for me, though, and I'll make sure you guys are square with the authorities once this bullshit is all settled."

"And?"

Fucking Dave. "And I will put in a good word with both my friends so maybe they'll provide you with a few tissue samples."

"I might need more than a few."

"As a freebie, I'll also give you ample warning that sticking a needle into either of them without proper precautions will most likely end with you as a smoldering pile of dust."

He blinked confusedly, seemingly unsure whether I was joking or not. Finally, when he saw that I wasn't laughing, he shrugged. "Fair enough. Deal."

"Good. So do you have anything for me?"

"Not much, but I have a few theories I'm working on."

"I'm listening."

Dave was right – he didn't have much. In fact, most of it sounded like Greek bullshit to me. But I had to trust him. Hell, anything at all was better than what I currently had.

I told him to get ready to hit the road as well as grab whatever he thought he needed.

"If we're being honest, I need my entire lab."

I looked around at the space – smaller than my bedroom in actuality. "So bring it. Need I remind you that you don't really have to worry about encumbrance these days? Besides, you've got three minions out there to help you pack up if need be."

"I'm not sure they're gonna be all too happy about me leaving. They're having way too much fun with this shit."

"I can see that. What the fuck were you thinking?"

"I told you..."

"Yeah, yeah, the coven bullshit. You had to know that wouldn't work."

"Well, I thought it had a shot."

I tapped my foot in annoyance, waiting for him to come up with something better.

"And honestly, I thought I was saving their lives."

"What? How? By killing them?"

"Have you looked at what's going on out there, Bill? The world is going nuts. Even with the extra stamina I seem to have gained from this condition, the hospital is still running me ragged on my shifts."

"Let me guess, you switched to nights?"

"Duh! They were happy to have me too. Used to be the late shift was dead, except maybe on the weekends. Now it's their rush hour."

I didn't doubt that for a second. "Fine, but how does that translate to turning everyone out there into the monster squad?"

"Seriously? Look at them. I got a taste of what was going on when we were trying to escape from that tattooed nutcase. I'm like you now, and I still almost shit myself. But those guys?" He waved toward the door leading back to his living room. "They wouldn't have lasted ten seconds. They're armchair heroes."

"Knights of the dinner table?" I offered with a smirk.

"Pretty much. But now, sure, they're causing some chaos..."

*"Some?"*

"Maybe *a bit* more than that," he conceded dismissively. "But really, can you honestly tell me you would rather them be the appetizers instead of the diners?"

What a fucking asshole. He had me over a barrel with that argument and knew it. Maybe I wasn't all that close with them, but hell, I'd known Adam since freshman orientation at NJIT.

Mind you, tearing their fucking throats out and turning them into monsters wouldn't have been my first choice when it came to saving them, but at least Dave's heart was in the right place.

"Besides," he added, "I got some awesome data from watching them turn. So much more useful than those mice I infected."

And by right place, I of course meant he was still an asshole.

Dave proceeded to start bundling up his supplies. That just left the rest of the group to deal with. I could have compelled them to be obedient henchmen, but that didn't feel right. Despite trying to act more the hero, there were still some lines of behavior I didn't care to cross lest they lead to me turning into a total twat.

There was also the little problem of how long such a compulsion would last. Sure, I could order them to stop eating delivery boys, but what happened then? They'd either starve or it would wear off and they'd go right back to being the scourge of guys just trying to earn a buck in this fucked-up world.

There was also the problem of them all being uncovened, despite Dave's bullshit proclamations. In short, there was only one solution – they needed to come with us too.

But what if they didn't want to? I could force them, but I had a feeling that would bite me in the ass as surely as any of Vehron's minions.

I stepped out of the lab, the question still on my mind, when I caught sight of them again. They were seated around the gaming table, two pizzas sitting open in front of them, and no corpses in sight – thank goodness.

"I see dinner arrived," I said idly.

"Yeah," Mike replied, taking a bite and then tossing the rest back onto a paper plate. "But it's not the same. The blood…"

"I know all about the blood," I interrupted. Vampires could eat regular food, but it lacked the luster it had when we'd been alive. It went in one end and came out the other, with no real benefit to us save the minor joy of how it tasted.

At least I knew one human would make it home tonight because of my actions … assuming something else didn't eat him before that happened. Oh well, not my circus, not my monkey. "Just pretend the tomato sauce is blood and…"

Hold on. Pretend! *That was it!* That was how I was going to get them to play ball with me – using the same concept that had brought us back to this apartment week after week.

"You okay, Bill?" Adam asked.

"Dave probably told him what happened to his character," Carl replied. "The shock is finally catching up."

"It's not that," I said. "I don't care about what happened to Kelvin." The fuck? "Well, I do care. Just not right now."

"Not even about the demon orgy where they passed your corpse around for six days straight?"

"What?!" Oh, Dave was *so* gonna fucking get it when this was all over and done with. "Let's not worry about that for the moment. You can bring me up to speed on the way."

"What do you mean, on the way?" Adam asked between bites.

"You're all coming with me. Dave too."

"Why are we…"

"Because look at you. You fuckers are wasting your time here. You're a coven of vampires, top dogs amongst the undead – outside of liches maybe."

"Don't forget demi-liches," Carl added.

"Fuck them. They're just dumb fucking skulls with magic powers. Trust me. I know one, and he's an asshole."

"Really? You know a…"

Not wanting to get distracted again, especially not by the topic of Harry Decker, I kept talking over him. "Bottom line is you … *we* are too good for this shit. Who gives a fuck about some zero level delivery … err … merchants, I guess? We should be out there fucking up kingdoms and claiming them as our own."

Whereas before the pizza had held their thrall, now their attention was fully on me. Holy fuck, this might actually have a shot at working. I had no idea where to go with it, but I'd figure that out later.

"So what are you suggesting?" Adam asked.

"A real life Ravenloft – an adventure that puts every LARP ever played to shame." A few dubious eyebrows were raised, but I continued. "I shit you not. I'm talking real monsters. The type that would make your balls shrivel up. There's magic too."

"We talking weapons? Like vorpal blades?"

"Um … maybe. We'll see."

"The stakes?"

I inwardly groaned at the vampire pun, but went on. "The world itself. We lose and everyone loses. We win, though, and we will be fucking epic."

## 7

## HUNKERING DOWN

If there was a final carrot that convinced my friends to come along, it was the fact that we still had electricity at my place – courtesy of some witches friendly to our cause. Never discount a geek's need to charge his electronics.

Unfortunately, by the time I was finished with my tale of grand adventure, it was getting dangerously close to sunrise. There was no way we'd be able to make it back before it was bright and, judging by the clear sky, sunny out. That wouldn't have necessarily been the end of us. I mean, it's not like I hadn't had several forays out during the daylight hours and survived mostly unscathed.

Sadly, though, unlike me, most vampires weren't acclimated to daytime hours. I guess I was one of the lone fools who had tried to carry on with my normal life postmortem, including a 9-5 job. Hell, Carl was already snoozing by the time I stepped away from the window where I'd been watching the sky lighten.

I shot Ed a text that I was delayed and would be home later. I was sure they'd be pretty pissed by my unscheduled foray into Jersey. There was no point in making it worse for myself by maintaining radio silence.

I wasn't really worried about my roommates – they were easily ignored – but any of our three female neighbors were perfectly capable of giving me a good tongue lashing. Well, maybe not Sally, considering I was all but a stranger to her at the moment.

As my friends settled down for the day, I reflected upon that part. Sally's current memories of me and my friends was minimal at best – a few bits and pieces she'd managed to recover herself along with some scattered remembrances that Christy had been able to uncover. It wasn't much, but it seemed to be enough to prove to her that we weren't full of shit ... most of us anyway. Tom was really gonna get decked when she remembered everything.

*She's a danger to them, but you're too stupid to even consider that.*

Fuck! I hated when my subconscious pointed out something I really didn't want to dwell upon. At least, I hoped it was my subconscious. I truly wasn't sure. I'd been feeling stirrings in my head lately that suggested maybe Dr. Death was waking back up again – violent, sexually aggressive, or overly morose thoughts that seemed to pop into my mind from out of nowhere. It was possible the events of the recent past were just getting to me, but somehow, I didn't think that was the case.

That made my course of action with Christy more imperative than ever. I needed to find a way to chain up Dr. Death for good before he was back with a vengeance.

That was the fear I really didn't want to dwell upon. If that monster woke up, I could find myself once again occupying my mental apartment – blissfully unaware of the real world around me as he slaughtered everything he could get his claws on.

Yeah, thinking about Sally was far less disturbing. Well, maybe not really. That thought of her being dangerous might be worth listening to. She was a killer. I wasn't about to fool myself into thinking otherwise. She'd been a killer before she met me and, despite mellowing out a bit, still didn't have any problems with taking lives if the need arose. The Sally who was with my friends now was a bizarre mix of the past and present. I had no idea how she'd react if pushed the wrong way. Well, okay, it would probably be with snarky violence, but the real question was, how far would that violence go?

We'd only been living under the same roof for a few days and she hadn't given me cause to worry about anything other than her sense of self-entitlement, but then again, she was smart. More than smart enough to realize the capabilities the rest of us brought to the table, with maybe the exception of Tom.

This was maddening. I wasn't Batman; I wasn't used to distrusting the other members of my personal Justice League and forming contingencies just in case. Although, maybe the new me – the one trying to keep his head out of the sand of blissful ignorance – needed to.

Ugh! This line of thinking was giving me a headache – not helped by the loud snores that had begun to permeate the quiet of the room. Whoever coined the phrase "sleeping like the dead" was full of shit.

I grabbed a pillow from Dave's couch and threw it at Mike, who snorted once and then turned over – ending the worst of it for the time being.

The thing was, no matter which way I turned, there were potential pitfalls staring me in the face. Sally's memories were just one. We had prophecies, explosive powers, and more standing in our path. Hell, none of that even counted the big stuff, like the nigh-invincible vampire we were tasked with somehow killing.

"And that doesn't even scratch the surface about the world ending," I said to myself. Hah! Forget stepping into shit over my head. I was sinking in the Challenger Deep of latrines.

These thoughts and others haunted me as I closed my eyes and attempted to drift off to sleep.

An odd sensation, like something crawling on my skin, dragged me back to consciousness. Pity, too. Sally and my third grade teacher, Mrs. Moranisberg, had just asked me to be the judge in a best blowjob contest and were busy arguing over who would go first.

"Hurry up!" a whispered voice commanded.

"You can't rush art," came the equally quiet response.

What the?

I cracked my eyes open and found Mike and Carl standing over me. Before they could say a word, I followed their guilty gaze up to Mike's hand, which was holding a Sharpie right above my forehead.

*Oh, you have got to be fucking kidding me!*

"Um, hi, Bill," he said.

"I told you you were taking too long," Carl muttered.

"You're probably wondering what..."

I cut off Mike's pathetic excuse by way of an uppercut to the jaw, which sent him flying across the room.

I grabbed Carl by his shirt and flung him over my body in the same direction my other friend had just gone sailing, cutting short his look of stunned shock.

"The fuck, dude?" Adam sat up quickly. His body tensed, as if he was ready to bolt should I step in his direction.

"Number one rule of being a vampire – we're super strong and heal really fast, so violence is always an option."

Dave stepped out of his bedroom wearing a pair of hospital scrubs he'd obviously lifted to use as pajamas. "What the fuck are you assholes doing?" He glanced in the corner where Carl and Mike where busy untangling themselves from each other. "Jeez, get a room."

"Bill broke my fucking jaw," Mike complained, getting to his feet. His fangs had descended and his eyes blackened.

As way of response, I simply pointed to my face – which I was certain had been used as a canvas for all sorts of unpleasant things.

Dave's smirk more or less confirmed that. "Looks like a wash to me," he said at last. "We heading out soon?"

I nodded my affirmation.

"Good. Mike and Adam, you guys grab the stuff in my lab near the door. Carl, you empty out the freezer. I'll show you what to take. Bill, I'm gonna need you to grab a few things too."

"Oh, and what the hell are you carrying?" I asked.

"All my game books and campaign notes," he replied as if I'd just asked a particularly stupid question. "You think I trust you fuckers to not take a peek?"

The sun wasn't fully down yet which, interestingly enough, made me feel a bit more secure about starting our trip. Thankfully, it was low enough in the sky for the long shadows to provide more than adequate cover for us.

We'd lucked out more than I had any reason to hope. Adam's car was parked in back of the complex and had a full tank of gas. I'd been expecting an hours-long hike back to Brooklyn, loaded down like a pack mule, but I was happy to accept the ride – even if his little hatchback would be packed to the gills with the five of us and all of Dave's shit.

Dave tried to insist on shotgun, but took a seat in back once I threatened to tie his ass to the roof rack. As much as I was mourning my character, it was kind of liberating to not have that leverage hanging over my head. It wasn't normally like me to be so aggressive, but I figured if there was one group to test my new outlook on life with, it was these guys. Besides, I was feeling pretty good – oddly recharged having taken a rare daytime snooze. I'd never really stopped to consider how much it cost me to fight against my physical nature.

It seemed I'd been fighting against so much since being turned into a vampire that I never bothered to stop and realize maybe not all of it was a bad thing.

Sadly, it was a little late in the game for that revelation. If I survived the next few days, this tiger could rethink some of his stripes. Until then, I needed to keep my game face on.

With everything packed up, we headed out – the most lethal carload of road-tripping dorks the world had ever seen.

8

# WRATH OF THE DEFILERS

"When we get inside, I want everyone to be cool."

"We've been to your apartment before, Bill," Adam rightfully pointed out from the driver's seat.

"Yes, but never as demonic hell-spawn."

"That's actually not bad," Mike said.

"What isn't?"

"As a name for our group."

"Our group?"

"Yeah. If we're gonna follow you on this so-called epic adventure, then we need a name. We can't just take credit for saving the world as ourselves."

"Why not?" I asked, despite knowing deep down the chances of us getting credit for anything were pretty much nil.

"Because that's lame," Carl replied.

"Well, I guess that does makes some sense. I mean, the vampire world kind of does love their names for things. I used to be in charge of Village Coven."

"Lame," came Mike's reply from the backseat.

"Then I was a part of Pandora Coven."

"Better."

"Oh, and the guy who turned me into a vampire was named Jeff."

*"Jeff?"*

"But he insisted everyone call him Night Razor."

"Okay, now we're talking. That's pretty badass."

"You got the ass part right. He was one of the biggest ones I ever knew."

"Was?"

"Up until I killed him," I replied, embellishing things a bit. It's not like the one person who could contradict my story was up on the details anymore.

"You killed him?"

"Fuck yeah," I said. "I didn't tell you my name in the coven ... Dr. Death."

The laughter that ensued did little to mollify my fragile ego. Thankfully, Dave finally spoke up with something to take the spotlight off me.

"How about the Defilers?"

"Huh?" Adam asked.

"Isn't that what you fuckers called yourselves in the last campaign?" Dave replied.

"Oh yeah," Mike said. "But that adventure ended on a bit of a low note."

"Sorry, but when I told you those owlbears were in heat, you really should have fucking listened. Regardless, I thought the name was kind of cool."

There were a few murmurs of assent.

"Fine," I said with sigh. "We're the Defilers." In the back of my mind, a small part of me realized the pain Sally often expressed when dealing with those less cool than herself.

"Awesome," Adam replied. "But you gotta lose that gay-ass Dr. Death shit. We just can't be seen with you otherwise."

Deep down in my gut, I knew this was a bad idea. I should have left them all back where I found them. Hell, Newark was pretty much full of assholes anyway.

Any way you looked at things, this did nothing but add complications to the whole affair. Hell, I had no clue how my friends back at the apartment would react.

"I'm just gonna warn you all, well, most of you anyway, that the women in this building are hands off." I smirked at Adam, and he casually flipped me the finger.

"You afraid of the competition?" Mike asked.

"No, I'm afraid of cleaning up the mess." I pulled out my key and unlocked the front door. "In addition to me and my roommates, we have another vampire, a witch, and an Icon — any one of which is more than capable of killing you faster than you can say 'Hey, baby.'"

"What's an Icon?"

"I'll get to that in a moment. First off, yes, Christy is a real witch and I don't mean some stupid Wiccan. Think at least a tenth level magic user here ... maybe higher."

"Still not a lot of hit points," Carl commented as we started up the stairs.

"Maybe not, but that assumes you can survive one of her fireballs, which I assure you, you cannot."

"You don't know our saves."

"Oh yeah, I do. Trust me. Then there's the Icon. She's the legendary foe of all vampires. Imagine a high level paladin whose favored class enemy is us."

"Paladins are so fucking annoying."

"Yeah, well, tell that to her and her +5 Holy Avenger."

"She has a..."

I stopped and laughed, cutting off Adam's question. I'd been joking about magic weapons, but I'd forgotten about Sheila's sword. Holy shit. We really *were* living out a real life D&D adventure.

Sadly, the only resurrection spell I was aware of included being dipped in a glowing orange pool and emerging as a slave to the hordes of rock monsters known as the Jahabich. All things considered, I'd much sooner just gain a negative level.

I gave the guys the vacant apartment in our basement. I wasn't sure if it was a result of panic from the weirdness of the world, the doings of the witches who had briefly occupied the building during my three-month absence in Vegas, or some combination of the above, but the apartment building where I lived was now empty save for my friends. Nobody had shown up to change locks, collect belongings, or make repairs, for that matter.

Oh well, when in doubt, possession is nine-tenths of the law.

I had the guys drop their stuff off before taking them to meet the rest of the occupants. I'd hosted my game here on occasion, like that time Dave's place was being fumigated for roaches, so they all knew my roommates. However, I wanted to make certain no nasty surprises occurred if they ran into the other inhabitants – a far more lethal bunch, all told, than Ed or Tom.

There was no answer at the girls' apartment. That was

odd. It was long past sundown, but still relatively early as far as the night went.

I was tempted to use the spare key to let myself in and check things out, but it seemed I had a nasty habit of running into Sheila during those moments. Not that it was a bad thing. It was just that, despite her control over her powers, she had this tendency to *flare up* whenever I surprised her. I wasn't really in the mood to get blasted across the room this evening.

Still, if they were in there and awake, they'd have answered.

"I don't think anyone's home," Dave said, his tone bored.

"Shhh!" I took a deep breath and reached out with my senses. The scent of my gaming friends was overpowering at first. At least a couple of them had skipped showering for the past day or so, judging by things. However, I pushed past that, my nose filling with the smells of the building around me, followed by the lingering lilac moisturizer that Christy favored, Sheila's simple yet slightly sweet perfume, and the overly expensive shit Sally enjoyed.

"Lingering" was the keyword there. It was recent, but it told me nobody else currently occupied this floor. The lack of noise, aside from maybe Carl's heavy mouth breathing, confirmed that.

No, wait. Faint voices filtered down to me from above. Nobody was home down here, but upstairs was a different story. That wasn't overly surprising. My apartment had kind of turned into the unofficial meeting area of the place.

"C'mon." I turned and headed up the stairs.

I dispensed with any pretense of ceremony when we arrived on my floor and just pulled my key out of my pocket.

"Remember what I said about the girls. Be cool or become dust," I warned one last time before opening my front door – only to find a glowing red ball of death staring me in the face.

**9**

# MEET AND GREET

My options were limited. I could save myself, relying on my vampire reflexes, or I could eat the brunt of it and save my friends.

Fuck it. When faced with the choice of red wine or white, I'm of the mindset that you make room and down both those mothers.

While cries of "What the fuck?" and "Holy shit!" rang out, I threw myself backward with everything I had, slamming into my friends and scattering them like bowling pins, in the hope that the death ray would pass by overhead, doing little more than singeing our pride.

I landed on my back, looking up at the ceiling, but no fireball of doom appeared. Daring to sit up, I saw Christy standing about ten feet inside of my apartment, a red glow still around her, but rapidly diminishing.

"Bill?"

"No shit!" I snapped.

"Why didn't you knock first?"

"Because I live here." I forced my tone to remain calm. There was little to be gained by pissing off the hormonal witch who was very shortly going to be mucking about in my brain. "More importantly, since when have you decided I needed to be blasted into oblivion? Tom's the one who always leaves the toilet seat up."

Speaking of my roommate, he leaned back on the couch where he'd been sitting and waved as if nothing had just happened. Dick.

Christy took a deep breath, but the glow remained around her. Her eyes searched out the forms that still lay scattered in the hall behind me and narrowed. "I wasn't looking to hex you," she explained. "I put some blood wards on the front stoop to warn me if anyone other than the six of us tried to enter. I set them to tingle especially hard if it was vampires."

I stood up and smiled. It was hard to be mad at her, despite having just stared my own death in the face and had it give me the finger back. Her precautions were smart, doubly so since I had little doubt the Draculas were aware of my ... *our* ... every move.

They'd begrudgingly let us go, having ordered us to kill Vehron or die trying – most of their betting pool probably leaning toward that latter option. I wasn't dumb enough to think they'd sit back and patiently wait for us to call and tell them how things went, though. We probably had a week at most before they showed up at our doorstep and gave us a friendly *escort* to our fate.

"Who are they?" Christy asked at last.

Tom got to his feet, walked to her side, and said, "Hey, guys!" effectively draining the tension from the room.

I stepped to the side to allow my other friends to enter, hoping they didn't say anything stupid.

Christy grimaced when she saw Dave. I'd gotten the vibe, during the short time of their acquaintance, that she didn't particularly like him – not surprising, since on a good day his personality was about as abrasive as steel wool.

I quickly introduced the rest to her as they entered.

A look of confusion washed over her face when I was done. "I thought all the survivors of Village Coven were accounted for."

"Like these guys would hang with those preppy dickbags," Tom scoffed. "This is Bill's gaming group. S'up?" He stepped forward to shake their hands. Though he wasn't a regular, he'd sat with us on a few occasions when we were a man short.

Christy pulled me aside. I kept half my attention on the group anyway, noting how the nostrils of the three junior vamps in the room were working. They might be on good terms with Tom, but they'd all tasted a lot of blood recently, and I wasn't about to rule out them trying to make a snack out of him.

"You turned your gaming friends into vampires?" she hissed at me. "When did this happen, why didn't you tell us, and at what point did you think this was a good idea? Sally is going to be..." She trailed off as she realized the error in that last part. "Well, anyway, what were you thinking?"

"I didn't turn anybody," I said. "Dave did."

"Oh." Her eyes narrowed in his direction.

"It's a long story."

"What have you been doing all this..."

"Duh! Bill needed my research," Dave said from across the room. Some vampires apparently needed decades to get with the program, while others were quite obviously born for the job. Goddamn, I really needed to remember to buy him a copy of *How to Win Friends and Influence People* for his next birthday.

"Yes, but first of all, I wanted to make sure you were

okay," I countered, which was true. I turned back toward Christy. "He's my friend."

Her eyes softened and she nodded. It had taken me a while after our first disastrous meeting, but I had eventually convinced Christy that, no matter what bullshit spewed out of my pie hole, I was loyal to my friends – to the end, if need be. "So why are they...?"

I mouthed "later" to her. I couldn't quite say the truth, that I was keeping an eye on them so that they didn't go on an insane killing spree through the ranks of Dominos and Papa Johns. That wouldn't exactly endear her to them, especially since she would then – rightfully – assume it meant she and Tom were potentially on the menu.

Speaking of which, my fellow *Defilers* were paying way more attention to my roommate than a casual greeting warranted. "I just brought the guys up to meet the rest of the group."

I turned toward them and waved them over before any of them got some not-so-bright ideas. "Guys, this is Tom's fiancée, Christy." At my use of the F word, Tom's head spun toward me. He opened his mouth, but then apparently thought better of saying anything that would make Christy happily feed him to my friends.

What can I say? Even with the world on the brink of madness, there was still always time to stick it in and break it off.

Adam walked over and held out his hand, which Christy accepted warily. Mike and Carl were a little slower to do so.

"Which one is she again?" Mike asked.

Christy turned toward me with a raised eyebrow, to which I grinned sheepishly. "She's the magic user."

"We prefer to be called Magi," she corrected.

That got my friends' attention, and all of them converged on Christy as if she was wearing a chainmail bikini.

"So can you cast Cloudkill?"

"What about Summon Monster Six?"

"Do you have a familiar?"

"Do you prefer wands or rods?"

"You versus a similar level sorcerer, who wins?"

"Do you know Feeblemind?"

She stepped back, a look of confusion on her face. "I have no idea what any of you are talking about."

"Yeah, sorry about that," I said. "I think they already got hit with that Feeblemind spell."

That set Tom at least to laughing.

Christy composed herself and tried to explain that she wasn't up to speed with anything they were asking about because it didn't have a basis in real magic. My friends weren't overly happy with that. Their attention turned toward Tom again as she attempted to explain a little bit about spirits and other shit that, quite frankly, wasn't all that interesting.

"You can give them a lesson on the finer points of mage training later. I just brought them up to introduce them and let everyone know..." I muttered the rest.

"Excuse me?" Christy asked.

"That they'd be coming with us," I said with a guilty grin.

Her eyes narrowed. "All of them?"

"Yes, *all* of them."

Before any protests could be raised, I changed the subject. "Where are Ed, Sally, and Sheila?"

"Sheila?" Adam asked.

Without thinking, I replied, "She's the Icon ... the paladin I was telling you about."

"No no no," he said. "I meant this wouldn't happen to be Princess Sheila, would it?"

Oh fuck! I'd spent the last couple of years telling any sympathetic ear I could find about the goddess I worked with. That circle included my roommates and my gaming buddies.

Eventually, one of Dave's adventures had included the king of the realm being assassinated and us being tasked with finding the killer. His daughter, who Dave had introduced as Princess Sheila, presented us with medals of heroism following our investigation. It was his way of mocking my pain.

Ever since then, we'd been her champions, but – much like in real life – she was always just out of my reach.

I should have remembered that before bringing these fuckers here. Now I was either gonna have to listen to their shit or kill them, and believe me, that last option was starting to sound preferable.

Sadly, the few seconds I took to process this were more than enough to admit my guilt. The four shit-eating grins – make that five; Tom was enjoying this too – that met my gaze cemented it.

Unbidden thoughts filled my head – all of them ending with me surrounded by piles of recently dusted vampire.

*Kill them all.*

I tried my best to ignore what I really hoped was just my internal defense mechanisms reacting. "So are the others around?" I asked Christy through gritted teeth.

The look on her face reflected bemusement tinged with a wee bit of compassion, albeit not nearly enough for my liking. She kept from smiling as she replied, "Ed's in his room. Sally and Sheila still aren't back from Manhattan."

"They went there already?"

"Yeah. They left right after you went to prep the safe house."

"And they haven't gotten back yet?"

"Relax, Bill," she said, putting a hand upon my shoulder.

"Look how long you were gone. You came back fine. They will too."

She probably had a point. Both of them were easily as capable as ... oh fuck it, *more* capable than me. Downtown Manhattan couldn't be any more dangerous than Newark these days ... or so I hoped.

Even so, I was glad I'd gotten some sleep earlier because I had a feeling I wouldn't be resting easy until both of them were safe and sound. Quite the ask in this day and age.

There was no point in introducing Ed to people he already knew, but Dave insisted on knocking on his door and bugging him for a blood sample. My roommate raised a skeptical eye and said he'd think about it – probably more to get rid of Dave than anything else.

Then, before my former DM could push his luck and start asking for toes or other body parts, I *suggested* they all head back downstairs and settle in for the night.

My own supply of blood was starting to run low, but I offered to share what I had with them – knowing that once we were on the road, I'd almost certainly have to accept the fact that it was either actively hunting or going mad from hunger.

*No one can eat just one.*

Fuck, that was getting annoying. It also pointed to the fact that my time was running out.

Once the footsteps of the Defilers – gah, that was stupid – had retreated below, I quickly shut the door and turned to Christy.

"That blood thingee, is it still on?"

She nodded. "Yes, I made it so that the ward itself was persistent. Takes a bit of extra work, but it also saves me from having to run up and down the stairs to reset it every time." Her hands went to her stomach to help emphasize that probably wasn't a prospect she relished while carrying a bowling ball inside of her.

"Does it work the other way too?"

"Other way?"

"If something that's not us tries to leave."

"Oh, yeah, it's omnidirectional. Why?"

I hesitated for a moment. There was something about telling an already twitchy mage that her new housemates had a penchant for murderous mayhem that struck me as dicey. "I'm worried about them. They were off in the wild by themselves with nobody to guide them."

"Except that asshole."

"Yes, except for Dave," I acknowledged with a sigh. "I know. He can be a bit ... intense."

She cocked an eyebrow.

"And unlikable too. However, from what he told me, he was doing his best to keep them in check."

"He turned them."

"I know, but he was also trying to keep them stocked with hospital blood."

"Trying?" Ed took a seat on the couch. His tone was one of casual conversation – he'd long grown desensitized to the bloody quirks of the supernatural world – but I had a feeling his question wasn't going to make Christy particularly happy.

"They've had a few ... incidents," I admitted.

"Incidents?" she asked coldly.

"Mostly involving gang members."

"Oh."

"And maybe a few delivery guys."

"So let me get this straight. You just invited a small coven of vampires to move in on the ground floor, despite knowing they're not like you. That at any time they could snap."

"Sally's not like Bill either," Tom pointed out, coming to my rescue.

"Tom has a point," Ed replied. "As much as I like her, let's not kid ourselves. She's not gonna think twice about snacking on her fellow New Yorkers if she gets thirsty."

I was tempted to point out that any and all denizens of the supernatural world could at any time resort to brutal violence – including the Magi. Hell, I'd been on the receiving end of that more times than I preferred. In a sense, weren't we all – every single one of us – killers in our own right?

"They just need some guidance," I said quickly, not wanting to open that can of worms. "They'll listen to me. I've already established myself as the party leader."

"Party..."

"Coven master," I corrected, "but in a way they'll understand. Besides, it's not like everyone else here can't take care of themselves in a pinch."

"Bill's got a point."

"No he doesn't, and you know it," Christy snapped at Tom. "You're vulnerable."

"I'm fine, babe. Nobody's going to touch me."

"You are not fine!"

Okay, that was a bit harsh. "Is there something I'm missing here?"

"It's nothing important," Tom replied.

I glanced at Ed, and he just held up his hands, indicating he wanted no part of this.

"Define 'nothing important,'" I pressed.

It was Christy who finally answered.

"It's his faith. He can't channel it anymore."

## 10

## SHOULD I STAY OR SHOULD I GO?

"Huh?"

Yeah, maybe that wasn't the most eloquent way of questioning her revelation, but it was all I had. From the time I'd become a vampire, Tom had possessed an ability that I'd only seen a handful of other humans master – the ability to infuse an object with the power of faith.

My roommate wasn't exactly a holy roller, but faith magic itself was a misnomer. It didn't require devotion to God. It manifested as a powerful belief in something; anything, really. Technically, one could empower a roll of toilet paper as readily as a crucifix. More important was that it could really fuck up a vampire's day.

In my roommate's case, he was a collector. He maintained a storage unit in Jersey, close to where his parents lived, that was filled with toys, comics, and old trading cards. Pity that Tom was closer to being a crazed hoarder than a discerning connoisseur. Most of the stuff he had was crap, barely worth the effort it would take to burn.

The few items he did have of value, he displayed proudly

in his room – much to my and Ed's delight, as we'd occasionally fuck with them just to annoy him. However, there had been one toy that had truly set him off. Soon after my turning, he'd managed to find a mint condition Optimus Prime Transformer, which he'd picked up for a pittance at a flea market. Such was his joy, combined with the greed of overestimating its potential worth, that he'd managed to inadvertently tap into the hidden well of white-hot power known to mages and vampires alike as faith.

What should have just been a pretty cool find instead became a weapon that could be used against the undead with brutal efficiency.

Sadly for him, it was smashed to bits during my first real test as a vampire – our foray to take down Night Razor. However, soon after, Christy was able to fashion him an amulet of sorts – inscribed with the toy's likeness. It had served as a conduit for the crazed *love* he'd felt for his prized possession. He'd worn it ever since, saving my ass in the process more than once.

"I don't understand," I said, adding a bit more intelligence to my grunt of a few moments prior.

"Tell him," Christy said.

"It's not a big..." Tom began.

"*Tell him.*" A beam of yellowish energy coalesced in Christy's right hand and lanced out at my friend's backside.

Tom jumped as if he'd been shot with a BB gun. "Ouch, okay, okay! Goddamn, that stings." He looked me in the eye as if seeking help, but I couldn't help but grin. The poor fucker was whipped in more ways than one. "Your sympathy fills my heart with joy."

I shrugged and he went on.

"It started a few months back. Remember when we got jumped by those HBC fuckers?"

"At the safe house?"

"Yep."

"How could I forget, especially after Ed made that one explode? But, if I recall correctly, you managed to burn the shit out of one of them pretty good too."

"I know," he said. "The thing is, I'm pretty sure that guy wasn't all that old. He'd have knocked my head off if he was. He should have been toast. I mean, it worked about as well on him as it had with François and that fucker was a shit load stronger."

I hadn't considered that. All I'd noticed at the time was screaming vampire and the smell of sizzling flesh. It had been enough that we'd won. "Why didn't you say anything?"

"I thought I was just having an off day."

"Go on," Christy prodded.

"I'm getting to the point," he replied defensively. "Then those vamps jumped me about a week back when I was coming home from the coffee shop..."

He didn't need to remind me. The memory of our *trial* was still a raw wound. We'd just barely made it out of that one, and I couldn't even claim it was in one piece due to Sally. "Yeah, I remember. You weren't wearing your amulet when they dragged you in. I figured they caught you without it."

"He was wearing it," Christy said. "Ever since the world started getting weird, I've been making him wear it whenever he goes out."

Ed snickered a bit, no doubt because Tom's balls had clearly relocated to Christy's purse. He lamely covered it up by pretending he was coughing – probably didn't want to be on the receiving end of a magic missile.

"Yeah, I had it on," Tom continued, looking frustrated. "I don't know what the fuck went wrong, but it didn't do shit. I might as well have hit those fuckers with a battery-operated bug racket for all the good it did."

"Are you sure?" I asked, grasping at straws. "Maybe it was just another off day. You tend to have a lot of those."

He gave me a sour look, then pulled the amulet out of his pocket. "Here, see for yourself."

I looked down at his outstretched hand. "Um..."

"Pussy says what?" he asked with a smirk.

"Fuck you." I braced myself as I put my hand atop his – waiting for the oh-so-pleasant sensation of my flesh immolating. What happened instead was a jolt, not entirely enjoyable, mind you, but really no more jarring than licking a nine-volt.

"See?" he said. "It's pretty much the magical equivalent of a joy buzzer."

"So maybe you just need a new one."

"That won't work," Christy said. "The problem isn't the magic in the receptacle. That's working fine." She must have noticed the look on my face because her tone got a bit defensive. "I know what I'm doing. It's Tom's ability to channel faith that's diminished."

He nodded and stepped to her side, putting an arm around her shoulder. "It's true. Our time together was sweet, but cut short way too soon. Alas, I can barely remember the soft caress of Prime's jagged plastic edges."

Christy elbowed him. "This isn't a game. Faith magic is nothing to joke about. Do you know how rare it is to find a non-Magi who can utilize it, even sparingly? People just don't believe in anything these days – I mean, *really* believe. They're too jaded and their attention spans are too short. Sure, you hear about families going to church every day, praying before bed, all of that, but it's a sham for most of them, even if they don't want to admit it consciously."

"Yeah, but you can use it, right? I remember back when I first met you, you and Decker were keeping us tied up in..."

"It's different for those of us who are born Magi. We can

manipulate the latent energies around us. We can tap into the power that seeps through the cracks in the veil. Faith is just another form of that – leaking into our world from one of the higher planes."

"You're losing me here."

"I gotta side with Bill," Ed added. "What are you talking about?"

"Magic, the multiverse, all of it!" An angry red glow momentarily appeared around her, causing the rest of us to back up a step. "It's hard to explain in a hundred words or less, but suffice it to say you are all painfully aware that we're not alone in this world."

It wasn't a question. We'd all seen the freakiest of the freaky. Hell, I'd gotten up close and personal with a death god, for fuck's sake.

"Well, it's not like those things are coming from down the street. There are cracks in reality everywhere ... spots where the barriers between worlds are so thin that you can sometimes accidentally step through them."

"Like the Bermuda Triangle?" Tom asked.

"Something like that. Ley lines, places of power, vortexes; there are lots of names for them. And not all transgressions are accidental. There are beings who can sense these weak spots and cross over as they please, although it's not nearly as bad as it used to be."

"What do you mean by that?" I asked, intrigued.

"Think about it." She eased herself down into our love seat. For all her power, she was still bound by the physical laws of being a woman almost seven months pregnant. "For whatever reason, these cracks between worlds have been on the decline."

"How do you know?" Ed asked.

"It's common sense for anyone who's ever had a history lesson," she replied as if Ed were an idiot. "Look at our history as a species, even the sanitized stuff. Monsters, wizards, dragons; they appear in ancient texts to the point of being almost blasé about them. That's because they were. Thousands of years ago, during the time of Kala the White..." She trailed off.

"Wait," I said. "I've heard that before. Is that the White Mother?"

"One and the same," she replied, a touch of defensiveness to her voice.

"What are you guys talking about?" Tom asked.

Judging from the confused looks of my two roommates, Christy hadn't shared the revelations from a few days past, that the White Mother – venerated mentor of the Magi – had actually been a psycho bitch. I know I hadn't. It was probably stupid at this late stage in the game to be keeping secrets, but I didn't see any harm in this one.

We were already aware of the threat the Jahabich represented. Christy was also privy to the cave etchings we'd managed to snag some pictures of. That she was terrified of this knowledge somehow causing Sheila to snap and go on a wizard-hunting spree seemed to be a bit of a stretch for me. However, due to the overall uselessness of knowing a crazy woman, thousands of years dead, was responsible for their creation, I didn't see the harm in keeping my mouth shut.

However, that didn't mean I couldn't throw her a lifeline when she needed one. "It's just some ancient history crap. So your point?"

Her eyes flashed a quick look of gratitude my way. "Anyway, a long time ago, this was all commonplace. Humans, vampires, the forest folk, and many more beings of both light and darkness lived side by side. It wasn't always in harmony – but there's no denying there was familiarity. What we consider weird and strange today was mundane once upon a time."

"So what happened?"

"Nobody knows. Maybe it was a calamity, natural progression, or intelligent design, but whatever the case, it's all been on a slow decline. Old gods were forgotten, not necessarily because they wanted to be. What once was as easy as stepping around the corner eventually required effort. The ability to channel faith magic, vampires, and Magi being relegated to the world of myth and legend, all of it. It's indicative of that same decline. Heck, assuming the world doesn't get immolated first, one day the source might just finally dry up for good."

"The source?"

"Magi myth. Kind of like the tree of life – a place where it all originates from."

We all internalized this in silence, until Tom finally asked, "So what's this have to do with anything?"

To my surprise, Christy actually laughed. "Nothing really, I guess. I just sometimes get caught up in things. I'm a dying breed, one of the few people left who actually knows the real history of the world." Her tone hardened again. "Regardless, it still doesn't change the fact that you've lost your connection to your well of faith. Without it, you're vulnerable."

"Technically, he's always been."

"You know what I mean," Christy snapped. I quickly shut the fuck up. Perhaps Tom's balls weren't the only set currently taking up residence in her purse.

I half expected my subconscious to speak up and suggest I gut her, but even Dr. Death was apparently smart enough to know when to keep his trap shut.

"Well," Ed began cautiously – probably not wanting to be verbally castrated too, "what about the rest of his stuff? I mean, no offense, man, but you can get pretty bent out of shape when we touch any of your shit."

"Maybe that's because you should keep your fucking hands off it," Tom offered.

"It doesn't work that way," Christy replied. "You can't force faith. It has to come naturally."

"So what you're saying is he doesn't love the rest of his stuff like he loved Prime."

"Apparently not," she replied.

Tom just shrugged at this revelation. "Still doesn't mean you assholes should be touching any of it."

We spent some time trying to dissect the root of whatever had caused Tom's initial obsession to take hold, in an attempt to see if it could be replicated. Sure, Optimus had been a pretty good collector's item, but he had one or two pieces that were worth more. No matter the case, that was a great big nada. I could touch them, play with them, or pose them in obscene positions without so much as a spark.

Even Christy had to conclude that it made no sense, finally admitting that perhaps it was "the mystery of faith."

Sadly, that wasn't a particularly helpful answer. At the same time, it did give me an opening for something I had been wanting to suggest but, up until now, hadn't quite worked up the nerve to do.

I turned to Tom. "Maybe you should stay here."

"What?" he asked.

"Exactly what I said. Stay here, guard the home front, hold down the fort." I tried to make it sound more important than it probably was.

"No fucking way, dude."

"Hear him out," Ed said.

"Ganging up on me?"

"No," Ed replied. "I'm not siding with anyone. But Bill

has a point. Even Christy said you're vulnerable. She's right. Of all of us..."

"Don't even go there," Tom said, pointing a finger. "Or do you want to compare the number of scars we've both racked up over the past year?"

He was right on that one, but it was a weak argument. "Yes, Ed's gotten his ass kicked more than you..."

"Hey!"

"It's true. You'd either be dead or sucking blood clots if Sheila hadn't stepped in."

Tom opened his mouth, a look of triumph on his face, but I cut him off before he could say anything. "But he's not. He's also got his shotgun and..."

"And a full box of silver slugs," Ed added, a slight note of threat to his voice. Some people just couldn't handle criticism well.

"Yes, that. But, as I was going to say, you also have your blood."

"Oh, that's a great fucking defense," Tom cried. "If he gets his arms ripped off, he can at least take out any vamps standing around! Not bad, for a kamikaze pilot maybe."

"Yes, I admit that's a poor offensive tactic, but it does give him a measure of protection against anyone in the know. Also, the Jahabich want Ed for whatever crazy reason they might have. As much as I'd love to leave both your asses on the sidelines, there's a chance that the second the rest of us turn our backs, those fucking things could burrow up beneath this place."

I walked up and put a hand on Tom's shoulder, giving it a slight squeeze. "Sorry to say it, man, but the supernatural world isn't after your ass in any capacity other than as a snack. There's no reason for you to do this."

Christy had been silent up until now. I knew she was weighing the options. Bringing him along was dangerous.

Leaving him, though, meant hoping he was all right, but being unable to do much if he wasn't. Regardless, she knew his odds were much better staying put. "Listen, honey. Bill's right. I don't..."

"Not happening," he replied, cutting her off. "There's no way I'm letting you go without me."

"I can take care of myself."

"I know that, but what happens if you can't?" He stepped up, put his arms around her, and drew her in. "I can't let anything happen to you or little Legolas."

"Legolas?!" She tried to pull back, but he pulled her in tighter.

"Or Loki," he amended quickly. "I won't let anything out there hurt you. I ... well ... you know."

"Love her?" Ed offered.

"I was getting to that!" Tom snapped.

"We know that," I said, trying to pull him out of the hole he was digging – mainly by jumping into it myself. "And that's why I think you should both stay behind."

# 11

# THE BITCHING HOUR

There was no doubt I'd just ruined whatever tender moment Tom had been going for in his attempt to persuade Christy to let him come along.

She pulled out of his grasp and rounded on me, her eyes sparking briefly with power. "What did you just say?"

"You heard me. Both of you should stay behind."

"You know I can't do that."

"Why not?" Ed asked. "For once, Bill is making sense."

"You know what's at stake here," she continued as she took a step toward me. I considered turning tail and going to see what my gaming group was up to.

"We all know what's at stake here," Ed said.

"No you don't," she replied through gritted teeth.

"Listen, you know what we're walking into," I said at last, steeling myself for this battle. It might not be as physically painful as facing Vehron, but that didn't mean it would be any more pleasant. "Sheila, Sally, me ... we're at the top of our game, physically at least."

I held up a hand in Tom's direction, before he could even

open his mouth. Knowing a fucker since Kindergarten had its advantages.

"Hell, even that batch of dorks downstairs are on par with the strongest weightlifters in the world."

"I can..."

"Yes, I know. You can take care of yourself. We all know that, but let's be realistic here. You're not at your peak. Sure, you're holding up better than most. When my Aunt Annie was as pregnant as you, she could barely waddle to the fridge."

Christy's eyes narrowed. That might not have been the best tangent to veer off on.

"Even you have to admit you get tired faster than you used to. You don't have as much stamina, physically or even magically, I'd bet."

Her lip trembled. I was venturing into some potentially bad territory here.

"You're also not just putting your own life at risk going up there with us."

There it was – the one fact that couldn't be disputed. Now to only hope it stuck.

The funny thing was, a small part of me didn't want it to. Christy was smart and powerful. Losing her would be a massive blow to both our resources and my fragile confidence in our success. Even so, the woman was only a few short months away from popping. All it would take was one swipe from an enemy's claws or a punch to the midsection to end it. I could live with a lot of stuff ... including whatever shit I might have to do to get through this mess, but I wasn't sure I could live with that.

"And what happens if you fail?" she asked.

"What happens if we don't?"

"We were *all* sentenced by the First Coven to carry this out."

"You're a mage, not a vampire. They have no ground to stand on politically if it comes down to it."

"*Politics?* You're saying I should rely on politics?"

"It's better than any excuse I have."

"That didn't help me during the trial. You saw the Grand Mentor, how he poisoned them against me. How he somehow even got to my coven."

"We don't know that."

"Then where are they?"

"Well, have you tried reaching out to them?"

She was silent for a moment. "What's the use? Who knows how much damage he's done or is still doing?"

"I'm pretty sure he's not doing much anymore." Oh crap, did I say that out loud?

For a moment, I thought I might be off the hook, but then Ed, of all people, had to ask, "What do you mean by that?"

"Um..."

"Seriously. How do you know what he is or isn't doing? As far as I knew, we'd never met Gandalf before the trial."

I tried to think of something to say. Maybe that I'd spied on him using Harry Decker's skull ... no, that was probably an even worse thing to mention in front of Christy. Some days, I so wished I was a better liar.

"What is it?" Christy asked at last.

Fuck. "Gan," I admitted.

"What about her?"

I tensed up, expecting to be blown through the floor or something. "She may have ... intervened."

"You mean she fucked up his shit?" Tom asked a bit too brightly. Maybe that hole in the floor was gonna be big enough for two people. "Way to go for the little hellion."

"Is that what happened?" Christy asked, her eyes narrowing.

"Not quite in those words, but yes. Gan made sure the Mentor never left that building."

"And you asked her to do this?"

"Me? No. The asshole might've fucked us all over, but I never asked her to kill him. Hell, if anything, I wouldn't have minded having him around while the Jahabich were busy using me as a punching bag. Believe me, the little nutbag acted on her own accord." I paused for a moment, as this next part was gonna be the tricky one. "She told me that the witch who'd escaped caused her people great shame and it needed to be rectified."

Her eyes opened wide at that. "My sister?"

"Uh, yeah, the same one who ratted us out."

"But the Mentor didn't..."

"Gan said she didn't like witnesses. Too much paperwork to deal with for her liking." And there it was, yet another dirty secret out in the open courtesy of yours truly's big fucking mouth.

For a second there, silence reigned supreme in our living room. Hell, even Tom took a step back. I mean, Christy wasn't shitting us with her use of *sister* – or at least in a sense of the word. She'd been more or less raised by Decker as a part of his coven. He'd been a second father to her, so it probably wasn't a stretch to imagine she'd had a strong bond with the rest, at least before she'd been assigned to seduce Tom as way of keeping tabs on me, only to end up falling in love with the doofus.

"Good."

"What?" my roommates and I spat nearly simultaneously.

"I said good," Christy repeated.

"But..." I began.

"I mourned for my sisters and mentor when I first heard they'd fallen." For a moment, I could sense the pain behind

Christy's eyes, but then they hardened. "That's over and done with, though. I won't mourn anymore. As for the Grand Mentor, I hope the little bitch took her time and made it hurt."

Tom, Ed, and I exchanged glances. They each conveyed the same thing: *whoa*, this chick was ice cold. I'd never known Christy to be so casual about anything like this. Compared to the rest of us, she was usually our group's resident hippie chick.

"Don't be so surprised," she said at last, her voice devoid of emotion. "My sisters chose their path, and I chose mine." She glanced at Tom, and her gaze softened. "Theirs led to ruin. Mine ... well, that's still to be determined. The Grand Mentor, though, can rot. He could have convened a conclave, tried me by the laws of our people, and let me say my piece in my defense, but he threw me to the wolves instead." After a moment she added, "No offense, Bill."

"None taken. Werewolves don't exist anyway."

"At least not in the classical sense," she replied.

Really? Sadly, we didn't have time for that. "Fine, but that means the Dracs have lost their hold over you. You're free."

"None of us are free, Bill. I know you and Sally gave me that little speech about fate, but I'm not sure I'm quite ready to buy that."

"What speech?" Ed asked.

She ignored him. "This is my path to walk. I need to see this through. But now that I know the Mentor's dead and not out there spreading his bile against me, maybe I don't need to walk it alone..."

"You're not alone. We're with you," I said.

"Maybe I can repair some of the damage." She was quite obviously talking to herself, going down some mental corridor where we weren't invited. That wasn't good. From the sound of her voice, I'd made exactly zero progress in my argument.

It was time to take a stand.

I steeled my voice, imagining myself as the tough guy in the room. For all intents and purposes, I was the leader of this ragtag group. It was time to act it. "I'm serious about what I said. I don't want either of you coming along. That's final."

Christy turned toward me, almost as if noticing me for the first time. "Final, eh?" she asked with a hint of amusement. "And how do you plan to enforce that?"

"I'm a vampire, the scourge of the night."

"You can't even decide which woman you want to be with."

"Wait, what do you mean by that?" Ed asked, suddenly showing a lot more interest in the conversation than at any time in the past ten minutes.

"Ixnay," I hissed through gritted teeth. "We're talking about keeping you safe. Don't change the subject."

"Fine. So once again I ask *how* you plan to make me stay here."

Oh, fuck this shit. I channeled my inner Dr. Death – figuratively, of course. "A couple of broken legs can be marvelous motivation."

"Hold on," Tom said, stepping up to Christy. "You can't threaten to break my woman's legs. That's not cool."

"If it helps, I meant yours."

"Oh, well then ... wait, that would hurt."

"Bill's not breaking anyone's legs," Christy said dismissively.

Okay, now she was starting to tick me off. It was bad

enough I got dissed by just about every evil entity out there. I sure as fuck wasn't going to take any smack talk from a chick who'd soon be waist deep in shitty diapers and breast milk.

Fuck Kelvin Lightblade. I imagined myself as Conan facing off against Thulsa Doom. No way was I gonna end up on the motherfucking tree of woe in this standoff.

My eyes blackened as I said, "If I have to make you hate me to save your life, I'll do it. It's the end of the world. Hard choices are gonna need to be made."

Silence met my proclamation. Holy shit, was I actually winning this one?

"Hard choices. You mean like refusing to help you tame Dr. Death?"

"What?"

"Or maybe I could stop trying to chip away the wall in Sally's brain."

My threats had been idle, but something told me hers weren't. "You can't stop that."

"The hell I can't."

"She's your friend too."

Christy took a step back and placed her hands upon her hips. "I know that, but don't you dare think for a second I wouldn't sacrifice either of you. I would kill every vampire, every Icon, every single decent person on this planet if it meant saving my baby. I will see this monster in Boston dead. I will make sure that the White Mother's heresies are laid to rest. I will sacrifice everyone and everything I hold dear to make sure this prophecy doesn't come to pass."

Oh shit.

I turned and caught Tom's gaze. I expected to see the same iron there, but instead, his face held a look of worry that said he was sure she meant him too if it came down to it.

That was this argument's game, set, and match ... and none of it in my favor.

## 12

## THE TELEPHONE GAME

The next few hours were spent helping Christy shore up her wards on the exits of the building. She also added a few extras to the thresholds of both her and my apartments. As much as I hoped they would be wasted efforts, even I had to admit there was no point in taking chances where loose ends like my gaming group were concerned.

For the most part, they stayed put and settled in for the night. When I went to check on them, I found Dave running them all through a premade Call of Cthulhu module. They asked if I wanted to join, but I figured I had lost my share of sanity points already this day.

Sheila and Sally still hadn't returned, which had me increasingly worried, but Christy kept reassuring me they could take care of themselves.

"They'll be fine," she said, glowing softly as she inspected some sigils that had been etched into her apartment door. It was like some sort of magical black light. I hadn't even been aware they'd been there until she'd said a quiet incantation. "Remember, Manhattan's a big place, and public transportation isn't exactly running at peak schedule."

"I know."

She let out a breath and both the glow as well as the sigils vanished. "I need to lie down for a bit. Junior's been kicking the hell out of me this past hour."

"Junior?"

"I figured you'd like that better than Harry."

"It definitely doesn't make my skin crawl as much."

She chuckled softly. "If they're not back by the time I get up, I can try scrying for them, or Sally at least."

"Fair enough." I turned to leave.

"Bill," she called after me. "You're doing the right thing."

"Worrying about them? Why wouldn't I?"

"No, letting me come along."

I cocked an eyebrow. "You didn't give me much choice in the matter."

"True."

"I'm not happy about it."

She crossed her arms over her chest and looked away. "I don't think any of us are."

"So are you going to zap Tom?" Following Christy's winning argument, Tom had insisted that if she was going, then he was as well – completely ignoring everything that had been said about his current lack of faith. Another twenty minutes and he'd worn us down. Even so, that didn't mean I was cool with it.

"No. It wouldn't be fair to him."

"Keeping him safe isn't fair?"

"The betrayal of trust. I mean, he's the man I'm planning on spending the rest of my life with. I can't keep mind-wiping him whenever it's convenient for me. I think you can understand that."

She was right; I could. What she'd just described was

essentially how the vast majority of the vampire world handled things – compelling those weaker than them to do as bidden. Speaking of which... "Oh crap. Compulsion."

"What about it?" Christy asked, leaning against her door.

"Getting gutted is only half the danger out there. A vampire even a fraction of Vehron's age is gonna be able to throw around compulsions like a Frisbee. Me and Sheila are immune. I think Ed might be too, but who knows how things work with him now? You, Sally, and Tom aren't, though. Hell, I'm pretty sure Tom has some extra susceptibility to them."

"You're not incorrect. I have some mental defenses in place, but enough power can definitely overwhelm them." A small grin broke out on her face.

"You do realize that's not a good thing, right?"

"I know."

"So then why are you smiling?"

"Because that was going to be another trump card in case you decided to keep standing your ground."

"Huh? Not following."

"I'm not stupid, Bill. I know that the Destroyer could ensnare our minds, enslave us, force us to surrender without firing a shot."

"But ... there is a but, right?"

"A big one, and not just mine."

I held up my hands. "I didn't say anything."

"I know you didn't, but you're thinking it and you're right. Goddess, I can't wait for this kid to be born so I can get back on the treadmill."

"No magical diets?" I teased.

"Well, maybe a little help from that front."

I smiled. It couldn't be helped. There had been so much doom and gloom the past couple days. It was refreshing to hear someone talk about what they planned to do afterwards. A little positivity could go a long way in times like these. Still... "Okay, so you're not stupid. Your point?"

"My point is I've been mucking around in Sally's head – trying to make sense of what Alexander did to her."

"I'm well aware."

"Are you aware of how unprecedented that is?"

"For Alex to..."

"No, for someone else, someone with abilities like mine, to be able to study it up close. No offense, but I'm not just in there unraveling some compelled Gordian Knot. I've been taking notes, too." Her grin broadened as she continued. "Mind magic, the way my people use it anyway, is different. That's why a strong enough vampiric compulsion can get through. We've always assumed it worked more or less the same way with some nuances. I don't think any mage has ever gotten this close before – seen such a powerful compulsion in action. If they have, it was either really long ago, or they didn't live to talk about it."

I hadn't considered that. Damn, we really were living in an age of firsts – knocking down walls left and right. "Go on."

"Well, think about it in scientific terms. Once you understand a disease, then you can start to fight it."

"So you think you can stop him ... insulate yourself?"

"Maybe. I should be able to fortify my own defenses enough to do so. But I've been thinking beyond that too. I've been jotting down notes for a spell. If it works like I think it might, it could help filter things out – offer some additional protection to other humans."

It wasn't much. Fuck, it still wouldn't help Tom if a vamp decided to chew his face off, but it might be enough to keep him from willingly letting it. Hell, that was better than nothing.

But wait just a second; there was more than Tom and Christy at stake here. "Could it work on another vampire?"

She looked confused for a moment, her brows knitting. "Maybe. I mean, your minds seem to mostly work the same as the rest of us."

"Mostly?"

"It's hard to say. It's weird, but when I'm in Sally's mind, I almost get a sense of being watched. It's ridiculous, I know, but..."

"Maybe not."

"Oh?"

"Yeah, I always suspected she had a thing for voyeurism."

I got the impression Christy didn't appreciate my joke. Well, excuse me for living. As the one guy in the group with a real demon, or whatever the fuck, knocking around in my noggin, I didn't really have a lot of sympathy for anyone who might just have a few issues. I mean, yeah, poking around in Sally's brain was bound to be creepy. After all, she'd done some creepy-ass stuff in her day. I wouldn't imagine that would leave one's mindscape fresh as a summer breeze.

Oh well, I had bigger fish to fry, but first things first. I knew Sally's stash of bottled blood was larger than mine. I'd made sure she had plenty on tap so as to keep her indoors and sated. She wasn't fond of the refrigerated stuff, but things were bad enough without her drawing undue attention to this building. We already had to keep thick shades over the windows at night to hide the fact that we had steady power whilst the rest of the block suffered under the currently unreliable grid. Even so, I also had a sneaking suspicion that when she came back...

*If she came back.*

*When* she came back, she'd be oddly full – no questions asked or, more precisely, none answered. Sadly for her, I had a micro-coven of vamps downstairs who'd be getting peckish sooner or later. I decided she could open her heart to the concept of sharing and grabbed enough pint bags to hopefully keep my friends downstairs...

*They're going to live up to their name.*

...happy until such time as we hit the road on our suicide mission.

Then I really needed to get my ass back upstairs and follow Christy's lead by taking a nap. The stress of the day was starting to get to me.

The sound of footsteps reached my ears before I'd even opened the door to let myself out. I looked up to find Dave descending the stairs. His hands were covered in latex gloves and in them he held tubing and a syringe full of red liquid.

"Hey, Bill," he said absentmindedly, staring with almost reverent glee at his prize.

"What are you doing?"

"Heading down from your place."

"What about the game?"

"Broke up about forty minutes ago. The rest of the guys decided to take advantage of the power to set up a LAN so they could blow the shit out of each other in *Call of Duty*."

"What were you doing in my place?"

"Blood."

"Blood?" I raised an eyebrow.

"Relax. Ed promised me earlier, so I figured I'd pay a visit and collect."

"And he did this willingly?"

"He was a little hesitant at first. Made me promise not to take anything else. Some seriously paranoid fuckers you live with."

"Yeah, the end of the world will do that to a fella."

"Anyway, I told him you'd filled me in on his condition and that I could maybe help figure out what was going on with him."

"Can you?"

"Fucked if I know."

"Just be careful with it. It's not vampire friendly."

"So you said. Fortunately, I am a professional."

"A professional *what* is the question?"

He juggled everything into one hand so he could flip me off with the other.

"You heading back down?" I asked.

"Hell yeah. Can't wait to look at this under a microscope."

"Better than a girlfriend, ain't it?"

He gave me a snide glance. "At least it doesn't talk back like one and it whines less than you."

"Well, speaking of wine ... I don't have any. But I do have these for you and the guys." I held out the contents in my hands.

He glanced at them dubiously. "That won't last long."

"Make it last as long as you can. Another day or so and we'll be on the road."

"I figured. That's why I wanted to get this sample tonight; give me a chance to get in a little work before you drag us to God knows where."

"We're heading to Boston, and God has nothing to do with it."

"It ain't that bad – except maybe for that freaky fucking carwash you pulled me outta."

"You apparently haven't been there lately."

I handed the blood packs to Dave, happy to kill two birds with one stone and save myself the trip. Before heading upstairs, I told him to ask the guys to leave any hotspots they set up unsecured so I could join if the mood overtook me.

As I walked up to my place, I doubted it would, but then one never knew when a bout of insomnia would hit – making a late-night session of mindless machine gun rampaging the perfect way to kill some time.

I let myself in. Tom was nowhere to be seen and his door was shut. I couldn't blame him. He'd probably barricaded himself in after Christy's little "fuck everyone but my baby" speech. Some days, that chick could easily be as scary as any vamp.

A small part of me was glad that it had been her master, Harry Decker, and not her that had the mad-on for killing me. He'd been an egomaniacal dickhead, but I could handle that. The frothing-at-the-mouth lunatics were easy to spot coming. It was the quiet ones you had to watch out for.

Ed was sitting on the couch, a book in hand. He looked up at me and I saw a small bandage on the inside elbow of his right arm. I couldn't help but smirk.

"Hasn't even been a day and you already fall prey to Dr. Alucard's charms, eh? That's Dracula spelled..."

"I know what it is, dipshit."

"Don't get all testy with me. I'm not the one jabbing you with things."

"Think he'll figure anything out with it?"

"Dave? He's been fucking around with my blood for a full year and it's only now that he's starting to come up with anything."

"Oh?"

"Pretty minor shit, according to him at least." I opened our fridge to look for something to drink – maybe orange juice spiked with blood. "Even so, you never know when something insignificant can turn the tide."

"Might not help, but it can't hurt."

"Exactly." I poured my beverage into a mostly clean mug from our dish drain. "But who knows? He might spot something interesting in your sample."

"Maybe I'll get lucky and find out I only have a day left to live."

"I doubt that. Two or three days is likely, however, depending on how long it takes us to get up north."

"Your confidence fills me with inspired hope."

"That's what I'm here for."

Our phone rang. As the first of the chimes subsided, I glanced at Ed. He shrugged. Aside from my call home the night before, our last caller had just been a message from Tom's sister checking in from the newly relocated Pandora Coven, now of Sacramento, California. Maybe it was her again.

I picked up without bothering to check the display. Though the landlines still seemed to work fine, some of the advanced functions like Caller ID had been on the fritz.

"Home for supernatural rejects," I answered. "Bill speaking."

"Considering the current state of affairs, Dr. Death, I am not sure whether to consider that a joke or not," a smooth voice replied.

"James?"

"Indeed. Now, if you will pardon me for just a moment. ***CEASE RECORDING THIS CONVERSATION. HANG UP, AND FORGET IT EVER HAPPENED!!***"

I almost dropped the receiver as his voice rang out, piercing my skull like a diamond-tipped drill bit. "Ow!"

Ed spun from his place on the couch and asked, "You okay, Bill?"

"Didn't you fucking hear...?" Then I remembered that he probably didn't. Not a bad tradeoff for nearly dying. "Oh, never mind."

"Who is it?"

I mouthed "James" just as there came a slight clicking noise from the receiver.

"Are you still there, Dr. Death?"

Raising the phone back to my ear, I replied, "Yep. I'm here."

"Good. I apologize for the compulsion, but you have to know that the First would have agents keeping you under observation."

I'd suspected as much, but stupidly hadn't considered the phones.

"I would also caution you to please not put this conversation on speaker. I prefer it be between our ears only."

My finger paused right above the speaker button. "Wouldn't dream of it. It's good to hear from you. We didn't get much chance to talk during the trial."

"Nor did I expect us to. Any fraternization between us during such an event would almost certainly be frowned upon."

He probably had a point, especially since he'd been one of our jurors. "So ... how's the arm?"

"Quite fine. I am loathe to admit it, but I found my penance to be a terrible inconvenience. I was glad to see it end."

Inconvenience wasn't quite the word I'd use for having to chop off my own arm every time it started to regenerate, but different strokes and all that. "Me too." I would have loved to have chatted for a while, but knowing James, that wasn't in the cards. "I assume this isn't a social call."

"I am pleased to hear you say that. A part of me feared that you would be your usual flippant self, ignoring the issues in favor of idle banter. Alas, I am not certain whether to be gladdened or worried to find you answering this call."

"Oh?"

"When the First hand out a sentence such as was given to you, it is expected to be carried out posthaste unless the convicted should wish to face even more dire consequences."

"Call me crazy." I hesitated for a moment, unsure how much I should say, but then pushed that aside. This was James. I owed him a lot. I could at the very least afford him a little bit of trust. "But, I got the impression that Yehoshua was more saving our asses than handing us over to die."

"And indeed he was. Never doubt that. He is a man of utmost intellect and cunning. He no doubt saw the bigger picture at play – that you and your friends would best serve in your current capacity. Know, however, that his grief for Theodora is real. Should you survive the coming days, you may wish to warn the Icon to stay clear of him."

"Yeah, about her ... listen, I'm sorry. I shouldn't have lied. I..."

"You have already been tried and convicted of those crimes, Dr. Death. As far as I am concerned, justice has been served ... in a fashion at least. Suffice it to say I am not entirely innocent of the crime of keeping secrets myself." I was curious if he would spill anything juicy, but he just went on. "In some ways, I was glad to see it. It shows you have been paying some attention to our ways."

"When in Rome."

"Quite true. Nevertheless, Yehoshua may very well have spared your life for the moment, but have no doubt that Alexander will make it a point to see your sentence enforced."

"Let me guess; that means sooner rather than later."

"No. That means *now*."

"Wait, what?"

"That is partially what I was calling to tell you. Your grace period has ended. Alexander is vexed at the embarrassment you caused him. I do not pretend to know his mind, but I would wager that any liberties he has afforded you in the past have been stretched to their limit and beyond. If you are not already a student of history, you would do well to read up. You would learn that Alexander of Macedon was not one to suffer slights lightly."

Oh crap. "So when?"

"Did you not listen to what I just said? You and your friends need to finish whatever preparations you are making. If you are still where you are by the morrow's sunset, I dare say you will end up entertaining *guests* who will not easily be sated by dinner and drinks."

Well, he had part of that right anyway. At least two of my friends had the potential to become the main course if things got ugly. Still, it's not like I could pack up and leave with a moment's notice. Some of us were still unaccounted for. "Listen, I need more time..."

"That is not mine to give."

"But Sally and Sheila..."

"Must accompany you. It has been decreed." There came a pause from the other end of the line. When James again spoke, his voice was clearly pained. "I know what has befallen Sally."

"Alex told you what he did?"

"No, he did not. Though I am of the First, I am certain I do not hold his favor any longer. Were it not for us already having lost Theodora, I might worry about my own seat being prematurely vacated."

"He wouldn't."

"Hear me and hear me well, my friend. If you have any wisdom at all in your head, you will never assume there is anything that Alexander would not do. Such was the folly of many vanquished by him, both before and after he took his place among our kind."

"Gotcha. So I guess he's busy trying to fill that vacancy."

"Have you not heard? No, I suppose you wouldn't have."

"Heard what?"

There was a slight hesitation on the other end. "Never mind. It is of no matter at this moment. There are, as the humans say, bigger fish to fry."

Fuck, if that wasn't an understatement. I had enough to feed a small army. "So you were saying about Sally?"

"Yes. I am not the most learned man to ever walk this Earth, yet it was painfully obvious she was under compulsion. If I were to guess, I would say it happened sometime between the debacle when the Icon was first brought in and when next we were seated."

"Right on the money. The fucker did it to her with me in the room, even."

"Have a care, Dr. Death. Alexander and I are still of the First. Though we may not see eye to eye, I believe in the institutions of our people and will not hear them casually sullied by a child."

Gah! Sometimes, James was maddening in his adherence to the rules. Even so, I had enough enemies. I couldn't afford to make any new ones. "Sorry."

"I will consider your remark stricken from the official record. However, for the sake of both conversation and curiosity, if you wish to share precisely what the compulsion entailed, I shall entertain your words."

Okay, so maybe not as by-the-book as I thought. Oh, who was I kidding? James was a complex guy. I had about as much chance of figuring him out over the phone as I did of solving a Rubik's Cube with my eyes shut.

I relayed to him what happened in the jail cell that Sally, Tom, and I had shared – how Alex had informed us that he considered the two of us to be a formidable team right before commanding her to forget any history she had with me and my friends.

James was silent for a few moments. "I suspected as much. Her behavior toward me when next we met was curious – a throwback to an earlier time, if you will, as if the years in between had melted away."

At first, I wasn't sure what he meant, then remembered back to the not-so-innocent-looking peck on the cheek she'd given him. Normally, that wasn't something one picked up on, but a fellow like me – who'd been relegated to the friend zone far too many times in his life – had a bit of insight into the difference between a "you're my best bud" kiss and an "I want to fuck your brains out" one.

Don't get me wrong, Sally and James were a more pleasant picture than the thought of her banging Mark the rock monster. Even so... "Yeah, about that," I replied, unable to help myself. "So what did you mean by..."

"This is most troubling," he said, completely ignoring me. Big surprise there. Christ, it's not like I was going to ask for many details. "Alexander was not incorrect about you two. Sadly for us, he was more right than he had any reason to believe."

"Uh, okay."

"I am sorry to be cryptic, Dr. Death. However, I think we both know Sally plays it close to the vest when it comes to what she reveals about herself and her past."

"Trust issues," I muttered.

"Well earned."

"I have no doubt."

"You don't know the half of it, I'm afraid. And I am not at liberty to divulge," he added as if sensing my next question. "It will have to suffice for you to know you have had as much impact upon her as she upon you."

Numerous different scenarios ran through my head. A good deal of them ended with her pushing me down onto a bed in a sleazy motel room while saying how much she wanted me.

"You have helped her find her humanity," he continued, squashing that fantasy.

"Oh."

"I would hope you are understating your position because believe me when I say that is most certainly the case."

"No," I replied. "It's not that. I mean, I know she's changed. She ... well ... *cares* now. You should have seen her in Vegas. A couple more months, and the homeless there would have been ready to canonize her. I also know she hasn't forgotten that part. She's still her."

"For now."

"What do you mean?"

"She hasn't forgotten herself, but she has forgotten the reason she was able to find herself again. How soon, I wonder, before that fades and she begins to lose all she has gained."

"Oh come on; she wasn't that evil when I met her."

"No. Sally has never been evil. She is, however, complicated. She is also highly capable, as I am sure you're aware."

I shifted uncomfortably where I stood. Movement caught my eye, and I saw Ed rise from his seat. He glanced my way and mouthed a question. I nodded and gave him the thumbs up, not really certain what else to say.

He shrugged and headed toward his bedroom.

"Don't get too comfortable," I called after him, remembering James's words from earlier.

"Excuse me?"

"Not you," I said into the receiver. "Sorry, James, but I'm not sure I see the point in what you're saying. Sally's had her memories of me wiped. But we're working on it."

"Of that, I have no doubt. That is why I recommended she stay with you in the first place."

"Then what's the problem?"

"The issue at hand is that the trust and friendship you two had took the better part of a year and several close calls with death to cement. That is gone now and in its place ... I do not know."

"Go on."

"Though it pains me greatly to say this, we do not know her motivations right at the moment. She may wish to get her memories back, or it may be a ruse – a cover for something else."

"So what you're saying is..."

"What I am saying is that you would be wise to not trust her."

# 13

# VAMANOS, MUCHACHOS

I let James's words sink in. On the one hand, I didn't want to believe him. Hell, Sally and I had been through so much in so little time. During all of it, she'd stood by my side.

At the same time, this was James who was talking. If it had been anyone else, my roommates even, I'd have blown it off in a second. But what he said made sense. Though she was still Sally inside, she was essentially surrounded by strangers. Well-meaning strangers, sure, but could she really know that?

There was also Alex to consider. What else had he filled her head with during their time together after leaving me and Tom to rot in our cell? He could have told her anything – made her believe it too. Even Christy had to admit that her work in Sally's mind was akin to taking apart the Great Wall of China one brick at a time.

*She belongs to him now. She'll turn on you when you least expect it.*

Fuck me! Not now. I mentally screamed for the voice to shut the fuck up ... once more wondering if I was just talking to myself or not. Even so, the words of my inner Dr. Phil couldn't be dismissed so easily. Sally wasn't back yet. She hadn't given us any indication of where she'd been going or what she was doing.

Oh, enough of this! Sheila had done the same thing. Was I now gonna wonder if Alex had put the whammy on her too?

Okay, maybe that was a stretch. Even so, it's not like I was innocent in this matter either. I'd gone off half-cocked without telling anyone just the day before. The bottom line was we were all adults and didn't need to ask Mommy or Daddy's permission to go out and do something potentially stupid.

Finally, all of that having run through my mind in the space of only a second or two, I said, "I'll keep an eye on her." It was more than I wanted to commit to, but I had never known James to hand out warnings frivolously.

"That is all I can hope for."

"Have any good news to share before you leave me to my doom?"

He actually chuckled at that. It was nice to hear his penance at the hands of his fellow Draculas hadn't totally crushed his spirit. "Not much, but perhaps a little."

"Lay it on me."

"The majority of the covens between you and Boston have been assimilated into Vehron's fold, in one way or the other."

"*Great.*"

"But pockets of resistance loyal to the First remain. I have instructed them to assist you in any way they can."

"Excuse my skepticism, but I got the feeling that I'm not too high on a lot of vampires' friend lists right about now."

"This is not a matter of how they feel, whether they

believe in you, or even if they like you. They will aid you, or they will answer to me."

I considered that. James was a pretty scary guy when he wanted to be. He wasn't the meanest motor scooter in the parking lot, but he was high on the list. Probably just as important, he was both known and respected in the northeast. Unlike the rest of the First, he was real to the covens in this area – having served as prefect for however long he did.

I uttered my thanks, and he rattled off a short list of the covens that could be counted on. It was with some annoyance that I noted the 6-6 Miskatonic Coven of Cambridge among them. Hell, I didn't even know what the fuck that meant, aside from maybe a reference to HP Lovecraft. Fucking MIT – even their vampires were elitist cocksuckers.

He made me repeat back the names twice – probably because I let loose with an editorial on what those doctoral candidate vamps could go do with their diplomas – and then finally said, "Good enough."

"Do you really think it will be?"

James paused for a moment. "I know you fear Vehron, rightfully so."

"That's an understatement."

"But you must believe in yourself. I for one do not buy into the so-called hype, Dr. Death. I still have faith that you are the one of legend. If so, you will find a way to overcome him."

I was tempted to point out that my chances of overcoming him in even a thumb-wrestling match were nil, but I decided to be a bit more diplomatic. "I'm not sure how. He's older than me, stronger than me, has waged a fuck-ton more wars than me, and he can do everything I can do ... probably better too."

Damn, there was a thought I hadn't considered. Dr.

Death was a beast, one that had proven strong enough to kick the shit out of a monstrous Sasquatch named Turd. How the fuck more powerful was Vehron's inner demon?

"In that, you are wrong," he said. "You may not be aware of this, but..."

"But?"

I heard muffled voices at the other end of the line. It sounded as if a conversation was taking place while someone kept their hand over the receiver. Probably some minion asking James what he wanted for dinner. Finally, a sigh sounded from the other end of the line. "I'm afraid I have tarried longer than I hoped. You need to get your friends together and get moving."

"Wait, what did you mean by...?"

"You have all the information you need. Colin told me about the dossier he left you. I trust you have studied it well. Any answers you need lie within."

"Listen..."

"No. You must get moving now. I have little doubt it will take some time to rouse your companions and prepare whatever supplies you need."

"How do you know I'm not already packed?"

"Are you?"

Goddamn it! I so hated when people had me figured out. "Fine, but I don't see what the big deal is. By tomorrow, Sally and..."

"There is no tomorrow," he said. "I have just been informed that if you or your friends are still residing where you are when the sun comes up, the building will be burnt to the ground around you."

As far as motivations went, that was a pretty good one. Sadly, I couldn't act surprised either. I knew our time was short when they'd let us walk ... or zap ... out of the nuclear bunker that had served as our makeshift prison.

Even so ... shit!

I said my goodbyes to James, thanked him for his help, and expressed the hope that I lived long enough to see him again. Unlike his, my own personal faith wasn't quite as deep.

No, that was the wrong attitude. I had promised myself that I wouldn't do the whining bitch of a hero routine, denying my fate until the very end. Of course, that was easy to do when the scariest thing I faced were the dorks currently living downstairs. It was quite another knowing what lie ahead.

Oh fuck it... "***GODDAMNED MOTHERFUCKING COCKSUCKING DOUCHE-FILLED TWATS!!***"

It felt good to let out all my frustrations in one giant psychic outburst.

Almost as if on cue, Tom burst from his respective bedroom. He was wearing shorts and a t-shirt. Despite the *fun* of earlier, he'd apparently managed to get some shuteye. Oh, how I envied him his ability to be so cluelessly unconcerned.

"The fuck, man?"

I turned my eyes toward Ed's room, expecting a similar entrance, but then remembered that whatever had been done to him had somehow rendered him compulsion-blind. Oh well, sometimes you had to do things the old-fashioned way.

"Do me a favor," I said, casually turning back toward Tom. "Grab me a big glass of water and a few ice cubes."

Once Ed finished threatening to blast me full of silver-laden holes, I imparted upon my roommates the highlights of my conversation with James – emphasizing the part about us living through the song lyrics about not needing any water, because this motherfucker was gonna burn.

Thankfully, they'd gotten with the program long ago. Once they got the hint and headed back into their rooms to collect whatever meager belongings were necessary for this road trip – I couldn't quite bring myself to call it an assault yet – I left to head down and inform the others.

No doubt, Dave and the Defilers – a band name if ever there was one – were busy wondering what the hell was going on following my compulsion. They could wait a few more minutes, though. Christy was the far more important stop. It would also give me a chance to check whether our two wayward travelers had returned yet, although I already knew the answer to that, as nothing – no sound of footsteps returning, or the delicious odor of their respective perfumes – had set off my enhanced senses. Oh well, one could hope.

Christy met me before I'd even stepped off the stairs at her floor.

"I thought you said you could insulate yourself from compulsion," I said, mirth filling my voice despite the situation.

"I can," she replied, her eyes narrowing. "I didn't think I needed to do it just to get some sleep."

"Yeah, well, I think you might need to take a raincheck on those forty winks."

"I wasn't asleep yet anyway. I was..." She trailed off, her eyes widening. "It's time, isn't it?"

There was nothing I could do but nod. I only wished I knew whether we were ready and that we hadn't wasted what time we'd been given. Oh, who was I kidding? It was me who'd wasted his time. My friends had tried to strategize, and all I'd done was talk to myself in the bathroom mirror.

No! Enough with the fucking whining already. What was done was done. I couldn't go back in time to change things ... hmm, but maybe Christy could with her magic.

Nah, that was a bad idea. Despite what movies would have us believe, there was the butterfly effect to take into consideration. I might travel back two days, accidentally fart at the wrong time, and return to the present to find New York overrun with dragons or something.

"Bill?"

Oh crap. There wasn't time for my idle speculating. "Pack up whatever you need."

"Already done."

"Really?" She was about a thousand percent more prepared than either Tom or Ed had been.

"Early practice for when I go into labor."

"Gotcha."

I gave her the Cliff's Notes version of what James had said. She opened her mouth, probably to voice something about what assholes vampires were. Yeah, yeah, I knew that song and dance. I interrupted to tell her to head up and help the guys get ready while I went downstairs to gather the Defilers for the campaign of glory I had promised.

"Are you sure about them?" Christy asked.

I was about to respond with a resounding "no," but thankfully, the sound of screaming drifted up to us from below to save me from being a negative Nancy.

I leapt down the stairs, trying not to enjoy the fact that being a vampire made one an instant parkour star. As I reached the basement, the commotion definitely got louder. Multiple voices, all male, expressed various degrees of "What the fuck?!"

What had set them off? Had a woman called their apartment by mistake and offered to provide free blowjobs? Usually, geeks were pretty hard to rattle. We were well-versed in zombie apocalypses and shit. Once you accepted the bloody end of everything by ravaging monsters, the rest was pretty easy to take in stride.

I reached the door and opened it, praying to whatever gods there were that nobody was traipsing around in the nude. It was unlocked and swung open to a scene of chaos. Mike and Adam were shouting at Dave, who was busy shouting back.

"What the fuck did you do?"

"It was his own fucking fault."

"This is so not fucking cool, man."

Oh Jesus Christ.

"***ENOUGH!!***" I compelled, hoping that there weren't too many folks – vampire or otherwise – outside within earshot.

There was no real force behind my command, just enough clamor to get their attention, and get their attention it did. The trio immediately ceased their little bitch-fest and turned toward me.

Wait ... trio?

"Where's Carl?"

"Why don't you ask Dave?" Mike pointed a finger at my former DM. "He killed him."

"I didn't kill him."

"Oh, so he just exploded for shits and giggles?" Adam asked.

Why, oh why didn't I leave these fucktards back in

Newark when I had the chance? "Okay, slow down. Start from the beginning. What happened to Carl?"

"I just said…"

"The word beginning; it means from the start," I interrupted. "Not the start of time, or the start of this day, mind you, but the start of when you all decided to yell at each other."

"We were playing capture the flag over the LAN," Mike said, "nothing major."

"Yeah, it's not like there's a lot of folks online these days," Adam added.

"Anyway, Carl got up to go see if Dave wanted in."

"Where were you?" I asked Dave.

"He was locked in his bedroom," Adam said. "Came running in here about a half hour ago all excited and shit about something. Figured maybe he was going to jerk off."

Dave shot him a sour glance, but before he could say anything, I asked, "Were you, Dave? Were you jerking off?"

"Fuck you."

Okay, that wasn't helping. And it was ignoring one very important detail … one of our friends had just supposedly bitten the big one. I needed to keep that in mind. "Go on."

Adam nodded. "So anyway, after a few minutes when Dave didn't answer, Carl put his shoulder into it and shoved the door open."

"It was locked for a reason," Dave growled.

I held up a hand. "Chill. You'll get your turn."

He gritted his teeth in frustration, but then simply sighed and made a "go on" gesture with his hands.

"Thank you," Adam replied icily. "Anyway, a few seconds go by and I hear Dave freak out."

"About?"

"I don't know, man. Just then, this booming voice reverberated all throughout the place … something about sucking cock."

"Are you sure that's not what you normally hear in your head?" Mike teased.

"Not now," I warned him.

Adam continued, "It was loud as fuck … kind of like that thing you just did at the door."

"It was a compulsion. That was me sending it out from upstairs."

"You can do it from that far away?" he asked.

"Why do you want to suck cock?" Mike inquired.

"Yes, to the former." I turned to Mike. "Don't make me compel you to play in traffic on the latter." Back to Adam. "Keep going."

"So, needless to say, that freaked the fuck out of us," Adam continued. "I got up to check on things and made it to Dave's door just as Carl started screaming … except it got cut off, turned into a gurgle or something."

Oh crap.

"I stuck my head in the door to ask what was wrong and saw Carl fucking explode. One second, he was there. The next, there was this flash of like white fire from inside of him and *poof*, he blew apart into fucking ashes."

White fire?! Double crap.

"Tell me what the fuck happened," I said to Dave once we were alone.

I had sent the others to get packed and ready. They were upset, quite rightfully, so I had to compel it into them. I hated to force the issue, messing with their minds in the process, but I didn't see much choice in the matter. We didn't have the luxury of time on our side.

Following that, I'd dragged Dave outside into the hall with me. As I faced him, I was surprised to find myself far more annoyed than upset. That was odd. Carl – all of them – were friends. Hell, Starlight's death still stung like it had happened just yesterday. I'd even beaten myself up over biting some army guy I didn't even know. Oddly enough, though, I couldn't bring myself to mourn the passing of a guy I'd sat next to at the game table for over five years. What the hell?

First, I was compelling my friends, and now this?

*They're just cannon fodder ... meaningless to us.*

I forced myself to push it all down and found myself disturbed it came so easily. This was not like me.

"...and the dipshit grabbed it."

"Huh?" I asked, trying to focus. Finding out the circumstances behind Carl's untimely demise was more important than whatever was going on in my head.

"I said, I was in my room working on Ed's blood. I had just gotten a sample mounted onto a slide and was about to take a closer look when Carl came in and grabbed it off my desk."

"Your microscope?"

"No! The blood."

"The slide or what was left in the syringe?"

Dave averted his eyes.

"Spill," I commanded. "What happened?"

"It wasn't in a syringe. In my excitement, I sorta bumped into the door on the way in and snapped the needle. So I grabbed a clean coffee mug out of the kitchen and squirted the blood into it so I didn't lose any."

"You had Ed's blood in a coffee mug?"

"I think one of you dropped my box of test tubes on the way over."

"So why the hell did Carl take it?"

"I might have sort of forgot to put those spare blood packs you gave us in the fridge. I just dumped them on the desk, and I guess Carl thought I was taking a snack break. I was too busy paying attention to what I was doing and didn't notice him taking a swallow until it was too late."

"Motherfucker," I muttered.

"He was my friend too," Dave said.

"I know," I offered apologetically. It was stupid to assume he'd done it on purpose.

"But did you see what the fuck happened? He blew up like a fucking bomb! I really have to get some more from your roommate because that shit ain't normal. Think of the possibilities."

And just like that, I found myself wondering whether I should be more worried about myself or the psycho standing in front of me.

"You know it's in the rules. Look them up."

Adam eyed me skeptically, but Mike shrugged and said, "Bill's got a point. Is that really how it works, Dave?"

I had found myself stuck between the choice of two evils. I didn't want to keep compelling my friends. That was a slippery slope I'd already started to lose my footing on.

At the same time, the truth was going to seriously fuck shit up. I kept trying to convince myself that we didn't have time to grieve for anyone. It sucked. Carl was probably the biggest ass at my gaming table, having once spent an entire campaign embezzling gold from the mine I'd inherited from my family. Even so, he deserved better. But better would have to wait.

Thus, I had fallen back on game rules. Dozens of years of vampire movies and TV shows had taught us that when a vamp is dusted, that's it – sayonara, sucker. Aside from what I'd recently seen deep below the streets of Vegas, they were right too.

However, RPGs, in the name of making monsters tougher and giving GMs everywhere extra chances to fuck with their players, had changed things up a bit. When a vampire was defeated in D&D and other fantasy variants, they turned to mist and returned to their crypt to regenerate. That was the only place where they could be killed permanently.

Dave, having both been read the riot act by me, and also not wishing to lose his personal equipment mules, had gone along with it. "Yeah. He's probably reforming as we speak."

"At your apartment in Newark?"

"Seems a shitty place to always end back up in," Adam commented.

"Hey!" Dave protested.

"It's true. No offense, man, but you live in a dump."

"So why don't we go back and pick him up?" Mike asked, coming to the logical conclusion that I hoped they wouldn't.

"We don't have time for that," I said. "I just received new orders from the Draculas..."

"What the fuck are the Draculas?" Adam asked.

Mike jumped in. "Is Dracula real?"

"No on the second," I replied, "at least that I know of. As for the first, that's the nickname of the ruling vampire council. Just don't say that to their faces. Otherwise, they'll remove yours."

I ran with the distraction and spent several minutes bringing them up to speed on vampire politics. Fuck it; if any of them managed to survive, they'd need to know this shit anyway. Sadly, ignorance of vampire law was definitely not considered an excuse for breaking it.

It was only after I'd finished that I realized I'd been giving them the equivalent of an orientation speech, introducing them to the vampire world as if I now considered myself a part of it. That was a scary thought.

"So Carl will have to fend for himself for the time being," I concluded, hoping that was the end of that. At some point, I'd need to explain the harsh reality of the afterlife, but for now, it seemed to mollify them.

Just then, footsteps could be heard descending the stairs. Saved by the cavalry.

Tom and Ed appeared, their shoulders laden with backpacks. Tom's was much fuller and heavier in appearance, as he was no doubt Christy's designated pack mule. Ed was carrying a longish item wrapped in a blanket – his shotgun. Hopefully, the police wouldn't pick this night to start reasserting their presence on the streets. An insulated travel mug was in his other hand. End of the world it might be, but some folks weren't going out without one last swig of coffee.

Christy came last, following down the stairs as best as she could in her current state. She was also carrying a bag, but it was much smaller than the ones weighing down my roommates. Judging by the scent that hit my nostrils from her direction, it held pungent herbs I couldn't identify except to say they probably weren't pizza toppings.

"Everyone ready?" Ed asked, stepping to the open doorway of the basement apartment.

"Yep," I replied.

Tom joined him, peering inside. "Hey, where's..."

"We're ready to go," I interrupted, not wanting to open that can of worms again. Tom was a brother to me. I loved him as much as any man could love another without picking out matching floral drapes, but I trusted him to keep his fucking mouth shut about as much as I trusted myself to win a game of mercy against a four-armed Sasquatch.

"Where to?" he asked, thankfully easily distracted.

"We have work to do before we can really hit the road, and we're still two fellowship members short," I replied, earning grins from around the room. "There's only one place we can go for now and hope they catch up to us ... the Brooklyn safe house."

I just hoped it lived up to its name.

**14**

# A RARE BLOOD TYPE INDEED

We received no acknowledgements to the texts sent to our missing friends. That wasn't entirely surprising as the increasingly spotty cell service around the city seemed to get worse by the day. That I'd been able to call home the day before was probably a minor miracle.

So, to be safe, I left notes taped to both the front door and the girls' apartment informing Sheila and Sally that we'd be at the place "we discussed."

It wasn't exactly a top-notch cipher. Hell, pig-Latin would have been more esoteric, but it was the best I had. I just had to hope James had either been kidding about our place being burnt to the ground or that they'd hold off once they saw the bulk of us heading out.

That left the safe house. The big question was how safe it would actually be. On the one hand, it was known by the Boston staff. That being said, most of them, including their current Prefect – a tight-assed chick by the name of Calibra – were currently enslaved by Vehron. I had a feeling that didn't exactly put them on speaking terms with the Draculas. James knew about the place, having been there, but I had to trust that he wasn't looking to fuck us up the ass the second we turned our backs.

There was also the little problem of James confirming our phones were tapped and us being under constant surveillance. Oh well, at least that explained the feeling of being watched. Unfortunately, there was a chance the Brooklyn safe house would be about as a big of a secret as who Luke Skywalker's father was.

We had maybe a day at most before we'd be forced to get our asses on the move. That would allow our human contingent to catch up on their rest, but that was about all.

"Shit!" I muttered as we made our way through the pre-dawn streets of Brooklyn.

"What is it?" Tom asked.

"We're pretty much screwed."

"Just figuring that out now?"

"I meant the plan ... the one to help me control my little personality disorder."

"I'm pretty sure as far as that's concerned, you're a lost cause," Dave said.

"Bite me," I replied. "No. I mean, Christy and I were going to work together to..."

"What do you mean, *were*?" she asked.

I turned toward her on the dark sidewalk. "Exactly what I said. I doubt we're gonna have much time to get comfortable where we're going."

"So we'll get started right away."

"Except we have no idea where Sheila is. We all agreed this is dangerous enough even with her there. Without her, it's off. There's no way I can guarantee your safety."

"There were no guarantees to begin with."

"I know, but at least with her there, the chances of..." I

stopped mid-sentence. Multiple scents reached my nostrils a split second before a voice rudely interrupted our chat.

"I think we'll be taking your cash, bags, and your bitch too."

Call me crazy, but I almost laughed as a group of men stepped out of a recessed basement entryway ahead of us. My ears perked up and I turned my head to see an equal number coming up from behind us. Eight in all. Not much more than our number, but it was a safe bet to say these guys weren't regulars on the gaming circuit. They were a mix — some big, some wiry, and each one of them meaning business — all with eyes as soulless as any vampire's.

This was the true problem for most normal people. Even with the war approaching its zenith, the chances of stepping outside and having a random monster encounter were still probably not exactly super high. In any emergency situation, though, there were always going to be those who took advantage of things, becoming the predators in the night. Most folks didn't need to worry about Sasquatches and vampires. Other people were monsters enough.

All that being said ... *seriously*? I'm sorry, but when you've survived getting your face punched in by a monster ape, some dude holding a box cutter was simply not going to make you blink.

I didn't see any of our would-be assailants brandishing guns. They probably figured they didn't need them with their strength of numbers. In most cases, they were right.

Today wasn't one of those times, though.

I glanced to the side at Ed, his hand already working its way under the blanket to the boomstick beneath. A grin lit up his face. I had to match it. How funny was that? Little more than a year ago, we would have both called something like this our worst nightmare. Now it was barely a reason to break a sweat.

"You fucking deaf?" one of them asked, his voice the same one that had originally greeted us. He was a big guy, bald, and looking like he'd been beaten with the ugly stick upon birth. His eyes twinkled with greed, obviously expecting to get his way whether through violence or not – although judging from his expression, he was probably hoping for the former. "I better see those bags on the ground, your hands in the air, and your whore stepping my way."

"Please let us pass," Christy interrupted gently, her voice betraying neither fear nor threat. She was easily the closest our little group came to a diplomat. Hell, she'd even talked Alex a good game just a few days prior. "We don't have time for this."

"Bitch don't have time for us." The big goon let out a laugh and his friends in front of us joined him. Judging by the sound of footsteps, his buddies in back were closing in and spreading out – no doubt expecting some of us to run. "Maybe we can convince her otherwise. Make her scream while we cut that big belly of hers open and see what's inside."

Oh crap.

I saw the barest of sparks in her eye, and immediately put a hand on her shoulder. She turned toward me and I gave my head a single shake. There was no reason for her to waste her power on these goons. Also, I didn't quite trust her to not immolate the entire block – us included – in the process. "We got this."

The glow subsided, but the angry look in her eye didn't. "Make it hurt."

I had no intention of doing anything, hurtful or otherwise. I had friends and, after the events of the past hour, I probably owed them a thrown bone.

I turned and put a hand up to Adam's face.

"What are you doing?"

"Smell it," I whispered ... sensing the time before the first fist flew to be mere seconds away.

He took a quick breath and choked out, "Where the fuck have you been putting that thing?"

"Just remember the scent, shithead. Use it to catch up." I raised my voice, making sure it was good and loud. "Defilers, if you will."

"That's it?" Adam asked. "*That's* our battle cry?"

"I'm still working on it."

"Good enough for me," Mike replied, slipping his Cthulhu mask over his head. "To arms!"

I stepped aside as a blur of movement wearing a Cyberman head raced past me, slamming into the four goons and sending them sprawling.

"Let's go," I said to the rest of my friends. "This is gonna get messy."

Christy glanced in my direction and raised an eyebrow. "Weren't there three of them earlier?"

Oh crap.

I filled the rest in on Carl's fate as the Defilers leapt into the fray behind us, including the lies I had told to keep them from losing their shit.

Tom and Ed were saddened to hear it, having known Carl, but sympathetic to my reasons behind the deception.

Christy merely shrugged and said, "That's gonna come back to bite you."

On that point, I couldn't disagree.

I half-expected Dave to stay behind and join in the fight. I wouldn't have blamed him either. A small part of me wanted to as well. Attacking humans was still not cool in my book, but I was willing to make an exception for animals like that.

As we continued on our way, though, he caught up to us.

"Not in the mood for..."

"So what was that back there before those meatheads tried to fuck up our shit?" he interrupted.

"Huh?" I muttered, barely audible over the screams filling the night. I glanced at Christy to see what her reaction was, but from the expression on her face, you'd have thought we'd done nothing more than cross the street. I guess she meant what she said about protecting her child. Note to self: don't even joke about that shit with her.

"You were talking about cancelling something dangerous."

"Oh, that," Tom replied. "Bill's got some shit wrong with his head. Christy's gonna help him out with it, but if it goes wrong, then chances are he's gonna wig out and kill us all."

"Thanks," I replied dryly. "That's really helpful, a real vote of confidence."

"What? It's true."

I nodded. He had a point. "It is indeed. That's why we need to cancel it."

"What's different from before?" Dave asked.

I explained to him about Sheila, going into a bit more detail on her powers than I had earlier with the rest of the group around, and finished by explaining how the plan was for her to stand guard in case anything went wrong.

"Sounds like someone I probably don't want to piss off," he concluded.

"Nope. She can cut through vampires like butter. Hell, she killed one of the Draculas maybe a week ago." Seeing his confused expression, I explained, "That's a pretty damn tough thing to do."

Sure, it had been an accident, on our part at least. Alex, on the other hand, had set up the pieces that were our part to play and let them fall like perfectly aligned dominos. The whole thing was the very definition of clusterfuck. Alex had not only gained more leverage over us to use in his kangaroo court, but we'd lost a potentially valuable ally in the process.

"So she was your failsafe?"

"Yep."

"Against?"

"I'm not one hundred percent certain, but it's badass and it lives inside of me. The only other one of us here who probably stands a rat's chance in Hell against me if it goes badly is Christy and since she's gonna be a bit indisposed at the time ... well, as I said, we need to bag it."

We continued walking, the cries behind us eventually rising in pitch before falling silent.

"Sounds like the Defilers have earned some XP," I commented to no one in particular, waiting to see if any guilt struck me from the fact that I had essentially turned them loose to do as they pleased against those humans back there.

I was just about to conclude that wasn't going to happen when Dave spoke up again. "We may not need to."

"Not need to what?" Ed asked.

"Cancel the experiment."

A small chill ran up my spine. It was never a good thing when Dave considered something an experiment. I glanced his way and caught that familiar semi-psychotic gleam in his eye. "It's not an..."

"Of course it is. Everything like this is."

Christy rounded on him. "This is life and death we're talking about – not some rats in a maze."

Dave, for his part, seemed unfazed. It was usually hard to rattle him when his brain was busy going a mile a minute. "You say potato…"

"Get to the point," I said, sure that Christy was currently debating between ignoring him and turning him into a gecko.

"You said Princess Sheila was your failsafe."

Tom and Ed's snickers were like fingernails on a chalkboard. Assholes. "Just Sheila," I growled.

"Whatever. You say she's the only one who stands a chance of stopping you, but what if that's not true?"

"Believe me, dude, you ain't got what it takes."

"I'm not talking about me," he replied dismissively. "Leave the fighting to the fighters and barbarians, I say. I'm more the mage of the party." At Christy's quick glare toward him, he amended, "Or an alchemist. They're cool too. Anyway, what I meant was Ed."

"Me?" Ed asked.

"Well not you, but your blood." Dave turned to me. "You saw what it did to Carl. I'm betting you've seen it happen to other vampires too." He took my silence as affirmation and continued. "Well, why not use that?"

"You want Ed to bleed on me? Not a bad idea, but if he's doing that, then I have a feeling his day has already taken a turn for the worse."

Dave let out a heavy sigh. "How you ever graduated from college is a mystery to me. What I'm talking about is drawing some more blood and hooking it up to you via an IV."

"But won't that immediately blow me to bits?"

"I'll be there monitoring you. I'll clamp off the line to keep it out of your system, but if anything goes wrong…"

I stopped walking as I processed this. The others took a few extra steps before noticing.

Holy crap, it could work. I mean, I wasn't entirely sure I trusted Dave to not let some of Ed's explosive fluids – wow, that sounded wrong even in my head – flow into me just to see what would happen. Even so, it was a pretty good idea.

"What do you think?" he asked, his tone betraying that he already knew he'd made his argument.

"I think we're wasting time standing here bullshitting. Let's get where we're going and do this thing. If it works, we'll have maybe the best weapon we stand to gain against Vehron."

"And if it doesn't?" Ed asked.

"That one's easy," I replied with a smile. "I won't be around to care what happens next."

**15**

# DREAMSCAPE

"**J**ust for the record, I'm not sure I like this," Christy said as she lit the candles deep within the bowels of the safe house.

She wasn't talking about the procedure itself. Even had Sheila been there, the stakes would have been the same. It would either work, which would be great, or it might not, which would suck, but it wouldn't leave us any worse than we'd been. The third option was it went horrifically wrong, in which case the failsafe was to kill me before I could return the favor. If there was anyone who shouldn't like things, it was me.

What was bothering her was the change in our contingency plan. Christy believed in a prophecy that Sheila would be the one to eventually end her and all mage-kind. However, they also shared a certain level of comradery, Christy even confiding in me that she felt Sheila was on the right path ... for now, at least.

The flipside of this was she really didn't like Dave. Couldn't blame her there. He was an acquired taste along the lines of poorly prepared Fugu.

As Dave pulled Ed into one of the many empty rooms of the complex to draw more blood – hopefully, my roommate had brought cookies and juice along for the trip – Christy not-so-subtly suggested Tom should hang around to keep an eye on things, preferably borrowing Ed's shotgun to do so.

I had to put the kibosh on that, pointing out my roommates would better serve as lookouts near the main entrance. My heightened vampire senses would be useless while we were mucking around in my head, and I doubted Dave would notice much more than his finger on the proverbial trigger, probably drooling at the chance to see me go boom in the name of science.

As for Adam and Mike, I expected them to join us once they were finished eating their fill of street punk. The problem was they wouldn't be worth shit when it came to telling friend from foe.

Once Dave was finished with his bloodletting, holding up a partially filled drip bag like it was the Ark of the Covenant, I told Ed to inform the Defilers that their orders were to wait in the large conference room in the center of the building. It had once served as the site of a failed meeting between the HBC and Village Coven – ah, the memories. Should they balk at doing so, he was free to kneecap them both with a silver twelve-gauge slug.

That done, my roommates sealed the three of us into the room that would either prove to be our salvation or damnation.

Christy had me lie down in the middle of the circle I'd painted on the floor. She positioned me so that I was in alignment with other symbols that lay at even intervals just outside it, taking a few moments to double check my work as I got into position – only slightly insulting, mind you.

The floor was cold and uncomfortable, so I grabbed one of the backpacks we'd brought along and used it as a pillow. Christy then positioned herself behind me, her palms on either side of my head.

"Don't break the circle," she hissed at Dave as he set up the IV, causing him to miss the vein.

"Ow."

"Really?" she asked, looking down at me.

"What? I don't like needles."

"You know, I could just blow him up now," Dave offered.

"Do your job and stay silent, please," she replied frostily.

"How will I know if something goes wrong?" he asked, his tone indicating her dislike of him had gone right over his head.

I winced as he inserted the needle again. "Believe me, you'll know. If I do anything that reminds you of Dr. Jekyll and Mr. Hyde, don't hesitate. Otherwise, your arms will probably be ripped off."

He immediately scooted back a couple of steps. "Good thing I brought a few extra feet of tubing."

Christy's soft chanting, just barely audible, refocused me. After a few moments, I felt the slightest tingle in my temples. Things were about to get interesting.

"Are you ready?" she asked, her eyes closed.

"Yep," I lied. "How long will it..."

"Take?" I was no longer on the floor of the safe house. Gone were the harsh concrete walls, the burning incense, and Dave. I was standing upright in ... it was hard to tell. The whole place was fuzzy, as if I'd forgotten to put my glasses on that morning.

"Focus," a voice said.

Well duh! That's what I was trying to do. People with twenty-twenty vision just didn't understand what a pain in the ass it was to...

"Focus on where you wish to be," the female voice clarified.

Where I wanted to be. Well, fuck, that was easy.

I concentrated, and the scene around me shifted. Where before there was a sense of being nowhere, now things began to take on form. The area where I stood expanded, the edges pushing outward until I was standing in an opulent bedroom.

I immediately recognized it. It had belonged to Alexander the Great, his residence within Chillon Castle, the fortress that served as the nerve center for the vampire world – located, in all places, within Switzerland.

No, that wasn't right. I turned and surveyed the room, realizing that some things had changed. Where once stood a massive statue of the great conqueror now stood one far more familiar. My own countenance grinned down upon me, carved from the finest marble. Oh yeah, this was more like it.

There was a large bath the size of a swimming pool next to it that I knew would be heated to the perfect temperature. The only thing missing was...

A muffled giggle from somewhere behind me caused me to spin around. Ah, there it was, the massive bed, covered in silken pillows and sheets with a thread count higher than my bank account.

But that wasn't all.

There was a bulge in the center of the bed, something hidden beneath the blankets. No, someone ... or make that *two* someones.

"Come out, come out, wherever you are," I playfully called.

At my beckoning, the sheet was thrown off, revealing both Sally and Sheila.

"We were wondering when you'd join us, master," Sally said in a voice so hot I was surprised my pants didn't immediately immolate.

"Ignore her," Sheila replied with a pout that was both petulant and wicked at the same time. "It's time to fulfill your destiny. The Icon needs conquering."

Fuck yeah! Now *this* was what I was talking about.

I took one step toward the bed when everything in front of me froze.

An angry voice sounded from out of nowhere. "You have *got* to be kidding me!"

I spun around, wondering who had pressed pause on the most awesome scene in the history of mankind.

"This is not what I meant, Bill."

"Um, sorry, disembodied ... err ... ghost lady," I replied, having no clue what was going on. Jeez, the days I had sometimes.

Footsteps sounded in my periphery, and I turned to find a figure beginning to coalesce. At first, it was as fuzzy as my view of the bedroom had originally been, but then I was able to make out features – a slim body clad in a tight mini-dress, brown hair so dark it bordered on black, a pendant hanging from her neck of a woman in gleaming white robes with arms outstretched – and then, finally, her face came into focus.

"Christy?"

"Who else would it be?" She sounded annoyed.

All at once, it slammed into me, what we were doing and where we were supposed to be. Oh shit, we were inside my head.

I blinked and found myself gawking at her trim figure. I mean, Christy had always been way above Tom's pay grade looks-wise, but she'd usually been a fairly conservative dresser. Not prudish or anything, but nothing like this. Here, she looked like she was about to take on every rave in New York City and leave dozens of broken hearts in her wake. In short ... *damn!*

Glancing back toward the bed and the lusty wenches within, still frozen as if time itself had stopped, I had to ask, "Um, did I do..." I indicated what she was wearing. "...*that?*" Oh crap, if I was subconsciously in love with her too, then I was in some deep shit for sure.

She appeared confused for a moment, but then looked down. "Oh this? No, this was me. We can appear however we like in the mindscape. Let's just say once I push this kid out, I am getting back to the gym pronto."

"Okay, I get that, but you ... well, you look like ... you're dressed like..."

"Sally?"

"No offense, but yeah."

"I know. She kind of turned me on to this look when we were in Vegas. I guess I enjoyed it more than I wanted to admit at the time."

"And when was this?" The only time I'd seen her with Sally in Las Vegas was for the few minutes when she'd teleported me there and then left. I mean, she'd been less pregnant than she was now, but not quite in the shape to pour herself into the outfit she currently inhabited.

"We really don't have time for that. We're here for a reason, remember?"

"Yeah, of course I do," I said, not quite ready to focus yet. "What's with the necklace?"

She lifted it and looked it over, a sad smile on her face. "I guess I'm also not quite as willing as I thought to give up on everything I've held dear in my life." She idly caressed the white figurine hanging from the silver strand. For a moment, she looked like she was about to cry, but then her face hardened. "Let's not worry about that for now. We're here for Dr. Death. Let's go find him."

I hesitated for the barest of moments.

"He's not here, is he?" she asked, trying to keep the horror out of her voice.

"Oh God, no!" I replied. "Believe me, I don't like extra sausage on my sandwiches."

"I really didn't need to know that."

"Sorry. Uh, yeah, let's blow this pop stand." I took a breath, trying to clear my mind, but once more turned to her. "If it's all the same to you..."

"Don't worry. This little, whatever it is, is just between us."

"Not even Tom?"

"Not even Tom," she reassured.

Good. The last thing I wanted was for him giving me shit about ... well, stuff he could probably figure out on his own. Even so, he didn't need the visuals to go along with it.

I steadied myself again, silently promising my two lovely bedmates I'd visit them once I had a chance to catch up on my sleep without any third parties looking on. A small shiver of fear worked its way through me as I forced myself to think of the cage I'd been kept in. It wasn't quite the dank prison I'd been stuck in during my tenure in Switzerland, but what was in it was far worse than a bunch of damp rocks and a door thick enough to withstand a bazooka blast.

I felt a hand on my shoulder. It was Christy. Somehow, she'd moved to my side without my noticing. "It'll be okay. I'm here with you."

Smiling, I nodded, hoping she was right.

The dream gave way to nightmare as the scene before us shifted. Gone was the penthouse suite of my fantasies and in its place was the dull reality of the hallway on the top floor of my apartment building – the one right outside my door.

"This is a bad idea," I muttered.

Unfortunately, Christy didn't have any words of encouragement to offer other than, "Go on."

These things always seemed so much easier when they were far enough off into the future so as to not seem real. But she was right. We couldn't just stand here for all of eternity, or however long had passed since we entered my mind. Eventually, time would move on – the Draculas would find us, the world would burn to a cinder, I'd have to pee.

There was also the chance that Dave would eventually grow bored and tell the scientific method to go take a flying fuck.

Yep, there was no turning back.

I took another deep breath, reminding myself that I was a new Bill, one who was unafraid of his destiny. I put on my best tough guy sneer and raised my hand to give the door a manly knock.

No, fuck that. This was my apartment. I didn't need to knock. Hell, I could beat the fucking door down with impunity. It's not like some dream landlord would show up and dock me my security deposit.

Yeah, that was the ticket. I cocked back a fist and let it fly ... just as the door was opened from the inside.

My momentum carried me forward. I stumbled a step,

then tripped over something – a foot – and ended up eating a mouthful of scuffed hardwood floor.

Oh crap. I'd been afraid of this. Well, there was no way I would let him get the drop on me without a fight! I salvaged my pride and rolled over in one fluid motion so as to at least see my attacker.

What I found instead was a hand offered to me from above.

Dr. Death stood looking down at me, his devilishly handsome features marred only by the black orbs that stared out at me from behind disturbingly familiar glasses.

"So sorry about that," he said, grinning. "Please forgive my excitement. I get so little company these days. Can I offer you a cup of tea? I just put on a fresh pot."

The fuck indeed?

# 16

# THE CALL OF THE WILD

pparently, the dickhead was hoping to bamboozle me with some sort of mind fuck.

Well, this Freewill wasn't born yesterday. I grabbed hold of his hand, then enjoyed the momentary look of surprise on his face when I yanked him forward, got a foot beneath his body, and catapulted him over me into our – *my* – living room.

One of these days, I really needed to thank Sally for her insistence on combat training back when we were at Pandora. Oh well, one didn't need to offer thanks for something the other party didn't even remember.

That thought quickly dissolved ... hmm, how could one think when one was already in one's mind? Never mind that. I rolled to my feet and turned to face my alter-ego, who was already dusting himself off.

"So that's the way it's gonna be?" he asked with a grin, his fangs looking a lot sharper than they ever did in my mouth. "I figured I'd try to be nice, but deep down, I kind of hoped you'd do something like that."

"Be careful what you wish for, asshole, because genies are

motherfuckers when it comes to granting them." I launched myself in his direction, clearing the distance between us in one leap.

I didn't bother to wait for a rebuttal, throwing out a hard right that connected with his incredibly manly, yet intelligent-looking, jawline. Outside of my head, the blow would have been enough to turn a two-by-four into toothpicks. Here, though, my fist slowed just before impact, feeling like it was moving through molasses. What the hell?

"Ain't that just the problem with dreams? All our inadequacies play out in the damnedest of ways." He followed up with a backhanded bitch-slap that knocked me over our couch and onto the coffee table, smashing it in the process.

"Oh yeah?" I slurred, wondering if back in the real world my sleeping self was spitting out teeth. "Well, let's see what inadequacies *you* have."

He appeared right before me in the time it took for me to blink. A clawed hand shot out and grabbed me by the throat in an iron grip, lifting me from the floor. "That one is easy. I don't have any."

"Oh? I'd call pride a major failing," a voice said from the doorway. Hmm, I'd been wondering how long Christy was going to stand there letting me get my clock cleaned. Maybe she'd been waiting for an invitation to come in.

"Aw, what's this?" my alter ego asked as he continued to crush my windpipe. "You brought me a present, and it isn't even my birthday."

Had she been me, a witty retort would have certainly escaped her lips. Instead, she had to do things the boring way – taking swift and decisive action.

She murmured and, suddenly, my apartment was gone. It

wasn't even a quick fade. One moment, we were in my living room. The next, we were outside in the middle of the day. Judging from the buildings around us, we were in midtown Manhattan ... oh, and Dr. Death and I were standing smack dab in the middle of the street.

Three things happened nearly simultaneously. I raised my hands to shield my face from the unforgiving rays of the sun, Dr. Death cocked a bemused eyebrow in Christy's direction, and then a taxi plowed into him from his blindside.

I flew free from his grip as the car slammed into my evil alternate self, sending him flying. The sound of screeching tires filled the air as I landed on the pavement, ending up on my back, staring into the bright blue sky.

Once again, I tried to protect myself as I let out a decisively unmanly screech. Well, this was gonna suck big time.

"Get up," Christy called. "It's not real."

Or not. Oh yeah, that whole inside my head thing.

"I knew that," I offered lamely, rising and dusting myself off. For a moment, the danger of the situation escaped me and I lifted my chin to the sky – enjoying the warmth of the imaginary sun. "Been awhile since I could do this and not burn to a crisp."

"Can we focus here?" she admonished.

Even had she not been there to keep me from lying down and sunbathing right in the middle of 6th Avenue, the squeal of tearing metal would have almost certainly caught my attention.

Oh crud.

Dr. Death was busy extracting himself from the side of the bus he'd been pinned against by the runaway cab. I watched in horror as his nails sank knuckle deep into the hood of the vehicle. With a shove, he pushed it away. Hmm, I sure as shit couldn't do that, at least not without a bite from a vampire of maybe James's level.

"Did you really think that would stop me?" he asked with a malevolent grin.

Before I could voice the opinion that one could hope, Christy stepped up to spare me the embarrassment. "I can do this all day."

"Don't worry, bitch, you won't live that long."

He'd barely finished the sentence when our surroundings changed again.

Where there had been the familiar scarred façade of Manhattan, now lush greenery stood. We were in the middle of a dense forest, standing in a clearing maybe thirty feet in diameter. At first, I thought Christy had plucked Canada from my memories – not a place I really wanted to relive – but the vegetation looked different, unfamiliar to...

"What the fuck is this?" Dr. Death asked. "You become a fucking Eagle Scout while I was asleep?"

Well, I guess it was unfamiliar to both of us. That must have meant...

"Sorry, I thought we'd try one of *my* memories," Christy said calmly, the black slinky dress gone and in its place a loose-fitting white robe. A breeze blew across the clearing, lifting the edges of it and revealing her bare feet and legs.

Whoa. I really didn't want to have to explain to Tom if she decided to start dancing naked in the moonlight.

Dr. Death smiled, his fangs looking even longer in the deepening shadows of the trees around us. "What are you gonna do? Attack me with squirrels?"

"This is where I spent many a night meditating."

"Oh, so you're gonna bore me to death." His legs tensed as he prepared to spring at her.

"And learning to become one with nature."

Dr. Death leapt, but he didn't get far. No sooner had his feet left the ground than roots shot from the dirt and entangled his feet, stopping him mid-flight. Within the space of a second, he had regained his footing, reaching down to tear himself free. What he didn't notice was the way the surrounding trees all picked that moment to lean inward. Vines flew from their branches and wrapped around his arms, neck, and torso.

They pulled tight and my alter-ego found himself suspended in midair, his arms and legs splayed wide.

He struggled, but the vegetation proved stronger than it looked.

After a moment, I stepped forward. "And that is why you don't burn down the trees around Isengard, motherfucker!" I turned to Christy. "Oh yeah! Mother Nature ain't got nothing on you."

I held up a hand for a high five. For a moment, she looked at me, one brow raised. Then she shrugged and slapped my palm. Woo!

Unfortunately, that was the end of her victory celebration. Her face turned serious once more. "Enough of that. We need to move quickly to…"

"Aw, c'mon," Dr. Death said, spitting out a wad of vines he'd managed to chew through. "Aren't you gonna say it?"

"Say what?" I asked.

"That this was almost too easy, of course," he replied with an eye-roll.

*Oh no.*

"Because believe me, junior, it was."

**17**

# DEAL WITH THE DEVIL

The vines around him withered and died almost instantly.

Christy made an upward gesture with her arms, as if willing more vegetation to rise from the ground, but nothing happened because we were no longer standing upon the ground.

I looked down to find the familiar floor of my apartment. When I looked back up again, the forest was gone and we were back where we'd started. Only this time, Dr. Death wasn't offering any refreshments.

Quick as a flash, he crossed the living room and pinned Christy's arms to her sides. He stood looking down upon her, seeming to be much taller than the five foot ten inches I commanded.

"Did you really think that would work, whore? We're in my fucking mind. I am *God* here!"

"You did not just quote *The Lawnmower Man*, did you?" I asked.

"Huh?"

"Because that movie sucked ass. Didn't have shit to do

with the book." I was stalling, trying desperately to think of something to do.

He was right, though. We were in his mind. He could do anything he wanted.

Wait a second.

He wasn't the sole occupant. It so happened he had a roommate, however reluctant. And if that were the case, it meant...

I lifted my hand and pointed it at him. "Set phasers to maximum, Mr. Worf." A bright orange beam of light shot out of the tips of my fingers and struck him dead on. It didn't disintegrate him as I'd hoped – fucking Federation. I knew I should've imagined me some Klingon weapons! It did, however, throw him free of Christy.

Fuck yeah!

I was by her side in an instant, steadying her and making sure she was all right.

"Stand back," I said. "This cocksucker is about to see what twenty-five years of pop culture is all about."

Remembering all the lessons from the first *Matrix* movie, I forced myself to accept the unreality around me. It wasn't as hard as you'd think, because it allowed me to reach down to my waist and grab the sword that had appeared there.

"Thundercats, hoooooo!" I shouted as I raised the gleaming blade, hearing the familiar roar ring out – deafeningly loud in the cramped apartment, but oh so cool.

Dr. Death wasn't out of it yet, though. He dodged backward, making me miss with my first swing. Damn, how could he ... and that's when I realized my living room was much larger than normal. He knew how to play this game too. That was fine by me.

Or not! He reached into our kitchen nook, grabbed hold of the nearest thing he could – the coffeemaker – and flung it at me with enough speed to make its cheap plastic shell a deadly weapon.

Fuck that! I might be taken down, but it wouldn't be at the hands of Mr. Coffee.

*SNIKT* Just like that, a trio of adamantium blades erupted from the wrist of my left hand, skewering the would-be projectile mid-flight.

"I'm the best at what I do," I said, closing the gap between us. "And what I do isn't very ... OOF!"

Sadly, a metal skeleton still wasn't enough to stop my nose from being crushed or me being sent flying backward from the blow. Note to self: save the one-liners for when the battle is over.

I smashed into the TV, thanking whatever gods there might be that I wouldn't have to worry about replacing the damned thing, and then rolled back to my feet.

Sadly, Dr. Death was nearly upon me ... or would have been had a glowing ball of red death not blasted into him from the side.

Christy was back in the game and through playing. This was a weapon that I'd seen her kind use in the past to blow the shit out of their enemies. The kid gloves were off.

Sadly, my doppelganger was one tough hombre. He again stood, his side seared, but still very much alive.

"You're gonna need more firepower than that to stop me."

"Brought it," I replied in a chipper voice. With that, I snapped my fingers and the whole apartment began to shake. Cracks appeared along the walls, widening by the second until the ceiling of the apartment – hell, the entire fucking roof of the building – tore off and revealed the sky and what occupied it.

The USS Enterprise and Battlestar Galactica both floated above, their weapons at the ready. A squadron of Macross Valkyries flew in formation between them. X-men Sentinels, riders on gleaming black dragons, and even a fake-looking giant robot from some shitty Japanese movie I'd seen back in grade school joined them. Finally, further up in the sky, something gleamed white.

"That's no moon," I said as a green pinpoint of light appeared on its distant face. "So, Princess, do you want to hand over the rebel plans or should millions of voices – all yours, mind you – cry out in terror?"

I was just imagining myself up a portable force field generator for the impending boom when Dr. Death held up his hands in a gesture of surrender.

My response was to lift a hand of my own, but this was no peace offering. My imaginary friends were waiting and dropping it would be their signal to unleash Hell. Still...

"Do it," Christy said, moving to my side. Her slinky black dress was back, no small distraction as it was.

I took a moment to remind myself she was six months pregnant with Tom's kid. Love him like a brother I might, but I really didn't want his sloppy seconds ... no matter how unsloppy they currently looked.

The angry glow that enveloped her – red, the color that mages seemed to adopt when they were good and ready to fuck someone's shit up – also more than helped put me back on track.

"What's your game?" I asked Dr. Death, not really sure why I hesitated. I was itching to blow this motherfucker back to the Stone Age. Sure, it would all be a figment of my imagination, but then again, so was he.

"No game," he replied evenly, his voice changing – becoming less a growl and far closer to the cadence I found issuing from my own mouth day in and day out. Dr. Death blinked, and the black around his eyes immediately receded, replaced by brown irises. He smiled. The fangs were gone too. "You finally did it."

"Did what?" I glanced to the side and, noticing the ball of energy quickly gathering in front of my friend's body, put a hand on Christy's shoulder. "Let him finish." Dr. Death smiled again. "And he'd better make it good because chances are they'll be his last words."

She laid into me with a glare, probably still a wee bit pissed that he'd tried his best to manhandle her, but I held her gaze and gave a single nod. She backed off – a little bit, anyway. That red ball of doom remained, but she reined it in ever so slightly.

That was fine. If dickface over there – by which I meant his face looked *nothing* like a dick, just so we're clear – so much as twitched the wrong way, I was gonna send his ass to quantum torpedo heaven.

"Exactly that," he continued, his entire demeanor changing. "I've been waiting all this time for your balls to finally drop." He glanced up. "Offhand, I'd say they came out made of brass."

"You've been waiting for this?" I asked dubiously.

"Yeah."

"Color me ever-so-slightly skeptical."

He sighed, then took a slow step toward our couch, where he sat down. "Ask yourself, Bill, who am I?"

"That's easy. The crazy-ass psycho who lives in my head."

"In some ways, that might be true. In others, that just reflects poorly upon you."

"How so?"

"Because I *am* you, stupid."

I raised an eyebrow. "Just because you look like me..."

"It goes deeper than looks and I think you know it."

"Humor me."

"I'm your reptilian brain, your anger center. I'm the part of you that used to lie awake at night wishing you'd told someone off when you had the chance. The part that used to fantasize about kicking the ass of everyone who's ever tormented you."

"Go on."

"The little piece of you that yearns to be a hero."

"You have a funny way of showing it."

"And you've had a nasty habit of keeping me fully repressed. All that resentment builds up after a while. That's why everyone always tells you it's not healthy to bottle that shit up."

He was right. Mom used to tell me that all the time when I was growing up. Of course, that was usually right after Dad complained about me being a crying little pussy.

Okay, that wasn't helping.

I turned to Christy. "What do you think?"

She opened and closed her mouth a few times, seemingly unsure of how to answer. Finally, she replied, "It's *your* mind."

"That helps a lot."

"I'm sorry, but it's not like I do this every day."

Letting out a sigh of frustration, I once more faced myself. "Fine, then where have you been all this time? I mean, I don't recall ever hulking out into a murderous rage-beast back in elementary school."

"You also weren't bitten by a vampire until a year and a half ago."

"Yeah, I noticed that part. I've also noticed that most other vamps don't do that."

"Fucked if I know," he replied with a shrug. "Maybe it's because most of them aren't Freewills."

I opened my mouth to reply, but he continued. "All I know is that one moment I was just another part of you, and the next, we were staring at Sheila out on a date with that asshole Decker and, suddenly, it was like I was a whole other person. All those weak parts of you stayed where they were, locked up tight, but I was free ... except I wasn't. All I could do was stare out at the world from behind your eyes, feeling your frustration grow."

I kept my eyes on him, partially to avoid Christy's glare for his mentioning of Harry Decker. What he said sorta made sense, though. That was the first time I ever felt myself start to snap, lose control.

"Then, out of nowhere, I started to take over. One minute, I was impotent." He held up a hand. "Don't fucking start."

"Sorry."

"The next, I could feel your arms becoming *my* arms, your legs becoming my legs, me taking control."

"But then I panicked."

"Yeah, and that bitch didn't help matters either..." He trailed off for a moment, his eyes momentarily growing dark again. Or maybe it was just my imagination – it happened pretty quickly. When he next spoke, they were back to being just my eyes. "But later on, you let it happen and I was free."

"Don't remind me," I growled, looking up and making sure my armada was still at the ready. The thought of what I could possibly do in that state was enough to make me consider a turbolaser lobotomy right then and there.

"I've been fighting for control ever since."

"Except in Switzerland."

"As I told you back then, be careful what you wish for." He stood up and took a step toward me, palms up with no claws to be seen. "But now that's changed. I said before that I didn't think sharing control was in the cards. I meant it. As long as you kept running from what you could do, from what you were *meant* to do, that was gonna be true. Now, though, you finally manned up. You came in here, faced me, and ... I am loathe to admit it, actually beat me at my own game."

"So what does that mean?"

"It means that you won. I'm ready to be a part of you again."

"Oh, well, then scamper back off into my repressed memories. Maybe we'll meet again in a dream."

"Doesn't work that way. You have to accept me." He looked me in the eye and slowly said, "Only then will you be able to have what you want."

Those words resonated with me. What I wanted. Did he mean his power? That was why I was here.

Even so, a part of me wasn't entirely certain that was the case. There were other things – people – I wanted. I'd just been too big of a pussy to ever go for it, outside of facing certain death, at least.

If what he said was true, then he represented those parts of me that always seemed to be just out of my reach when I needed them – probably because I was simultaneously pushing them away, afraid of what would happen: rejection, scorn, even losing control of my temper.

"And what happens if I accept you?"

"You open yourself up to the possibilities you already seem to be on the verge of accepting, that maybe, *just maybe,* you can be the man you always wanted to be."

"Not sure that's ever..."

"It also means," he continued, ignoring my self-doubt,

"we fight side by side. Whatever brings me out, turns me into the ultimate expression of your Freewill powers, that's controlled by me. By opening your mind to that potential, I'll once again become you. And if I am you..."

"Then that thing is me too."

"Exactly. All that power will be at your fingertips. You just need to stop being afraid to wield it."

"But what if my friends get hurt?"

"Have you looked around?" Dr. Death had moved to a spot directly in front of me. "That's a possibility no matter where you go in this world. But ask yourself this. What if my power allows you to save them?" He raised a hand and put it on my shoulder. For a moment, I was sure his claws would extend and he'd bisect me, all while laughing merrily away. All he did, though, was grasp my arm. It was oddly comforting ... and kinda weird too.

I looked over at Christy. The glow around her had faded. Indecision reigned on her face for a second or two, but then she smiled and nodded at me. "Accepting your personal demons is never a bad thing."

A part of me wasn't sure ... hell, it was practically screaming at me to open fire on this fucker regardless. I pushed it away, though. It was probably just my insecurities acting up as usual. Call it habit. The benefit, though, was too good to pass up. Being able to call upon this power at will – power that seemed to dwarf what I gained from drinking all but the most powerful of vampire blood. It was the prize I'd been seeking.

I had to take the chance. "Deal," I said, holding out a hand.

## 18

## FIRE AND BRIMSTONE

As the door to my apartment shut behind us, I turned to Christy. "That went better than expected."

"I agree. I'm glad I didn't have to restrain him deep in your subconscious."

"Or lobotomize me?"

"That too. That first one, though, carried more risk with it."

"Oh, as opposed to carving your initials into my brainstem?"

"Yes, that would have been unfortunate. However, in the other case, it would have been more worrisome."

I glanced back and the door was gone. The walls around us started to become unfocused as well. "How so?"

"Well, for starters, one can never tell how permanent of a solution that will be. However, it would have also verified that something wasn't right inside of you."

"Hold on for a second." All at once, Alex's former bedroom sprang up around us again. I could hear giggling coming from behind me where the bed stood.

Christy placed her hands on her hips. "Really?"

"Sorry, it's my happy place. Ignore it for the moment. What do you mean something's not right inside of me? I'd call my aggression splitting off into its own independent state to be pretty screwy."

"And it is," she replied, obviously making a conscious effort to not look at the pillow fight happening over my shoulder. "But not as wrong as ... it's hard to explain. I told you about being in Sally's head."

"Tearing down walls."

"Not just that, but how there was this strange sensation of not being alone. I wasn't sure if it was just her or maybe a vampire thing in general. If the latter..."

She trailed off, and I didn't ask her to finish. I had no idea what that might mean, and meaningless speculation wasn't going to solve any of our issues right at that moment. "Let's just chalk it up to Sally having some issues," I said.

"I hope so."

"So ... I don't suppose you'd let me hang out here for a while."

The last thing I saw in my mind was Christy's smile; amusement and a little pity coloring it. All at once, the dreamscape faded to nothing, and I became aware of the cold concrete upon which I had been lying.

The rest of my senses came flooding back as I wondered when I might get a chance to test out the tag team of the Dr. Death brothers.

My eyes fluttered, and damp air assaulted my nostrils, bringing with it the smell of decay, dirt, cleaning supplies, and people ... lots of people.

"Look, it's waking up. Get ready, men. It's powerless against our faith."

Perhaps I was going to get a chance to test out those new powers sooner than I thought.

"Uh, Bill…"

Christy's voice tapered off, the confusion evident. That wasn't good.

I opened my eyes and sat up.

"Be still, beast!" a deep voice commanded. It sounded like someone who had smoked far too many cigarettes in their lifetime. It was also familiar.

Sadly, all I could see were blurs of red … quite a few of them.

*Oh shit.*

I felt around where I sat. Sure enough, my glasses had slipped off at some point during my little exercise in theater of the mind. I popped them back on and everything swam back into focus … particularly ugly focus as I looked up to see a fat old lady clad in the red robes of a Templar brandishing a cross at me.

It was Sheila's former *neighbor*, the one I had punched out rather unchivalrously when she'd tried to stop us from leaving her apartment building. The look on her face suggested she hadn't forgotten.

That in itself wasn't much of an issue. Hell, I might not have James's or Alex's powers, but I could sure as hell take out a pudgy geriatric bitch if the situation called for it. Sadly, she wasn't alone.

Gone was Dave, and in his place stood at least half a dozen Templar warriors – most of them brandishing their holy fetishes, but two being somewhat more practical and wielding swords.

I put my hands up in a conciliatory gesture and slowly got to my feet. "Listen, guys, I don't know what the issue here is, but we don't want any trouble." I turned toward Christy, noting her form had filled out considerably from her mental avatar's state. She was still sitting on the floor, her eyes trying to take in the situation. I reached out a hand to help her up.

One of the Templar, a young and eager fellow – perhaps a bit too eager – sprang forward and slammed his metal cross down upon my knuckles. Fucking A! "Touch her not, filth. I command thee in the name of our Lord and savior!"

My hand wasn't on fire, meaning Sir Lancelot's faith wasn't worth the breath he wasted on it. Even so, that still fucking hurt.

*Do it*, a voice from deep within commanded.

"Huh?" I asked to nobody in particular. "What was that?"

*It's time*, Dr. Death repeated. *Kill them before they attack you ... before they hurt the witch.*

"That seems a little extreme." I mean, sure, these guys were assholes, but that didn't mean they needed to die because of it.

"Who is he talking to?" the young Templar asked.

The fat Templar stepped in front of him. "Be wary, my brothers. For surely he is receiving orders from his master ... Satan."

She might as well have just walked into a DC Comics convention and pointed out the one guy wearing a t-shirt that read "Fuck Batman." The Templar might have been cautiously holding back before, but now they took on a much more aggressive stance, converging upon my location.

It wasn't just me in danger either. The second Christy tried to use her magic, they'd no doubt remember those dictates along the lines of not suffering witches to live. I couldn't allow that.

*We'll make it quick, merciful.*

I nodded to myself. I'd closed my eyes to a situation that had been under control and came back out again to find myself smack dab in the middle of a shit storm. Sure, I stood a good chance of taking these clowns by myself, but it wasn't a guarantee. I was trapped with no way out, save the lone door beyond a sea of red cloaks, and with little room to maneuver. There were also my friends to think about.

*Your roommates. They were guarding the door. What happened to them?*

He was right. What had these fuckers done to them?

I didn't need a mirror to know my eyes had turned black as night. I could feel the slight prick on my bottom lips that said my fangs were descending. My claws were next and then it would continue.

"Let's do this, partner."

I'd been told to accept his presence. So I did. I opened myself up, willing myself to let him in, and felt a cold void of raw rage begin to seep into me.

When next I blinked, the room had taken on a decisively red tint.

I tensed my arms and realized my sleeves felt tight. This was it. Fear bubbled up in me as I felt the change begin. All of my defenses screamed out for me to stop what was happening. It was a learned response, little more than a subconscious version of Pavlov's dog. I needed to push it down, repress it for once.

*Yes, let it happen.*

"That's enough!"

The voice carried with it authority and determination. Everyone in the room turned toward it.

*No!*

I did too, the rage subsiding in me as quickly as it had risen. Hers was a voice I knew well, one that I often dreamt of … and not just in the way Christy had seen a few minutes prior.

Well, okay, mostly in that way.

The Templar parted as Sheila stepped to the doorway. I found myself surprised to find her wearing regular clothes – half expecting to see her clad in her Templar armor, and not just because she looked hot in it.

"Really, guys? I told you to just guard the room."

"The beast is not to be trusted," Fatty spat.

"For the last time, he's on our side. There's a far greater evil to be dealt with."

"Wait, far greater evil?" I asked as it hit me.

"Sorry. You know what I mean."

"Apologize not to this thing," one of the Templar, the faithless one who'd smacked my hand, said. Christ, these fuckers really needed to get laid. "You are far above it in the…"

"Thank you, Brother Thomas," Sheila said curtly. Though she'd had nothing to do with them since the battle in Upstate New York, as far as I knew, they still seemed to venerate her words as that of an authority figure. Speaking of which…

"Um, what are these guys doing here?"

Ton o' Templar spoke up. "You mean besides protecting this sweet child, heavy with babe as she is, from your voracious appetite?" She took a step toward Christy, who scrambled to her feet and away. "You need not fear, child."

"I'm *not* your child." Christy's eyes flashed, and a purplish glow began to suffuse her body. "I know what you are. All Magi know the crimes the zealots have committed against our kind."

Oh crap, here we go again.

If my presence had been a slap across the face to the Templar, learning that Christy was a witch was the accompanying kick to the nuts. Murmurs of prayer rose up in the room, and so too did their weapons.

"I said that's enough," Sheila said again, a glow erupting from her body – one that made Christy's seem like a night-light by comparison.

"You said nothing of a daughter of Lucifer being present."

"And if you still think that's how it works, then it shows you know nothing of us," Christy retorted.

"Sister Bernadette," Sheila said, stepping forward and putting a hand on the tubby Templar's sloped shoulder. The glow from her spread to the old woman, and a look akin to rapture passed through her face. "These are my friends. Please trust my judgment in this."

The look of pure joy at being touched by Sheila's power – harmless to humans, but probably making the Templar think God himself was giving them a handjob – immediately fled Bernie's face, seemingly replaced by a bad smell. "We will trust you, your Holiness. But know that we will not trust them."

"That is all I can ask for," Sheila replied, her voice remaining pleasant. "Everything is under control here. Please take the faithful upstairs and keep guard. I'll join you shortly."

Bernadette hesitated, throwing me and Christy the stink eye.

"Worry not, Sister," Sheila continued. "I have nothing to fear. You know the damned cannot enthrall me."

Sheila shut the thick door once her asshole buddies had passed beyond. Though it would keep them from eavesdropping, it still wasn't enough to stop me from hearing them muttering as they walked away.

"She says she isn't enthralled, but..."

"Have faith, brother; the Lord's will shall prevail in the end."

Their voices faded away to several cries of hallelujah as they reached the stairs. Fucking Bible thumpers.

"Damned, eh?" I asked, an eyebrow raised.

"Sorry. Sister Bernadette would only believe so much of what I tried telling her. I had to walk a fine line to get them to come along. Things almost got ugly as they were."

"I have a feeling ugly's a concept she's quite intimate with." The glares from the two ladies, both of them nuclear bombs to my firecracker, caused me to cease with the insults – true though they might be. "Why are they here?"

"I was kind of hoping they'd turn you down," Christy said, causing my head to snap toward her.

"What the hell do you mean by that?"

"You know we need them," Sheila replied, ignoring my outburst.

I stepped between them and held up my hands. "Okay, red light! Let's back up just a step here. What the fuck are the Templar doing in this safe house and," I turned toward Christy, "why do you know about this?"

"You do realize that while you've been off doing whatever it is you do, the rest of us have been planning, right?"

I spun toward Sheila, meeting her silver eyes with my own. "I mean, I figured you guys were talking about it, but..."

"But without you to lead the discussion, we'd just flounder about like fish out of water?"

"Well, not exactly." Her eyes blared white for a moment, and I added, "Okay, maybe a little."

"Seriously?" She threw up her hands and paced across the

room. "Your entire plan was to march us up to Boston and attack them ... with just the six of us?"

"I..." Fuck! She had me there. "Fine. I'm more of an adjust-on-the-fly type of guy anyway." I turned around and pointed a finger at Christy. "And you knew?"

"I live there too. Now you know."

"And none of you said anything because...?"

"A couple of reasons," Sheila said.

"Oh? Care to enlighten me?"

"For starters, we weren't sure any of it would work. The Templar and I didn't exactly part ways on the best of terms. An entire chapter was wiped out in Westchester, and then you had to go and punch Bernadette in the face while we were standing together."

Ah yes, quite the pleasant memory. "Okay, and..."

"That was on me," Christy said. "After you told me your plan, I thought it best to keep you in the dark on this. I didn't think the extra stress would help while you were preparing yourself."

"Oh, and waking up to a bunch of crosses about to be shoved up my ass wasn't stressful?"

"Sorry about that," Sheila said. "Bad timing. Took longer to gather them together than I thought. Believe it or not, they've been doing a lot of good in the city – fighting off monsters and protecting people where they can. A lot of them were out on the street when I made it to their sanctuary."

"Took you long enough."

"I also stopped by my old place for a few changes of clothes," she admitted with a guilty grin.

"Fine. What's done is done. I don't like them much, but I won't lie and say they won't be useful. Lord knows – and yes, I will refrain from saying such things around them – but we could use the help." That thought caused me to look around the room and remember the distinct lack of Dave. I quickly scanned the floor, looking for signs of dust. "Where is..."

"That one's my bad too. I didn't realize you were bringing other vampires. Apparently, I'm not the only one who's been keeping secrets."

"In all fairness, I wasn't originally planning on bringing them along. It just sort of worked out that way."

"Whatever the case, we found two strange vampires upstairs with your roommates and then a third standing over you both, holding an IV of blood that was attached to your arm."

"You didn't hurt them, did you?"

"It was close. The two upstairs started pointing at me and yelling stuff about holy avenging something or other."

"Your sword. I told them it was a plus five Holy Avenger."

"Uh, yeah. Well, either way, they got real lucky. I saw they were covered in blood and was..." She averted her gaze from mine. "I was afraid for the worst. But then they threw up their hands and surrendered."

"You don't fuck with a high level paladin," I commented.

"Anyway, I have some more Templar upstairs guarding them all."

I let out a sigh of relief. Things had already gone bad with Carl. I didn't need shit escalating with the rest.

"Thank you. They're friends ... weird though they might be."

"And the blood?"

Thankfully, Christy was there to bail me out on that one. "A necessary evil. We wouldn't have made it here without their help." A bit of an exaggeration, but it sounded a whole lot better than what really happened.

That was all Sheila apparently needed, because she nodded somberly. "I have a feeling there's going to be a lot of that in the days ahead." She smiled and turned back to me. "Sorry I wasn't here to help, but I assume you went ahead with things anyway, even without precautions?"

I explained to her Dave's presence with the bag of Ed's blood. She nodded, a look of admiration upon her face. "Not bad. But more importantly, did it work?"

I opened my mouth, not entirely sure what I was going to say. I mean, I *thought* it worked. However, pointing out that we would have known for sure had she made her grand entrance just a few moments later didn't seem particularly wise.

Thankfully, one of the Templar popped his head back in the door and spared me from having to sputter something about learning to sing Kumbaya with my inner self.

"Blessed one, come quick. A figure approaches from the night. She has the form of a harlot, but moves with the grace of one of *them*."

His inflection toward me carried with it enough venom to down a rhino, but I didn't care. The description he'd given was the important part and it pointed to only one person.

Sally was finally back.

**19**

# LIKE OIL IN HOLY WATER

I pushed my way past the Templar minion and headed upstairs. The last thing I needed was for Sally's return to be interrupted by a bunch of asshats trying to turn her into a fried Twinkie with their crosses.

Sheila hurried to keep up. I wondered why she was suddenly so interested in Sally, but then when I reached the main floor, I realized it wasn't Sally so much as me.

She'd done her part in spades. The group of Templar I'd met upon my rude awakening was just the tip of the iceberg. She'd gone all out. The place was packed with them, albeit it was hard to tell how many due to the multiple rooms that made up the main floor.

The one thing they all had in common, though, was an adverse reaction to me – like I was a walking vine of poison ivy. Each group immediately reached for their weapons when they saw me. Guess they were still a bit steamed over what happened to their buddies up in Westchester. Either that or they were just of the kill first, ask questions later mindset when it came to vampire filth.

Sheila was probably the only reason I made it upstairs

both unharmed and without having to bust some heads on the way – that latter prospect something I found myself oddly okay with. Go figure, beating up on righteous assholes – a victimless crime if ever there was one.

Regardless, her presence served to remind them that they weren't here on a search-and-destroy mission.

As I neared the door, I overheard a loud argument off in one of the side rooms.

"For the last time, I'm not a goddamned thrall!"

It was Ed.

"Take not the Lord's name in vain, thrall. Your lies fall upon deaf ears, for why else would a righteous man cavort with one of Lucifer's fell demons?"

Cavort?

"Because he pays his share of the fucking rent, that's why."

"Sorry," Sheila said with an exasperated sigh. "Let me go take care of that."

I chuckled and kept walking. "Nah, leave them. Sounds like he's fine."

"Get out of the way," I snarled as I reached the door.

The two Templar guarding it glared at me, but stepped aside nevertheless.

"You know, you might catch more flies with honey than vinegar," Sheila said from behind me.

"I'm pretty sure that myth was busted."

"You know what I mean."

An irrational surge of anger flooded through me. *Tell her to go fuck herself!*

What the hell? I told my inner problem-child to chill out and then took a deep breath, waiting to see if Dr. Death reared his head again. When he didn't, I replied, "I know and I'm sorry. It's just that I'm stressed and these guys are all staring at me as if I'm gonna pull a baby out of my backpack and start eating it in front of them."

"I'll have another word with them."

"Thanks."

Approaching footsteps from outside reached my ears. Judging from the clicking on the pavement, sensible shoes weren't a part of the equation. Oh well, there was only one person I knew with the audacity to face the apocalypse while wearing five-inch heels.

I flung the door open only for the business end of a massive handgun to greet me. Damn, the barrel looked wide from this angle.

"Hey, Sally," I squeaked, hoping there was no pee leaking out of me.

The gun lowered, and my partner's blonde visage stared back at me. She was wearing a trench coat, no doubt meant to conceal the hand cannon she stuffed back inside of a pocket. Across her shoulder was slung a heavy-looking duffel bag.

"Sorry," she said. "I found your note."

"Then what's with the fifty-caliber greeting?"

"Because someone else could have found it too. Your genius cipher left a lot to be desired."

"Cryptography isn't one of my specialties."

"No shit." She stepped past me. "So, any reason for the sudden upheav..."

I didn't need to ask to know Sally had just noticed the red-robed figures standing inside the doorway.

"Well, this is nice." Her voice betrayed no hint of panic as she glanced over her shoulder. "Is this your great plan for beating Vehron? Enthralling an army of cosplayers?"

"They're with me," Sheila said from a few steps further in.

"Oh. Those Templar jokers you were telling us about."

"You knew too?" I asked.

"Of course," she replied dismissively.

I secured the door and left our Templar guards to resume their duty as I walked after the two wayward members of our group. Out of the corner of my eye, I noticed Christy had likewise caught up – albeit looking pretty winded. Whether it was from the stairs or from the trip inside my noggin, I wasn't sure. Probably a bit of both. That the eastern sky was just now starting to get light wasn't helping matters. She hadn't gotten any rest all night.

Sally glanced around, taking in the hostile glares the assembled Templar were giving her. She stepped fearlessly up to one and ran a finger over his red robe. "Not the most inconspicuous bunch I've ever seen."

Judging from the Templar's face, you'd have thought she was a leper rather than a beautiful woman. Oh well, maybe I could point Adam in this one's direction.

"You've met them before, you know," Sheila said with a wry smile.

"Oh? Well, they obviously didn't make all that big of an impression."

Amazingly enough, I found myself stepping in to put a stop to that. "They're here to help us." I sensed multiple sets of eyeballs boring into me, so I quickly amended, "I mean, they're here to help the *Blessed One* on her holy crusade for justice, of which we – the evil shit stains of the world – are joining in our attempts to repent our wicked ways."

I couldn't have spread more sarcasm over that had I tried, yet it seemed to mollify them nevertheless. Oh yeah, this was gonna be a fun bunch to travel with.

Sheila spent the next fifteen minutes or so sorting things out with the Templar. Ed had really been the only one inconvenienced by the whole ordeal, looking kinda pissed when they finally let him out of the room they were holding him in.

Meanwhile, Tom, Adam, and Mike were busy playing cards off in a corner as if they hadn't noticed the holy rollers milling about.

Dave had set up some of his equipment in one room and was busy scribbling notes on a pad. If he was bothered by having been dragged away from babysitting me, it didn't show.

In the end, the Templar had no problem honoring a truce with their fellow humans, something Ed really wasn't, but nobody seemed willing to volunteer that information. No matter what Sheila said, though, it was obvious they weren't going to let the rest of us go about our business without keeping an eye on us. Oh well, they'd just best hope I didn't need to take a shit anytime soon.

A fragile peace thus established, I suggested to my friends we take some time and get each other caught up – on everything this time. They'd been planning without me, and I'd been guilty of doing the same. The time for secrets needed to end. It sure as shit wasn't Christmas, so I had a feeling more surprises wouldn't be to our advantage.

Tom waved us off, obviously caught up with his game. Judging from the stack of bills in front of him, they were playing for cash and he was winning. That was fine. He most certainly wasn't the Rommel to our war council.

The only downside was Sister Bernadette. Despite Sheila's assurances, she was unwilling for her men to be kept in the dark. Quite the amusing concept for a group that looked like they had stopped keeping up with fashion sometime around the fifteenth century. I wouldn't have been surprised to learn they all thought the world was flat and considered women to be property.

I really didn't care to call for an entire assembly. I'd done more than enough speaking in front of hostile crowds lately. This meeting was for the generals only. As such, we agreed to let Bernadette be their emissary. I wasn't big on taking her into my confidence, and I'm sure she wasn't either, but fuck it. What was the worst that could happen? I mean, it's not like this entire operation wasn't about to blow up in our faces as it was.

I led the group to a conference room deep inside the building, hoping that this conclave proved slightly more successful than the last time I'd been here.

We straightened up a bit, locked the doors, and sat.

"Time to lay all the cards on the table," I began. "It's safe to say we've all had enough surprises as of late to make us wonder where the big fat guy in the red suit and sleigh is."

"Christmas is the time to celebrate the birth of our..."

"Oh please shut up," Sheila snapped at Bernadette. "Can we focus here and save the vitriol for later?"

Judging from the look on Bernadette's face, you'd have thought she'd been branded with a pentagram instead of told to keep her ample pie-hole closed. I could have hugged Sheila for doing that, but I had a feeling that wouldn't do much to cement the fragile alliance we had going with the Templar.

*We don't need them!*

Dr. Death had gotten awfully chatty ever since our little soiree. I found myself wondering when he was going to get reabsorbed back into my subconscious. Couldn't be soon enough.

*I heard that.*

Fuck!

Okay, enough of this crap. I turned to the rest and got us

started, telling the assembled of how I went to visit Dave and my reasons for doing so.

"Wait a second," Sally interrupted. "You've been letting someone experiment on your blood? You do know that is particularly frowned upon, right?"

Yeah, that. I nodded. "I know how it fucked François up the ass." She probably didn't remember him, so I moved on. "Yes, I know the consequences, but I don't care. We need any edge we can get."

To my surprise, she actually smiled. "Maybe you own a set after all."

"Not if I get caught. Regardless, he could come in useful. I've asked him to take a look at Ed's blood as well. See if he has any clue what's wrong with him." My roommate glared at me, to which I added, "Well, more wrong than usual."

"Do you think he can really help?" Sheila asked, her tone dubious.

I decided to leave out the results, or lack thereof, of Dave's experiments so far. "He's a smart guy."

"What is wrong with his blood that this vampire need examine it?" Bernadette asked.

Oh crap. I really should watch what I say around certain company. It wouldn't behoove our cause for the Templar to know my roommate had been reclassified from "human" to "who fucking knows?"

"Um, Ed's feeling a bit under the weather," I replied lamely. "I want to make sure he's healthy for the trip." I kicked my roommate under the table, at which point he caught the hint and let out an unconvincing cough.

The Templar headmistress narrowed her eyes, but before she could question me further, Sheila steered us back on track. "Can we trust your friend to be … discreet?"

"Dave's a recent convert. He got turned by Vehron and hasn't been exposed to the greater vampire world, so he's not contaminated by their dogma. He's got one other thing going for him in that regard. He's a self-absorbed asshole. There's no way he's going to share his research with someone else, at least not before he can make a fortune off of it."

To my surprise, Sheila said, "Okay, if you trust him, I will too. If it'll help Ed, he can have some of my blood as well."

"Blessed one," Sister Bernadette intoned, "this is unwise, giving of yourself to the enemy."

"If it will help a friend, then it's for the greater good. Could I do any less?"

That shut the Templar bitch up. I smiled toward Sheila, then switched things up to inform them of how I couldn't leave my former gaming group behind.

"Oh, so you *did* bring other gaming dorks with you?" Sally asked dismissively. "Just keep them away from me. I already took a shower today."

"Relax. I already warned the Defilers about you."

Sister Bernadette leaned forward, her beady little eyes boring into me. "Defilers?"

Son of a bitch. "It was just a party name from our D&D game."

Judging by her increasingly sour look, that explanation wasn't winning me any points either. Damn, I felt sorry for any kids who had to visit her on the holidays.

Quickly changing gears, I next brought the team up to speed on my Dr. Death issue and the progress made there.

"So you're saying he's just some offshoot of your powers combined with your subconscious?" Sheila asked.

"Seems like it."

Sally leaned forward, eyeing me curiously. "You ever maybe consider group therapy? Because that shit doesn't sound normal."

"What do you think?" Sheila asked Christy.

"Fingers crossed, but it sounded reasonable to me," she replied.

My tale finished, Sheila told of how she, Sally, and the rest of my friends had discussed things and realized the Templar would be a potentially powerful ally against the forces Vehron was mustering up in Boston.

Her speech put a lot of emphasis on their faith and how it would be tested – no doubt buttering up a big cinnamon roll full of bullshit for Bernadette to chow down on. I could dig that.

Sister Bernadette corroborated this, informing us that so long as we didn't stray into darkness, then our truce would hold.

Yeah, that was gonna take a wee bit of a miracle to pull off. Bottom line was vampires needed blood to survive, and our stash of the bottled stuff was close to empty.

Thankfully, Sheila seemed to sense my trepidation because she had the perfect answer.

"We're going to split our forces when the time comes. The Templar will work to clean up the streets of Boston and rescue anyone they can. The rest of us will focus on the main complex."

It wasn't much, but the separate missions might give us the breathing room to do what we needed to, while not ticking off our allies too badly.

When all was said and done, I had to admit she'd thought this through in much greater detail than me. I mean, neither of us were exactly trained in military strategy, and that showed. However, at the end of the day, she had much more of a claim to leading this party than I did. I'd need to tell her that when I got the chance.

For now, though, it was Sally's turn to enlighten us all as to what she'd been up to. She lifted up the duffel bag she'd come in with onto the table. The creak of the wood beneath it was testament to its weight. She unzipped it and threw back the cover, revealing a whole shitload of firepower within.

Whoa. Sheila might have invited the party guests, but Sally had brought the noisemakers.

"I was hoping to find any remnants of Village Coven," she explained. "Even a couple of seasoned vampires could be helpful to our cause."

I let out a sigh. We'd been through this. "I told you, anyone with any experience was wiped out. As for the new recruits, Vehron got them all."

"Yeah, I know you *said* that, but I also know me. I have a hard time believing there wouldn't have been a few nooks and crannies that I hadn't told you about."

"Sorry to douse your paranoia with some reality, but I knew every..."

"And I was right."

She was?

"I found traces of recent vampire activity at some of our less-frequented locations."

"Whoa. Hold on. What do you mean *less-frequented locations?*"

"Like the apartment up on 22nd."

"What apartment?"

"Or the basement below that bistro on Canal Street."

"Huh?" Motherfucking son of a bitch! "I was the master of that coven. Why the fuck didn't you..."

It was a stupid question to ask, considering her state of mind and, thankfully, she spared me from finishing it by talking right over me. "Unfortunately, I was also too late."

"What do you mean?"

She turned toward Sister Bernadette. "I found piles of ash inside that last place. Your people were thorough."

"Once the signs of Armageddon were clear, my people

fought to protect the innocent and ensure our place in the Rapture."

"Yeah, thanks for that. You also fucked us out of some potential cannon fodder. Thankfully, you weren't *that* thorough, and I was able to get my hands on some consolation prizes." She indicated the big bag of guns in front of her.

I was just about to comment when she pulled one other item from the bag. It was a big heaping ball of bubble wrap, but I could see something within through the translucent material.

Before anyone could ask what it was, though, a voice rang out from both everywhere and nowhere at once, answering the question.

*Many will be called, but few shall stand. In the end, the white rises and the darkness falls.*

It was the remains of Harry Decker: wizard, asshole, and my late, unlamented nemesis.

I had no idea what the fuck he meant by that. Unfortunately, our game of Blue's Clues was going to have to wait.

An angry red glow erupted in the room as Christy stood, her fists clenched so tight that her knuckles shone white even against the crimson fire building around her.

I think it was safe to say she was a wee bit ticked off.

# 20

# UNEASY ALLIANCES

"What is that?" Christy hissed as the lighting in the room changed to match what was obviously a reflection of her mood.

Needless to say, this didn't sit too well with Bernadette. She waddled to her feet in … well, slightly more than a moment, and produced a silvered dagger, pointing it at Christy. "Betrayer! Whore to Satan!"

Sheila rose to her feet next to the Templar. White fire flared around her, a distinct clash to that which swirled around Christy.

Bernadette noticed it and grinned. "Now you finally see. These creatures cannot be trusted."

"*Sit down*," Sheila growled at her so fiercely that I found myself keeping my own ass planted despite the situation.

To my amazement, Bernadette complied, although she kept her weapon in hand. That left only the three ladies standing, Sally the only one among them who didn't look particularly perturbed.

I glanced to Ed, who was sitting next to me, and whispered, "Did you know she was gonna bring that?"

He shook his head.

"Christy," Sheila said, the glow around her subsiding now that Bernadette was contained, "please calm down."

"I want to know what is in that package and why it sounds like Harry," she replied, tears forming in her eyes. Combined with her hormones and current lack of sleep, this revelation was definitely not having a positive effect on her mood.

"Sally," I warned. She'd opened the bottle on this genie for some insane reason. She needed to seal it back up again.

"What's the issue?" she asked, sounding genuinely surprised. The claws on her right hand extended, and she sliced easily through the wrap, shredding it ... and making several popping noises in the process. Ah, no matter the situation, that never failed to sound soothing.

Unfortunately, it didn't have a similar effect on Christy, who let out a gasp when Sally produced a skull from within and set it upon the table. "Is that...?"

"This?" Sally asked. "No idea really. Not sure who owned it or why I have it, but it helped out a bit in Vegas. Some of the mages there owed me favors, so I phoned and asked if it was still in my old office and if they could zap it over to me. Figured it might come in handy. Didn't realize it would be such a problem."

Fuck me! Sally's memory loss. Her dealings with Decker had pretty much all been around me. She'd obviously forgotten about him and the reason we had kept her little paperweight a secret from Christy ... the reason that had the potential to bring this whole building down around us.

Christy's voice turned to steel. "Why do you have my mentor's skull?"

Sally, finally grasping that this was indeed a big fucking deal to at least one person in the room, seemed to realize things were escalating toward potential violence. So, of course, rather than try to make things better, her eyes flashed black and her hand slid inside her coat to where her weapon of choice, a Desert Eagle, was holstered.

Shit on toast!

"It's because it tells the future," I cried out, hoping I wasn't too late to stop things from completely devolving.

"You knew?" Christy asked accusingly. Sheila likewise turned toward me, one eyebrow raised quizzically.

I opened my mouth, wondering what answer I was going to stammer as way of apology.

*You're not going to win this by pussing out. Man the fuck up.*

That wasn't helping. Christy was my friend. There was no way I was attacking her and ... wait. Dr. Death hadn't actually said to rend her limb from limb. Was it possible he was actually giving me some useful advice for a change? Maybe he was right – mewling was just going to make things worse.

"Yes, I knew," I said, willing my voice to be steady. "Tom and Ed did too." I felt the stink eye coming from the direction of my roommate, but fuck him. Besides, if I was sailing into a sea of shit, I was sure as hell taking some boating buddies with me.

"How could you?"

"Okay, you need to calm down so we can..."

"*Do not* tell me to calm down!"

Oh, fuck this shit. "***SIT DOWN AND KNOCK IT OFF!!***"

The compulsion took them all by surprise ... well, except for the two in the room who seemed immune to them, but they at least heard my voice.

Christy, for her part, looked as if I'd just slapped her in

the face. For a moment, I was certain she would blow large chunks out of my favorite torso as way of response. After a second or two, however, she averted her gaze and sat. Unfortunately, the red glow around her continued to emanate.

The door to the conference room suddenly burst open and two Templar strode in, crosses at the ready, because this situation obviously wasn't explosive enough.

Thankfully, Sheila was on her feet in a heartbeat, ushering them out of the room. That was good, because I really didn't want to take my attention off of Christy right then.

I needed to talk fast. "I'm not going to tell you to be happy about this, or that this is no big deal. I'm sorry, but..."

"You hated him," she spat.

"You're right. He was a dick. I'm not sorry for what happened to him. I'm also not sorry that we inadvertently found a use for him as he is now. What I am sorry about is hurting you because you're my friend and I know he meant a lot to you."

"He was like a father to me," she replied, the glow around her subsiding as tears began to fall from her eyes. "He raised me after my powers manifested, after my real parents became terrified of me. He took me in, taught me about our people, made me the witch I am today. He helped me in so many ways."

"I know," I replied, feeling like quite the stepped-in pile of dog shit. "The thing is, he can still help. I don't know whether it's dumb luck or fate..." Yeah, I really shouldn't have been walking down that path, but damn, sometimes circumstance ended up being a little too freaky for even me. "But whatever the case, a part of him is still here."

She glanced at me, her brows furrowing.

"I mean in more ways than just ... *that*." I gestured toward the skull grinning up at us from the table, the look on it somehow smug even in death. Asshole. "There's still a piece of him there. You heard it."

"He's not at rest."

"No, he's not." I had no idea what afterlife awaited the Magi, but I had to hope it was more than just becoming the metaphysical equivalent of a fortune cookie. "The thing is..."

"He won't be until this is all over," she said, finishing my sentence for me. That was good, because I really had no idea where I was going with that thought. Even better, she seemed to be calming down. I had a feeling we were all gonna be on her shit list for a while to come, even Tom, but it seemed the danger of being blown to bits had passed. "You said he could see the future?"

"Yes," I replied carefully. "Every time he speaks up, it's about an event that eventually comes to pass. He foresaw the fall of Boston and the rise of Vehron." I left out the minor bullshit he'd spouted, like the time in Vegas he'd screamed out a warning about the terror of the endless night, only for it to foretell no more than the power grid failing. There was also the nonsense. Back right before Ed had been kidnapped, the skull had spouted some shit about purity and the first ... whatever the hell that meant. Oh well, it always seemed to have some disdain where Sally and I were concerned. I wouldn't have been surprised to know that was the eldritch version of his spirit fucking with us.

"Knowledge of the future is dangerous," Christy said. "Long foretold prophecy is one thing. Scholars and mystics can debate them for eons. But knowing the immediate future is tricky. One can run the risk of causing the very event they're trying to escape."

"Yeah..."

"But I also believe that the future is malleable and can be rewritten," she continued. "Harry was so afraid of the coming of the Shining One, the downfall of our people.

Perhaps this is his way of still trying to keep that from coming to pass. Maybe he knew this day would come and we would be reunited."

"He could still be trying to protect you," Sheila said.

Christy turned toward her and flashed a grateful smile. "What if he's trying to protect me from you?"

"Then I'm happy he's around to do so."

Amazing. The person to defuse the situation was also the same one Decker had been purposefully trying to rid the world of ... first by destroying me, and then by giving up all pretense of sanity and forming an alliance with the vampires. Funny how the world worked sometimes.

That didn't mean Christy wasn't still ticked at the rest of us. I had a feeling we'd all be getting an earful of that. For now, though, she made it clear in no uncertain terms that she'd be holding on to her master's skull until such time as our mission was over, at which point – assuming we weren't in a position for our skulls to become matching bookends to his – she'd give him proper last rites as a Mentor and Magi.

Sally came close to ruining that, opening her mouth when Christy claimed the skull and managing to emit a "Hey!"

Thankfully, I was on hand to mutter, "Shut the fuck up *now!*" under my breath. It was probably just barely audible to Ed, who was seated right next to me, but Sally heard me plain and clear. She locked eyes with me and I held her gaze, willing her to get the hint.

For a moment, it was touch and go. Sally's glare was an alien one; no trace of the familiar fuck-you attitude that usually permeated such exchanges. James's warning began to play out in my mind, but then she relaxed her gaze, rolled her eyes, and nodded ever so slightly.

That was too close.

We spent the next hour hashing out details – mostly petty squabbling between the rest of us and Bernadette over what the Templar would and wouldn't tolerate from us. We decided my group would get the pick of the weapons Sally had brought, albeit I wasn't entirely certain I wanted the Defilers to be armed. Sounded like a good recipe for being shot in the back, even if by accident. Bernadette had originally refused to take any of them – citing that her men had faith to back them up and needed nothing else.

She was none too pleased when I pointed out that at least one of her Templar's faith wasn't worth the paper his Bible tracts were written on. If there was one, there would undoubtedly be more – quite likely the majority. She didn't want to hear that faith was a tricky thing, far easier to profess having than to actually possess, but I could see it in her eyes that she knew I wasn't bullshitting her.

In the end, Ed was the one who offered the compromise of outing the posers by having me go down the line, touching each of their preferred items of holy ass-kickery. Note to self: beat the shit out of Ed when the opportunity presents itself.

Oddly enough, Bernadette didn't seem to have any issue with causing me unjust pain – fat, hotdog-sucking bitch.

The smirk on Sally's face said all there was to say there, and Christy had stayed quiet ever since the row about Decker's noggin. Sheila was the only one to pipe up with any concern, but – even to my own amazement – I found myself ratifying the idea.

"It's okay. I can take it," I lied, glancing down at my watch. It was late enough for the sun to be shining. "If we do it soon, I'll have plenty of time to heal up. It's not like we're probably going anywhere for the next several hours anyway."

Sheila tilted her head at me and shrugged, her meaning clear – this was my choice to make.

"Once we determine who has the mojo and who doesn't, we can split up the guns accordingly."

"Are we sure these clowns aren't going to just shoot themselves in the feet instead?" Sally asked rather undiplomatically. Oh yeah, I was sure she and they were going to be the best of buds on this little field trip.

"Don't doubt the prowess of my brothers," Bernadette spat. "You see only that which we wish you to see. Though we may prefer the traditional weapons of our order, we are well-versed in the trappings of the modern age." She reached her stubby fingers across the table and grabbed one of the handguns from Sally's pile of happy boom-booms.

She expertly slid the magazine out, checked the slide, and did a few more things that I probably should have paid more attention to during my firearms training back in Vegas. She glanced at the ammo in the magazine. "Silver?"

"Of course," Sally replied, sounding almost insulted.

Bernadette loaded the gun again and glanced between Sally and me, her thoughts no doubt turning to the opportunity at hand. I subtly gripped the edge of the table, ready to push off if need be. Even Sheila seemed a bit on edge, her hand sliding closer to the hilt of her sword. Sally's response was to lean back in her chair and put her feet up on the table.

"There's plenty of regular ammo too," she said casually. "I'd recommend using that for the trip up and only loading the good stuff when we get into the Boston city limits. No point in wasting it on roving gangs of crackheads."

For a moment, Bernadette continued to look at the

weapons, then she placed the gun on the table and eased her considerable mass back into the chair. "A sound strategy. Agreed."

And with that, the tension eased ever so slightly in the room ... not by much, mind you, but down from DEFCON 2 at least.

It seemed as if we had a plan for the imminent trip north. I was about to adjourn so everyone could go to their respective corners and try not to kill each other for a little while, when I realized not everyone had spoken regarding their contributions to this cluster-fuck of a campaign.

Oh crap. I didn't relish this after the little interlude from earlier, but I needed to give her a chance to add anything she needed to. "Christy?"

She looked up, the circles under her eyes dark – no doubt a combination of sleep deprivation, the work we'd done in my head, and her current emotional state. She looked like someone in desperate need of a full eight hours. I just hoped she'd be able to relax. The shit Christy had been forced to swallow as of late was easily the equal of my issues, and I didn't have the burden of trying to figure out how I was gonna raise a kid in a world that could very possibly be overrun by Sasquatches.

"What?" she asked.

"Do you have anything to add to our discussion?"

She pulled out a piece of paper and a pen and scribbled something down. I found myself hoping it wasn't some oddball resignation letter. *"Dear Bill, Fuck you for defiling my mentor's body. I'm joining the bad guys. – Love Christy."*

Another thought crossed my mind – explosive runes. Nah. If she was going to blast us all to oblivion, why bother with the theatrics? Well, hopefully, that was the case anyway.

She slid it across the table toward me. Our eyes met, and she read the question in them. "It's the address where I'll be.

I have to take care of some stuff and, quite frankly, I need some time to think. Meet me there when you can."

"It's not safe to leave."

She stood from the table, clutching Decker's skull to her side, and turned away from us all. "Right now, it's not safe to be around me either."

**21**

# THE FIRST STEP OF MANY

A true friend knows when someone needs their space and gives it to them. However, a true friend also watches the other person's back, even when they don't want them to. And a nosy friend will use their vampire hearing to find out what the fuck is going on.

Ed, Sheila, and I trailed Christy at a distance through the safe house as she wordlessly went about her way to retrieve her stuff.

"Are we just going to let her go?" Ed asked.

"Not sure we have a choice in the matter."

"Do you think she'll be okay?" I had a feeling Sheila was asking about more than Christy taking a trip on her own, but I wasn't quite ready to address much beyond that.

"It's daylight. Things are gonna be about as normal as possible out there. As long as she stays out of the bad neighborhoods, she should be fine."

Ed glanced between us. "Think one of us should go with her?"

"Bill can't," Sheila said, stating the bleedingly obvious. "She's probably too ticked off at you anyway."

"You're out as well," Ed pointed out. "You're the only one keeping the Templar from throwing a mad staking party."

We stood in the main hallway and bickered about this for a few when I noticed Christy heading toward the door of the building. Tom came running after her.

"Hey, babe," he called obliviously. "Where you going?"

She turned, her eyes practically skewering him.

"Where'd you get the skull?" he asked. Her gaze o'death had obviously gone right over his head.

Christy looked as if she was about to turn away in disgust, but then stopped. She reached out, grabbed him by the shirt, and dragged him so that he was face to face with her. "You and I are going to have a *long* talk."

A look of surprise showed on his face for a moment, and then a blinding ball of light erupted from her, enveloping them both. When it subsided, they were gone.

"And it looks like we have our volunteer," Ed said.

"Somehow, I'm thinking better him than us."

Christy's vanishing act had the possibly intended consequence of unnerving the Templar who'd witnessed it. The rest of us – minus Sally, who'd stayed with Bernadette to take stock of all the weapons – had to do some damage control to convince them that Satan's wrath wasn't descending upon their heads.

Unfortunately, Christy and Tom were on their own for now. Nobody else in our group could zap themselves away like she could. That it was daytime made it risky for the undead amongst our party. Unfortunately, the address she'd given us had turned out to be upstate, some miles north of the city. It wasn't far, but the subways definitely didn't run that way, and it wasn't exactly within walking distance either.

There was also the fact that when I went to check on my other friends, I found Mike and Adam – true to their vampire nature – conked out. Lazy fucks.

The Templar could have made the trip without any issue, but Sheila and I discussed it and came to the conclusion that it was premature to split our party – at least until such time as we were ready to hit Boston with our planned pincer movement.

As for the Templar, Bernadette got them all lined up a little past noon – crosses, rosaries, and the like at the ready. They were a mixed bag. Some looked worried, others far too eager to see how badly they could burn a vampire.

My friends joined me as the gauntlet was readied. I had hoped maybe Sally or Dave would volunteer to share some of the fun, but no such luck. He pulled out a notepad and pen while she found a comfortable section of wall to lean against and watch.

Assholes.

*Kill the faithful, turn the rest.*

Tempting, I considered while approaching the first in line, but probably not the best tactic with regard to keeping our fragile alliance intact. The first Templar before me was a young man, not even my age. He had acne on his face and a wooden cross in his hand.

"Care to show me what you got, buddy?" I asked flippantly, dreading what was to come next.

"I am not your friend, beast. This cross belonged to my mother and hers before. I only present it to you so that you might burn at its touch."

"So I'm assuming lunch at the BFFs club is out."

I held out a finger. Fuck this. If I was gonna get burned, I wasn't going to be stupid about it. One touch was all they got. If I got zapped, I could hopefully pull back before I had to be doused with an extinguisher.

I placed my finger against the cross with a wince, hoping Dr. Death didn't notice my mental cry of "Mommy, don't let the bad man hurt me."

When nothing happened, I glanced down, saw my hand intact, and smirked. "Ain't so bad."

Well, maybe not for me anyway.

Sister Bernadette was right there behind the Templar, and damn if she didn't look pissed.

So it went. Any Templar who turned out to be firing blanks had their name jotted down so as to be properly armed before we left. Until then, Bernadette sent each and every one of the posers off to pray for forgiveness for their lack of true faith.

Sadly, that amusement only served as a minor distraction, as greater than half – more than I expected – turned out to be the real deal. I had to take a break once all ten of my fingers were singed.

It also gave me a chance to take note of who to avoid if they got in a mood to play crucifix tag. The upside, though, was that the faithful were a plus for our mission. A bunch of regular humans, trained or not, weren't going to be as much use to us once shit got real. Forget what the comic books tell you. In a battle between super-powers, folks like Black Widow and Hawkeye would get squished real quick.

Unfortunately, it wasn't all good. The Templar were just barely tolerating me and only because Sheila had told them I was pathetically repentant of my sins. More than one had me worried for entirely different reasons. The thing about having vampire hearing is you can't help but eavesdrop. Back in grade school, that would have been awesome – overhearing who liked who and who thought who smelled. Now, though, it made me privy that some of the Templar weren't all too keen on stopping the events that had been set in motion.

Judging by a few conversations, many considered the stupidity I had started in the Woods of Mourning to be the actual Biblical Armageddon. They were convinced this was all part of God's plan and wondered whether they should let it play out accordingly ... waiting in line for their respective places in the Rapture, while the rest of us dirtbags got to live out Hell on Earth.

For all my Freewill powers, I found myself instead wishing for eyes in the back of my head around this bunch.

Finally, the sun began to set. By then, I'd started getting real twitchy. We were well past the deadline that James had given me. I had to wonder if my apartment was still standing or had been reduced to a pile of smoldering ash. I hoped for the former – I still had a lot of stuff there. Regardless, I had a feeling we didn't have long before the same threat was levied against this place.

There was also the possibility of some HBC stragglers returning from whatever the fuck they did when they weren't busy being pissed at me. That wouldn't end well for them, but it was another distraction we didn't need.

We needed to get moving and catch up with Christy, wherever it was that she'd apparated to in a huff. I just had to hope that bridge wasn't burnt. Hopefully, Tom had taken the brunt of it for us.

I gathered Sally and Bernadette to discuss the issue of our conveyance. The distance wasn't one a vampire couldn't handle, but last I checked, the majority of our group was human, with an Icon and Ed thrown in for good measure.

"I need your talents for this one," I said to Sally.

"Oh?" She furrowed her brows. "Sorry to say, but I was hoping we could just be friends."

"Not *those* talents. Save that shit for the stripper pole. We need wheels, lots of them. Think you can do that?"

"Your kind keeps a fleet of cars in reserve?" Bernadette asked.

"Not quite."

Sally turned to her. "Bill wants me to go on a hot-wiring party."

Bernadette made a sour face. It didn't do much to make her look less unpleasant. "Thou shalt not steal," she whispered in an acid tone.

"It's a necessary evil," I pointed out.

"One no doubt meant to drag us off the righteous path. Don't think I am unable to see the serpents in the garden for what they are."

"Just as I'm sure you're unable to miss any pies in the oven."

She cocked her head to the side, looking like a particularly stupid bulldog as my sarcasm sailed right over her head.

I sighed and decided on the direct approach. "Unless you plan to walk to Boston, this is pretty much our best shot."

"I could grab us a few buses," Sally offered.

"No. That would get us there, but it would also put us in a jam if we got stopped."

"I don't foresee cops being a particularly big obstacle."

"Ixnay on the urdermay," I said through gritted teeth.

"The Night Spawn is correct," Bernadette said, although it was painfully obvious from her tone that she'd rather take selfies of her face buried in the Pope's crotch than agree with me on anything. "Stolen buses could be too easily noticed. Also, if the news which has reached our ears is correct, the roads north may not be passable by larger vehicles." She turned toward me. "It still doesn't mean I'm comfortable with being an accomplice to this."

"Relax. As long as most folks have kept up their GEICO payments, I'm sure they'll be fine. Besides, if push comes to shove, what would you rather admit to in confession: that you stole a car or let mankind be overthrown by the forces of darkness?"

"It shan't happen with the Blessed One by our side."

"Yeah, well, God helps those who help themselves. So we'll make sure Sheila has the chance by getting ourselves to a spot where we can make a difference."

Sally took Ed and maybe a half dozen Templar with her. Everyone who went had a license and enough experience behind the wheel so as to give us a good chance of getting there alive. Their mission was to procure SUVs or other vehicles large enough for multiple passengers and tough enough for going off road if need be.

Adam offered to go fetch his car, but it was too small for our needs. Also, having driven in it recently, I was also aware it kinda smelled.

The plan was simple. As each stolen vehicle pulled up in front of the safe house, a pre-designated group would load up and drive off ... thus hopefully not attracting too much suspicion by having a full convoy parked outside.

We also kept it nice and segregated: Templar would go with other Templar, and the rest of us would try to stick together. The only X-factor there was that both Ed and Sally were driving, but Sheila had the solution to that. Me and the Defilers would go with whichever of them showed up first. She'd go with the other. This also allowed us to allay

Bernadette's paranoia by staggering the order in which we left, as she didn't trust my group to go first or last.

As luck would have it, Ed was the first of my friends to arrive – driving a beat up Ford Explorer. Maybe it was for the best. My feelings for Sally had potential to cloud my judgment for her. Despite James's warnings, I couldn't quite bring myself to see anything but the Sally I knew and was *fond* of. If there was something out of sorts with her, Sheila would probably spot it far sooner.

Of course, that also opened up the possibility of them both talking about me during the drive up ... something potentially awesome and terrifying at the same time.

Regardless, there wasn't anything I could do about it ... short of maybe constantly calling and annoying the shit out of them.

In the end, though, I decided against anything so petty. Besides, my battery was just about dead.

We pulled away from the safe house and began our journey north. As we reached the city limits, I looked back upon its familiar façade and took in as much as I could. I tried to fool myself that it was only a matter of time before I'd see it again, but the truth was, I couldn't quite convince myself of that.

**22**

# THE SISTERHOOD OF
# THE TRAVELING SKULL

The drive up was slow, but mostly uneventful. There were a lot of broken down cars along the side of the road, with "along the side" being the operative phrase. Things hadn't quite devolved into total chaos yet.

Our caravan was spaced far enough apart so all we could see of each other were taillights in the distance. That was good for keeping things from looking too weird for anyone who happened to be observing us. However, as the buildings gave way to trees, I couldn't help but wonder whether that could also prove to be to our detriment should we come across anything unfriendly.

Despite my fledging can-do attitude and the promise of Dr. Death being in my ring corner, I was pretty freaked out. There were a lot of miles ahead of us, and I couldn't help but think most would be filled with nasty things.

Thankfully ... sorta ... Adam and Mike were there to keep us distracted by their talk of grand adventure and the treasure – that I never promised them, by the way – which would no doubt come from it. More than once, they expressed the hope that Carl had been able to come with us, but decided he was probably having fun back in Newark. Ed, Dave, and I wisely kept our mouths shut during those moments.

Fortunately, there was plenty of other stuff to talk about … mostly making fun of the Templar, or as Adam put it, "Fucking newb paladins." Yep, that pretty much summed it up.

Eventually, we found the place we'd been looking for – it was maybe twenty miles north of the city, off a dark road that looked suspiciously perfect for an ambush. My paranoia proved unfounded, though, as we pulled into a long driveway that led us to an isolated farmhouse surrounded by fields on two sides and trees in the rear. Dim light shone from the windows – candles were my guess.

"This it?" I asked.

"According to GPS, it is," Ed replied. "Look." He pointed out some other cars parked haphazardly about the front yard, presumably members of our party who'd arrived before us.

That wasn't all, though. My night vision was far superior to his. From my place riding shotgun, I made out several red-robed figures skulking in the shadows – no doubt acting as sentries for the arrival of the rest.

I just had to hope, with Sister Bernadette behind us, that these guys didn't decide to be proactive in their pledge to cleanse the Earth of evil – of which they certainly grouped me.

I should have hoped for a Templar ambush, because what I got instead was Tom waiting for us on the porch.

"Thanks for the heads up, Bill," he called out after we'd parked our SUV. "I really appreciate spending the entire day being bitched out over a fucking skull."

"She still angry?" I asked gingerly.

"Probably, but I think she used me to get it out of her system."

"And you wanted to leave him back at the apartment," Ed said to me with a grin. "See? We all have our part to play."

"Had I known mine would've been to take one for the team, I'd have taken you up on that," Tom replied. "Why the fuck did you assholes rat me out?"

"Simple." I grabbed a backpack from the trunk and slipped it on. "She could have flat-out vaporized us. You at least get a slow death."

"Yeah, well, safe to say it's gonna be a while before I get any again."

"Welcome to the club, buddy." I clapped him on the shoulder. "Welcome to the club."

It didn't appear that Sally, Sheila, or the dumpy bitch in charge of the Templar had arrived yet, and I didn't particularly care to wait outside in the open – especially with that copse of trees out back. I had no idea how deep it was or what it contained.

Of course, if it *was* full of Sasquatches, then it stood to reason there would probably be no need for them to stay their hand. I had no doubt the Templar would serve as little more than a distraction for a Bigfoot – like a fly a kid might capture so as to tear its wings off.

Besides, I figured that I'd earned the right to be a bit jumpy at the prospect of being in or near the woods at night. "So, can we go in or is that a no Bill zone?" I asked Tom.

"I think you're safe." He turned toward the entrance.

"She took a nap earlier, which helped, and then she spent the rest of the evening bitching all of us out to her coven."

"Wait, her coven?"

"Yep," Tom replied.

"Hey, they got anything to eat in there?" Adam asked before I could question my roommate further. "I don't know about the rest of you fuckers, but I'm getting kind of hungry."

Oh crap.

"There's a barn off that way," Tom said casually, pointing to the left of the house. "I was walking around earlier while Christy was asleep. I think there's a cow or two in there."

Adam seemed to consider this for a moment, then shrugged. "Any port in a storm."

Mike and Dave decided to join him, and together, they all walked off in that direction.

"Be careful," I called after them, more as a warning to not do anything stupid.

"Sure it's okay for them to be doing that?" Ed asked Tom.

"Fuck if I know or care," he replied. "It's not my place."

"If anyone asks, we play dumb," I said.

"Works for me. Hey, Bill?"

"Yeah?"

"Do you think a vampire cow is possible?"

"Hopefully, we'll be far away from this place before we have to find out."

Tom led the way in. The house was large and well kept. Definitely made our apartment back in Brooklyn look like a shithole in comparison. Well, okay, the cardboard sleeping bag of a homeless methhead would probably also do that.

Anyway, it seemed like a good place to raise kids ... assuming the world wasn't about to be consumed in fire and blood, of course. Such things tended to trump decisions such as whether to build the kiddies a treehouse or swing set.

As we approached what I guessed to be the living room, Tom turned and raised a finger to his lips. He needn't have bothered. I smelled the incense the moment we stepped through the doorway and heard the low chanting coming from inside. The light pouring out of the room ahead also had a decisively odd bent to it – a pulsating glow that seemed to change colors every few seconds. Either magic was afoot or we were in a stoner's dream den.

I distantly heard the engine of a car approaching outside. More of our merry little bunch was arriving, but I wanted to see what was going on before turning around and playing welcome wagon to a bunch of red-robed douches.

"So you admit that he spoke true?" a female voice from the living room asked, drawing my attention in that direction.

The three of us stepped to the doorway of what was once a fairly large family room – complete with a sixty-inch flat-screen TV on the wall. Damn – Farmer Brown, or whoever this place belonged to, certainly wasn't taking the whole *Little House on the Prairie* vibe to heart.

Whatever the room had been, though, was of no consequence. All the furniture had been pushed off to the side. The center was what mattered, and that was a bit of a doozy.

Four women sat in a circle outside of a pentagram that had been painted into the floor, along with other symbols I wouldn't even try to identify. Three were unfamiliar, but the last one was Christy. Although the black circles under her eyes appeared to be gone, she looked no less stressed. I immediately understood why.

In the middle of the pentagram, and seemingly the source for the weird light show, sat Decker's skull.

No wonder the Templar had all chosen to remain outside.

I took a step forward, but Tom caught my arm. I glanced at him, and the look on his face said it all – are you outta your fucking mind?

Yeah, he probably had a point there.

Ed pushed forward to get a look, but that was as far as the three of us went. Whatever was going on in there had the look of a closed meeting.

"I say that the events recounted by the Grand Mentor of the Plains happened," Christy replied to the challenge, which had obviously been directed her way. "However, as we are all aware, there are many points of view in life. His was but one of them – one which I do not agree with."

"Holy crap!" one of them, a petite auburn-haired girl, cried out. "So you really killed them?"

"Please keep this hearing formal, Sister Veronica," Christy admonished, the authority in her voice unmistakable. Yeah, witch culture was kinda weird if you asked me.

"Sorry."

Christy's demeanor softened for a moment, and she offered a small smile toward the other woman before addressing a raven-haired witch of average height and build. "As you were saying, Sister Meg?"

Meg, or so I presumed, had a book open in front of her. It was a large tome with a feeling of age about it – probably not a loaner from the local library.

"It's not the Necronomicon, in case you were wondering," Tom whispered in my ear. "I already asked."

At least none of us would hopefully end the evening being anally violated by possessed trees. Although a chainsaw hand sure could come in handy.

"The charges the Grand Mentor laid down were quite serious," the black-haired witch said.

"I am aware."

"Please tell us your account of events, and then we shall seek to corroborate via remote commune."

"That will be difficult."

"How so?"

"I have been informed that the Grand Mentor, as well as my former sister, are both deceased."

Whatever was going on was obviously some kind of formality in Magi circles. Nevertheless, I could have sworn I heard a bit of scorn thrown in there at the Mentor's expense. Oh well, the guy had been a dick.

"What?" Veronica asked, her tone shocked. At least one of these witches was fairly green.

"Yes," Christy replied, her tone once more neutral. "The Grand Mentor met his fate at the hands of the vampire who led the effort to hunt down my former coven."

"But why?" the third witch asked. She had short brown hair, wore glasses, and a *Lord of the Rings* t-shirt. Finally, someone with some fashion sense.

Christy sighed and tried to explain Gansetseg's twisted sense of honor.

"Holy shit," the nerd witch exclaimed.

"Sister Kelly!" Meg warned.

"Sorry."

"So," Meg continued, "you were allied with this vampire while your former coven hunted for the Icon?"

"I wouldn't exactly say that," Christy replied, breaking formality for a moment. "My apologies. I say that this vampire is no friend of mine or our kind. I did not learn until later her part in things. By then, it was too late for most of my brethren."

"Most?"

"To the best of my knowledge, there were three other survivors."

"And you aided them?"

"No."

"Why?"

"Because they were holding my fiancé hostage."

Ed and I glanced over at Tom. "Not a fucking word," he hissed.

I smirked in his direction and then turned back to the proceedings at hand, barely registering the sound of more car doors slamming outside. This was far more interesting anyway.

Christy summed up the rest of the events that occurred during our battle with Remington's forces. Interestingly enough, her account was far more accurate than the bullshit Sally had spread – and I'd perpetuated – following that incident. Who knows? Maybe the light pouring out of Decker's skull was some sort of magical lie detector.

When Christy finished her tale, I expected the session to wrap up – maybe for the three witches in attendance to vote, then hand down some sort of sentence or penance. What that would be, I had no idea.

In the vampire world, there were usually only two punishments: immediate death or having your head chopped off and stuck in a jar for eternity. The Draculas had apparently never heard of the concept of community service. I wondered if Magi society was as harsh. If so, I had no idea why Christy would seemingly volunteer herself for this, and I had to assume she had, as it seemed painfully obvious the others were deferring to her as a person of authority.

Finally, Meg, who seemed to be running this Q&A, said,

"Very well. We shall now call upon the other in attendance so that we might hear his account."

Once more, I glanced at Tom, but he just held up his hands and shook his head.

"Anyone else here?" I asked in a low tone.

"Not that I know. They were waiting for some other chick to arrive, but she never showed."

"Well, then who?"

"Harry Decker," Meg continued, "we summon you from beyond the veil. Hear us and be drawn back to your earthly remains to stand in judgment of your daughter."

What!?

All four witches in the circle joined hands and began to chant. After a few moments, their tempo increased, along with the pulsing lights coming from Decker's disembodied noggin.

No, they couldn't...

Could they?

Almost as if in answer, a rush of wind came from out of nowhere and blew past us, knocking pictures off the walls and ruffling the curtains. For a moment, a swirl of air and dust could be seen above Decker's skull, yet the witches kept at their chanting as if none of this was out of the ordinary.

All at once, their chanting ceased and the mini tornado was sucked into the skull.

"Anyone else find that a bit weird?" Ed asked.

I was about to reply when a flash of sickly purplish light blazed from within the skull's eye sockets followed by a voice I knew all too well.

*Beware, the end is near,* Decker's voice shot out from everywhere, *for the Icon has arrived.*

## 23

# HEAD GAMES

*I see the buffoon of a Freewill is present too.*

"Fuck you, dude," I said from the doorway. All eyes – living ones, anyway – in the living room turned my way. "Don't listen to this asshole. He's full of..."

Just then, the front door opened in the hall behind us. I glanced back and saw, sure enough, Sheila stride through the entranceway. Okay, well, point one to Decker.

Before I could say anything further, Decker's voice again bellowed out. *Destroy her! It is too late for me, but you can still save yourselves.*

The three witches who'd been questioning Christy immediately clambered to their feet. Christy started to rise too, but she needed a nearby chair as leverage. By the time she was standing, the three other witches were gathering energy around them.

Much to my horror, but not even remotely to my surprise, Sheila joined us at the doorway in that moment. "Sorry I'm late. We ran into some..."

Her voice faded at the freaky sight in the living room –

three witches arming for battle, with a talking skull egging them on.

Oh yeah, this was right where I wanted to be – smack dab in between them.

Sheila's aura sprang to life in response, and I closed my eyes to prepare myself for the oh-so-wonderful feeling of being blasted.

A second passed and that didn't happen. I dared to open my eyes and found my roommates had both awesomely stepped between me and Sheila – her faith aura washing harmlessly over them for a moment until she reined it in.

"Sorry," she said.

"Enough of this!" Christy snapped. "I told you guys she was coming."

*Listen not to my misguided pupil,* Decker urged. *She has been enthralled by this beast's lackey and knows not what she says.*

"He talking about me?" Tom asked.

"Yeah, pretty sure," I replied.

"He is my betrothed," Christy said to the witches. "I am of sound mind and have not been enthralled."

"Except by my penis," Tom proudly added, perhaps a wee bit louder than intended.

She threw a glare his way that would have melted an iceberg and, for a moment, I was certain she was going to let the other witches blow us to hell.

Amazingly enough, though, my roommate's dumbass remark had defused the situation as two of the witches – Veronica and Kelly – immediately powered down and dissolved into giggles.

For a moment, the third didn't quite seem to know what to do, but then she covered her mouth and joined them.

Tom turned to me and smirked. "Do I know how to work a crowd or what?"

"You do have a way with words, I'll give you that," I replied before stepping forward and raising my voice. "Is it safe to assume nobody's going to be disintegrated, or should I come back later when you've all gotten it out of your system?"

"Technically, that was defensive magic," the one with the glasses, Kelly, said. "You must be Bill. Christy told us all about you." She held out a hand.

*Beware, for the Freewill corrupts all he touches.*

"Bite me, asshole," I said to the skull as I shook her hand. "Oh, and all your marketing campaigns were fucking stupid too."

"Marketing?" Kelly asked.

"He was a VP at my old job."

"Oh."

*Yes, and I made a lot more in that short time than Mr. Ryder could ever hope to earn in his entire mediocre lifetime.*

"Goddamn, how I wish I had taped Gan ganking your ass for YouTube."

*Laugh while you can, filth, for soon you shall meet your end.*

"That another half-assed prophecy?"

*No. Just common sense for an idiot such as yourself.*

I opened my mouth to give Decker another piece of my mind when I realized everyone in the room was staring. Glancing over at Kelly, I asked, "I'm having an argument with an inanimate object, aren't I?"

"Pretty much."

Sadly for Decker, his craziness proved Christy's innocence in the eyes of her coven. All one needed to do was listen to his whacked-out noggin for a few minutes to see he'd gone off the deep end and was still swimming out to sea.

Sheila's presence was another matter entirely. It was one thing to understand someone's motives in doing something normally deigned undesirable. It was quite another to shake off dogma that pointed to someone being your own personal Antichrist.

I could see what Christy was doing, though. While Decker's skull continued to rave about death, destruction, and what a dipshit I was for bringing it all to fruition – prick – Christy introduced Sheila around. In doing so, she humanized the boogeyman. It was easy to fear an abstract concept, but a bit harder when you had a name, face, and enough personal interaction to see that someone wasn't a giant walking cock with a hard-on for killing your ass.

Regardless, the stigma wouldn't be erased overnight. After all, I'm sure there were people in history who'd briefly met Hitler and thought he was a swell guy, and look how that turned out. Assuming Christy's new sisters weren't idiots, and so far, I didn't get that vibe, they'd be optimistic but still cautious enough to sleep with one fireball readied.

There was one other bright side to all this. Whatever they had done to summon Decker's specter seemed to have mellowed out Christy's anger. I wasn't sure I was back on the guest list for her wedding, but I decided to take a chance and sidled up to her.

"How are you doing?" I asked casually.

"I got some rest. That helped."

"Good to hear."

"I'm still pissed at you."

"Not surprising. I'm trying to put myself in your shoes right now. I can imagine my reaction walking in to a neighbor's house and seeing Grandpa's skull up on the mantel."

"Yeah, it's something like that."

"Albeit I'm pretty sure he wouldn't be quite so vocal either."

"I will admit, seeing ... or hearing him like this is putting things into perspective for me. In my head, I only remembered..."

"The good parts?" I led her over to a corner so we could talk a bit without being overhead. "Yeah, I know what you mean. I tend to remember sitting on Pop's lap while he told me stories from his days in the service. Oddly enough, most of those memories tend to ignore that half the time I was coughing my lungs out because he was chain smoking and blowing it in my face. If he showed up here right now, I know deep down his first thought before giving me a hug would be to ask if I'd run to the store and grab him a carton of Pall Malls."

"Still better than trying to incite a race war."

"Oh, he might've done that too. He always did have a major mad-on for the Irish."

She smiled. Although it was half sad in its acknowledgement, it told me enough to know that we were still friends.

"So..."

"Yes?"

"How long is he gonna keep doing that?"

"Normally, a spirit tether is a tentative thing. Mediums, the real ones anyway, use them to get bits and pieces – usually just glimpses. It's like talking to someone through a TV full of static."

"Shades of *Poltergeist*."

"This one is a lot stronger, though. For starters, most people don't have access to body parts." She threw a glare at me that I did my best to ignore. "We used blood magic before you arrived. Each of us donated a little piece of our life force to draw him fully back from the veil. It's not something to be done lightly, as it will keep his spirit from finding rest."

Somehow, that sounded way more ominous than I'd been

hoping for. "I guess that's understandable. I mean, he was like a father to you and..."

Christy lowered her voice to a level that she knew only I'd hear. "That's what I told my sisters, but it's only partially true."

"Oh?"

"Those pictures, the ones from the Jahabich lair?" I nodded and she continued. "I've been studying them, trying to make sense of it all. There's definitely a spell in that final pictograph."

"You mean the..." I looked around, saw Kelly and Veronica throw a glance my way, and then lowered my voice to match Christy's. "You mean the one that showed them being beaten?"

"Exactly. The problem is twofold. There're some symbols I don't understand. Enochian is very old. Even with the most dedicated of teachers, there were bound to be changes over the centuries. Losses too. All you need is one person to transcribe a symbol slightly wrong and, over time, it takes on a whole new meaning. I'm hoping Harry can help. You may not know this, but he was considered a respected historian of my people."

Nope, didn't know that. Didn't really care either. "Um, you're gonna bring him up to speed on all of that?"

"I have to. My sisters too. It's heresy, but the truth needs to be told. Besides, it might be our only chance."

"At stopping them?"

"That, and maybe stopping other things from happening..."

Christy trailed off, but her meaning was clear. The doctrines the Magi had followed for thousands of years were based off of the White Mother. The thing was, Christy was now convinced that she was pure in the color of her clothing only. If others could be convinced that their entire way of life was based off a pack of lies, then perhaps they could be swayed from the path that fate had supposedly set them upon.

It was most likely a fool's errand, one that could get her ostracized just as surely as the crime she'd been accused of. Even so, it gave her hope.

Considering everything she'd been through, I wasn't about to deny her that.

# 24

# WAR PARTY

Christy convened a closed session upstairs with her sisters and Decker's skull to bring them up to speed on our findings from the Jahabich lair. With the Templar keeping guard outside and the Defilers off ... well, supposedly defiling barnyard animals, it seemed like the perfect time for the mages to do so without interruption and with minimal people overhearing.

Mind you, minimal didn't mean nobody.

With the magical freakiness over for now, my roommates and I moved the furniture back into the living room so as to relax a bit. The large living space just so happened to be conveniently located right beneath where Christy and her coven were talking, allowing me to pick up everything being said above a whisper while pretending to engage my friends in some idle chitchat regarding who would win in a fight: a platoon of Sith warriors or the X-men.

Sheila joined us soon after, having gone to check in with Sister Bernadette, who'd set up a Templar command center in – where else – the kitchen.

"How's it going with the holy rollers?" I asked, having

just crushed Tom's argument by pointing out that Jean Grey and the Phoenix Force could fuck up Emperor Palpatine six ways to Sunday.

"Not bad. They're a bit on edge, but putting them on guard duty is helping to distract them from the distaste most of them are still feeling."

"Teaming up with me?"

"It's not just you, but yeah."

"Maybe we should pass the collection plate around," Ed suggested. "That always seemed to work when I went to Sunday mass as a kid."

"I draw the line at confession," Tom joked.

"Believe me, nobody wants to hear that," I said idly, focusing on the conversation at hand since all Christy seemed to be doing upstairs at the moment was passing around the photos I'd taken of the Jahabich-be-good spell. "Although I'm sure Sally would have some snide comment. Speaking of which, where is she?"

"Still outside, I think," Sheila said. "She drove Bernadette and me up. When we got here, she said she wanted to take a walk, scope out our perimeter."

"I bet that was a fun ride."

"It was ... uncomfortably quiet."

"Sally? Quiet?" I asked. "I can see Sister Dumpling not wanting to lower herself to speaking to garbage such as us, but I'm having a hard time picturing Sally not getting in every dig she could."

"Yeah," Ed agreed. "She's never been shy about her opinions."

We shared a glance, which I broke off quickly. He and I still had one hell of an uncomfortable discussion ahead of us. I couldn't pretend forever that he hadn't noticed my feelings for Sally had changed ever so slightly. As one of the few folks in this world I considered a true friend, I'd need to come clean at some point, albeit that could certainly wait until after we discovered whether we'd live or die in Boston. Death was potentially the best plausible deniability excuse of them all.

Thankfully, the awkward moment was shattered just then as *Blasphemy!* psychically reverberated throughout the house.

I refocused my attention back upstairs. Yep, Christy had gotten to the White Mother and what a bitch she really was. Things were finally getting interesting.

"What are they talking about?" Sheila asked.

"Huh?"

"You're eavesdropping, aren't you?"

"Um..."

"Every few seconds, your eyes lose focus. Also, you tilt your head so your right ear is facing upward."

"I do?"

"He does?" Tom echoed.

"Yes. Don't you guys ever play poker? Bill's tells are obvious from across the room."

"Yep," Ed replied. "Hence why I always win."

I pointed at him. "You said it was just luck."

"I lied."

"Ass."

"Don't change the subject," Sheila chided. "Are you listening or not?" My silence was apparently a confession of guilt because she added, "So spill."

"Dude, are you listening in on my girlfriend?" Tom asked.

"Fine. Yes, I'm listening."

"Have you ever done that before?"

"On occasion," I admitted.

"Like what about when we're doing it in my room?"

"Oh, fuck no!" I lied. Truth was, it was kinda hard to tune out. Tom liked to pant "oh yeah, baby" over and over again like he was in a bad seventies porno. Try sleeping through that shit.

"And no," I said, turning to Sheila, "I don't listen to you guys either when you're downstairs in the shower."

She blinked a few times, her expression blank. "I didn't ask."

"Yeah ... well ... in case you were wondering." Oh boy. "Anyway, let's focus on the important stuff right now."

"So what are they talking about? Sounded like that ... *thing* ... Harry, I guess, wasn't happy."

"You mostly only had to deal with him at work," I said, purposely ignoring the date he'd taken her on once. "Believe me, Decker was a psycho asshole for the most part. I sincerely doubt dying has given him any new insight into things. But anyway, he's all bent out of shape because..." I trailed off for a moment, remembering my discussion with Christy from a few days prior. The discovery we'd made far below ground had shaken her to her core. She'd had a not-so-minor freak-out about that, not the least of which was because of the mage prophecy that Sheila would be the destroyer of their race.

Though Sheila had professed to have no desire to harm her or her child, much less commit genocide, Christy believed this info could be the catalyst to change all of that. If one mage could create such unholy abominations, didn't that potentially make them all capable of such atrocities? While I didn't believe for one second that would cause Sheila to change her attitude from helpful to stabby, I also realized it was Christy's tale to tell. I'd already broken her trust enough for one lifetime.

That being said, there were some parts I didn't see any harm in sharing.

"Sorry, they started mumbling," I said as way of covering myself. "Lost them for a moment there. Seems they're arguing over some spell that could stop the Jahabich."

"A spell?" she asked.

"Yeah. Right before we got put on trial, Sally and I had to go deep underground to save Ed's useless ass."

"Fuck you," he said.

"Make that his useless and *ungrateful* ass. Anyway, while we were in their lair, we saw some pictographs written on the wall. Seemed like hieroglyphics to me. But anyway, I thought it looked kinda neat, so I took a picture. Glad I did because Christy thinks it might actually be a spell that could be used against them. They're discussing it now."

"Oh. That could be useful."

"Tell me about it."

Christy and her group spent more time arguing over beliefs and dogma, at times heated enough that one didn't need vampire hearing to listen in. Most of what was audible to the living were more cries of heresy or, a few times, Decker went off on a rant about what an oaf I was. Such a likeable guy.

Finally, they got down to business, and that was about when I decided to tune out. Listening to mages discussing whether a symbol meant earth or some other stupid fucking thing was not nearly as interesting as one might think. It was kind of like watching *Raiders of the Lost Ark*, followed by the crushing realization that most field archaeology involved a lot of scrubbing rocks with toothbrushes.

By then, it was getting late. Ed and Sheila were both snoozing in their respective chairs and Tom didn't look too far behind. Some of the Templar had returned to the house to find places to crash, and daylight wasn't too far off.

I heard voices from the foyer. Dave, Mike, and Adam had

returned. It was probably time to see what kind of chaos they'd caused. Afterwards, I needed to find Sally. That she'd been off wandering for so long was a bit worrisome.

I stood and stretched, then took an extra-long moment to stare at Sheila as she slept. Yeah, it was probably borderline creepy, but I didn't think I'd ever seen her in such a state of peace – especially since she'd become the Icon. It was nice to see her like that, and to hope she was having pleasant dreams free of the nastiness around us. She was also drooling, quite a bit. Eww.

I was tempted to wake her up or maybe turn her over, but then hesitated. Her powers were basically a hand grenade as far as I was concerned. Awake, she was in control, but being rudely awakened could be akin to pulling the pin out. Yeah, best to let her drool.

I walked out and turned toward the exit before stopping dead in my tracks.

"There a shower in this place?" Adam asked.

I could only dumbly point to the stairs leading up. "What the fuck happened to you guys?" I'd seen vampires bloodied up before, but these fuckers looked like they just came back from the rave scene at the beginning of *Blade*.

The exception was Mike, who was both bloody and had several muddy hoof prints on the chest of his shirt.

"I'd stay out of the barn if I were you," Adam replied.

"What the hell happened? Did you drink from that cow or throw it into a wood chipper?"

"The cow wasn't really all too cooperative," Mike replied, gritting his teeth.

"Oh and it wasn't a cow," Dave, the least messed up of the bunch, added. "It was a bull."

"I call dibs on first shower," Mike said, heading upstairs.

Adam followed. "Why do you get to go first?" he complained.

"Because I'm the one it fucking trampled."

"Hey." Dave tried to clap me on the shoulder, which I used my vampire reflexes to narrowly avoid. I liked the shirt I was wearing. "At least it wasn't a person."

"Better hope none of these Templar are members of PETA."

He shrugged, then handed over a plastic container he'd been holding in his other hand. "Here. We saved you some."

"Thanks, I think," I replied, taking it from him. True enough, it was full of a thick red liquid.

"Oh, speaking of blood," he started as I stepped past him to the door, "is Princess Sheila..."

"She's asleep. Wait until she wakes up. Oh, and definitely don't surprise her looking like that. Trust me on this."

I stepped outside into the cool night air. The steps leading up to the porch were covered in bloody footprints. Subtle, my friends were not.

I took a moment to look around, found a garden hose, and spent a few minutes washing out the worst of it. No point in freaking out any Templar heading this way.

Once done, I figured I'd earned a drink, so I took a swig of the cow blood. Not bad. Definitely different than what I was used to – more earthy, grassy than human blood. Either way, it seemed to do the trick. I wasn't sure if it was a sustainable way to survive, but for the moment my stomach didn't seem to object.

I drained the container, hungrier than I realized I'd been, and immediately regretted doing so. I should have saved some. If I was feeling peckish after the past day of craziness, then Sally would be too. Sure, she'd probably topped off in Manhattan. Hell, knowing her, that was a certainty. Even so, it might've stopped her from wanting a snack break some-where down the line.

Oh well, it's not like I was a mama bird and going to regurgitate it for her. I tossed the emptied container aside and let my nose take over. Sally was a lot of things, but cheap when it came to her personal hygiene was not one of them. Unless one of the Templar was Emma Frost having found religion, I sincerely doubted any of them used her particular over-priced brand of perfume.

Once I reached the lineup of stolen cars, enough to keep a chop-shop happy for a week, it was easy to single Sally out from the crowd. Her scent led off into the night and I followed cautiously, conscious of surprising any red cloaks out patrolling the place.

The land surrounding the farmhouse was vaster than I'd imagined, certainly a lot bigger than a city boy was used to. I'd only been walking for a few minutes, but when I looked back, I realized the house was already hidden from view. A small part of me wondered what it would be like to live out in the sticks ... being able to camp out yet still be on one's own property. Of course, camping wasn't really a bright idea for vampires. Our ancient enemies tended to take a dim view of our presence in or around the woods.

I crested a rise and saw another field in front of me, this one covered in low growing vines – pumpkins or gourds judging from the few times I'd been out pumpkin picking with my parents as a kid. However, it was what lay in the middle of the field that caused my breath to catch.

It was a body and, judging by its shapely curves, one I knew all too well.

**25**

# CATCHING UP

Oh crap! I raced forward, fearing the worst. Unfortunately, my feet got tangled in the vines and I tripped, got tangled again, and went down face first. When I got back to my feet, I saw Sally sitting up and staring in my direction.

"Some real stealth you got going on there," she replied before casually lying down on her back again, putting her hands behind her head. "You must've been a ninja in a former life."

"You're okay?" I made my way toward her, a bit more carefully this time.

"Of course."

"Then what are you doing?"

"Looking up at the stars. I..." She trailed off, almost as if she'd said too much.

"What?"

Sally let out a loud sigh. "Fine. I used to do this as a girl, except it was on my roof. I used to sneak out of our attic window at night."

"Really?"

"Yeah." She glanced in my direction, apparently saw my look of confusion, and added, "What? I got blood on my face or something?"

"No, it's just ... I didn't know that."

"Huh. Interesting." She turned her head skyward and continued stargazing.

I reached the section she was in, a small clearing in the patch, and sat down next to her. "You almost never talk about your life ... before."

"I thought you said we were friends."

"We are! You just, well, tend to live in the present and..."

The sound of her laughter cut me off. "Relax, Bill. That's not too surprising to hear. It was a different life, a different me. I don't care to mix the world of today with one that's dead and buried."

I lay down next to her and gazed upward. She was right – it was quite the view. The experience was only diminished by the certainty that something nasty was probably gonna crawl all over me lying down in the dirt like this. Yeah, I'm a wuss when it comes to the outdoors. "Well, if you ever want to talk about it..."

"I won't," she replied brusquely. After a few moments, she said, "Sorry. Didn't mean to snap."

"It's okay. I can imagine things are a bit stressful for you."

"Can you really? It's like there are two different versions of me – the way I was back when Jeff was lording over Village Coven, and me today. That's not a lot of time difference, yet there've been some pretty major changes."

"Indeed there have." I enjoyed the feeling of being alone with her with nothing trying to kill us for a change.

"The problem is, I don't remember why. It's like one minute I was Jeff's slave, the next I was in charge of Village Coven."

"Actually, *I* was in charge of Village Coven."

"Well, since I don't remember you, that's hearsay at best, now isn't it?"

"You said you remembered Jeff's death and my part in it."

"Vaguely. Almost like a dream that you can't discern from reality. There are other bits and pieces too, parts the witch has been helping me uncover."

"Like what?"

"Like, I sorta remember being up in Canada for some reason."

"Oh?"

"Yeah, lots of weird stuff went on up there, didn't it?"

"Definitely."

"Did you shove me into a pool of Sasquatch shit?"

"Um ... that part was just a dream."

She raised up on one elbow for a second and glared at me while I continued to try staring innocently up at the sky above.

"Then there's you and that human."

"Tom?"

"No, the one with half a brain."

"He's not entirely human, I don't think."

"Whatever the fuck," she said, waving me off as if she wasn't interested in the details. "What's going on with you two?"

"What do you mean?"

"I'm not stupid. You both might think you're slick, but I keep catching the puppy dog eyes slipping my way. It's borderline creepy."

"Oh."

"It's okay. I'm used to it. Hell, I even got a few eyefuls from some of those Templar assbags. I mean, why wouldn't they?"

"Humility, thy name is Sally."

"Just stating the truth. Anyway, what bugs me is the

feeling of only knowing half the story. It's like you've both got something to say, but lack the balls to say it."

She might've had a memory that was about as aerodynamic as Swiss cheese, but she was still sharp as a tack. It was what made her such a great friend to have by my side, and probably also what made her so dangerous to any who dared cross her path. I lay there for a few moments, contemplating my next words.

*Just take her already!*

What the...? Goddamned Dr. Death. Oh well, it was refreshing to learn his interests lay in more than just killing everything. So nice to know being rapey was in his repertoire as well. Sorry to say for him, but this current scenario wasn't quite the one I had in mind for testing out our little alliance. I sent him a mental note to please pipe down.

Still...

Oh fuck it. She deserved to know the truth.

"You and Ed have been out on a few dates." Well, okay, some of the truth. Besides, I was sure he wouldn't mind me throwing him a bone like that.

"We have? He doesn't seem my type."

"Sure he is. He has a credit card. Or do you only take cash?"

"I'm sure you'd know all about paying for it."

I smiled at her dig. It was familiar, comforting. A small piece of the Sally I'd known, lost, and hoped to find again. "Anyway, it's true. I even caught you two making out up in Canada."

"Was this before or after the Bigfoot shit?"

"Probably best not to ask."

"Kinky."

"That's one word for it."

She let out a long sigh. "Whatever was there is a blank now. Try as I might, I can't see him even standing in the shadows of my dreams. He might as well be a stranger on the street. Don't get me wrong, I don't mind playing with my food for a bit, but I can't even do that with him."

"Nope. Probably a point to him, though."

"Definitely ups his chances for survival."

"That it does."

"So what about you?"

"Me?"

"That explains why he's always staring at me like I left him at the altar."

"I wouldn't go that far."

"To know me is to love me," she replied with a snicker.

Funny how just a few short months ago, I'd have had a pithy response to that. Now, though, I just let it pass in silence.

"So anyway, what's your deal in all this?" she asked. "Maybe it's just me, but I get that same vibe from you. I thought you were supposed to be in love with the Icon. Wasn't that what you were on trial for?"

"I was never convicted."

"And yet here we are."

"It's kinda complicated between me and Sheila."

She turned her head and stared hard at me. "Is that because she can kill you with a kiss or because of me?"

"Mostly the former."

*"Mostly?"*

Ugh! Talk about your Freudian slips. The assertive part of me that wasn't a psychopath said this was it – my chance to put all my cards on the table. They say confession is good for the soul. I'm sure the Templar would argue that I had no soul or that it was condemned to hell anyway, but fuck them. Either way, there was no more perfect opportunity to clear the air.

Even so, would it really count? I mean, shit, I had seen

that movie with Drew Barrymore where she had no short term memory. Sure, I'd been high as balls when I'd watched it, but even so, I'd found it just a wee bit creepy. Of course, that might have just been because of Adam Sandler.

Whatever the case, the concern was still valid. Would it truly be a confession right now, or would it just be dumping even more shit on her already overburdened plate?

The answer was sadly obvious. My feelings for Sally were too strong to do otherwise.

"I just want my friend back. I miss her."

Sally smiled in return, no sense of sarcasm in it. She was gorgeous on any given day of the week, but seeing something genuine on her face really accentuated that fact. "Your friend sounds like a pretty awesome person."

"On occasion. The rest of the time, she's a bitch."

"Asshole."

"Yep."

Sally chuckled and then sat up. "I guess we should be getting back."

I didn't want the moment to end, but sadly, immortal or not, eternity wasn't on our side right now. "I guess so."

Together, we got to our feet and began the trek back toward the house.

"Hey," I said, a thought popping into my head.

"What is it?"

"What did you mean back there about having blood on your face?"

"Oh that? I got thirsty earlier and killed one of the Templar. Figured he wouldn't be missed."

# 26

# DOWN ON THE FARM

"Are you..." I started to yell before stopping to look around. Lowering my voice to a loud whisper, I continued, "...fucking insane?"

"Relax. This is not my first rodeo," Sally replied as we neared the farmhouse.

"Did you have to kill him?"

"What do you think? I have a feeling these guys wouldn't be cool with letting me take a drink and then keeping their fucking mouths shut afterwards."

"Is he ... did you..."

"Don't worry. He won't be coming back ... or found anytime soon either."

"And you think they won't notice?"

"Relax. It'll be fine. A few of the cars didn't make it. We passed one that actually got pulled over by the cops. I bet that was an awkward traffic stop. There was another on the side of the road with a flat." She stopped walking for a second, a thoughtful look on her face. "You'd think those whack-jobs would maybe be subtle about things, take off those road-flare-colored capes just to change a tire. You'd be wrong. Either way you look at it, we're a few weirdos short. With the way the world is today, I doubt one or two not showing up for roll call will cause too much suspicion."

"One *or two?*"

"It's just a figure of speech."

I furrowed my eyebrows and gave her the once over. It wasn't just for thrills either.

She noticed my not-so-subtle inspection and added, "I took off my top first. Figured I'd give him the first and last thrill of his life."

"You're too kind."

"I know."

"Maybe you should give a few lessons to my gaming group. They came back from the barn looking like they'd been rolling in ... oh crap."

"What is it?"

"The Defilers, they..." I stopped as her brows raised questioningly. "That's what they call themselves. What? It's no dumber than Sally Sunset."

Her confused look turned into a glare.

"Anyway, they went off to the barn earlier and had themselves a regular vampire hoedown with a cow."

"Ewww. You really need new friends."

"I mean they ate it, but not like how you did things. They were drenched with blood."

"So?"

"*So* ... the Templar are paranoid about us as it is. They're gonna see that and flip the fuck out."

"And probably end up turning a more critical eye to who made it back and who didn't," she rightly concluded.

"Exactly."

"Oh well. Should be fun to watch."

"That's it? You're just gonna let them take the fall for what you did?"

"Hell yeah. The best alibis are the ones that create themselves."

The most I could do was cross my fingers and hope for the best. Fortunately, it seemed that I was in luck. All was quiet as we entered the house. I passed the living room, and saw both my roommates were sacked out. Call me paranoid, but I checked them until I saw the rise and fall of both their chests.

"It's so cute that you care for your pets," Sally said.

"Don't you have a pole you should be shaking your ass on?" A smile crossed my lips as I said it. It felt like one of our normal exchanges. Though it had only been a few days since she'd been mind-wiped, I hadn't realized how much I missed them.

A door on the far side of the living room opened and Dave emerged. He had a full vial of blood in one hand, some nasty burns covering his other, and a big shit-eating grin on his face.

I opened my mouth to say something, but he brushed past me. "Can't talk. My Nobel Prize awaits."

"That one worries me," Sally commented once he'd left.

"Me too." I turned back toward the room and saw Sheila emerge from the same door Dave had. She was holding a glowing hand to the crook of her right arm, the sleeve rolled up. I'd seen her do that before. She was healing herself. She looked up, noticed us just as the glow subsided, and rolled her sleeve down again.

"Hey, guys," she called out quietly so as to not wake my slumbering roommates.

"You actually let that nutcase near you?" Sally asked.

"Was the only way to shut him up," Sheila replied. "Well, maybe not the *only* way, but since he's your friend, Bill..."

The meaning was clear enough, and I nodded my thanks.

"Anyway," she continued, "if it's all the same with both of you, let's not tell Bernadette about this. I'm really not in the mood to get a lecture."

I mimed zipping my lips. "No problem there. And like I told you before, you don't have to worry about Dave. He's a self-absorbed douche, but he's a self-absorbed douche who only serves himself."

"Let's hope so."

"Any more fireworks from upstairs?"

Sheila nodded and glanced up. "There were a few more outbursts from Harry. Hard to miss them. Those seem to come right through the walls."

"I think it's psychic."

She shrugged. "As good an explanation as any. It's been quiet the last half hour or so. I heard some shuffling around up there, but nothing major, so I'm gonna assume they didn't kill each other."

"I'll go check on them. It's almost dawn. Assuming I don't find a bloodbath, why don't we all try to crash for a few hours and then..."

I left the words unspoken. It was painfully obvious what came next. The time for preparation was over. It was time to head north toward our destiny.

A quick check on things showed that Christy and her coven had turned in. They'd apparently been at it all night.

Something in the middle of one of the rooms was covered in a black shroud – no doubt Decker's skull and probably something I didn't want to disturb without hearing him laughing about how doomed I was. Even in death, the guy was still a gigantic cock.

I next stuck my head in the room that Adam and Mike had appropriated, finding them snoozing away in thankfully clean clothes.

All was actually peaceful. Maybe, just maybe, we'd get out of this place without any incidents.

Of course, hope is a fool's errand. I found that out a few hours later when I was abruptly kicked awake. I opened my eyes to find Sally staring down at me. "Rise and shine, cupcake. The natives are getting restless."

"I don't want to go to school, Mom."

And with that, I found myself airborne. One moment, I was snuggled up fairly comfortably in a guest bedroom, and the next, I was in the hallway picking myself off the floor.

"Just for conversation's sake," Sally said, stepping out into the hall, "do me a favor and don't *ever* call me Mommy."

"Noted," I croaked, righting myself. Jeez, some people sure were cranky in the... "What time is it?"

"Afternoon. Still plenty of daylight left, though."

"Then why..."

"The Templar, why else? Get moving and you'll see."

I quickly shook off my rather rude awakening, grabbed my glasses, and followed Sally downstairs – the sound of angry voices below already beginning to reach my ears.

Just as we made it to the main floor, one of Christy's friends said, "Calm down."

"Do not tell me to calm down, harlot of the Adversary!" an unfamiliar male voice, one of the Templar, no doubt, replied.

"Just for the record, my boyfriend is a bouncer at the local bar. I'd love for you to say that to his face."

I stepped into the kitchen just in time to see it was Meg who'd made that remark. She and the geek witch Kelly faced off against three Templar knights. None of them looked particularly happy.

"All right," I said, stepping in, "quit the foreplay and get a room."

The glares that met me said my joke had fallen flat. Tough crowd.

Sally chuckled behind me, obviously at my expense, and then turned and walked off – presumably to rouse the rest of the troops.

"Fine. All joking aside, what's going on?"

"I do not answer to your kind," the Templar who'd been arguing with Meg replied. "I am a holy warrior and, as such, I answer to none but..."

"You can stop right there, buddy," I snapped, recognizing him from our impromptu testing the day before. "We both know your faith isn't worth shit. So stop pretending to be all holier than thou before I beat some manners into you."

The Templar glared at me and his hand inched ever so closer to his waist.

"And don't even think of going for that gun," I added almost as an afterthought, hoping the asshole didn't try to call my bluff.

Judging from the appreciative looks from the witches, I scored at least a few points with the ladies on that one. Ah, if only my prospective dance card wasn't already fuller than I'd intended it to be.

Unfortunately, a pissing match wasn't the best way to cement an already uneasy alliance between factions who naturally hated one another. So I swallowed my pride and quickly added, "Okay, enough. I apologize for any offense, but Sheila ... the Blessed One and your leader have already spoken on this matter. We're in this together whether we like it or not, so let's try to be civil and work this out like reasonable people. So I ask again, what's going on?"

For a moment, I thought nobody was going to say anything, but then Kelly broke the silence. "Some of their men didn't come back from patrol, and now they're blaming us."

Oh crap, I was afraid of this. "Us?"

"Anyone who falls under the category of supernatural being."

What a surprise. "Ah, thanks."

"Do not understate the problem, witch," another of the Templar, a young guy with a nasty scar down the left side of his face, said. "Six of our brothers have gone missing since night fell."

"*Six?*" I asked, mentally making a note to have a word with Sally once she got back. "Are you sure? I mean, I heard there were a few cars that didn't..."

"We're aware of those," he replied acidly. "I'm not talking about them. These were brothers who were present and accounted for yesterday."

"Okay, fine." I was tempted to offer the old standby about being sure there was a rational explanation, but then remembered the group I was dealing with. "So, that begs the question of why you're naturally assuming one of us did it."

"We found these downstairs in the laundry." The third Templar tossed a t-shirt and pair of jeans onto the floor in front of him. The jeans were discolored, but it was the shirt that was damning. Though faded from washing, it was pretty obviously covered in what could have been dried blood stains.

Oh, who was I kidding? I recognized the shirt as Mike's.

He'd been wearing it yesterday when he, Adam, and Dave had gone cow sipping.

Fucking morons, all of them.

"I can explain that," I said, knowing how that probably sounded as all eyes in the room turned toward me. I swear, once this was all over, I was getting a job as a janitor, considering all the experience I had cleaning up other people's messes. "There's a barn out back. If you go out there and check, you'll find ... well, I'm not one-hundred percent certain of what you'll find, but I'm sure it'll account for this."

"Wait," Meg said. "What do you mean out in the barn? You mean the stable where the livestock are kept?"

"Uh yeah. My friends might have sort of paid a visit there yesterday. They said there was a cow and..."

"What the fuck did they do to Benny?"

"Benny?"

"My shorthorn bull. I raised him from a calf."

"You named your bull Benny?"

"Don't judge me."

Needless to say, Meg was not pleased to discover that Benny had been *defiled*, so to speak. Thankfully, Sally picked that moment to return with both Sheila and Christy in tow.

The Templar's attitude took a one-hundred-eighty-degree turn in Sheila's presence. She was able to calm them down, make them sit tight until Bernadette – who was out scouring the property for signs of her missing people – could return.

Sadly, Christy wasn't in nearly as conciliatory of a mood. She joined Meg in bitching me out for my friends' actions – as if I'd turned into a wholesale butcher overnight.

While this was going on, the Templar sent runners to the barn to confirm my story. Thankfully, it checked out. While there were plenty of remains to be found – jeez, they'd even killed a couple of ducks, fucking weirdos – none were human. This didn't do much to dissuade the present company from thinking that vampires were assholes, but it pointed away from my friends being murdering assholes. Thank goodness nobody said shit about what they'd done back in Brooklyn.

As things got sorted out, I managed to slip away and pull Sally aside. Once out of earshot, I said, "Six Templar are missing."

"So?"

"So," I hissed, "is there anything you want to tell me?"

"Nothing I haven't already said."

"Are you sure?"

"Do I look like someone who can't count?"

I opened my mouth to say something pithy, but then quickly closed it. I had no desire to be force-fed my own teeth. Also, there was no reason to assume she was lying. Why bother confessing to killing one Templar just to cover up killing six? There was also the fact of her unsoiled clothing. I could buy taking down one guy in a way that didn't leave a mess, but a half dozen? Sally was good, but that would have required Navy SEAL-like training ... or maybe her stripping naked first, killing them, then finding a place to shower off.

Tempting as that imagery was, it didn't add up.

"You think there's someone else out there?" she asked.

"Someone, maybe more ... or some*thing*." That last part gave me the willies. I might be a vampire, but I'd gotten a taste of the weird-ass things that lurked just outside of humanity's perception. Sadly, I had a good enough imagination to fill in the blanks on any of a hundred different unsavory horrors that might be stalking us.

"The Draculas' welcome wagon maybe?" Sally asked,

apparently not nearly as fazed by this as I was. "They might be here to prod us on."

"Could be," I admitted, "but I'm not sure that makes sense. We've only been here a day, and last time James called to give me a heads up that we needed to..."

"Wait, when did James call?"

Oh crap.

Me and my big mouth. I relayed to her the gist of James's call, mostly sticking to the stuff about our apartment building being burnt to the ground if we hadn't gotten moving when we had. "You were out when this happened, and after that, things sort of moved quickly. Otherwise, I would have told you."

For a moment, her eyes narrowed at me, as if questioning my motives. In the back of my head, James's warning played out again, but then she softened her gaze and nodded. "If he calls again, tell him I said hi."

"Will do."

"Fine, so maybe it's not the Draculas. Wouldn't make sense for them to kill off the Templar anyway. I mean, sure, those guys are assholes, but why fuck with our chances even more than they already are?"

I shrugged, not having an answer. It could've been on Colin's orders, but I had the feeling if that were the case, there would have been a lot more incriminating evidence pointing toward me. Hell, he'd have probably Photoshopped me doing the deed. No, not his style to let such an opportunity pass. "As much as I hate to admit it, you might be right. There might be something else here on this farm with us."

"So what do we do?"

"What we're supposed to – get the fuck out of here and back to the mission."

It wasn't long before Bernadette got back to the house, her sour puss looking homelier than ever. Thankfully, she was willing to listen to reason – not mine, mind you, but Sheila's. By that time, my other friends were up and about. Well, okay, Dave didn't look like he'd slept at all – he had a wild look in his eye. No doubt he'd been playing doctor all day, and not the sexy kind either.

Meg wasn't happy at all when Mike and Adam joined us, but thankfully, Christy was there to talk reason to her. Sure, that reason consisted of "save it for later," but I was happy to have it for the time being.

At last, the sun started dipping low on the horizon. We gathered everyone out in the front yard to give them the lowdown on what was happening.

"... and that's pretty much what we know," Sheila said. "Our choices are limited. We could search for the missing..." That elicited some mumbling among the Templar. "... or we could stake this place out and hunt down whatever is out there." That brought even more assent. A few of the Templar drew their blades and raised them skyward. Hell, even Meg seemed in favor of that one. "Sadly, that brings with it risk too. We don't know what we're up against, how many, or where they are. It's possible we could be wasting our time, or worse, more could lay down their lives."

"We are not afraid!" a Templar near the back shouted.

"Nor do I doubt that for a second, brother," Bernadette said from Sheila's side. Feh, Icon suck-up.

"Thank you," Sheila replied. "As Sister Bernadette said, your bravery is not in doubt. But the road ahead of us is long and filled with danger. The foe we seek is powerful and has resources without number. As much as my heart screams for justice..." I had to suppress a smirk at the bullshit being piled on here. "... I know that we must press on toward the greater good. The world must be rid of this evil. Too many are counting on us. Who will stand with me?"

The Templar, good little zealots that they were, couldn't raise their hands fast enough. Goddamn. I couldn't help but wince a little. It was a like a small army of cockblockers. Oh well, where we were going, sex was bound to be the furthest thing from my mind.

Oh, who the fuck was I kidding?

Still, it would probably serve me best to keep my mind away from such things – especially that little fantasy Christy had seen in my mind.

"Not bad, Bill," Adam said, stepping up to me. "It's like we have our own Dumbledore's Army."

"Fuck that shit," Mike replied. "He has his own Stormtroopers."

Adam seemed to consider this before adding, "Dibs on being Tarkin."

"Fine, you got him. Me, I think I'd prefer to be General Grievous, or maybe a Ringwraith."

"What do you say, Bill?"

I shook my head with a sigh. "I say you guys are fucking dorks."

With the troops rallied, the real generals met inside for a pow-wow to discuss things.

"Meg is going to kill your friends," Christy said. "She loved that stupid cow."

"Bull," I corrected.

"Whatever. I'm tempted to let her."

"Let's not waste the cannon fodder so quickly," Sally replied. "We may need to use them as meat shields at some point."

"Can we please focus here?" Sheila asked, being about as close to a voice of reason as our group apparently had. "Nobody is killing anyone right now."

"But..."

"But I also don't want to risk any accidents happening along the way. That would be counterproductive."

"Fun, though," Sally commented under her breath.

Oh yeah, it would be a miracle if we made it to Boston alive.

Sheila ignored Sally's snark and continued. "We were already planning on splitting our forces, to hit Boston from both the north and south. So what I propose is sending Meg, Kelly, and Veronica with the Templar."

Christy appeared to contemplate this. "I'm not sure I'm comfortable sending my sisters with that group."

"It's probably better than sending Bill's friends with them. No offense, Bill."

"None taken," I replied. "Pairing up those yahoos sounds like a clusterfuck in the making."

"If it's just because of what happened with the cow..."

"No, this actually makes sense," I interrupted. "As much as I'd like for us to have the extra firepower, the goal was for the northern group to be small and the southern offense to be the bigger distraction. Also, the Templar are a bunch of sanctimonious assholes, but the truth is they probably need the backup more. You weren't there with us in Westchester, Christy, when we rescued Sheila."

"Rescued?"

"Okay, fine. Before we realized you didn't need rescuing. Anyway, between Remington's vamps and your old coven, the Templar were torn to pieces. They didn't stand a chance. We have no idea what we're facing up in Boston, but I'd bet my life savings that whatever it is, it's a lot worse. Some witches could make all the difference between them punching through and ending up as a box lunch."

"Bill's right," Sheila said. "They won't admit it, but they need the help."

"The thing is, will that ugly cun ... err, I mean Bernadette go for it?"

Sheila raised an eyebrow for a moment. "She's not stupid. She knows the odds. Despite what they might say about not being afraid to die, I'm pretty sure the majority aren't all too keen on this being a suicide mission. Besides, I'll put in a good word for them. They won't like it, but if their *blessed one* makes them swear to play nice, then they will."

"Starting to like having your own cult?" I asked with a grin.

"Not really. It's actually kind of creepy, but I might as well make the most of what I've got."

She had a point on all fronts. Christy still wasn't pleased, but she agreed to speak to her sisters about it. Considering that we still had no idea what was lurking out there somewhere on this farm, it seemed a safe bet they'd accept the safety of numbers rather than be left behind.

A short while later, everything was set. As expected, Bernadette wasn't happy – fuck, I'm pretty sure nothing short of seeing us all burnt at the stake would've put a smile on her pugface – but she accepted the necessity. Besides which, it wasn't like she hadn't already accepted us as the lesser of evils.

That set, the arrangements were next. The Templar-backed force would head up in much the same way we'd gotten to the farmhouse – they'd drive. Yeah, it wasn't exactly a tactic up there with the Invasion of Normandy, but it's not like we had much else to work with. The goal was to get as close to the city limits as they could. The majority of the trip would be taken under cover of darkness – dangerous, but necessary, as that would allow them to converge upon the city at as close as possible to sunrise. Say what you will about their odds, but they'd be magnified at least a hundredfold while the sun was shining.

Sadly, my group would be using a similar tactic. It was smart to do so during daylight, but it meant me, Sally, and the rest of the undead in our party would need to be extra careful.

As for how we were going to get in position, I was letting our resident master mages work that one out.

"I think Medford is your best bet," Kelly said. "Puts you just a few miles away. Should be an easy trek."

"Too close," Christy argued.

"You don't want to end up too far away either," Meg protested. "Not in your condition anyway."

"Don't worry about my *condition*," Christy snapped. "I'll be fine."

She was definitely getting testy. Must've been all those hormones eating away at her brain. I stepped in to defend her. "Christy's right. During our trial, for lack of a better word, Alex told me about Vehron's growing circle of influence. He's been subjugating covens all around that area. He's probably been recruiting new troops too. Who knows how many Bostonians are now bloodsuckers? Might be best to apparate further away rather than poofing right into the lion's den."

Christy frowned, although whether at *apparate* or *poof* I wasn't sure, but she didn't correct me. Probably realized a lost cause when she saw one. "Bill's got a point. Tired feet is preferable to being torn limb from limb the second we arrive."

"Fine," Meg relented. "Medford's out. Then where?"

"There's only one place that makes sense," Christy said, pointing at the map. She turned to me and grinned.

I looked down and saw where her finger rested. Damn, she really had been hanging out with us too much.

Oh well, I guess it was time for us to prepare for a trip to Salem, Massachusetts.

Now to just hope that town's history wasn't of a mind to repeat itself.

# 27

# THE LONG KISS GOODBYE

The plan was for both groups to head out at the same time – just a little past midnight. My group would obviously arrive at our location first, magic being far more efficient a travel method than anything the automotive industry would ever dream up, but since we'd be on foot from the start, it would probably all even out in the end.

The Templar busied themselves in those last few hours by – wait for it – praying. Yeah, a real mind blower, right? Who'd a thunk it?

Christy and her coven locked themselves away for some … err … magical stuff, no doubt.

Dave was still off by himself, hopefully not doing something with Sheila's blood that he'd end up regretting. The rest busied themselves with Sally's stash of guns, making sure they were locked and loaded – or whatever the term is. I don't know. I only really understood the point and shoot part. Seemed about all I needed to know.

As the time to depart drew near, I found myself in the kitchen brewing a pot of coffee. Say what you will about everyone else's prep work, but I had a feeling the next several hours would be a lot more pleasant with some caffeine in me. Sue me for being a traditionalist.

I smelled her sweet scent a moment before the footsteps signaled her entrance into the kitchen. Goddamn, even out here on this farm, right at the edge of us marching off into oblivion, she still smelled better than just about anything in the world. Hell, I'd have taken a whiff of her over the scent of sizzling bacon on a Sunday morning.

"Just about ready?" Sheila asked from behind me.

"Getting there." I turned around, two cups in hand. "One for the road?"

"How can I say no to that?" she replied with a smile. "Who knows when we're going to get a taste of civilization again?"

"Not sure I'd call this sludge civilized. It's instant."

"Any port in a storm." She took the cup from me.

"Want anything in it?"

"Black is fine."

"Suit yourself. I like mine just like I like my ladies, sweet and ... err ... creamy, I guess."

She giggled at my lameness. Yeah, some things never changed. Even with the world teetering on the precipice of chaos, I could still somehow manage to sound like a moron in front of her. "Bloody too?" she asked after a moment.

"Sadly, no. We're all out of the bagged stuff."

"That gonna be a problem?"

"Hopefully not. The boys were good enough to share a cup of cow with me. That should tide me over for a bit."

"And if not?"

I wanted to reassure her that I wasn't a monster, that I'd find some way to get through the coming days without resorting to unsavory means, but that seemed insincere. She deserved better. "I'll do what I need to do, but I..."

She reached out and put a hand on my shoulder. "I can't ask you to starve."

"I don't want to hurt anybody."

"I know that, Bill. I don't want to either. But I also know that neither of us should make any promises we can't keep. The world is too messy for that now. The best we can do is try."

"Thanks for understanding."

"Just don't offer me any leftovers."

I smiled over my cup of coffee. "Don't worry. I save that stuff for grossing out my roommates."

"I still don't know if it's smart bringing them."

I put my cup down and leaned against the counter. "Fuck that. I *know* it's stupid to let them tag along. Tom's faith is kaput and Ed ... well, he seems to be everyone's favorite dance partner these days for some reason. Unfortunately, it's a case of damned if we do, damned if we don't."

"The First Coven," she replied, pretty much answering everything. "When this is through..."

"James is a friend," I warned. "He's helped me more than once. Hell, he's been helping me from the very start. Yehoshua seems like he's a halfway decent fellow too."

"Yeah, him. His name ... listening to him talk. I almost get the sense he's..." She trailed off.

"He's what?"

"Not what, but who." She shook her head as if clearing her thoughts. "It's probably nothing. Never mind."

"Whatever. Anyway, as I was saying, the rest of them, well, have as much fun with those fuckers as you want. Hell, I might help you."

"Would you?" She raised an eyebrow questioningly. "I mean, they are your leaders."

"They aren't shit to me. Assholes, the whole bunch of them, and Alex is their king hemorrhoid. If you manage to get that cocksucker down, I'll hammer the fucking stake into him myself. He and I have unfinished business."

She stared at me for a moment as if weighing what I'd just said. Then she smiled, nodded, and took another sip of her coffee before putting her mug down. She took a step toward me, and I wasn't sure whether it was the look in her eye or maybe her Icon powers flaring up, but I could've sworn the temperature in the room shot up several degrees. "You know, you and he aren't the only ones with unfinished business."

All at once, my throat went dry and any of the thousand or so witty quips I usually had at the tip of my tongue went flying away like doves released before the Olympics. "Um ... unfinished business?"

*Don't let her fool you!*

What? Dr. Death wanted to have a chat *now*?! I mentally told him to get the fuck back in his box. Goddamn, that dickhead had some poor timing.

When I looked up again, Sheila was a step closer. "You okay?"

"Yeah, fine."

"You looked like you zoned out for a moment there."

"It was nothing. I just..."

"Need to shut up?" she asked, leaning in. "Yeah, I'd say so."

With that, her lips met mine. Every worry in the world, every bit of stress weighing me down, hell, every fucking thought I had in my head evaporated away. I stiffened for just a moment, expecting to be blown through a wall. Sad that had become such a commonality between us. But then nothing happened.

Well, okay, not nothing. Something was *definitely* happening ... something so freaking awesome I couldn't begin to describe it if I tried.

So rather than offer the boring details, let's just get right to the point. I stepped in and put my arms around her, drawing her close and feeling her body pressed against mine.

Everything was perfect. Her lips tasted so sweet, her hair smelled so clean, and her body was so warm, so full of life.

She groaned ever so slightly in response to our kiss...

...and that's when my lips caught fire.

I'd like to say I said something romantic as I disengaged from her, such as, "Oh dearest, your soul has sparked something deep inside of me. My love for you is a roaring flame of desire."

However, the reality was more an incoherent scream as I ran to the sink with my mouth ablaze, turned on the faucet, and stuck my face under the gush of water.

Steam exploded around me as the cold torrent hit the magical fire. For a moment, I was afraid that nothing would happen, that her power was the equivalent of supernatural napalm, but then, finally, I felt the flames being doused.

"Oh my god, Bill! Are you all right?"

After a couple more seconds of drowning my sorrows in the sink, I felt sure the fire was out. Wincing at the horrific pain, I turned around to reassure her that I was much better off than I actually was, only to see her eyes go wide and her take a step back. Duh! I probably looked like a fucking horror show. Probing with my tongue, I confirmed it. Yep, no lips. Bet that looked pretty as all hell.

"Ust ive it a second. They'll row back." Hmm, go figure, eloquent speech wasn't the easiest thing in the world when half your face was exposed jaw.

"I'm so sorry," she said, backing up another step.

Jeez, talk about killing my ego. "Ot or ault."

Apparently, I was less coherent than I thought, because she seemed to ignore me. "I thought I had it under control..."

"Iss o-tay."

"...I worked so hard."

"Hese tings appen."

"...but I couldn't stop it."

Oh crap. She was rambling. Worse, panic filled her eyes.

"Issen ooh ee..." I took a step toward her, and her power flared to life full force.

I wasn't sure if it was the sight of me or the fact that she was sorta freaking the fuck out, but it really didn't matter. One moment, I was reaching for her, and the next, I was hit by the metaphysical equivalent of a flaming Mack truck.

A wall of hot force punched me in the face and I went flying, slamming through the window above the sink and sailing out into the dark night.

Lucky me, I landed in a small garden out back – or more precisely, in the mulch pile of that garden. The smell of burning manure filled the air, but thankfully – sorta – the pile was moist enough to douse the flames covering me.

Oh yeah, a shower was definitely going to be a necessity before we poofed outta here, or at least it would be as soon as I...

*That's it! The bitch needs to die!*

What the...?

I tried to sit up, but immediately my guts cramped as a shudder racked my body. I curled up into the fetal position to let it pass, and that's when I caught sight of my hand. Charred from the flames of faith, the claws extended at the end of it were still plainly visible – but they were longer than usual and still growing.

"Oh no!"

All at once, my mouth felt cramped and I realized my fangs were likewise elongating past their usual length.

"What are you doing?" I asked to nobody but myself.

*She attacked us. I'm coming out.*

"No!"

I tried to force Dr. Death back down, but he felt like an irresistible force in my head – raging to be set free.

"Go away!"

Rather than focus on fighting Dr. Death, adding to the anger I could feel radiating from inside of me, I instead tried to think good thoughts – the Nintendo system my parents had gotten me one Christmas, the first time I'd felt a girl up in college, that time Tom and me got shitfaced on cheap tequila and the cops caught him taking a shit in my mother's herb garden, Sheila ... not as the unstoppable warrior of faith, but as I'd first met her. Her smile, the only thing I remembered from the day I first interviewed with Hopskotchgames.com.

Yes, focus on the good things in life.

It was touch and go for a moment, but at last, I felt the change within me reaching a parity with my thoughts.

*What are you doing?*

"Now is not the time," I replied to myself. "Leave me alone!"

*She...*

"Doesn't deserve this." I concentrated on the good, forcing every negative thing in my life to the back of my head.

I don't know how long I lay there in a pile of smoldering cow shit. Could have been seconds or hours. I wasn't sure. Sights and sounds filtered through to me – voices, movement above me, the rumbling of engines. However, nothing really registered for a while. I was too busy, locked in a contest of wills, focusing every inch of my being internally.

What I do know is that when I finally looked up and saw Sally's face staring down upon me, I felt like me again. Probing with my tongue, I was delighted to find I had lips again. Whatever time had passed had been enough for my healing to take over.

She reached a hand down to me, then scrunched up her nose and apparently thought better of it. She was a real sweetheart, I tell ya.

"Want to talk about it?" she asked, her look not entirely unsympathetic.

I sat up and brushed myself off a bit for all the good it did. "How's Sheila?"

"Fine, I guess."

"You guess?"

"She's gone."

"What?"

"Yeah, she told you she was leaving."

"She did?"

"Uh, yeah." She backed up and leaned against the house, looking at me like I had two heads. "Half the place came out here looking for you after we heard the explosion, but you were all like 'Go away! Leave me alone!'"

"What?"

"Yeah, you looked kinda pissed ... rolling around in your shit pile there."

"Wait," I said, standing up. "Did she say anything?"

"Well, once everyone saw you were okay, they decided to give you guys some alone time."

"Oh."

"But I might have overheard a little."

Normally, I would've been pissed, but right then, I was grateful that Sally was a nosy busybody.

"Spill."

"You don't remember?"

"Would I be asking if I did?"

"Beats the fuck out of me. You might have some weird-ass quirks I don't know about."

A small part of me was tempted to ask Dr. Death if he wanted to come out and play now, but I held my temper and paused for a moment to consider things. I wasn't sure what had just happened with regard to my inner psycho. Until I was, it was probably best to keep it to myself. "The ... *incident* sort of scrambled my circuits for a little while there."

"No shit. What did you do to piss her off?"

"I kissed her."

"Must've been one heck of a bad kiss."

It had been quite the opposite, in fact, but rather than bask in the moment, I was far more interested in hearing why Sheila had disappeared. I expressed as much to Sally.

"She seemed pretty upset about what happened."

I looked down at myself and shrugged.

"Not about blowing you up, although maybe she felt bad about that too. She didn't really elaborate."

"Go on," I said through gritted teeth.

"Well, all the while you just kept mumbling things about leaving you alone, so I'm pretty sure that didn't help, but anyway, she kept apologizing, saying she thought she had it under control, but it got away from her..."

"Her power?"

"I guess so. But she said something about getting caught up in the moment."

"Caught up in the moment? You mean she liked kissing me?"

"I don't fucking know! Like I said, I was eavesdropping,

not hitting her up with a survey." After a few moments, she added, "Maybe. That could be the case. After a few minutes of you ignoring her, she kind of broke down. Was sort of pathetic to watch."

"And?"

"And she said that maybe it was fate."

Oh crap.

"That maybe Icons and Freewills weren't meant to be together and that trying to go against it was maybe tempting destiny in a way that wasn't meant to be."

The tale Alex had told me of the doomed lovers – Edgar and Vara – briefly flashed in my memory before I was able to push it away. "So she left? Where? Is she coming back? Is she..."

"Relax, Don Juan. She left with the Templar. The plan hasn't changed ... well, much anyway."

"So that means..."

"You still have a shot at meeting up with her in the middle, assuming we all don't come down with a bad case of being dead."

For a moment, my spirits lifted, but it didn't last. How many times were we going to go through this before I accepted it – that it just wasn't going to work, at least not without one of us perpetually being blown to smithereens?

Christ, other couples had issues like hating each other's friends or not liking the same TV shows. I had to pick a girl for whom seemingly any emotional upheaval – good or bad – could lead to a fiery blast of anti-Bill magic.

I shook my head, having no fucking clue what to do, and then went and leaned against the house alongside Sally.

She wrinkled her nose. "You might want to do that upwind of me."

"Sorry."

In response, she smiled. "It's okay. I probably shouldn't kick you when you're down."

"Never stopped you before."

"Hah! Now that *does* sound like me. I just wish I could remember those good memories."

"Me too," I replied softly.

"Although I doubt there's anything nearly as good as you kissing an Icon and blowing half your face off."

"Oh, I don't know. The first time *we* kissed, it kinda blew your mind."

She stopped and stared at me. "Wait a second. We kissed?"

"Yep."

"Us?"

"Uh huh."

"As in you and me?"

"That's pretty much the gist of it."

"How ... why?"

Geez, talk about another ego boost to make my night. Oh well, there was probably no need to outright torture her. "It was right before we did it." Okay, maybe a little torture wouldn't hurt.

"What?!"

I couldn't help but let the grin escape onto my face. "Gotcha!"

"I was gonna say, since when did my standards drop so..."

"But the kissing part was real." At her dubious glare, I continued. "It was the first time you met Sheila ... or almost met her. She was out on a date with Harry Decker."

"The skull?"

"He wasn't a skull at that point, but he was still a walking cum stain."

She turned toward me, interest in her eye. "Go on."

"Anyway, we were out grabbing a coffee when I saw

them. She turned toward me, I panicked, and so I planted one on you so she wouldn't recognize me."

Her eyes grew wide, so I held up a hand. "Relax. It was just to cover my..."

"Not that," she said, her eyes turning glassy. "Keep going."

I didn't like the look she had on her face, as if she suddenly felt sick. "Are you okay?"

"Yes ... *keep talking.*"

"Okie dokie, then. So anyway, after that, we ended up in an alleyway where I might've said a few things and..."

"And it was ... deep, wasn't it?"

"Well, not what I was saying. I pretty much just wanted to kill the dick, but you..."

Sally suddenly doubled over. Tremors racked her body and then turned into a full-on seizure.

"Oh no." I grabbed hold of her to keep her from tumbling over into the mulch pile, but she was shaking so badly I was certain I'd lose my grip. "Sally! What's wrong? Talk to me!"

Just as quickly as it began, the spasms stopped. For a moment, she went limp in my arms. Quick as a flash, though, she seemed to recover. One little wobble and then she was standing back up straight. The hell?

She looked me in the eye and, for just a second, I saw what appeared to be recognition. "I told you to hold on to your humanity for a little while longer."

Holy shit! "Yeah, you did."

"I told you it was one of your more endearing traits."

"You remember that?"

"Clear as day. I..." She hesitated.

"What?"

"I probably shouldn't say this, but I was proud of you. You held on to yourself where I ... err ... a lesser vampire, that is, might have given way to the anger and torn Decker's throat out."

"In retrospect, that might not have been a bad idea."

"I don't know, don't remember that much, but you didn't. That's the important part. You stayed *you*. That's when I first suspected that maybe I..."

"You what?"

"It's ... fuzzy. I'm not sure."

Fuck it; it didn't matter. What did was that she'd gotten another little piece of herself back, that once again she'd managed to tap into some emotion that allowed her to knock down another piece of the wall in her brain, the wall put there by the most powerful vampire on the planet.

I couldn't help myself – I threw my arms around her in a great big hug. It had been a kiss that had ruined part of my life this night, but in some strange sort of cosmic symmetry, it had likewise been a kiss that gave a small piece of my friend back to me. Maybe fate wasn't so cruel after all.

"Bill?"

"Yes?"

"Don't take this the wrong way, but get your fucking mitts off of me. You smell like ten pounds of shit in a five-pound bag."

No, maybe fate wasn't cruel. People, on the other hand ... they could be assholes.

# PART II

28

# RAISING THE STAKES

Our plan had originally been to leave at the same time as the Templar contingent, but since we'd already blown that, I figured a quick shower wouldn't hurt us too much more. Besides, Sally was right – I did reek.

By the time I came back downstairs, smelling nice and soapy with maybe a spritz of some cologne I'd found in the medicine cabinet, I found everyone in the living room.

Tom, Ed, and Sally were busy pulling guns out of her duffle bag. Adam and Mike stood nearby, hopeful looks on their faces as they stared almost rapturously at the weapons. Oh God, those two packing heat. That was gonna be lots of fun.

Dave was off to the side, a large backpack slung over his shoulder and a notepad in his hands that he was busy scribbling on. I made a mental note to see what he was writing about and, if necessary, burn it.

Christy was checking a large circle that had been drawn on the floor. I stepped forward and felt a slight hum of power coming from it. Our conveyance for the evening, I presumed. Off to the side, just outside the circle, lay Harry Decker's skull. A dim purple glow continued to emanate from its empty eye sockets. I'd been kind of hoping his spirit had departed back to whatever Hell he was damned to be sodomized in, but that wasn't the case. So much for this being a pleasant journey.

"Everyone present and accounted for?" I asked, knowing that at least one of our number – perhaps the most powerful among us – had been driven away by our aborted tryst earlier.

"Hey, Bill," Tom said amicably, "you get all the shit outta your teeth?"

"No, but I see you haven't gotten all of it out of your brain either, so I guess we'll both have to deal."

He chuckled, and I stepped past him.

"How's it looking?" I asked Christy.

She turned toward me. For a moment, her gaze was hard, a testament to the fact that she was still angry, but then – thankfully – it softened a bit. Guess she'd been one of the folks who'd checked on me and probably put two and two together. The hell with it. I'd take some pity forgiveness. I wasn't proud. "I'm just about ready."

"Are you going to be ... okay doing this? Apparating us to..." Her glare cut me short. "I mean, sending all of us?"

A small smile crossed her face. "That's not going to be a problem. My sisters charged up the circle before they left. There isn't really much for me to do other than to release the power."

"Sounds like a capacitor."

"In a sense. At the end of the day, magic is just another form of energy. It can be harnessed and contained."

"Cool." I glanced to the side where I had the eerie feeling Decker's skull was watching me. Holding up my left hand to cover that I was pointing with my right, I asked, "So, is *everyone* coming with us?"

*If only your subtlety was as great as your stupidity,* Decker mind-blasted, *you might have a chance of coming out of this endeavor alive.*

Gah, what an asshole. "Listen, you skinless shithead, I will gladly skull fuck the magic right out of your gourd."

Silence descended upon the room for a moment, until Tom added, "You tell him, Bill!"

*Try it and I shall show you the true meaning of power, you pathetic excuse for...*

"That's enough, both of you!" Christy snapped. "Yes, Bill, everyone is coming. Harry too. I need his help with that Jahabich binding spell. His knowledge of ancient arcana is superior to mine and..." She hesitated for a moment, as if she found what she was about to say distasteful. "...his time beyond the veil seems to have given him some extra insight."

That immediately set off Adam and Mike, talking among themselves and wondering which of the myriad D&D pantheons he'd ended up in. Dorks. Besides, it was painfully obvious that someone like Decker would end up in a place where he'd be polishing Demogorgon's knob for eternity.

"Is that a good thing?" Ed asked, speaking above them.

"It's ... it's not natural," Christy replied, a pained look on her face. "What awaits us is supposed to be an unfathomable mystery. Breaking that wall is wrong."

*But quite useful, my ward,* Decker opined. *I have seen things that would have melted the eyes from my mortal head, conversed with beings forgotten for eons, gained knowledge that could shake the world to its very foundation.*

"Prove it," I said, smelling bullshit from a mile away. "Make good with the vulgar displays of power."

*Brainless dolt! As if I need to answer to you, the one who was my undoing in this...*

"It was your own damn fault," Christy blurted out, her face turning red. "If you hadn't become obsessed, had considered for even a moment that your damned prophecy might be wrong, then maybe you wouldn't have been killed."

*Blasphemy!*

"It's a fact. I've spent time with the Icon. She no more wants to kill us than anyone else." She glanced around the room and shrugged. "*Most* people in this room anyway."

*And that will be your undoing, child.*

"No, it was your undoing." She sounded sad for a moment, but then her voice hardened again. "I've decided to make my own fate, forge my own path."

*Then you will die.*

"If so, I will die as my own person, not a slave to the..."

"This is all truly fascinating," Sally interrupted, her tone saying otherwise, "but are we going to argue metaphysics all night or go and kick Vehron's ass before the Templar get there and fuck it all up?"

"Hard to argue with that logic," Ed said, the look on his face mirroring what I was feeling – she sounded like the Sally we knew.

Christy apologized and went back to her preparations, but not before – much to my amusement – picking up Decker's skull and stuffing it into a velvet bag. I shared a smug grin with Adam and Mike. It was pretty much the strategy we used when Dave had once burdened us with a wisecracking sword that he used to mercilessly mock us in-game.

Within minutes, she was ready. We all gathered inside the circle, a tight fit for our group, as Christy chanted a few words. When she was done, she started to say, "May the White Mo..." before catching herself. "May fate smile upon us."

I had just enough time to add, "I sure as hell hope

someone will," and then there was a bright flash of light as reality blinked out around us.

I've said it before, but I am really not a big fan of being poofed from one place to another. It's kind of like those freefall rides they have at amusement parks, except instead of falling down, it feels like you're falling in all directions at once. It's hard to explain otherwise, except to say that I was glad I hadn't eaten a big meal before doing so.

Although I'm sure it all happened in the space of a second, it felt like hours before the world coalesced around us again. When it did, I was surprised at the view, or lack thereof.

"Holy Dimension Door, Batman!" Adam exclaimed. "That was fucking wild."

"Wild is one word for it," Ed remarked, no doubt due to the fact that we had seemingly reappeared in the middle of a forest. It was a small miracle none of us had rematerialized inside a tree trunk.

I was about to ask Christy if maybe she hadn't gotten her directions mixed up when I spied something through the trees. It was overgrown and in heavy shadow, but enough remained of the billboard to clearly make out "Visit the Salem Witch Museum, 2 miles on the right."

"Oh shit."

"This is not natural," Christy warned, no worse for the wear from our teleportation.

Ed and I shared a glance. We'd seen this before. Sally had too, but we had the benefit of remembering it. "It's worse than that. It means we are potentially double-fucked."

"What's the big deal?" Dave asked, finally looking up from his precious notes. "So we're in someone's backyard."

"Except we're not." I pointed down at the broken asphalt peeking up through the dirt at our feet. "We're standing in the middle of a fucking road."

Ed and I filled them in on things. An unnatural growth of trees, no sign of life otherwise. It all pointed to Sasquatch magic. Hadn't Alex mentioned something about there being a potentially large Bigfoot invasion force nipping at our heels from the North? Guess he hadn't been shitting me.

Great! In addition to everything else, now we needed to worry about how many of the ugly fuckers were standing between us and Boston.

I took a deep breath through my nose to try to gauge that. Ugh! Son of a bitch! I really needed to remember not to do that where the Feet were concerned.

"We need to get off the street," I choked out, a pinprick of sweat trickling down the back of my neck.

"Maybe not," Christy said. "The Forest Folk have no quarrel with the Magi. If we run into any, I can..."

"You can explain to them why you're hanging out with a group of their archenemies," I pointed out. "I have a feeling they'd love to hear the story, maybe even before they tore all of our arms off."

"Bill's right," Ed said. "Let's find somewhere defensible and hash out a way to get through this."

"So you're saying we're trying to avoid Bigfoot?" Mike asked. "I can't imagine it'll be hard to avoid a pack of giant screaming apes."

I turned toward him, keeping my voice low. "Imagine those giant screaming apes with a stealth modifier of fifty. Trust me, they make for much better thieves than you ever did."

We definitely didn't need the delay, especially considering that seemed to be all we were doing lately – perhaps subconsciously avoiding the inevitable – but the Feet had a nasty habit of stepping out from behind trees and pummeling the shit out of their enemies before they even knew what was happening. Sure, we were armed, but that wouldn't help us much if we ran into an entire army of them.

Thankfully, it didn't take much effort to find something. Despite the thick foliage, it soon became obvious we were in a residential area. Bigfoot magic seemed to affect organic life, but it left buildings intact. Kind of like a neutron bomb, except filled with triffid chlorophyll. Once you knew what to look for, it was pretty easy to spot buildings through the brush, even ones that had been overgrown at an alarming rate.

Even better, the neighborhood we chanced upon was a nice one. Before long, we found ourselves standing on the torn-up driveway leading to a big-ass McMansion.

Fuck it, if we were going to plan some strategy, it might as well be in style.

We didn't waste any time breaking in. Locked doors aren't much of a deterrent to vamps. Most of them aren't designed with beings of supernatural strength in mind. It was child's play to turn the knob until the tumbler snapped. Even better, it seemed the power was out. No power meant no loud security system blaring out to every Squatch within half a mile.

I pushed open the door and took a quick sniff of the air. No stench of rotten forest ass assaulted me. I did catch the smell of humans, but it was stale. Nobody had been through here in perhaps a day or more.

Even so, just to be safe, I called out, "Anyone home?"

"Yeah, *we are*." Sally pushed her way past me. "Enough with the welcome wagon bullshit. If anyone is here, they really don't have much choice in their new roomies."

Thankfully, no angry residents met us with shotguns blazing. The place, as my nose attested, seemed to be abandoned.

Well, maybe not entirely. A few trees appeared to have grown straight up through the floorboards. I had a feeling it wasn't a random act. If what I knew about Sasquatch magic was correct, they were what remained of the original residents.

Oh well, any port in a storm. While the rest of our group fanned out to see if maybe there was anything in this place we could use, Christy pulled Decker out of his bag, and together they set to work in the spacious living room.

"Any ideas?" I asked.

*Be gone, fool*, Decker's skull hissed. *There is nothing here which a buffoon such as yourself could possibly pretend to understand.*

Christy, thankfully, was far more generous than her former mentor. "A glamour might work. A powerful enough one can mask scent as well as form. The only problem is the number of us involved. That's going to take a decent amount of effort to keep up. And even then..."

"Then what?"

"As I said, the Forest Folk have always respected Magi neutrality. But that doesn't mean they're allies. They're secretive, and they have a bond with nature that's strong."

"So basically what you're saying is you have no idea if it'll work against them."

"More or less. I mean, I can fool their physical senses. I'm pretty certain about that. Eyesight, sense of smell, touch; all of that – those are known quantities. They all play by the same rules, just at different levels. The problem is, we're surrounded by growth that's an outcropping of their own magic. They're going to be extra attuned to that. I might be able to fool it, I might not. For all I know, it's warded in ways I've never seen. Magic can be tricky like that – especially without time to study it."

"Well, that's just dandy like candy."

*I'm certain our passage will not be helped by your utter uselessness. Perhaps we should split up. You and your strumpet would make for excellent bait to cover our retreat.*

Goddamn, what a dick.

I was about to say as much, but then a cry caught my ear. It was from somewhere off in the massive household, far too low in volume for Christy to hear. As for Decker, who knows? The fucker didn't even have ears.

Regardless, I knew immediately who had made it.

I'd lived with Tom long enough to recognize his voice anywhere. My friend was in trouble, and he needed me.

# 29

# SCORE OF A LIFETIME

"Fuck me!" the cry came again, as I navigated down into the basement. Holy shit, this place was huge. One could have crammed my entire apartment into just a small corner.

Downstairs was no different. It was like these people had their own fucking bat cave.

"Yes!" Tom's voice was much louder now, and ... sounding less distressed. What the hell?

"This is so fucking awesome!"

Yeah, definitely a wee bit less distressed. What? Had he come across the owner's porn collection and a battery powered DVD player?

I passed a big screen TV set in front of a massive and disturbingly comfortable-looking leather couch. Impressive setup, but as dead as the rest of the house. So much for that theory.

Such a pity. Following my little incident with Sheila, a part of me wanted nothing more than to drown my sorrows in a sea of booze, weed, and surgically enhanced breasts.

I spied an open doorway ahead – the paneling around it

all scuffed up and the beam of a flashlight visible from within.

Tom was somewhere inside. His excited mutterings of "Fuck yeah!" and "Hit the mother lode!" would have been painfully obvious even to someone without vampiric hearing. What interested me more at the moment were the nicks and scratches on the door frame, almost as if...

"Did you kick this door in?" I stepped through the threshold, my eyes immediately opening wide with understanding as I beheld what lay within.

"Yeah," he replied, his arms full. "It was locked and I was like fuck that noise, I want to see what's in there. Glad I did. Do you see this fucking place?"

Hell yeah, I saw it. We were in what could best be described as my roommate's idea of heaven. The entire room was dedicated to collectible toys – some far older than us. I saw Furbies, stacks of Magic The Gathering cards, A GI Joe USS Flagg, and more – much more. Tom, proving that he was neither blind nor overly burdened by morals, had already grabbed a bunch of the nicer pieces.

His arms were full of mint-condition, unopened figures – Han Solo's plastic eyes stared back at me from within his clear plastic carbonite. I saw a few Masters of the Universe toys, a Stretch Armstrong, and, of course, at least one Transformer – Soundwave, from the looks of it. He was also holding a toy I didn't immediately recognize – a Barbie-sized action figure wearing camo fatigues and sporting a pornostache.

I crossed my arms over my chest and stared at my friend. "What the fuck are you doing?"

"Investing in the future."

"You're robbing this place blind."

"It's only stealing if it belongs to someone else," he said

idly, his eyes drifting back to the shelves. I was half-surprised he wasn't drooling.

"This is someone's house."

"*Was* someone's house."

"They might still be alive."

"Doubt it."

"What if they come back?"

Tom turned back to me and, for a moment, a solemn look appeared on his face. It was pure bullshit since the mad gleam never quite left his eyes. "I thought of that, Bill. Really, I did. But look around us. The Sasquatches either killed everyone or drove them off. The way I see it is, I could either leave this stuff here to rot, or I could honor their memory by cherishing that which they've left behind."

"Honor their memory?"

He shrugged. "Or something like that."

"What are you going to do with this shit anyway? The world is about to end. I doubt..."

"Fuck that nonsense right in its big fat ass. Unlike everyone else, I have faith that you're gonna find a way to end this bullshit. Then, when it's all over, the world will get back to normal – which means eBay will be there, waiting for a smart investor such as myself to offer his treasures up to those who are nostalgic for the old days ... and have the cash to pony up."

I was tempted to slug him and drag him out. "Put that stuff back."

"Not gonna happen."

"I'm serious."

"And I'm serious when I say you have a better chance of me sucking your dick than you do of me dropping this haul." He looked me in the eye. "Oh, and just for the record, the chances of me sucking your dick are less than zero."

"Glad to hear it." I took a step forward, and Tom – paranoia on full display – took one back. I reached out for him, but then stopped as I remembered the day he'd come home with his precious Optimus. He'd had the same look in his eye then as he did now. Hmm, was it possible? "How do you feel?"

"What the fuck? I feel fine."

"Not quite what I meant. Do you feel like ... your old self?"

"Are we still talking about my dick?"

"Oh, fuck this shit!" Bracing myself, I walked up and made to grab the toys in his arms. Thankfully, I was aware of the potential consequences. Had I not, I'd have certainly regretted it.

My fingers had barely grazed Darth Vader's plastic packaging when the cool material suddenly turned red hot. I jerked my hand back in time to avoid the worst, but still came away with smoking fingertips.

Tom look at my singed hand and a grin lit up his face, so wide I thought it might split his head in two. "FUCKING A! I am back, motherfucker!"

I shook my fingers, waiting for my healing to kick in. "So it would seem."

The law-abiding part of me still felt that what he was doing was scummy to the nth degree, but I had to admit it was good to see his insane faith once more flare to life. It didn't mean he was safe, but he would be a whole lot less vulnerable than when he started this journey.

"There's only one problem," he said, looking thoughtful for a moment.

"What?"

"Last time something like this happened, I ended up with nothing more than a pile of broken plastic. No fucking way. Not again."

"Sorry. I can't guarantee safe passage for Greedo, Prince

Adam, or..." I pointed toward the oddball of the bunch. "What the fuck is that one anyway? Did someone sell a Child Molesters of the Seventies line at some point and I didn't hear about it?"

"Oh, this guy?" Tom held up the creepy doll in the camouflage outfit. "It's Max Adventure."

"Who?"

"Don't you remember?"

"Um..."

"My dad had one when he was a kid. Gave it to me when I was eight. Remember that Fourth of July?"

I thought back. "Hold on. Was that the doll we blew up with those firecrackers?"

"Yep. Sadly, the Teenage Mutant Ninja Turtles refused to pay the ransom, so the bad guys had no choice."

"Wait, that stupid toy was your dad's?"

"Yeah, and believe me, he was fucking pissed." He held it up and smiled. "Oh man, good times. It isn't worth shit, don't get me wrong, but damn, does it bring back the memories."

"Okay, whatever. Bottom line is, I'm glad you got your faith back, but there's no way I'm giving you a warranty."

"I know. So I'm gonna split my stash. Bring a few, enough to cover my ass, but hide the rest for after."

"I don't think we have time to..."

**"*GET YOUR ASS IN HERE, BILL!!*"**

Sally's compulsion rang throughout the house, easily reaching the far confines of the basement. It was better than a PA system, although far less pleasant. Judging by the way Tom was rubbing his ears, he concurred.

"What the hell was that?" he asked.

"I don't know. We should..." Oh fuck it. "Stay here. I'll see what's going on."

"No problem-o. I need to find a box for all this shit anyway."

I left Tom where he was and raced back upstairs. Heck, it's not like I could have dragged him with me had I tried. His find was truly awesome – and I didn't mean from a monetary perspective either. It meant that he would be protected from vampires like me. That in itself gave me some small comfort as I finally stepped onto the main floor, having made at least one wrong turn in the cavernous basement.

I found the rest of the group in the living room, standing in front of a picture window and looking out toward what would have normally been a well-manicured front yard, but was now a forest primeval.

"Jesus Christ, Sally. Lay low with the compulsions. Otherwise, every Bigfoot within a mile is going to find us."

She stopped me with a glare. "It's too late. They already have."

# 30

## SHIT STORM

"I don't see anything."

"That's kind of the point with them," Christy said. "You won't see them until they want you to."

"Well, that's useful," Dave groused.

"They're near," she continued.

"Yeah," Sally added. "It's little things – a crunch of leaves, a tree branch swaying the wrong way."

"How many?"

"Who the fuck knows?"

"This is bullshit," Mike said. "Everyone knows vampires beat out dire apes. We should just go out there and kick their asses."

I turned toward him, somehow repressing the urge to smack the piss out of his stupid self. "This is one case where the Monster Manual got its stats dead wrong. They're not just apes, they're spirits."

"Ghosts?"

"Not quite ... unless you want to go with ghosts strong enough to rip off your head and shit down your throat. Oh, and believe me, if that latter happens, you're gonna wish for the former."

"So what do we do?" Adam asked. His tone, however, suggested he didn't feel all that worried. I really needed to remind these guys that there were different tiers of super powers. The Green Goblin might seem tough to Spider-man, but against a guy like Thor, there wasn't going to be much of a fight.

"Lock and load," Ed replied. He already had his shotgun in hand. "We know that bullets can kill these things."

"A lot of bullets," I corrected.

"Dead is still dead."

"Yeah, if there's one or two of them. If there's a hundred..."

"Too risky," Sally said. "Christy, can you get us out of here?"

"Already on it." She'd placed Decker back in his bag – thank God – and was busy drawing a circle on the floor in chalk. "Guess we should have aimed for Medford after all."

"How long do you need?" Ed asked.

"If it were just a couple of us, we'd be gone already. But I need a few minutes to set up a sending circle for a group this size."

Sally grabbed her Desert Eagle from the big duffel bag o'doom. "We'll give you what we can, With any luck, they don't even know we're in here yet."

Sadly for us, luck *was* on our side – bad luck, that is. Sally had barely closed her mouth when there came a crash from the back of the house – loud enough so that I had little doubt a wall had just been caved in.

"I really hope you've got some more weapons in that bag of holding," Mike said nervously.

"Way ahead of you." She'd already started pulling more

guns out, checking to make sure the safeties were off for the inept among us and passing them around. We quickly formed a crude defensive line around Christy's chalk circle. The plan was simple enough that it didn't need to be spoken – we keep the ugly fuckers off of us long enough to poof out of Dodge.

All at once, the ripe scent of woodland ass reached my nostrils. Ugh. Did these things have no fucking concept of bathing?

Sadly, such musings would need to wait, for I spied a monstrous shape step into the hall leading to the living room. It was large, hairy, and took up the entire space.

"Holy fuck, they're real," Adam gasped.

"No shit."

"If there's any chance of getting any samples, let's..." Dave began.

"Do a fucking autopsy on its corpse when we're done," I snapped. "For now, concentrate on making it into one."

More sounds of walls being broken through were heard as the creature we'd spotted moved in our direction. It wasn't alone. Just fucking great.

"How's it going, Christy?"

"I just need a few more..." Her voice trailed off. Not a good sign.

"What? What's wrong?"

"Tom!" she cried. "Where's Tom?"

Fuck! I'd completely forgotten I'd left him downstairs in his own personal Toys R Us wet dream. The dumb shit was probably so enamored of his ill-gotten goods that he didn't have a clue as to what was going on just above his head.

"What are you doing?" Sally snapped.

I turned and found Christy stepping out of the circle. She tried to push past me, but I risked a fireball to the face by grabbing hold of her arm. "No!"

"Let me go. I need to find him."

"You need to finish the spell. I know where he is. I'll go get..."

Alas, fate decided that wasn't gonna happen. At that moment, the Bigfoot we'd spied in the hall burst into the living room. Its massive form shattered the doorframe around it as if it were made of candy glass.

"What the fuck?" Mike cried at the sight of it full-on.

He'd probably been expecting *Harry and the Hendersons*. I'd forgotten to mention that these things had a four-armed, armored, and scary as fuck battle mode.

Regardless, terrifying though it might be, it still lived by the cardinal rule of Arnold Schwarzenegger movies – if it bled, we could kill it. The creature snarled, ropes of drool hanging from its ugly mouth. Too bad for it, at least half our group had our wits about us. Sally, Ed, and I raised our weapons and prepared to bring the pain.

The pain came all right, but it was on us. Two more of the beasts came crashing through the walls – one near its friend, another through the front, flanking us.

Before we could compensate, two of them raised their fists and smashed them into the plaster above their heads. The high ceiling, no doubt already strained by the damage the beasts had caused, shattered from the impact and came raining down upon us.

Thank goodness for vampire reflexes. I threw myself onto Christy, shielding her from the worst of it. The debris that fell upon us wasn't exactly pleasant, but at least nothing large – like a full bedroom set – came crashing down from the floor above onto our heads.

"Are you o ... shit!"

A massive paw grabbed me from above, lifted me up, and

threw me. I went flying through the picture window, smashed into a tree, and landed dazed on the comparatively soft lawn.

Multiple roars of rage sounded from back inside the house. There came a single gunshot – loud enough to be nearly deafening to my sensitive ears. A high-pitched scream, definitely inhuman, followed, and then came the sound of more stuff breaking.

"*Kill the T'lunta!*" one of the monsters cried.

I tried to stand, only for a massive foot to stomp down on my back and pin me to the ground, half crushing me in the process.

"*No!*" the beast who stood atop me ordered, loud enough that I'm sure his buddies in the house heard. "*We take prisoners.*"

Okay, that was definitely better than killing us indiscriminately. The beauty of being a prisoner was that it offered the hope of escape.

Sadly, the creature wasn't finished, as what he added next was enough to make me wish they'd gone with their original plan.

"*We take T'lunta to leader. We take them to Turd.*"

# 31

# A TURD IN THE HAND

Of all the Sasquatches to be brought before, not that I knew a lot of them by name, Turd was the last on my wish list.

It was bad enough that he was larger, scarier, and a metric fuck-ton meaner than the others I'd met. What made it worse was that I'd embarrassed the ever-living shit out of him not too long ago. Turd wasn't the brightest bulb, but I had a feeling it was too much to ask that he didn't remember my face.

The raiding party turned out to be seven Sasquatches strong. That would have been a daunting number even had we a defensible position and been armed with rocket launchers. Seeing my friends dragged out of the house, disarmed and defeated, I knew that our chances of escape were rapidly moving out of the slim area code and to the town of none.

Sally was the worst of the lot. Her right arm was bent at several unnatural angles, and one side of her face looked like it had gone ten rounds with a meat tenderizer. They threw her to the ground at my feet, where I tried to help her up as gently as I could.

Adam and Mike were bruised up, but otherwise seemed intact. Well, that was until Adam tried asking one of the brutes something and got a fist to the face as an answer. Yeah, I probably should have mentioned that these things *really* didn't like vampires. Oh well, guess that at least answered any stupid questions they might have had.

Dave, obviously the smartest of that bunch, walked out with his hands held high in surrender and his mouth zipped shut. So much for his master vampire bullshit, but at least he seemed to grasp that now was not a good time to do anything other than what we were told.

Ed and Christy brought up the rear. I was happy to see both were unharmed outside of a few scratches. The Feet seemed to be treating Christy in particular about as well as could be expected. I wasn't sure if she'd be able to pull off some diplomatic immunity, but her status as a Magi seemed to give her a bit more leeway than the rest of us.

There was no sign of Tom. Though my mind insisted on a few worst case scenarios, I held on to the hope that he was still safe and sound in the vast basement – probably too far in for the Sasquatches to notice, especially when they had us in their sights. Now to only hope the fool stayed put and out of trouble. With any luck, he'd be okay.

"*What this one?*" one of the Feet asked, towering over Ed and sniffing him. "*Smell funny.*"

"You're one to talk," my roommate replied, risking a pummeling.

Thankfully, none came, but another of the creatures – the one who'd shit-stomped me a few moments earlier – stepped in and likewise gave Ed a good long smell.

"*Not know ... strange.*"

It turned to us, then pointed a finger between me and Christy. "*Your cub?*"

Our what?!

I glanced at Christy, and she shrugged.

"*T'lunta asked question,*" the creature growled, raising a menacing fist. "*T'lunta answer question or T'lunta be crushed.*"

That didn't sound particularly pleasant. At the same time, I had no fucking idea what the correct answer was. Somehow, I had a feeling explaining to them that I had no clue what Ed was wouldn't be particularly helpful for us. For all I knew, their way of finding out would be to eat him.

"Yes. He's our darling ... cub."

Even injured as she was, Sally snorted a brief chuckle of laughter from my side. Bitch!

Ed's eyes narrowed at me. "Are you out of your goddamned mind?"

The Sasquatch ignored my roommate's outburst. It pointed one large finger at my face, the nail on it encrusted with some sort of sludge that I silently prayed was just mud. "*Cub ours now. We keep safe as long as T'lunta no try anything.*"

Though a part of me wanted to comment as to the lack of anything even remotely resembling intelligence on the part of our captors, I didn't dare look a gift horse in the mouth. So long as I acted my part, Ed would be safe. For the time being, that seemed a pretty good offer compared to everything else going on lately. "It's a deal. Keep my cub safe and I won't try anything."

"Wonderful," Ed commented disgustedly.

"Oh, relax, junior," I replied. "Maybe you'll get lucky and one of them will volunteer to wet nurse you."

The beasts marched us through the woods, away from the house we'd mistakenly taken shelter in. Within a few minutes, Sally's healing factor had kicked in and she was soon able to walk unaided. Thankfully, aside from their initial assault, the worst we were subjected to were more threats. Nobody in the group seemed to want to test them on that, though.

Even Christy, who I was afraid might try to blast her way out so as to search for Tom, kept herself in check. Hopefully, she'd reached the same conclusion as me. The Sasquatches were focused on their enemies – vampires. So long as Tom kept out of sight, they probably had no interest in a lone human. Not sure how that would help him in the long run, especially since there was no way of knowing how vast this unnatural forest was, but I'd settle for baby steps.

As stealthy as the beasts had been on their approach toward us, their ambush complete, they made no attempt to cover their tracks as they marched us through the woods. We left a trail wide enough for ... well, someone like me to follow. That was good. If an opportunity presented itself, we'd have a shot at being able to find our way back.

It soon became apparent why. We probably hadn't gone a half mile before the stench hit my nostrils – Sasquatches ahead, a shitload of them. Though the area around us remained overgrown, I began to see massive crude huts in between the trees, strewn about in haphazard formation. I couldn't see any other life, but I got the distinct impression there were eyes watching us – a lot of them.

Almost as if to prove that was indeed the case, the lead squatch stopped mid-stride – nearly causing me to walk face-first into his dingleberry-laden ass. He lifted his head and let out a screech.

The cries of dozens of beings answered in response. As freaky as that was, it was nothing compared to a deafening roar that came from somewhere up ahead. Talk about making one want to shit their pants.

Apparently, I wasn't alone either. I glanced around and saw my gaming buddies – their eyes wide. They finally understood this was no game.

As the hoots and hollers subsided, shapes stepped out from behind the trees – some with two arms, others with four, but all of them massive in form. There were a lot of them, far more than just a raiding party.

Holy shit. We'd practically teleported ourselves right onto the front stoop of what was apparently a major offensive. Medford was sounding better and better all the time.

We resumed our forward march, passing by several Feet, all of whom looked like they wanted nothing better than to smash our heads with a rock. I found myself hoping that the supernatural world had the equivalent of a Geneva Convention. Otherwise, things were gonna get mighty unpleasant for us in the short term.

We were soon marched into a clearing maybe fifty feet across and roughly circular in shape. Sasquatches lined the perimeter, a living wall of muscle. Even the smallest could have played center guard for the NBA. We looked like a group of midgets among them.

All of that, however, paled in comparison to what awaited us on the opposing end. Upon the ground sat a crude throne made of logs, hides, and assorted other gunk. It was adorned with skulls – some human, some animal, some I had no fucking clue. That was all foreboding enough, but it was the giant pile of shag carpet that sat upon it that had me far more worried.

Turd was kinda like Grape Ape's little cousin, except far meaner, uglier, and probably a lot worse smelling. Oh, and he wasn't purple either ... or maybe he was. Who knew? It's not like the filthy fucker had probably ever been near a shower, much less taken one.

As we were paraded before him, the Sasquatches

surrounding us all began to chant his name. "*Turd, Turd, Turd...*"

Oh God! I couldn't help it. It was still too fucking funny. I bit down on my lip, but I'm pretty sure even that wasn't enough to keep the grin from spreading onto my lips. I glanced around and saw I wasn't alone. In fact, of our group, only Sally and Christy appeared capable of maintaining a straight face.

Still, the Feet continued their idiotic chant. Much more and I'd lose my shit. As it was, tears began to stream down my cheeks, and my face began to shake with the effort it took to keep the laughter in. Judging from the looks our captors were giving us, busting a gut would not go over well with them.

Finally, the chanting stopped and, as it died down, one of beasts next to Turd shouted, "*Behold how the T'lunta trembles at the sight of Turd.*"

Oh, Jesus Christ. Quick, stupid, think of something, *anything*: marrying Gan, Sally never getting her memory back, Sheila walking out after that ill-fated kiss.

Combined, those did the trick and I managed to sober up, at least enough to get myself under control.

Turd stood up. Over ten feet tall, he made the rest look almost compact in comparison. He only sported the normal two arms of his kind, but then, he probably didn't need anything else. If he tipped the scales at anything less than half-a-ton, all of it muscle, I'd have been surprised.

He looked me in the eye and smiled – I think. Humor and the Feet didn't seem to really go hand in hand. Even smiling, their faces still looked about five paces north of pissed-off. "*Freewill, T'lunta. Turd remember you.*"

The Sasquatches who'd brought us in shoved me and the other vamps in my group forward. Turd glanced at the leader of the raiding party and raised a brow questioningly.

"*This Magi and cub were traveling with T'lunta, mighty Turd,*" it said reverently.

Turd cocked his head to the side, making him look extra stupid for a moment. "*Cub?*" He pointed a finger at Ed and snarled.

My roommate in turn gave a sheepish grin, no doubt hoping Turd didn't remember how he'd taken a shit on their so-called sacred trees.

"*That not cub. That human who accompanied T'lunta to Woods of Mourning.*"

"*T'lunta claim he his and Magi's cub.*"

Turd looked back at me and took a single step my way, his stride enough to cover most of the distance between us. "*You think to trick Turd?*"

"Um, no. It's just that..."

"*T'lunta's friends kill Turd's daughter. You try to hide that you brought cub with you to Woods of Mourning so Turd no take revenge!*"

What?!

"*Now Turd knows your secret.*"

"Um, you do?"

"*Turd claims what is yours. Will raise cub as my own clan.*"

Okay, that was unexpected.

"Oh, for Christ's sake!" Ed shouted from somewhere behind me. "I'm not his cub, you fucking moron!"

Turd made a dismissive motion with his hand. "*Take cub away. Turd train him later.*"

I glanced back to see the leader of the ambush dragging my protesting roommate away. Ed put up a fight, but he might as well have been a squirming kitten compared to the Sasquatch. His eyes locked with mine and I shrugged, giving him what I hoped was my best apologetic smile. Right before he was dragged into one of the huts, he flipped me the finger.

Such an ungrateful cub I'd raised.

# 32

# PRISONERS OF WAR

Turd cleared his throat, no doubt to remind me that he was still there – as if I had any chance in hell of forgetting.

I turned back, debating how best to handle this. I could cry and beg for mercy, and Lord knows a part of me really wanted to do that, but I had a feeling that would be about as useful as just asking him to let us go. There was little doubt that my near future involved a lot of pain.

Fuck it, I might as well deserve it.

"So, Turd, how ya been?"

"*Turd happy to see you, Freewill T'lunta.*" He smiled, showing off the chipped and rotting teeth in his mouth framed by two sets of canines, long enough to put a vampire's to shame. "*Turd very happy.*"

His tone turned my blood cold. His was the voice of a kid who had been denied a long desired toy for far too long, only to find it sitting out in the open on his brother's bed.

"Listen to any good tunes lately?"

As expected, that wiped the smile right off his face. As I'd learned during my brief foray up in Canada, Turd had one weakness. Unfortunately for him, that weakness was one of the Feet's chief taboos: he liked technology. Exposing that truth had caused Turd to lose a lot of face. Hell, up until I saw him sitting on the throne a few minutes back, I'd entertained the fantasy that maybe he'd been busted down to janitor.

Turd leaned in close, bathing me in the eyebrow-melting rancidity of his breath. "*You embarrass Turd, cause others to doubt Turd. Turd repay the favor many times over.*"

Huh. Gotta love self-absorbed assholes. Forget the fact that the bullshit from the Woods of Mourning had plunged us into a war, that supernatural creatures not seen for eons had overrun whole swathes of the planet. No, the thing that pissed him off the most was that I'd embarrassed him. And here I thought vampires were arrogant.

He stepped past me, then stood glowering down at Sally. "*Turd remembers your mate too.*"

"His mate?" she asked, turning toward me.

"Long story," I mouthed. Needless to say, I hadn't had time to bring her up to speed on *everything*. Guess that was gonna be a fun recap.

"*Not know the rest of you, but T'lunta enemies. You are all Turd's prisoners now. Turd will decide your fate. Turd will decide when you die.*"

Christy stepped forward. "The Magi have never had a quarrel with the Forest Folk."

"*True,*" Turd replied, turning her way. "*You were prisoner of T'lunta?*"

"No, they are my friends."

He folded his hands across his massive chest, as if considering what she'd said. "*If friends with enemies, then enemy you are.*"

"They are my allies in this venture, and thus should be afforded the same neutrality as I hold."

Turd was silent at this for a moment. He gestured for her to continue, apparently curious to see where she was going with this. I had to admit, I was too.

"We ask for safe passage through these woods."

"*Why?*"

"Ours is a mission that may benefit your people. An evil has arisen. He has claimed one of the great cities to the southwest. We have come to stop him."

Turd's eyes opened wide. He turned toward me. "*This true?*"

Holy crap, was this actually working? I had to wonder if Christy was using the Force or something on this piece of shit's weak mind. If so, she really needed to start doing it more often. "Yes, it's true. A great power has taken over the city of Boston. His influence has been spreading for months now. What Christy – the Magi – says is true about helping you too. I've seen the bodies of your people, broken and left for dead by this enemy to us all. I've come up here to end this. I've come to kill him."

Turd was silent for a moment, shock evident on his face.

And then he started laughing.

Guess maybe Christy's powers of suggestion needed a little work after all.

The rest of the Sasquatches around us followed Turd's lead, filling the air with grating laughter that would have creeped out even the Joker.

Turd pointed a finger in my face. I'd have bitten it off if I wasn't certain I'd have caught something nasty from putting it in my mouth. "*You,*" he said, still cackling, "*puny Freewill T'lunta, seek to kill mighty Freewill T'lunta warrior?*"

I glanced at Sally, my lips a thin line across my face. She merely shrugged. "He does sort of have a point."

"Thanks, I appreciate the help," I muttered before turning my attention back to Turd. "I take it you've heard of Vehron."

Turd's laughter finally died down, and he spat upon the ground at my feet. Ugh, that was definitely a loogie I was glad hadn't hit me. "*Turd has heard of warrior from the past, reborn. Turd's people have died at his hands, many tribes slain by him. Turd is here to hunt him, kill him. Turd is here to reclaim our lands and slaughter all T'lunta we find.*"

"So we're on the same mission?" I asked. Well, okay, maybe excluding that last part anyway.

"Save your breath, Bill," Sally whispered from behind me, so low that I barely heard her.

Fucking negative Nelly. Nothing ventured...

"We could help you. We..."

A massive fist met the side of my face, lifting me off the ground and sending me flying.

Yep, nothing gained.

Thank goodness part of my healing abilities included growing my teeth back. I'd have hated to face eternity with dentures. At the rate things were going, it would only be a few hours before my face was convex again.

As I had lain there on the ground, contemplating all the pretty colors my jaw was probably turning, Turd had leaned over me – hocked another disgusting wad of phlegm, one which landed square on my chest with a nasty splash – and said, "*Turd hates great T'lunta warrior, but Turd hates you more. Turd will only help you do one thing – die.*"

He'd turned and made a dismissive gesture, at which

point I was scraped off the ground and dragged, along with my friends, out of the clearing. Once more, they gave Christy deferential treatment, in that they at least didn't rough her up, but apparently her status as a neutral party was now null and void in their eyes. Poor girl. At some point, she was going to conclude that her life had taken a definite turn for the worse since she'd started associating with me. I could only hope that when this happened, it didn't give her cause to reconsider her former master's words.

On the subject of Decker, there was at least one small consolation. We'd been forced to abandon our weapons and possessions back at the house. Seeing Christy's hands free, I garnered Decker had been among those items left behind. At least I wouldn't have to spend the duration of my torture and eventual execution listening to that asshole. Victories – take them where you can, I say.

I was expecting us to be thrown into one of the huts. They all looked big enough to serve as prisoner barracks. However, apparently some of the Sasquatch were smarter than they looked. The huts, although large, didn't appear to be the most reinforced structures. Busting through a wall of moss and twigs wouldn't have presented much of a challenge.

The giant pit we were led to, however, was a different story.

Fifteen feet deep, it was covered in a tight net of heavy logs bound with thick vines. The rocky sides appeared wet and slick – probably greased to hamper anyone trying to climb them. At least, I hoped it was grease. I couldn't help but picture a bunch of Feet circling the area, smearing their asses against the walls. Ugh. I was so gonna need to bathe in hand sanitizer if I ever got out of this mess.

Speaking of smeared assholes, though, as the Feet lifted a hatch on the crude prison, I saw that, while the accommodations could be worse, the company couldn't. Several vampires already occupied the pit. Most of them were strangers, the random faceless cannon fodder one might find in a bad fantasy novel. However, despite the dim light below and the dirt upon his smudged face, one figure in the bunch was easily recognizable.

"So, Freewill," François spat as he stood, straightening his tattered sports jacket, "to what do I owe the displeasure?"

"Any chance I can get put into a different ... oof!" A pair of frying-pan-sized hands shoved me into the empty space of the open hatch.

The drop itself was nothing, but, caught off guard, I still landed face first onto the cold hard ground below. A cruel snicker met my abrupt descent – fucking asshole surrender monkey.

Sally was smart enough to take the hint and leap down into the pit, landing smoothly on her feet before she could be pushed. Adam, Mike, and Dave followed, landing with considerably less grace than my partner.

Christy came last, one of the Feet holding her by the arms and lowering her down as far as he could reach. She dropped the remaining few feet and landed unsteadily.

"You okay?" Sally asked her.

"Yeah, just need to sit down for a bit."

"*No magic,*" one of the Sasquatches above warned. "*We watch you.*" He then shut the trap door, locking us below. Oh well, so much for plan A – teleporting the fuck out of here the second they turned their backs.

I got back to my feet and turned to my friends. "Is everyone else okay?"

"Those fucking things hit really hard," Adam said, worry

showing on his face for the first time since I'd met him in his vampire form.

"No shit," I replied, feeling the skin of my bruised jaw as my healing finally decided to take over.

"I am surprised our friend Turd did not rip your arms off like a child might tear the wings off a fly," François said.

"Maybe he remembers what happened last time," I replied, turning to face him.

He scowled as he strode up to me. "Oh, I am certain he remembers. I know I do."

**33**

# THE LAST TO BE FIRST

"**I** take it your little deal with him is null and void since we're sharing this executive suite here."

François's eyes narrowed at me, and several of the other vampires sitting in our cell tensed up. No doubt they were his men. Out of the fire and definitely into the frying pan.

"Ah yes," he replied, painting the most unpleasant of smiles upon his face, "you were truly in rare form that day, you and your strumpet." His eyes never left mine, but I wondered if Sally realized he was talking about her. "Despite everything, you somehow managed to ruin a mutually lucrative business arrangement, destroy my chances of rightfully ascending to the First Coven, and start a war in the process."

"What can I say? When I'm hot, I'm hot."

"Yo, Bill," Mike said. "Who the fuck is this guy?"

"***DO NOT INTERRUPT YOUR BETTERS!!***"

The compulsion caught me by surprise and knocked me flat on my ass, sending me skidding back several feet.

Fuck! I'd forgotten how powerful François was. He was a vampire some seven centuries in age. Though I'd since gotten

299

a taste of both Alex's and Vehron's strength, it was stupid to forget that this guy was no slouch. He could've fucked me up six ways to Sunday and, in the current tight confines, there probably wasn't dick I could do about it.

His voice still ringing in my mind, I glanced around. Sure enough, Dave, Mike, and Adam were standing still as statues, their eyes glazed over. Although I considered my DM to have a pretty forceful personality, his will was nothing compared to such raw power.

Christy was leaning against the wall. Her hands were on her knees, but her eyes were clear.

"You okay?"

"Don't worry about me." She smiled, and that's when I remembered what she'd said about developing a way to insulate herself against compulsions. Apparently, she'd put her plan into action at some point, using herself as a guinea pig. That only left...

I glanced over and saw Sally. She had been caught off guard as much as I'd been, but where the others were deep under François's spell, her eyes were clear.

"Curious," he said, stepping past me.

I stood up and put a hand on his shoulder. "Listen, asshole. Leave her al ... ACK!"

His claws extended at lightning speed, and before I knew what had happened, my throat had been slit. It wasn't deep, but I nevertheless found myself gagging on my own blood.

I staggered back, clutching at the wound.

"Much better," he said as he neared Sally.

She glanced toward me, concern showing on her face for a moment, but then turned to meet him.

As I continued to gag, the area in which we were held took on a red hue. For a moment, I thought it was Dr. Death forcing his way to the surface again. I was just about to conclude that this time I was more than likely to let him when I realized it wasn't me. The crimson glare was originating from Christy. Her body was alight with power, and she did not look happy.

Even had I been able to speak, there was no way I was gonna say shit. Christy was pregnant, tired, angry, and her boyfriend was currently MIA. If she wanted to take out all of those frustrations against an asshole like François, then who was I to tell her no?

Sadly, not everyone shared that view.

"*No magic!*" a voice roared from above. "*Bung give you last warning.*"

Bung? Goddamn, these things were fucking ridiculous.

For a moment, Christy looked like she was about to tell Bung what to go do with his hole, but then she thought better of it. The glow around her subsided.

François let out a chuckle, but then something dark and wet splattered against his face.

"*No compulsion either, T'lunta,*" Bung said. Through the bars at the top of our cage, I could see him wiping his fingers off on his fur. Judging from the Bigfoot-reek that now emanated from François, I guessed he hadn't just been hit with dirt.

A better asshole to be shit-encrusted I couldn't think of.

Sally backed up a step, a disgusted look upon her face – probably because she'd caught some of the splatter on her blouse.

François's eyes flashed black for a moment, but another growl from above apparently caused him to think better of any response. He merely held out a hand. One of his vamp minions immediately raced to his side and placed a handkerchief in it.

The prissy cocksucker took several seconds to wipe himself as clean as he could. By that point, the wound on my throat had closed up, and I could again breathe without inhaling a lungful of my own blood.

He glanced once more at Sally and then turned back to me. I thought perhaps he meant to continue slicing me to shreds, but instead, he smiled.

Somehow, I found that far worse.

"Your strumpet has been compelled," he said.

"Okay, now I know you're talking about me," she said from behind him.

François ignored her, however, and continued to grin at me. "It would have to be someone powerful to ignore my will, far stronger than Ogedai's lackey."

I faced him with a grin of my own. "Oh, you mean the lackey who now outranks you."

"*Used* to outrank me," he spat, quite literally.

Gross. What was it with assholes and spittle? Goddamn, did nobody ever teach these fuckwads to say it not ... wait a second. "What do you mean 'used to'? What happened to James?"

"Nothing, fool, so far that I am aware – unless I were supremely lucky. Alas, my presence here with you would seem to suggest I am not."

"I think I get what he's saying," Christy said from her place against the wall.

That's when realization sank in. "No way."

"Theodora's death. It left a vacuum of power within the thirteen," he said, circling me as I took it in. "With what happened: the ambush, the loss of face in front of their allies, the embarrassment of being caught so *utterly* by surprise, they had little choice. Even Alex, supremely arrogant as he is, could not deny that doing anything other than immediately filling the void dear Thea left would be tantamount to courting disaster."

"But you ... well, not to mince words, but I sort of got the impression Alex didn't like you."

François shrugged. "Nor I him. But there was no other. I am an elder among our kind, twice denied. There was no time for him to find a loyal scapegoat, nor anyone present with near my level of experience. Of course, he did not say this to my face. Even he is aware that such folly is best kept out of the political arena. After you and your pack of fools left, he turned to me, embraced me as a brother and I him – swearing undying loyalty to my brothers and sisters. Thus, the pact was sealed."

"You can't be serious."

"Oh, I am. I shall let your slights of the past few moments pass for now. We shall call it a circumstance of your exceptional ignorance. But know this. I am of the First, boy, and should you ever cross me again, I will care not what anyone says nor what any prophecy proclaims. I will *end* you without a moment's hesitation. Am I clear?"

An eternity passed in my head as I weighed my options. We were outnumbered, and three of my team had been sent to la-la land with a single sentence. I was trapped with an enemy who was several times faster and stronger than me. I had a monster in me that could probably even the odds, but he was best kept bottled up until I really needed him. Settling petty scores didn't strike me as the most judicious use of that power. Oh well, it's during times like these that you sometimes gotta tell pride to take one for the team.

"Crystal clear ... François of the First."

That seemed to mollify the asshole, at least partially. He glanced back at Sally, but she was no moron. She'd overheard everything and, even with a Swiss cheese memory, probably understood it all. She gave François a deferential nod of her head.

"I am pleased to see you choose reason for a change, Freewill – however surprising that might be."

Goddamn, the snide digs just kept coming. Suck it up, Bill.

"Now that we have all established the hierarchy of our situation..." François lowered his voice to a bare whisper, so low that even I strained to hear it, "it is time we planned our escape."

## 34

## THE REBEL ALLIANCE

Fuck it. If forced to choose between a smarmy asshole who hated me and a giant slobbering ape that smelled like ass and hated me, the choice seemed pretty goddamned clear. I was sure at some point I'd regret it, but for now, I just nodded.

"Good," he replied. "Your allies?"

The Defilers were still doing their mannequin impersonations, but I had little doubt they'd help in the name of getting us out of here. Even if they didn't want to, it wasn't like François couldn't compel them with no more effort than it took to breathe. I glanced at Sally and she rolled her eyes as if to say, "Of course I'm in, numb nuts." Jeez, even in my imagination she was a bitch.

There was little chance of Christy having overheard our whispers, but there was no doubt in my mind she'd take any opportunity presented to her. "The witch is with me. She'll help," I replied softly.

"Good. We will need her. Turd has brought considerable forces to bear. This is a much larger offensive than we anticipated and much sooner too."

"That's bad for Vehron," I pointed out.

"Perhaps, but worse for us since we are in the middle of it."

"How did you end up here anyway?"

He glared at me, his ego probably amplified at least tenfold by his promotion.

"Please, sir. I'd like to know. It might help us in our efforts." Goddamn, why couldn't James have mentioned this shit to me when he called? Well, it probably wasn't any of my business to begin with. Also, how was he to know that I'd run into this asshole? My God, the world was a small place when it wanted to be.

"I was returning to my troops in Canada when I decided to make a stopover to check on our covens north of here. I didn't realize my trip coincided with the Sasquatches' push south. I had barely touched down when the trees began to grow at an abnormal rate. I did my best to rally our people, but there were too many of them. We were quickly overrun."

Something in his voice told me that was bullshit. The fucker probably ran back to his plane double-time, but chances are the runway was already overgrown by then. However, I kept these doubts to myself.

"Turd was not at all pleased to see me following our botched dealings in the Northwest Territories. If not for my new station, he would have surely had me executed by now. Thankfully, the fool thinks to use me as a pawn, as leverage once The Destroyer is defeated."

"Any chance of a rescue party?" I doubted the Draculas were in a position to let their newest member rot, no matter how much they disliked him. I, for one, wouldn't say no to some heavy duty backup right about then. Hell, maybe I could even convince them to help me retake Boston.

"If they knew of my predicament, perhaps," he replied with a pained sigh. "Alas, I was not given the chance to contact them. Turd's ambush was too quick, too overwhelming. We are on our own for now, but once we have an opportunity, then I have no doubt my *dear siblings* will come to my aid."

I couldn't help but notice it was *his* aid and not ours. I glanced at Sally and then at Christy, who'd moved close enough so that she'd probably gotten the gist of what we were talking about. The look on their faces echoed what I was thinking. If we relaxed our guard for even a second, we'd be thrown to the wolves or worse.

We didn't have much choice in the matter, but that didn't mean we needed to go into this with our eyes closed. A silent agreement passed between the three of us, hopefully more than my imagination, and I turned back to François. "What's the plan?"

"The plan for now is to wait. Once the time is right, then François of the First and the legendary Freewill shall show our enemies how truly formidable a pairing we can be."

Ugh. I felt like Superman being forced to team up with Lex Luthor to stop Darkseid.

No matter who won, I had a feeling I'd lose.

"I'm telling you, you should have taken lunge as a feat for Kelvin. Would've saved you from getting your ass handed to you over and over again. You're not a melee tank."

"Well, it might make more sense if *someone*," I glared at Dave, "didn't give every single monster we fought extended reach. I mean, seriously, how the hell did that beggar in Oncara hit me from fifteen feet away?"

Dave shrugged from where he lay sprawled out on the rocky ground. "He was enchanted."

"If he was so fucking enchanted, then why was he still living in the fucking gutter?"

"You don't know. Next time, don't whiff your diplomacy roll and maybe he'll tell you before he kicks your ass."

Fucking cock. I swear, if I wasn't afraid of getting a Sasquatch-sized shit ball tossed down at me, I'd compel the fucker to stop being such a dick.

Oh well, talking game strategy helped to pass the time. It was either that or fraternize with François and his minions. I'd have sooner risked the shit ball.

Sally and Christy had gone off to their own corner. Christy wasn't going to risk using magic, at least not until it made sense to, but she was still trying to help Sally with some meditation techniques – or so I gathered from my eavesdropping. Sadly for them, our cell wasn't quite large enough to afford us the comforts of privacy.

That definitely didn't help when it came to taking a piss. The Feet apparently didn't believe in toilets or even a freaking chamber pot. I prayed that François would put his plan into effect before the need to drop a deuce arose.

I only hoped Ed was doing better than we were. Maybe he'd gotten lucky and some mother Sasquatch was picking nits out of his hair and grooming him. It was probably too much to hope that he took any selfies of his predicament.

A lone screech sounded from above, catching my attention. It was followed by the shuffling of large feet. Within a few seconds, more cries filtered down to us – a few cutting off abruptly.

"What's going on?" Dave asked.

"Maybe Turd let one loose and now they're evacuating the village."

My friends chuckled, but François's voice cut in and immediately silenced them.

"Freewill," he hissed, "to my side." Pushy motherfucker, wasn't he? "Our time is now."

I signaled for Sally and Christy to join us as I walked over. All of François's men were still seated, but upon closer look, I could see it was a ruse. Though appearing to relax, each was coiled and ready to strike.

"What's going on?"

"It matters not, child," François replied. "Listen. There is something afoot."

Ugh, the puns, they burned. "I gathered that, but we don't know what."

"It is a distraction. That's all that is important."

"It could be anything," I protested. "A passing deer, a hiker wandering into the area."

"I think not."

"Fine, but think about where we are. It could be Vehron making a counterattack. He could..."

"*SILENCE!!*" The compulsion wasn't full power, but it was more than enough to hit me in the head like a brick. "Remember your place, boy."

God, I so wanted to wipe that fucking smirk off his face, but for now, I simply nodded like an obedient child.

He had a point anyway. We had maybe an hour or two of darkness left. Although the canopy of trees above us was thick, I had little doubt our odds of escape wouldn't be made easier with the sun shining above.

"Even if it is our great enemy, do you propose we wait down here for him to arrive?" François asked, a sneer on his face. "Would that not be convenient, for you to offer yourself up to him already a prisoner?"

"What are you getting at?"

"Alexander's court proceedings stunk worse than this place. It was one misdirection after another, ignoring the true facts."

"True facts?"

"You were the one who released Vehron upon the world. That much my spies have gathered. Who is to say that you did not manipulate events? Perhaps your mission's true intent is to merely mask that you're journeying to Boston to join your Freewill brethren?"

What? This fucker thought I was in cahoots with that muscle-bound cock-knocker? "We're heading there to kill him. End of story."

"Very well, so then prove it. Join me now and together we shall see."

Motherfucker! I should have followed after Sheila. Hell, dealing with the pomposity of the Templar beat spending even a minute with this asshole.

Regardless, it still struck me as stupid to act without having any idea what was going on above us. For all we knew, it was just some military drill and we'd pop out of this hole to find Turd and his buddies waiting to smash our heads with rocks.

Fuck. We needed to act, but maybe it didn't need to be stupidly. "Christy," I asked, "I know they said no magic, but is there any chance you could maybe do some subtle sort of scrying up top? Something to let us know if the coast is clear?"

"I can try," she replied with a sly grin. A red glow erupted from her body. Before I could question what she was trying to do, a lance of pure power shot out of her. It hit the beams at the top of our prison and exploded, sending a shower of splinters raining down on us.

"That subtle enough for you?" After a moment, when no guards appeared, she added, "Looks like the way is clear."

"Umm, yeah ... let's go find Tom."

"Somehow, I knew you'd say that."

I turned back toward François, mentally reminding

myself to never ever piss Christy off again. "Looks like we're committed. Let's..."

I stopped when I saw that he was busy tearing off a sleeve from his jacket.

He held out his arm to me. "Drink."

"What?"

"It is as distasteful for me as it is for you – more so, I can assure you – but we need every advantage we can get."

He had a point. I'd gotten a taste of his blood during the fracas in Canada. His power was immense, more than enough to take down the average Squatch. We were still badly outnumbered, but maybe it could make a difference.

"One Battlestar is badass, but let's see how these Cylon fuckers handle two."

François took a half step back, confusion on his face.

"Never mind. Let's do this."

"So be it." He held out his arm, and I clamped my teeth down upon his wrist. "But know, Freewill, that should you dare try to use my own power against me, I shall compel your friends to do things to themselves that will give you endless nightmares."

This asshole needed to get in line because I already had enough of those for centuries to come.

35

# FIRST TO ESCAPE

I had to admit, biting an elder vamp was a lot easier for me to swallow – pun intended – than handing the reins over to Dr. Death. Despite our agreement, it seemed he only wanted to come out and play during times when it really wouldn't behoove me. I mean, the dude seemed to have a serious mad-on for Sheila. The Templar I could understand, but her? For now, though, he was oddly quiet. I decided not to look that gift horse in the mouth.

The bars to our cell in pieces, it was child's play to escape from the pit even with the greased walls. I gave Christy a piggyback out of there, while the others had little problem jumping the distance and pulling themselves out.

"Being a vampire is so fucking boss!" Mike said as he climbed out. "I couldn't even do one pull-up during those stupid Presidential fitness tests in school. Now look at me."

"Keep your head on," I admonished him, "because, otherwise, all I'm going to be looking at is a pile of ashes. These fucking apes aren't playing around."

Sure enough, we'd just barely gotten out when a roar sounded from nearby. The Sasquatches had been in the process of scrambling about chaotically, but it had been stupid of us to assume they'd all abandoned their posts.

No sooner had the warning come than one of François's minions was taken down, his head pulverized by a rock winged at him with a disturbing amount of power.

Thankfully, the smarmy asshole hadn't surrounded himself with newbs. Three of François's men swarmed the Foot responsible and made sure he suffered a similar fate.

One down, probably far more than I dared count to go. There was no way we could win this. We needed to amscray post-haste and keep moving. I didn't want to flatter myself that I was Turd's archenemy or anything. I mean, who knew how many beings the ugly fucker had pissed off in his time? Even so, I'd seen the glee in his eyes. I'd embarrassed the shit out of him, exposed him as being an iPod lover. I had the feeling I was one prize he wasn't going to let get away easily.

"Bill!" Christy's voice cried.

Shit! I'd been so worried about what everyone else was up to that I forgot to cover the one ass I cared about most here – my own. I turned to find one of the Sasquatches charging, about to barrel through me like I was nothing.

But I wasn't nothing. In fact, I was supercharged on the blood of a seven-hundred-year-old vampire. The irresistible force met the immovable object of my fist, and I was pleased to win that contest.

The Squatch doubled over from the blow to his stomach, and I followed through with an uppercut that sent eight feet of soiled fur flying.

Oh yeah! That felt good, damn good.

Unfortunately, it was about to start feeling real bad again. I turned from my downed foe and found about a dozen more ready to converge on us.

I was about to tell my friends to run like hell. Even with Christy's magic backing us up, there was no way our odds looked good. Of my group, she and I were the only ones who stood a chance against these monsters. Hell, even Sally was going to be hard pressed to survive, unarmed as she was.

Before I could open my mouth, though, François rallied his men. They gathered round and charged the Sasquatches. Holy, crap. Who'd have guessed that in the end he would actually step up and keep his word?

"*FIGHT TO THE LAST!! DEFEND YOUR MASTER!! THE FIRST MUST SURVIVE AT ALL COSTS!!*"

Not me, that's for sure.

As soon as the compulsion left his mouth, he turned and took the fuck off, disappearing from sight before my jaw could hit the ground.

Sadly, I was in no position to hunt him down. His compulsion had taken hold of Dave, Adam, and Mike. They raced forward, heedless of the danger – screaming battle cries as if this was one of our many games. Hell, for all I knew of what was going on in their heads, maybe they thought it was.

I glanced over and saw Sally standing close by, a bit dazed, but otherwise alert. For once, I found myself glad for Alex's compulsion. Whatever he had done, it had apparently included orders preventing others from imposing their will upon her. I'd be sure to thank the asshole – maybe right after I shanked him with a stake.

That would need to wait, though. I couldn't have cared less about François's lackeys. Those fuckers could play cannon fodder all they wanted and it didn't mean shit to me, but I didn't want to see my friends charge forward into the slaughter – and a slaughter it was. Several more Sasquatches ran from the nearby trees, disengaging from whatever chaos had sent them scrambling so as to provide backup to their brethren.

"Help me stop them!" I screamed at my two coherent friends before launching myself forward.

Thank goodness for being amped up, because I managed to overtake Dave before he'd done more than get to the rear of François's chicken-shit offensive.

There was no time to fuck around. I drove a fist into the back of his head and he went down, lights out. Not a second too soon. Several flashes of light caught my attention as at least three of the compelled vamps were torn limb from limb, bursting aflame as they died.

Christy had my six. A beam of sickly green power lanced out from her, striking Adam in the back. He convulsed for a moment and then collapsed in a heap. Sadly, her second shot went wide, missing Mike and gouging a chunk from the ground where he'd stood just a moment before. Damnit!

Now where was ... shit! I turned back to find one of the beasts had snuck up from the rear and engaged Sally. It had her on her knees, clubbing away as she tried to mount a defense.

My indecision cost me, because in the split second I hesitated, two of François's men were knocked back and sent flying into me.

I went down, low man on the pile, as the sounds of battle intensified all around us.

I shoved the stunned vamps off me and took a look around. Much to my delight, Sally had rallied. Claws extended, she waited until the Sasquatch had raised both of its fists so as to pummel her into paste, and then slashed upward – right into the monster's crotch.

Ouch.

He instantly became a she, and it doubled over screeching in pain. That was one, now to...

"DEFILERS!"

Oh crap. I spun to see Mike, still compelled to action, leap into the fray – right into the arms of no less than three waiting Feet.

Nothing, not even Alex's power, would have given me enough speed to reach him in time. I watched, helpless, as he disappeared beneath a torrent of massive fists – the telltale flash of light letting me know that it was all over for him.

No!

This was my fault. I'd dragged them out of Newark with promises of a grand adventure. I'd sacrificed my friends so as to save the nameless strangers they'd been preying upon. To save people from the monsters they'd become, I'd perhaps become something even worse.

There was nothing I could do for Mike, but I could still avenge him, save the others, and then find François and put my foot up his craven ass.

The two lackeys that had gotten thrown into me began to shake off the blow and rise. I kicked one in the head and then dragged the other to me.

Before she'd been mind-wiped, Sally had tested a theory about my powers. It had proven quite useful then, and it was going to prove even more useful now.

I sank my teeth into the vampire's neck and drank deep, letting his power bolster the already massive burst of strength I had flowing through my body.

Unlike back at Pandora, François's men weren't youngsters barely a few years old. I drank from the one, shoved him back into the fight, and then took blood from his friend – feeling their centuries enter me, pushing my abilities past even François's frightening strength.

One of the Feet broke through and came at me as I finished my snack break. He swung a club-sized fist at my face, and I caught it with my own hand as if it were in slow motion.

I spun, gave its arm a twist, and heard the crack of bone.

I lifted the beast over my head, its fur slick and ... well, gross, and threw it into an onrush of its friends, bowling them over.

Glancing around, I saw that François's forces had been reduced to a few stragglers and now the monsters were turning my way. They thought it was over. They were wrong.

I was going to give them a fight to remember. They'd been on their way south to face Vehron, but they were going to learn that there was more than one Freewill worth fearing in this world. They were going to sing songs of the time they...

...were all struck down by arrows?

What the fuck?

# 36

# NOT YOU AGAIN!

It had been me in a heroic last stand against maybe eight of the ugly monsters. Then, without warning, the air had filled with the sound of things going *thpppt*.

Before I knew what had happened, all of the Feet in front of me fell to the ground, arrows and crossbow bolts sticking out of their faces, necks, and torsos.

I spun to find Christy and Sally back to back, looks of confusion upon their faces. They'd been prepared to defend each other, to fight off monsters that were all now dead or dying.

I didn't pretend to think we'd won. From the smell in the air, Turd had a lot more *things* at his disposal, but for a moment, the area around us was disturbingly still.

Then multiple roars of anger rose up from the surrounding forest, screeches of rage that told me the main force of our enemies was very much still alive. Standing around gawking wasn't going to get our asses out of this fire.

Sally looked at me and held up her hands to indicate she had no idea what was going on. That wasn't promising.

I took a deep breath through my nose, almost retching at

Sasquatch stink, and forced my way through it to try to pick up other scents. Trees, my friends, more trees ... maybe a squirrel or two. That was it. I didn't sense anything else. The fuck? Was this place haunted or something?

Ghosts or not, the Feet definitely weren't alone in their outrage. Voices rose up from the trees behind us in answer — more battle-cries, but these weren't the screams of monster apes. A horn sounded from somewhere close by and orders were shouted.

The voices sounded human.

No, wait — make that more than human. Though I didn't recognize the words themselves, their guttural cadence struck a primal cord deep inside of me. I'd heard that language spoken before. It was Chinese or maybe Mandarin, or what-ever the fuck they spoke in Mongolia. I don't know. I took two fucking years of Spanish in high school and that was it. When the UN put out job postings for interpreters, I was most definitely not at the top of their call list.

All I knew was that I suddenly found myself in the middle of the party I least wanted to attend in this world. Turd on one side, François on the other, and now...

Speak of the little devil and she shall appear.

A squad of armored warriors burst from the trees with a battle cry. Swords, spears, and crossbows were their weapons of choice. As they passed us, another group of Sasquatches emerged from the far end of the village to engage them. Jesus Christ, we were in the middle of fucking *Apocalypse Now*, the director's cut.

"Beloved!" a voice cried from near the tree line where the warriors had just emerged.

Had Gan not spoken, I might have remained in blissful ignorance. I still registered no scent from her brethren. The hell?

As for her, she was decked out in a miniature version of

the fur-lined armor her people wore. A saber hung from her side and she held a ridiculously large bow in one hand. Strapped to her back was a wicked-looking spiked mace. If I hadn't been aware of her power, I'd have certainly thought she might tip over from the extra weight.

"Well, she *did* say she'd see you soon," Christy said, stepping to my side, a grimace on her face. "Guess she's a murderous hell-spawn of her word."

"Lucky me," I replied.

This was still no place for us to be. Gan's forces seemed to have the upper hand, no doubt thanks to the element of surprise – they'd certainly surprised the shit out of me. But there was no telling how long it would last. There was no sign of Turd, but I had a feeling when he reappeared, it would be in force.

Sally ran over and helped me get Dave and Adam back to their feet. Both were still dazed from being roughed up, but their eyes told me that the moment they got an opportunity they'd probably go right back to following François's asshole orders. Well, fuck that. It wouldn't last long, but right now, there was a bigger dog in these woods than him.

"*SNAP OUT OF IT!!*"

Gan reached us just as my friends did as told, their eyes clearing and looks of confusion taking over.

"No time to discuss things. We need to get out of here," I explained to them.

"That was marvelous, beloved," Gan said, making my skin crawl with her insane devotion. "You are truly coming into your power."

A not-so-small part of me was tempted to use and abuse that power, maybe compel her to forget ever meeting me. That would be nice.

At the same time, I couldn't deny that she'd just saved my ass – *again*. Holy crap. When this was all over and done with, I'd owe her for so many times that the only way to repay her would probably be to marry her. Hell, she probably planned it that way.

"Where did you come from?" Sally asked her.

Gan glanced sidelong at her for a moment, as if studying a bug under glass, before turning back to me. "I see your whore is still compelled."

"Why do you keep calling me that?"

Gan ignored her, though. "Sadly, as marvelous a display of strength as that was, I fear it will still not be enough to undo Alexander's mischief."

Fuck! Well, there went that theory. Unfortunately, it didn't look like there were many more of François's men around to bite. There were Gan's forces, but I had a feeling they might take offense to that, not to mention they were armed to the fucking teeth.

Still, nothing ventured, nothing gained.

"***YOU TOO!!***" I compelled at Sally.

She staggered and, for a moment, her eyes glazed before clearing.

"Remember anything?" I asked.

A partial answer came in the form of a fist to my jaw. Thankfully, with the stolen power racing through my system, I barely flinched from the impact.

"Yeah, I remember that you're a fucking asshole," she snapped.

"That's it?"

"Sorry. All you did was give me a goddamned migraine."

Trying to mask my disappointment, I turned back to Gan.

"I told you, beloved," she said, sounding about as emotional as if she'd predicted rain and instead gotten sunshine.

"So you did." No point in dwelling on my failure. "So

how *did* you find us? How did you get here? Hell, are you even here? I'm standing three feet away from you, but I can't smell a thing from you or your troops."

She laughed. "Ah, my love. When this is over, I shall enjoy schooling you in the ways of war. The Alma's sense of smell is superior even to ours. One does not engage them without proper preparations. Here." She pulled a small bladder from a pocket and handed it to me. "One of my herbalists prepared that. Apply it to your body, and your scent will be masked for half a day."

"Thanks. Is this enough for all of us?"

Gan looked at my friends, pretty much dismissing Adam and Dave, then at Sally, and finally, she narrowed her eyes at Christy. "I suppose. Although it would last longer if you were to perhaps reconsider your alliance with the witch."

"Don't start with me," Christy said, her eyes flashing red. "I still owe you for Harry."

"Yes, and you likewise still owe me for dealing with the Magi who had accused you of treason. If anything, I would say your debt is fulfilled. Mine, however, is not."

"Enough!" I said, getting between them. Goddamn, would these two ever kiss and make up? On second thought, perhaps I didn't really want to see that. Pushing that disturbing image from my mind, I quickly changed subjects. "You still haven't said how you found me."

Once more, a bright smile creased Gan's face. "I have had my people watching you ever since the trial."

"But we teleported out of there..."

"And straight back to your home. A mere child could have predicted that."

Apparently, one had. "Fine. But what about you showing up here? You had no way of knowing we'd be up in Salem. What, do you have me bugged or something?"

Gan appeared to consider this for a moment. "That is

an excellent idea, my love. I shall have to consult with my advisors on it. However, no, not at this time. We did, however, track you to the farmhouse you stayed in for two days."

"And..."

"And it was a minor matter to abduct a handful of the Templar and torture the information out of them."

Well, that was one mystery solved. At least Sheila wasn't here to listen to this. "You couldn't have just knocked and asked?"

"Alexander's orders were more than clear on the matter. So as to not arouse suspicion, I thought it best to keep my forces in check until such time as you needed my assistance."

"Until such time?"

"You do have a singular talent for walking into situations which you are not even remotely prepared for. Such childish ignorance is endearing in you. I will almost be saddened when you finally learn otherwise."

Sally chuckled, drawing a glare from me.

"Fine," I grumbled. "We can discuss this later. For now, we need to get the fuck out of here."

"Very well," Gan said. "You are welcome to stay by my side, beloved. It would be an honor to dispatch our foes together."

"Uh yeah, maybe next time," I replied. "Two of my friends are missing and..."

"As you wish," she said with a shrug. "I can tarry no longer. My men require my leadership if we are to win this day. I shall find you when the battle is over."

Judging by the way her people were fighting, I sincerely doubted they needed the leader of the Lollipop Guild at their vanguard, but I wasn't about to say shit. Her reappearance had been beyond creepy. She'd graduated from infatuated to full-on stalker mode. It made me glad that I didn't keep pets, for I'd surely find them boiling on the stove when I got home.

Hmm, considering what she thought of humans, that didn't bode well for my roommates in the foreseeable future.

I looked down to find the nut job preteen still smiling up at me as if in anticipation. "Um, can I help you with something?"

"Perhaps a token of your appreciation to send me off – I believe your people often give a kiss for luck."

For one moment, I actually gave thanks that my roommates were missing and Sally was mind-fucked. Otherwise, I'm certain of the comments that would have flowed like fine wine.

Fuck it, I wasn't proud. Feigning a cough, I said, "Sorry. Think I'm coming down with something. Wouldn't want to pass it on." I began to back up. "Uh, try not to die."

My pathetic attempt at a blow-off apparently did nothing to dissuade her. Gan smiled again, waved at me eagerly, and shouted, "You too, my love! Fear not, for I shall find you soon. It is our destiny!" She turned, let out a battle screech, and raced to join her warriors.

That was all the impetus I needed to pop open the bottle of magical deodorant she'd given me.

"Not if I can help it."

## 37

# POUND PUPPIES

"That one worries me," Sally said, finishing with the de-scenting agent from our hiding spot behind one of the massive huts.

"You have no idea," I replied.

"What's in this stuff anyway?"

"Knowing Gan, you probably don't want to ask."

Sally held the bladder out to Christy, but she held up a hand.

"I don't want anything from that creature."

"Trust me," I replied, "neither do I, but if it'll help us get out of this mess..."

"I can use a glamour to mask myself," she said. "Since it's just me now, it won't take as much effort. Let's just hurry up."

"Hold on," Adam said, applying his portion of Gan's concoction. "Where's Mike?"

"Back in Newark," I replied, trying not to think about it. Fucking François. That asshole was gonna pay if we ran into him again, especially if we did so before the vampire blood I'd ingested wore off.

Before Adam could ask anything else, I pointed to him and Dave. "You two go with Christy." She raised a questioning eyebrow. "Oh, don't look at me that way. I know better than to stop you from trying to find Tom."

"You're going after Ed?" she asked.

"Yeah. We can't risk leaving and then coming back for him. We need to grab his ass now and haul ours. Sally and me will find him and then rendezvous with the four of you." I glanced at Sally. "That okay with you?"

"Not really sure I want to risk my life for one human."

Her blunt reply caught me by surprise, but then James's warning again echoed in my head. I pushed it aside for now, though. Time enough to consider that later. "One human who everyone else seems to want. Besides, that's my cub you're talking about."

Sally looked as if she was about to protest again, but then just said, "Fine. But you're carrying junior if we need to run."

"Sound like a plan, everyone?"

"Not yet," Christy replied. I thought she was about to argue with me since she wasn't overly fond of Dave, but instead, she said, "Give me your arm." Using one of her fingernails, she cut her own wrist and dabbed a finger into the blood.

I recognized what she was doing from our time in NORAD – blood magic. "Good idea."

"It makes sense to do so." She drew a bloody symbol on her forearm and then did the same on mine. "You won't be able to smell us and the unnatural growth might interfere with my ability to scry you quickly. This way, it'll lead us straight to you if ... *once* we find Tom."

She'd been all business, but in that moment, I saw the deep worry in her eyes. I put a hand on her shoulder. "Relax. He's fine. Probably hasn't even realized we're gone. Just try to not let him rob that place completely blind, okay?"

She met my eyes and a small smile creased her face. "Thanks, Bill."

"No problem." I turned to Dave and Adam. "Keep her safe. As leader of the Defilers, I command it. Oh, and Christy, you might want to put something on that cut. Sanitary, this place is not."

"Not an issue," she replied with a wry grin. She lifted a finger, and it glowed red as she used it to cauterize the wound shut.

Yeah, I definitely needed to stay on her good side.

"Get down," Sally hissed as she dragged me next to her.

Searching through the Sasquatch encampment felt oddly right. Not prowling through a den of monsters who wanted us dead, mind you. No, that part was as fucking stupid as they come. It was Sally and me working together. Despite her memory loss and the warnings I'd gotten, a part of me was still certain that, together, we could do anything.

Thankfully, we didn't need to. We just needed to find one human in the crowd – the proverbial needle in a haystack. Fortunately, I had the equivalent of a high-grade metal detector. My senses, still amped high as fuck on vampire blood, were more than up to the task.

Even though our scents were currently masked from the Feet, that didn't mean my nose had stopped working. If anything, it was putting in some overtime – Sally normally smelled damn good, but with the masking agent doing its job, those distractions were at a minimum. With all the Sasquatch stink in the air, it still wasn't a pleasant task. More than once, I had to wipe tears from my eyes when their pungent odor became overbearing, but it was necessary.

It was also fruitful, as I was able to lock on to Ed's scent after just a few minutes.

Though all the Sasquatch huts looked the same to me, we were able to find the one he'd been dragged into by virtue of my nostrils.

Now, hunkered down behind some brush, we waited for the perfect moment to make our move.

Gan's forces had certainly succeeded in causing chaos. Though I had no idea how many warriors she had with her, the surprise attack had left the Feet in disarray. The monster apes raced back and forth through our line of sight. Some were in formation and had the bearings of disciplined troops. Others, however, appeared to be just as confused as I would be in such a situation.

The problem was in their numbers. As strong as my body felt with the added power boost, I still didn't fancy rumbling with a dozen or so of these fucks no matter how disorganized they might be.

Sadly, time wasn't on our side. I had no idea how long my current boost would last; therefore, waiting for the perfect moment wasn't in the cards.

Well, okay, the perfect moment would have been if Turd had given up and marched all of his troops home. Since that didn't seem likely, though...

"Now," Sally said.

"Huh?"

"It's not going to get any better. Let's fucking do this."

The area in front of us was mostly clear – "mostly" being the keyword there. Three of the brutes had gathered and were busy chattering among themselves. Better yet, they were all veritable runts of the litter, maybe no more than seven feet tall. Hah! That still made them all the size of Andre the Giant. What a world we lived in where I considered that to be favorable odds. "Maybe we should give it a few..."

Sally was already on the move, though. Fuck me! But then again, maybe she was right. Better to jump into a winnable fight than lose an opportunity that might not come again.

Well, hopefully, it was winnable.

By the time I stepped out from our cover, she'd closed half the distance between us and them. Yeah, well, fuck that noise. She might be fast, but she wasn't turbocharged. I put on a burst of speed, accelerating so quickly that I was certain the soles of my sneakers would melt.

I caught up to her just as she leapt at the nearest of our foes. That left two for me. I could do this.

The beasts heard us coming at the last second, and one spun to meet me just as I was about to tackle it. Ugh! Something soft, fleshy, and hairy hit my face, blotting out my vision as I plowed into the creature and drove it into its friend.

Bones snapped and both of them cried out as we all went down, me on top. I excised myself from what I realized, much to my horror, was a pair of flappy Sasquatch breasts.

Oh crap. We'd just attacked a trio of Bigfoot women. Ugh! I never thought a little T&A would ever be such a turn off. Even so, it caught me by surprise. I backed off, hesitating in what I knew I had to do.

"Get with the fucking program," Sally snarled, stepping past me and delivering a vicious boot to the face of the one I'd taken down.

"But they're…"

"Chivalry is dead, dipshit, and so are these things." She extended her claws and sank them into the neck of the third as it was trying to scramble its way out from beneath its fallen friend.

I backed up a step, then glanced to the side. The first Sasquatch lay dead. Sally's attack had been quick, efficient, and messy as all fuck. Mercy had never been a part of the equation.

"Please don't tell me you were going all soft on these things just because they had tits."

"Well, no. I just wasn't expecting it."

"Two things," she said, stepping up to me. She held up a bloody hand, index finger raised. "One, that weaker sex bullshit doesn't apply in the supernatural world." Her middle finger joined the first. "And two, pretending that it does *really* pisses me off. Are we clear?"

"Crystal."

"Good, so let's cut the crap and go get your meatwad of a friend."

I had never given thought to what a Sasquatch nursery would be like. Seeing one now, it made me really rethink ever wanting kids of my own. I remember attending kindergarten. I also have a few younger cousins. Little kids are loud, messy, sticky, and pretty much all around stupid.

Now imagine those kids at least five feet tall, covered in matted fur, and smelling like they just spent the day making mud pies out of dog shit.

That's pretty much the sight that greeted us when we entered the now unguarded hut. The hoots and grunts coming from within were now more distinct than the sounds of battle outside. As we stepped in, though, silence descended as half a dozen pairs of wide eyes turned our way.

Great! First a couple of chicks, and now I had to beat the snot out of Sasquatch children. Some legendary vampire warrior I was. What was next, pimp-slapping a newborn?

Thankfully, the adolescents in the room didn't appear to want to fight us any more than I did them. After a few seconds of silent staring, they screeched in terror and retreated to a far corner where they all stood huddling and – ewww – pissing themselves in fear.

"It's about fucking time!"

The voice was familiar; Ed's obviously, but the form wasn't.

For a moment, I thought it might be my eyes, but then I remembered that the dim light of the hut wouldn't mean shit to my vampiric vision. "What the fuck did they do to you?"

Behind me, I could hear Sally try, and fail, to contain a snort of laughter.

Ed walked toward us, looking none too pleased. "Well, first they tore off my clothes. Said they smelled bad. Then, after I protested that I wasn't all too keen on my dick swaying in the wind, they gave me this wonderful *outfit*." He pointed to the filthy-looking garment – a deer hide maybe – tied around his waist. "Oh, and just because they could, my *litter mates* over there decided to finger paint on me, except they don't stock paint in this daycare so they used..."

"I get the picture."

He stepped up to me, the look on his face one of pure murder. "*Do you?*"

"Relax, Tarzan," I said. "You look ... *fine.*"

"That's one word for it," Sally added, smirking in the gloom of the place. "But let me just be the first to say, if you're thinking about hugging us as way of thanks for our daring rescue, do yourself a favor and don't. You'll live longer. Trust me."

# 38

# THE MONSTER SQUAD

"So what's the plan?"

"What do you think, Mowgli?" I replied. "We get the fuck out of here."

"I know that, dickhead. More specifically."

"We're heading back to the house," Sally said. "Christy and the others went there to find Tom."

"Yeah," I added. "With any luck, they made it with no problems and found him. If so, we can meet up with them and teleport the fuck out of here."

We scrambled through the brush, having finally left the Sasquatch encampment. As feared, Ed's clothes had been shredded, leaving him stuck in his jungle boy attire until we could find something better. At least we'd found his shoes still relatively intact. One of the Sasquatch toddlers had been using them as a chew toy. Teeth marks aside, it was a fuckload better than running barefoot through the woods.

Screeches, cries, and occasional gunfire – guess Gan had brought more than just medieval toys to the party – still sounded, but they were to our back. With any luck, the worst was behind us.

Yeah, one should never even think something like that. It's an instant invitation for fate to flip you a big middle finger.

And this middle finger was big indeed.

One moment, we'd stepped into a clearing so as to gather our bearings, and the next, the scent of Sasquatch surrounded us – appearing as if out of nowhere.

Fuck! I'd forgotten they had some magical affinity for the forest and could use it in ways that I had no fucking clue about. Four Sasquatches stepped out from behind the trees surrounding us. That was bad enough, but then a fifth, bigger and uglier than the rest, joined his brothers.

Turd wore a bandolier of skulls, similar to the one he'd worn up in the Woods of Mourning, although it was a fair bet he didn't have an iPod hidden in them this time.

"*Stupid, T'lunta,*" he growled, drool pouring over his bottom lip. "*You no escape Turd.*"

How the fuck was he here? Sally and I were doused in Gan's potion. We smelled absolutely neutral. He couldn't have sniffed us ... oh shit. I glanced at Ed, standing there smelling ripe as a month-old pile of fruit.

As if in confirmation of this, Turd smiled. "*Your cub. Or now Turd's cub.*" He clasped his hands behind his back, an almost human-looking gesture. "*Stupid cub. Turd would have raised you well. Now Turd think he smash your skull instead.*"

"All things considered, asshole," Ed replied, "I'd sooner go with the smashed skull."

"Really?" Sally asked.

"It's just a figure of speech."

"*Perhaps Turd will keep T'lunta's mate as his own.*"

Sally raised an eyebrow and turned to Ed. "I see what you mean about preferring the smashed skull."

"Oh, c'mon," I protested, "I thought girls like you were always on the lookout for a sugar daddy."

"Syrup *is* a six-billion-dollar industry," Ed casually remarked.

Sadly, the mention of his busted deal with François did not go over well with Turd. He let out a roar of rage and swung a fist – shattering a nearby tree into splinters. "*Leave.*"

Huh? Did he mean us?

"*Mighty Turd?*" one of the other Sasquatches asked.

Oh yeah. Guess that was just wishful thinking on my part.

"*Leave!*" Turd repeated. "*T'lunta, she-T'lunta, and cub are mine.*"

Great. At least we were going to die as one big happy family.

Without a single word of protest, the four Sasquatch reinforcements stepped behind nearby trees and disappeared from sight. All trace of them, even their scent, was gone.

That definitely changed the odds a bit. We went from being outnumbered five to three, to – well, probably still being outnumbered. Pumped up as I was on all the vampire blood I'd ingested – and I had a feeling my time was running short there – I still didn't like our odds.

"What do we do?" Ed asked.

"*We* don't do anything. Stay the fuck out of this. Let Sally and me handle it."

"Sounds like a plan," she said. "This asshole doesn't look so tough."

"Let me guess. You don't remember the last time we fought him."

"Should I?"

"Probably best you don't."

"*Enough talk!*" Turd roared, eloquent as ever. The monster ape charged us, giving me a momentary feel for what it felt like to be in the path of a runaway train.

Thankfully, it only lasted a moment. Sasquatches like Turd had an advantage when it came to size, strength, and being scary as all fuck, but they couldn't match a vampire's speed.

Mind-wiped or not, Sally dove out of his way. I grabbed Ed and did the same in the opposite direction. Turd flew past us, unable to stop his forward momentum in time.

Sadly, I landed atop Ed – made all the more uncomfortable by his current state of undress. Why couldn't this shit ever happen when it was a hot chick wrapped in a dirty deer pelt? Fuck it, my fantasies weren't picky.

"Run!"

"It's dark," he complained. "I can't see shit. Where the fuck should I run to?"

"For starters, anywhere but here would probably be good."

"Fuck that. I'm not leaving..."

Another roar of rage interrupted him and I glanced up just in time to see about ten feet of tree trunk flying at us. I grabbed hold of Ed again and rolled us out of the way a split second before it smashed into the ground where we'd been lying just a moment earlier.

Ed looked to where it landed, then back at me wide-eyed. "On second thought, you might have a point."

"No shit. Now run, Forrest, run!"

Ed might have been loyal to a fault, but he wasn't stupid. Without his shotgun, he knew he was essentially useless in this fight. The best he could hope to do was bleed all over Turd and, since neither of us had any clue whether that would do jack shit to a Sasquatch, that seemed a poor strategy at best.

We both got back to our feet just as Sally tackled Turd from the side. He barely budged, taking a step at most before swatting her away like a fly.

Shit!

"She'll be fine. Go!" I gave him a shove before he got any bright ideas. "We'll find you later." The way he smelled, it wouldn't be hard. There was also no way I could concentrate on this fight with him around. Thankfully, he finally got the hint.

As I turned to face Turd, I heard Ed's footsteps retreating behind me.

"Just you and me now, cupcake," I said, hoping he wasn't about to pound me into batter.

What happened next was a whirlwind of movement. Turd would swing at me with his boulder-sized fists, I'd do my best to duck or block, and then throw one of my own. Thankfully, Turd's style of fighting was of the crude "keep hitting something until it stops moving" variety. Every punch was a haymaker, but that also meant it was telegraphed from a half mile away, allowing me to use my speed to parry the worst of it.

I got a few blows in, eliciting some angry grunts from Turd. It wasn't quite a fair fight, strength-wise, but I had enough firepower backing me to be effective.

"Hey, fuck-face!" a voice said.

Turd turned his head toward the sound just in time for a

good-sized rock to smash into his face. Sally was back in the game!

Sadly, I think the rock got the worst end of that deal. I wasn't about to ignore the opportunity for a cheap shot, though. I stepped forward and brought up my fist in an uppercut that was meant to send Turd's balls into his chin.

Much to my dismay, though, he picked that moment to stumble forward. The horror was twofold. His bigfoot-sized junk smashed into my face, and my punch flew wide from its intended target, landing somewhere moist and tight – oh so tight. It was only then that I realized the ugly truth of my predicament.

Oh, sweet merciful God, no! My hand was stuck in Turd's ass!

*"Get away, T'lunta! Turd already have enough mates."*

What?! Sadly, I couldn't respond with anything appropriately pithy. Otherwise, I would have ended up with a mouthful of Sasquatch dick.

"What the hell are you doing, Bill?"

Oh great, now I was gonna hear it from Sally too.

I was tempted to stay where I was and let Turd pummel me to death. Surely that would have been a kinder fate, but alas, I still had friends to save.

Before Turd could bring his massive fists down upon me, I dropped to my knees and excised myself from his rear orifice. My hand pulled free with a disturbing *schlupp* sound and I knew that no amount of paper towels would be enough to wipe Turd's ass-grease from it.

When, oh when, will the world stop shitting on me?

Apparently not yet, for, just then, I caught a massive kick to the chest. I exhaled a cloud of blood as my ribs shattered and I flew back, helpless to do anything except skid along the forest floor until my body came to rest.

I expected to be back on my feet within a few seconds at most, but instead, my body took its sweet time to heal.

Oh no! Not now.

Another roar sounded and only then did the burden of breathing begin to slowly lessen. My stolen power was rapidly leaving me, the last of it exerted in a move that had netted the end result of giving a rectal exam to my foe – not quite the game ender I had hoped for.

"Chew on this, you hairy fuck!"

Shit! I couldn't let Sally face off against that monster alone. As quick and brutal as she was, she didn't stand a chance. Turd was a walking brick wall. Short of some heavy firepower, there wasn't much she was going to do except piss him off even more.

*You need my help.*

Huh?

*You heard me.*

Dr. Death had been silent ever since my rebuke of his attitude toward Sheila. I hadn't been sure if he'd gone back to sleep in my head or was just sulking. Regardless, he was obviously paying attention.

"I'm not..."

She *needs my help.*

As if to emphasize this, a cry of pain rang out – Sally. I struggled to sit up, my healing finally catching up to the damage inflicted. Sadly, that was it. I felt certain that effort had used up the last of the power I'd stolen from François and his minions.

Unfortunately, now was when I needed it most. Sally had done her part to keep Turd off me when I'd fallen, but she'd paid for it.

She staggered, holding a hand to her side, through which blood flowed freely. Though she still managed to dodge the mammoth-sized monster, it was only a matter of time. She slowed with every step, even if she was still defiant, managing to throw out, "That all you got, pussy?"

I took a step, feeling my insides shifting around uncomfortably.

*You can't win this alone.*

He was right. Templars, a misunderstanding with Sheila ... hell, any of the crap of the past week – that stuff I could handle. But this? Had I not dallied, perhaps I could have taken him, but now there was no chance. Even taking a sip of Sally's blood wouldn't get me anywhere close to where I needed to be.

But Dr. Death could.

"Our deal?" I asked quietly.

*Still in play. You let me out and we'll do this together.*

Turd sniffed the air and then turned toward me. For a moment, I thought he was going to charge again, but then he grinned – showing off his massive canines. "*Good. Freewill T'lunta can watch as Turd crush his mate. Then Turd crush you next.*"

He turned his back on me, writing me off as no longer a threat. It was a mistake, one I'd make sure he'd regret.

"Let's do this."

*Are you sure?*

"We need to stop him. Teach him a lesson. Just tell me what I have to do."

*Nothing. Just let it happen. Let the rage flow.*

I did as he said. It wasn't hard. Although Turd hadn't been responsible for everything bad that had ever happened to me, he held stock in his fair share. The whole sham in the Woods of Mourning, trying to kill my friends, starting the war that threatened to engulf the world. All of it fell on his shoulders.

As these thoughts crossed through my mind, I began to

see red – the world around me appearing as if it were bathed in blood.

I shuddered, letting the anger fill me, taking over, starting the change.

Just as it began to take hold, crossing the point of no return, a moment of clarity hit me. I had no idea what would come next, but one thing was certain: I was afraid.

At that thought, a low chuckle rumbled through my mind.

*You should be.*

# 39

# WAR OF THE GARGANTUAS

There was no time to wonder what Dr. Death meant. I fell to my knees, then to all fours as I experienced the odd sensation of every square inch of my flesh rippling. My clothes, up until now a comfortable fit, suddenly felt way too tight.

It wasn't just all in my mind either. The distinct sound of fabric tearing met my ears, now as sensitive as they had been under the influence of François's blood. No, more so. I began to hear sounds that I shouldn't have – Turd's stomach gurgling from something he'd ate, Sally's labored breathing, Ed's footsteps, faint and still retreating but audible nevertheless.

My glasses slipped from my face and fell into the dirt, yet when I looked down everything was still in clear focus. The claws at the tips of each of my fingers expanded beyond their normal size, turning into cruel talons that I somehow knew would rend flesh and bone as easily as paper.

My mouth opened of its own accord and I let out a snarl, feeling my canines extend until they felt like sabers that would tear my lips to shreds if I dared try to close my mouth.

Turd's heartbeat sped up at the sound and he turned back toward me, his eyes widening ever so slightly.

*"Freewill T'lunta. Turd remembers you this way."*

I meant to reply, "Then you remember what happened last time," but for some reason, all that escaped was a feral growl.

I stood, not remembering giving my nerves the signal to. When I faced Turd, he still towered over me, but not by as much. I'd changed, but I was still me inside. Holy crap, Dr. Death hadn't been shitting me after all.

I made to glance down, take a look at what I'd become, but my eyes continued to focus on Turd. That's when the worry took hold. I tried to flex my fingers, but nothing happened.

My mouth opened and a word, barely a whisper, escaped. "Sucker."

*"Turd not sucker. Turd chieftain. Turd your killer!"*

The pity was, I had a feeling Dr. Death's decree hadn't been aimed at him.

*Wait, you said...*

"I lied," a voice – mine, yet not – answered.

*But you're a part of me.*

"Obviously the better part," he replied.

Although my eyes remained focused on Turd, I caught a glimpse of Sally beyond him, her mouth agape. Whether it was in surprise or fear, I didn't know, but I hoped it was the latter.

I wanted to shout for her to run, but instead, my body did the running – straight at Turd.

Everything seemed to be moving in slow motion, but then I realized it was just him. I could see every movement he made, every ripple of every muscle, every hair on his body fluttering in the breeze. It was pretty wild. Sort of like having spider-sense.

He hesitated ever so slightly, so minor I would have never noticed – even hopped up on blood as powerful as François's. Yet now it was plain as day, as if I'd been blind to not notice such things.

Then he sprang into savage action, throwing a fist in my – our – direction. The thing was, even that seemed to move at a ridiculously slow pace. It was as if I could have sat down and read a book in the time it took him to throw the haymaker.

My left arm came up, and I marveled at the torn sleeve and bulging muscles. Hell, if I didn't know that it was attached to me, I would have thought a professional wrestler had just stepped in to be my personal bodyguard.

Either way, Dr. Death easily deflected the blow. It was weird. I couldn't control any part of me, save my thoughts, yet I could feel it all. That was one really fucking strange sensation – like wearing someone else's meat suit while they drove.

Sadly, pain was a part of the deal too. Turd and I locked arms, each trying to force the other back. I wanted to cry out to Dr. Death, tell him to watch what the fuck he was doing, but if he heard me, it was ignored.

Turd opened his mouth and bit down upon my shoulder, his teeth sinking to the bone. Motherfucker! It hurt like a son of a bitch. Worse, who the fuck knew what germs were swimming around in that guy's mouth? Vampire healing was great and all, but some things were beyond gross.

Dr. Death merely laughed. Dude had one fucked-up sense of humor.

My jaw opened wide, obviously under orders from the new landlord, and I saw what he was planning.

*Don't do it!*

I chomped down on Turd, in the spot where his massive head met his shoulders. Sadly, in addition to pain, I also got to experience the wonderful sensation of taste. I swear, if I live to be a thousand, I will never ever forget the taste of Turd. Pity that my gag reflex wasn't under my control because I would have loved nothing better than to puke my guts up at that point.

As if to rub it in, my tongue washed over the bloody fur I was biting into.

*You're a real fucking asshole, know that?*

There we stood, fighting back and forth – each taking a chunk out of the other and refusing to let go. I swallowed, a goodly amount of flesh and blood slithering down my throat. At least Sasquatch blood didn't taste like the rest of them. I can't say I would have been happy living off a diet of it, but I'd tasted worse.

Sadly, no power boost came from it, but then, it didn't seem like Dr. Death needed one. Little by little, Turd gave ground. It seemed an impossible task, yet I was forcing him back.

Or at least I was until Turd used his superior height and leverage to lift me off the ground and throw me.

Dr. Death refused to let go easily, though, so along with us came a chunk of Turd's immense tricep hanging from my mouth.

We landed twenty feet away, rolled with it, and bounced back to our feet nimbly. Goddamn, it was weird to think about myself in third person. Made me feel like I should have been wearing a lucha libre mask or something.

*Okay, you've made your point. Put me in control now before you do something stupid.*

"Stupid? You're one to talk."

*You let Turd take a chunk out of us! Is that your plan, to keep biting each other and see who falls first?*

"Might be." We glanced to our left, and I saw my arm whole again. The shoulder had been torn out of my shirt and jacket, but the flesh beneath it showed no sign of having been wounded. Hell, I hadn't even noticed the pain was gone, it had been so fast.

Okay, so maybe as far as plans went, it wasn't *that* bad.

Turd wasn't faring nearly as well. He stood there, several paces away, his hand over the gaping wound we'd left where we'd bitten down. It wasn't fatal by any stretch, but it looked like it hurt like a motherfucker. Can't say I felt too bad for him.

*"Turd done playing. Now T'lunta die!"*

The ugly asshole threw back his head and let out a sighing howl.

"What the hell's he doing?"

I glanced to my side and saw Sally had made her way over to me. What the fuck? Had she gone insane? Didn't she see that I wasn't in control?

"No idea. Let's find out," Dr. Death replied, sounding quite reasonable.

I guess she didn't realize it. The old Sally would have probably sensed something was wrong. She knew me too well to be fooled, or I thought she did anyway. This new, mind-wiped Sally, however, didn't seem to realize that what Dr. Death had just said was far from my normal mannerisms. I wasn't one to stand by and wait for the enemy to power-up to Super Saiyan 3.

And that seemed to be what Turd was doing. I'd thought maybe he'd been calling for reinforcements. He was, but they weren't from anyone else. His body shimmered and, for a moment, it was hard to tell him from the forest behind him, but then I saw him change – adding an extra foot in height.

Bony protrusions burst from his body, covering him in armor of sorts. He raised his arms and two more immediately grew out from his sides, each as dangerous-looking as the originals.

*Brilliant fucking move, Einstein. Shall we sit here while he runs into town and buys a howitzer too?*

"Should we run?" Sally asked, looking up at me, her eyes trailing over my form.

"No need," Dr. Death replied smoothly.

"So then what's the plan?"

*Run!*

My teeth ground together. Apparently, my other half was getting annoyed, although I wasn't sure if it was from me or her. That wasn't good. If he tried to hurt her, I'd...

"Stay out of this, darling," he replied, no trace of anger in his voice. "Papa's got some work to do."

*You didn't actually say that, did you? Christ, that was lame even by my standards.*

Dr. Death chose to ignore me, instead rushing forward again toward Turd. Oh crap. It was like being on a roller coaster, except having no idea what was coming next.

Turd smiled, both sets of hands cracking their knuckles as I came at him. This was insane. We'd wounded him, and a wounded Turd didn't sound like something I really wanted to corner.

Dr. Death had other plans, though. He took one more step and then we were airborne, sailing over Turd's outstretched arms. We did a somersault mid-air and landed behind him.

Before Turd could spin around, we kicked a leg out from under him and sent him to one knee. A punch, harder than anything I'd ever thrown before, flew into the back of the Sasquatch's head and momentarily stunned him.

Dr. Death grabbed hold of Turd's two upper arms and planted a knee in his back for leverage as he began to apply pressure.

Turd was still dangerous, but we were in a position where his other arms couldn't reach back and grab hold.

I looked up, caught sight of Sally's face on the other side of the clearing, and – holy shit – I actually winked at her. What a cock!

She gave a somewhat uncomfortable glance back and then rushed forward as Dr. Death continued to match strength with Turd, slowly pulling the big ape's arms back.

Sally, proving that she gave far more shits about fashion than fair combat, ran up and planted a kick to Turd's face.

"I thought I told you to stay out of this," Dr. Death growled, his claws now extended and digging into Turd's arms at the elbow.

Sally smiled. "Since when the fuck do I listen to what you say?"

"Since..." I could feel my own muscles straining against the massive Sasquatch, but then... ***crack*** "...now."

Turd screamed, both in rage and pain, as his two upper arms were broken. Holy shit! I wouldn't have guessed doing anything less than running him over with a semi would have done that.

Dr. Death let go of the now useless appendages and Turd flopped forward, just barely missing Sally, who jumped out of the way at the last second.

The Sasquatch pushed himself back up using his remaining two arms, but he otherwise looked to be in pretty rough shape. "*Turd kill you all,*" he growled, but it seemed to fall short of being a threat.

"He's done," Sally said. "Let's get the fuck out of here before more of them show up."

My body took a step toward her. "We're done when I say we're done."

"*Turd say you done now!*" All at once, Turd sprang back up and spun. His broken arm went flying wide, almost like a ragdoll's, but his other was the true threat. It caught us on the jaw full-on with a backhand. Our lip split and we went flying through the air.

Had I been my normal self, the blow would have sent my head in a different direction than my body. Instead, it did little more than momentarily daze me.

Sadly, that was more than enough for Turd. He shoved Sally to the side as if she were nothing and then charged us, all reason gone from his eyes, not that there had been a lot there to begin with.

*You deserved that!*

"Are you done being a distraction?" Dr. Death growled, pulling us to our feet.

*It's what I do best.* Although perhaps he did have a point. Turd winning this fight wasn't really in any of our best interests, no matter who was in control of my body.

We dove at Turd, a sloppy maneuver that did little more than land us in his arms – the working ones, sadly.

He closed them around us in a bear hug and, all at once, I knew how it felt to be stuffed into a trash compactor.

"*Now Turd crush you like bug you are.*"

I thought Dr. Death would try to power his way out, but instead, he just freed his arms, leaving Turd to continue crushing the rest of our shared form. My ribs creaked from the pressure and though the lungs of my body weren't currently under my control, I still felt the air forced out of them.

What the fuck. Was Dr. Death waiting for an invitation

or something? Eye gouge the motherfucker already. *Do something!*

"Say please." His voice was barely a whisper due to our current lack of oxygen, but there was no mistaking what he mouthed.

*What?!*

"Do it. Beg me to save us."

*Fuck you!*

"*Turd no beg. Turd eat face!*"

Oh fuck! The King Kong wannabe opened his mouth and snapped at us. Dr. Death pulled back at the last second, almost costing us a nose.

*Jesus Christ! Punch him at least!*

Again, Turd tried to take a bite, offering me a close-up view of the back of his throat.

*Okay, okay! Please kill this fucker or something.*

"Much better. Now was that so hard?"

As Turd continued to put on the pressure, enough so that I was surprised my eyes hadn't popped out of my head yet, Dr. Death finally took action. With his left hand, he held Turd's snapping jaws at bay. He then extended the claws of his right and used them to dig into the still gushing wound on Turd's neck.

Turd screamed as the razor sharp talons dug their way in. Muscle, tendons, and more gave way to the assault. Ugh, so gross, although I had to admit it was still preferable to shoving my fist up Turd's ass.

At last, when Dr. Death was elbow deep, Turd let go and tried to tear us off. Sadly for him, he was too late. My hand closed around something hard and sharp deep inside of him and squeezed.

It wasn't until the bone shattered under my grasp that I realized what it was – Turd's spine.

With a final shudder, Turd fell to his knees. For a second, he just stared at me, a mixture of hatred and confusion etched upon his stupid face. Then his eyes glazed, he fell over, and let out one last fart to let the underworld know he was on his way.

Turd had finally been flushed for good.

*Way to go! We did it!*

Dr. Death lifted a hand to our lips and licked the blood off the fingers – the act being far less pornographic than it probably sounded.

*Okay, fight's over. You can give me control again.*

My gaze shifted and I caught sight of Sally picking herself up off the forest floor and dusting herself free of dirt and pine needles.

*Yep, it sure will be great when you're a part of my subconscious again.*

"Holy shit, Bill, you did it," Sally said, walking over and standing alongside me. She gave Turd's corpse one last kick for good measure.

*Yoo-hoo! You listening to me?*

"And I have to admit," she continued, giving me a cursory once-over, "you clean up pretty well when you want to."

I did? Where was a fucking mirror when you needed one? I...

"I was never a part of you."

*What?*

"What?" Sally asked. "I didn't quite catch that."

"You thought I was a piece of you. How pathetic. As if a being as magnificent as I could ever be a subset of you."

"Bill, you okay? Something get knocked loose during the fight?" Sally chuckled, but it had an uneasy air to it. She no doubt sensed something was off ... probably because the stuff Dr. Death spouted sounded batshit crazy even to me, the guy he was conversing with.

"You know nothing of your kind," he continued. "I was dragged into you when you were turned, but unlike most, I got lucky. You were different, special, a Freewill. A means to an end, a means to be ... *free*."

He turned toward Sally. I was normally a good head taller than her diminutive frame, but now, I practically towered over her.

"Sadly, there's not enough room in the old apartment for both of us. It's time for you to get yours, but first..." He took a step toward Sally, who wisely backed up two, "...it's your turn to get what's coming to you, bitch."

*NO! Leave her alone. I swear to God I'll...*

"Time for baby boy to take a nap. Don't worry. I'll wake you when it's all over."

My vision once more turned to red, a bloody haze descending upon the world as he advanced upon Sally. Bodiless, formless, helpless, I fought against it to no avail. As the red tint deepened, blotting out all vision, closing in upon me, the last thing I saw was her eyes widening in fear.

I cried out silently without a voice to be heard and then knew no more.

**40**

## MIDNIGHT TRYST

"No. I'm not gonna let you. I'll die first."

My eyes flew open and I sat up, drawing in a huge gasp of air, feeling as if I'd been drowning.

I glanced up and saw swirls of green and dark blue. Everything was blurry as fuck, but from the color, it appeared that the sky had lightened. Apparently, dawn was approaching. Normally, that would be a point of concern, but then realization hit. I couldn't be turned to dust inside my own head, or at least I didn't think so.

Dr. Death had said something about getting rid of me. Back when Christy had been helping me to get in touch with my inner problem child, I'd threatened to blast him to bits with all sorts of sci-fi awesomeness and he'd seemed pretty goddamned afraid. Maybe all that bullshit about dying in your dreams was true in a fashion.

So, then maybe if I believed an imaginary sun could burn me to a crisp, then it would. If that happened, then Dr. Death would get the joy of owning my body forever. Except it wasn't really my body. If it was, I'd be almost tempted to let him. Somehow, it had metamorphosed into something else ... something bigger, meaner, and built for a day at the beach.

Well, fuck that shit. No way was he getting off that easily. He might have the advantage, but that didn't mean I needed to make it easy for him to snuff me out.

I sat up, marveling at how real the ground felt beneath me when a groan at my side caused me to nearly jump out of my skin.

Was the asshole already here and waiting to ... wait a second. Dr. Death didn't have blonde hair, or at least I didn't think he did. Squinting, I made out a petite form next to me, clothing in tatters, with a head of blonde hair with blue highlights.

"Sally?"

Fuck me. Was this his plan — to torture me with her image before letting me die?

"Yeah, Bill?" she asked with a barely stifled yawn.

"Get the fuck out of my head."

"What are you talking about?" She sat up and I saw that her exposed flesh — and damn, there was quite a lot of it — was covered in bruises and bite marks.

"You can stop it now."

"Okay, you're weirding me the fuck out ... even more so than a few minutes ago."

"I'm not a moron." I stood up. "I'm ... where are my pants?"

"Around, I guess. You were kind of in a hurry so you just tore them off."

Huh? Despite being in my own head, I was still too self-conscious to stand there and have a conversation with my dick flapping in the wind. I peeled off the remains of my jacket — torn to shreds as if something had burst the seams — and wrapped it around my midsection.

Wait. There was no need for this crap. "Oh, forget this." I closed my eyes and concentrated.

"What are you doing?"

"Hold on," I replied.

"You look like you need to take a shit or something and if that's the case, I'm just going to get the fuck out of here. I mean, I'm into some kinky stuff, but I have to draw the line somewhere."

"There." I opened my eyes and looked down, certain I'd be dressed again ... except that I wasn't. My clothes were in the same state of disrepair as when I'd last checked. "Why didn't it work?"

"Why didn't *what* work?"

"I willed my clothes back together."

"Is that some new Freewill power I've never heard of? I didn't realize you could create instant textiles. If I'd known that, I might not have spent two hundred bucks on this bra ... which is of course now ruined, thanks to you."

Unable to help myself, I glanced again at her, but was unable to make out nearly enough details for my personal edification. "Fuck, why couldn't I have at least made my glasses appear?"

"I think you dropped them over there."

"What?"

"When you were changing. Over there, past Turd's body. It's right ... oh never mind. I'll go find them myself."

Sally's out-of-focus form stood and adjusted her clothing as best she could. After that, she stalked off past a large brown shape.

Wait, why was Turd's corpse in my imagination? I mean, I guess Dr. Death could have been messing with me, but if so, then why not just make Turd alive again and have him chase my half-naked ass from here all the way back to Canada?

Oh, maybe *that* was his ruse. Make me think Turd was dead and then, out of nowhere, zombie Turd would rise up, craving my flabby white flesh.

While Sally was busying herself beyond the range of my clear vision, I walked over to the mound of putrid fur. Turd was fucked up beyond repair. We're talking broken arms, rent meat, a shank of vertebrae sticking out the side of his neck. Ugh! If anything, he smelled even worse in death than he had in life.

"Okay, you can cut the shit. I'm ready for the chase scene."

"What are you babbling about?" Sally called from where she was still off supposedly searching for my glasses. I only hoped Dr. Death would be sporting and allow her to find them before Turd played like a spring-loaded cat and popped up to give chase.

"Let's go, shitball." I gave him a good solid kick with sneakers barely held together by a few strands of canvas. Ouch! Even dead, the fucker was solid as a rock.

Sally walked back over, her form gradually appearing from the blurred forest around me. "Did you get your head knocked loose during the fight? Or is this just some weird ritual you always do that I don't remember?"

"Just trying to save us all a little time," I replied.

"Yeah. Anyway, here you go." She held out her hand and I was relieved to find my glasses in them. The earpiece was a little bent, but that was a quick fix. A second later, my vision was restored and ... whoa. Sally looked like one of the covers from those old men's magazines – the ones where a muscular hero fought off cannibals and killer snakes while a damsel in distress – in shredded clothes – stared helplessly from the background.

I was forced to admit, as hot as my bedroom fantasy with

her and Sheila was, this was potentially even better. "Damn, I have an awesome subconscious."

Sally sighed, her eyes narrowing. "Okay, that's enough. What the fuck are you talking about? And, I swear, if you ignore me one more time to talk to yourself, I'm going to fuck you up – and not in the fun way this time."

"Like you don't know."

Her hand shot out and she grabbed my throat. She dragged me close, lifted me off the ground, and held me with my feet dangling. "Pretend I'm stupid."

"Fair enough," I gasped.

She let go, and I landed on my feet, giving a quick cough to catch my breath. Oh well, there were probably worse ways for her to get my attention. "Fine. You're not real, none of this is."

"Oh?"

"Yeah. We're all in Dr. Death's head ... well, my head. The head we share."

"You're making zero sense."

"When Dr. Death took over, when I changed, it turns out he lied. He didn't give me control. He just let me watch. Then, when it was all over, he shoved me into the background of my own fucking mind as he was about to..." My eyes popped open wide. "Oh shit! I have to save Sally."

"I'm right here."

"The real Sally, I mean. Dr. Death was about to..."

"Wait, hold on. So you mean that wasn't you?"

"Huh?"

"During the fight?"

"No, it was him. Couldn't you tell, the way he was acting like an asshole when you were trying to help?"

"Not really. I thought maybe you'd grown a set when you changed. I mean, hell, your other form was nothing like ... you are now. No offense."

"None taken," I replied offhandedly. "How bad was it?"

"Bad?"

"Yeah. I mean, I saw my muscles and all, those were kind of cool, but I can only imagine how horrible the rest was. Was I drooling pus? Please tell me no, because that's just fucking gross."

She looked like she was contemplating things, then shrugged. "Nope, nothing gross about you. You were ... ugh, I really shouldn't say it."

"Say what?"

"You were actually pretty hot."

"Wait, hot?"

"See, I knew I shouldn't have said it. Now it's gonna go straight to your head."

"Didn't happen to get a picture, did you?"

"You see any place for me to hide a camera?"

I allowed myself another glance at her – her clothes barely clinging to all her fun lady parts. I really needed to find my pants because my makeshift kilt sure as shit wasn't going to do much to conceal the mega-boner I was about to sport.

"Err, anyway," I said, glancing away and trying to fill my head with thoughts of Turd, "after the battle, I saw him – me – advancing on you. He said you were gonna get what you deserved. Then everything went blank and I woke up here in my mind."

"You definitely got hit in the head too hard."

"Whatever. I need to wake up and rescue Sally before it's too late."

"Too late for what?"

"For me to stop him from killing you."

"You didn't kill me, genius. Hell, quite the opposite. I mean, you were a little forceful, sure, but I kinda like the rough stuff anyway..."

"Whoa there, Hoss. I'm not following."

"You mean you don't remember?"

"Like I said, Dr. Death shoved me into the back of my own mind, knocked me the fuck out. I..." I stopped and glanced down at her again, then remembered my own missing pants. "Oh God! Are you saying I *raped* you?"

"I wouldn't put it that way. I mean, it surprised the fuck out of me at first, but it's not like that's the first time I've done it following the heat of battle. If anything, there's something about a warm corpse nearby that really gets me going."

I turned away, unable to believe I'd done something so reprehensible. I was no better than the others, just an animal – a monster like the rest of them.

"You okay, Bill?"

"I'm so sorry."

"What for? No complaints here. I came."

I spun back toward her, my jaw agape. The fuck? "Are you serious? How can you be so ... nonchalant about this?"

"Don't let it go to your head. I was sorta in the moment."

"Not that! I..." Goddamn, vampires were weird.

Wait a second. This didn't add up. As bad as this was, I'd been certain the bastard had intended far worse for her. "I thought Dr. Death was going to kill you."

"You *were* a little extra bitey, I'll admit. Oh, and you did have me worried there for one little second."

"How so?"

"After you ... finished, you bared your fangs, pinned me to the ground, and raised your fist. For a moment there, I thought you were *really* into the rough shit, but then all of a sudden your eyes rolled into the back of your head. You started mumbling some weird shit, rolled off me, and then out of nowhere you shrank back down to ... you. Let me tell you, that was trippy as all fuck to watch."

"Mumbled what?"

"It was right before you started going off about being in your head. Something about not letting you do whatever, and wanting to die first. Just for the record, those aren't words a girl wants to hear in the afterglow."

Holy crap. He *was* going to kill her.

But then what stopped him?

After a moment, Sally's eyes opened wide as she apparently began to catch on. "Wait, so you're saying that wasn't you?"

"No."

"Then how did you reassert control?"

"Who knows? Maybe shooting his load affects him just like any other guy."

Sally raised a dubious eyebrow. "Or maybe it was you. I know I don't remember much, just bits and pieces, but I'm not stupid. I get the sense we're friends. Not sure how that happened, but I've seen the things you've done, the limbs you're willing to climb out on for others. Other vampires wouldn't do that sort of thing."

She was right, far more than she knew. Sally was a friend, maybe more. I still wasn't certain. What I did know, though, is that I would have died for her if need be.

Holy crap! Maybe that was it. A strong emotion could break a compulsion. Wasn't Dr. Death's control of me not entirely dissimilar? Hah! What a joke that would be. I was the Freewill, but at the end of the day, I was just vulnerable to a different type of control – one from within.

If so, maybe that made sense. If Dr. Death was truly about to kill her and some part of me was even vaguely aware, then I would have fought tooth and nail to stop it. I'd done it before. When Dr. Death had gone on a bloody rampage, I'd awoken to find my friends untouched. More than ever, I was convinced he was a murderous asshole with no love for anyone, but maybe he wasn't as fully in control as he claimed.

"Penny for your thoughts."

"I'm just trying to make sense of this shit. I think you're right about what you said. Maybe deep down there was some part of me still aware enough to fight back. But if so, then that means this is all real."

"That's what I've been trying to tell you!"

"I'm awake and in charge of me again."

"Yep."

I glanced sidelong at her. "It also means ... we sorta boned."

Her eyes narrowed and she sighed. "Pity you can't remember it. In fact, I'm pretty sure that means it never happened."

"Wait, what?"

"Let's go. We need to find the others and get the fuck out of here." She turned with an eye-roll and started walking.

I quickly caught up to her. "But it *was* good, wasn't it?"

"I guess you'll never know."

# 41

# PILLOW WALK

Sally was mum as we continued our trek away from the sounds of battle that still continued off in the distance.

As much as I didn't want to run into Gan again, I silently wished her well. Batfuck crazy that she was, she'd rushed into a lion's den to help where others had run. That one of those others was now a member of the Draculas said a lot to me.

I didn't fancy ever crossing paths with Alexander again, but if we did, I'd make it a point to bring him up to speed on François's heroism when it came to saving his own ass. Although the leader of the Draculas was a douche-canoe the size of an ocean liner, I was pretty certain his attitude when it came to battle was to lead by example. After all, one didn't become the greatest conqueror in history by making a habit of letting everyone else lead the way.

A part of me was still certain I was stuck in some sort of *Total Recall* nightmare and that the walls of reality would start melting around me at any moment. The more time that passed, though – and the lack of any Death Stars showing up in the morning sky – began to convince me that I'd somehow come out on top again.

However, there were a lot of questions left unanswered. I had my little compulsion theory, and it sort of made sense, but that still didn't tell me how it all happened. Then there was the part of Dr. Death spouting off about never being a part of me. What the fuck was up with that? I didn't recall ever being possessed. At no point during the last couple of years did I end up in a bed projectile-vomiting pea soup onto a priest. I mean, sure that was that time Tom, Ed, and I went on a bender of mind erasers and screaming Nazis, but I had a feeling those spirits were more the type to require aspirin the next day as opposed to a full-on exorcism.

As for the beast himself, he had been quiet ever since I'd woken up. Nary a peep out of him. Can't say I was sad for the silence in my head, but at the same time, I found it a bit disconcerting. It was probably too much to hope he was gone for good or lobotomized, for that matter.

I'd need to discuss this with Christy. I wasn't sure if I wanted to repeat our head-trip of an experiment, but if we did, then I'd make certain to nuke Dr. Death from orbit the next time. It was the only way to be sure. It would also prove to be fun. Some assholes just needed wiping – right off the face of the fucking planet.

Alas, that would have to wait. Sally stopped so suddenly in front of me I almost bumped into her nearly uncovered ass.

"I think we found your friend."

"Tom?"

"No, the shit-covered one that everyone seems to want for whatever reason."

That meant Ed. Poor guy would probably be consider-ably displeased to hear how Sally was referring to him. But ticked off was better than being lost in the woods of ... well, former suburbia.

Still, I'd gotten to home plate whereas he'd been able to hit a single at best when it came to her. No, that wasn't right. Ed was a friend and, my feelings for Sally aside, taking that attitude was a shitty thing to rub in his face. I probably still would, mind you, but I needed to also make sure I wasn't being a total prick to him. He'd had eyes for her first and had been making some headway before being turned into a walking vampire time bomb. "You might want to be a bit nicer to him."

"Why?"

I struggled, almost biting my tongue, but in the end, Ed's friendship meant a lot to me. I didn't care to casually stomp it into the ground, drop my pants, and take a big steaming dump on it. "I told you, you and he sorta had something going on before you got compelled."

"Were we a steady item?"

"Not that I'm aware of. I mean, I know you guys went out for coffee."

"Coffee. You don't *say*. I'm surprised we didn't move in together. I mean, going out for a cup of Joe isn't a commitment I take lightly."

"I'm serious. Oh, and don't forget what you two were doing up in Canada."

"Oh yeah. So how'd that one work out?"

"I might have interrupted."

"Freewill *and* cockblocker. Quite the resume you've got going there, champ."

"I didn't mean to."

She eyed me for a second or two, a smirk creasing her face. "Really?"

All at once, despite my lack of clothing, it began to feel

really hot beneath her gaze. "Yes ... I mean, no. I mean, I was too busy worrying about..."

Her gaze softened and she put a hand on my shoulder. "Relax, *Dr. Death*. I was kidding. Here's the thing – telling me all of this is meaningless. I remember a few things, but most of it is a jumble. Him ... he's a total blank and no, I have no idea if that means anything. How about this? Our little encounter back there aside, why don't we agree that discussions about the worlds I might or might not be contemplating rocking should probably wait. If we can break these blocks in my head, then we can talk."

"And if we can't?"

"Then we'll *all* have to start over."

If that wasn't the story of my life, then I didn't know what was.

Ed's scent, a mix of human and putrid Sasquatch ass, was pretty easy to follow from a ways off. As we trailed him, a tingle lit up my forearm. "What the...?"

"What's wrong?" Sally asked idly, still facing the way we were headed.

"Not sure. Think something bit me." Okay, that was silly, although it did lead one to wonder what would happen to any mosquito dumb enough to land upon a vamp. I mean, they were already like little vampires as it was. Gah! I didn't have time for stupid thoughts like that.

I glanced down at my arm and saw that my speculation was pointless anyway. The tingling was coming from the blood mark Christy had drawn, still there despite everything. Must have been the magic in it.

"Check this out," I said, looking down at the mark as it

glowed ever so slightly – pulsing with the tiny bit of power invested into it.

"In a sec," Sally replied.

"I think Christy found Tom. We should probably stop moving in case she decides to zap back here."

"I think we should stop moving regardless," she said.

"Why?"

"Your friend. He's not alone."

"What? Did he meet up with the others?"

"Maybe, and maybe they all got a chance to shower off that de-scenting stuff your Chinese friend gave us."

"Mongolian."

"Whatever the fuck."

She had a point. Gan had claimed it would last half a day. Hell, despite all we'd been through, I could smell the dirt on our bodies and the trees around us, but had Sally stepped around a tree to play hide-n-seek, there was no way I'd have been able to track her. Had Ed not stunk up the forest around us, we'd have surely gotten away scot-free.

"Who then?" I asked after a moment. The point was moot, though. I, too, caught the scent from up ahead.

"Vampires," we blurted out simultaneously.

"Jinx!" she said, then slugged me in the arm. "You owe me a drink."

"Ow."

"Pussy."

"Any idea who they are?"

"They're not the ones who pulled our asses out of the fire."

"Gan's troops?"

"Yeah. We never smelled them coming. These, they don't

smell nearly that good. Whoever they are, they've had run-ins with the Feet. I can smell their lingering stench."

The whole fucking forest still stunk of Feet to me. It was weird, because when I was hopped up on the blood of other vamps, it all seemed so clear to me. Yet another perk that came with age, I suppose.

An unpleasant thought hit me. "I doubt it's any covens out here sightseeing. That leaves two possibilities: François or Vehron's lackeys."

"Yep."

For the first time ever, I found myself actually hoping to see François's unpleasantly smarmy face. Who'd a thunk it? The end of the world had truly taken me to some strange places indeed. "What are we going to do?"

"I'm not sure we have much of a choice."

"Why?"

"Because they're heading this way."

"Do we hide?"

"I don't know," she replied. "This would be so much easier if we had my big bag of guns. Never a bad idea to say hello with a cocked fifty-caliber piece in your hand."

"How did they find us?"

"I don't know that they did. Maybe they're just walking in this direction, or maybe they're following your friend's back trail."

"They can do that?"

"The way he smells, I doubt it would take much effort."

"Oh fuck this." I grabbed her hand. "Come with me."

Sally didn't put up any resistance as I dragged her into a bramble of bushes. She wasn't dumb by any stretch of the imagination. Being caught out in the open with no weapons and looking like we were auditioning for parts in a porno didn't seem smart.

"If they're friendly, we step out and say hi," I whispered. By now, the others were close enough so that I could hear the crunch of leaves as they approached. Whoever they were, there was a decent number of them.

"No shit," she hissed back. "What if they're not?"

"If they're not, then they still have Ed. They don't get to keep him."

She nodded. "If we can take them, we do. If not, we follow and wait for an opportunity."

"There will be no need for that, I can assure you!" a voice cried out to us, close by, but still several dozen yards off.

The smarmy French accent gave it away. Even if it hadn't, the owner's ability to hear us from that distance spoke volumes to his age and power.

François had returned, and he had Ed with him.

# 42

# GEE, DIDN'T SEE THAT COMING

Sally and I shared a shrug and stepped from our hiding spot.

Unsurprisingly, the newcomers headed our way. Even through the trees, I could tell it was a ragtag band, not even remotely resembling Gan's disciplined troops. If they had any advantage over her men, though, it was their armament. A mishmash of guns – pistols, rifles, a few submachine guns – were pointed in our direction.

"There is no need for that," François said from somewhere behind the vanguard.

The guns were lowered, slightly anyway, and the vampires in the middle parted ways to reveal him – looking smarmy as ever, even if he wasn't dressed quite as crisply as I'm sure he preferred.

"Are you certain, sir?" one of the vamps nearest him asked, his tone belaying the fact that he obviously didn't want to speak up. Yeah, the Draculas had that effect on the rubes. "They smell..."

"Neutral, I am well aware," François replied with a dismissive wave. "I am impressed, Freewill," he said to us as his people approached and started to fan out around us. "Where did you happen upon manticore gland out here?"

"Huh?"

"Your scent, or lack thereof. Shall I assume you had friends among that force that appeared, quite conveniently, I might add, at the time of our escape."

"We know people," Sally replied in a non-committal tone.

"I can see that," he replied sourly before turning back to me. Gah! Turd wasn't the only big shit in these woods. "I would hope they too survived. I would like to commandeer them for my mission."

"I somehow doubt that's going to happen. They tend to be a *willful* bunch."

He waved a dismissive hand. "Free will is not something the First often worry about."

I raised one side of my mouth in a half smile at his double-entendre pun. "Where's my friend?"

"Friend? I believe you mean that in the plural."

What the...? I sniffed the air again. Ed ... he was definitely close. In fact, if my nose was telling me correctly, he was right in back of the line of vampires who stood guard behind François. The rest, well, I couldn't have sniffed them out while they were wearing that gland ... except that I did, for at least one of them.

I glanced at Sally and saw that she realized it too.

One of our wayward party had insisted on refusing Gan's scent-masking agent. Maybe she'd known it was made from manticore glands. Ugh! I had a feeling that was one recipe I didn't want to ask for.

With a smile, François stepped aside. So, too, did the armed vamps behind him. They revealed Christy and Ed, standing side by side. Christy's hands were bound in manacles. I didn't need to get closer to guess they had magicdebuffing runes carved into them. As for why those two hadn't shouted a warning to us sooner, the reason was blindingly obvious. Dave and Adam stood to either side of them, guns pointed at my friends, and the glazed look in their eyes indicating they were both under compulsion.

Shit!

I had meant to ask something a bit more conversational, perhaps, "What is the meaning of this affront?" Instead, it came out sounding more like, "What the fuck, asshole?" What can I say? It's one of the reasons I never joined the debate team in college.

"Your flippancy continues to get the better of you, boy," François replied with a tone that practically dripped icicles. "I cannot begin to fathom why that fool Alexander tolerates your tongue remaining in your mouth."

"That fool is your boss," I pointed out, lame of a comeback as it was.

"Not so, for the First are equals, or so Alexander would have his fawning minions believe. However, tis all meaningless conjecture, for I would sooner call your trollop my sibling than acknowledge that fool on his obsidian throne."

"So what's the plan? Try to use me as a bartering tool for safe passage? Because that's not going to work. Your buddy Turd is dead."

A greasy smile creased François's face, making me want to tear the ratty little mustache on his upper lip right off. "Is he now? That is fortuitous indeed. If so, it will take some time for our foes to regroup. There will be meetings of their war council to decide who shall take Turd's place. The Sasquatch will pull back until that happens. Do I have your friends to thank for this happy event?"

"Nope, you're looking at him."

François appeared to be doubtful, but he didn't say anything. He knew firsthand that I had more than one trick up my sleeve, although I'd have bet anything the asshole would have sooner stapled his mouth shut than acknowledge it.

"Very well," he said after a moment. "I offer you this, and before you say no, please be aware my terms are nonnegotiable. Any attempt to even discuss them otherwise will result in a most painful death for your friends."

"Oh well, in that case, hit me."

"My terms are simple, even for a fool such as yourself – unconditional surrender." François nodded toward one of the other vamps in his honor guard. "Shackle him. Should he make any attempt to remove them or otherwise escape, shoot his friends in the face, starting with the pregnant Magi."

A vamp walked over, producing a pair of handcuffs. These weren't the old magic-dampening sort they liked to use on mages. This was a pair of modern, heavy-duty cuffs. I doubted I'd be breaking free of those anytime soon, at least without Dr. Death's assistance – assistance that I didn't plan on calling upon.

I couldn't help but notice that the vamp snapping them on likewise appeared to be compelled.

"Where'd you dig up these guys so quickly?" I asked conversationally, trying to keep things friendly. "Some of your group that managed to escape Turd?"

"Hardly," François replied with a disdainful sniff. "Had they been loyalists, they would surely have died trying to rescue me. I was lucky enough to find the remnants of Salem coven, one of the few holdouts against Vehron's reign. They have proven most useful."

"Yeah, speaking of Mr. Destroyer," I said before I could be shuffled back to my friends, "you do realize this isn't going to work, right? Marching us north to your stronghold? Alex gave us specific orders to head to Boston to end this creep. When he finds out..."

"He will not," François replied, his back to me. "Besides, you are mistaken. We are not marching north."

"I thought you were supposed to be checking on covens in..."

"A ruse, you blathering fool. Nevertheless, you will happy to know that I am allowing you to complete at least part of your mission. You shall indeed reach Boston. I shall see to it personally. As for killing Vehron the Destroyer, you may find him a wee bit more difficult of an opponent than that oaf Turd."

"You're giving us an escort?"

"I don't think so," Sally replied from behind me.

"The strumpet is correct. Imagine my delight upon learning that you foolishly brought the abomination with you."

Wait, isn't that what Vehron kept calling Ed?

"Mighty Vehron will reward me most handsomely. Imagine it; not only will he have all the knowledge one of the First may offer, but I will also present him with both the Freewill and the one he has been seeking out. My glory shall be limitless."

"Wait, you're joining that douche?" I asked.

"I prefer to consider it a partnership, but yes."

Gunshots sounded from off to the left. They were followed by a roar of rage and then silence. Subtle our little parade was not, but perhaps that was to our advantage. If we got lucky, we might be ambushed, which could give us a chance to escape in the chaos. Or we might be ambushed and all die horrible deaths. At least in that latter case, I wouldn't have to drown in François's smarm any longer than was absolutely necessary.

"That makes no sense. Haven't you wanted to join the Drac ... err, First Coven since like forever?"

"Your usage of their common name does not bother me in the least, Freewill. I am beyond such hubris."

I sincerely doubted that.

"But to answer your question, yes. I have longed to ascend to the First. It was my right as an elder. Yet, twice I was denied, both times at the hands of the Wanderer. I had watched eagerly as he lost face. His defeat at Vehron's hands was an embarrassment the First had not known in centuries. But then he was vindicated, just before the First finally saw reason and gave to me what was rightfully mine. Do you think for one moment I would serve alongside the man who twice made me look the fool?"

I glanced around at my friends. Sally shrugged. Christy had hung her head and was breathing hard. Obviously, the exertion was catching up to her. Ed appeared in okay shape, but as I glanced his way, he made an up and down motion with his hand, stroking the invisible dick he held. Yeah, that about summed up what François was spewing.

"As a member of the First," François continued, in full-on monologue mode, "I was tasked with overseeing the torture of those who had betrayed us to our enemies. In all the chaos following the battle, it was a simple matter to allow one to escape, claiming he had perished at my hands. I sent him to Boston with an offer, one that was accepted gladly."

"But why?"

"Better to rule in Hell than be a slave in Heaven," he replied simply.

"Yeah, but you aren't going to rule. Veh..."

In a flash, François turned and was in my face. "I am well aware of the situation, fool, as I am aware that I would gladly bend a knee to one who would lay low those who have dared humiliate me. The world is a large place, and Vehron one man. The Cult of Ib will rise again, but in order to do so, even one as powerful as he must acknowledge that it cannot be done alone. I am perfectly willing to be a general in the army that shall burn away our stagnant ways."

"And when it is all over," he continued, "I shall know power beyond what meager crumbs the First afford me and I shall not have to answer to Alexander when I decide to utilize it. If you cannot see that, then I pity you – even more so than I already do."

**43**

## SIGHT SEEING

**F**ollowing François's spittle-soaked tirade, his minions shoved me back with my friends as he marched on ahead, obviously disgusted with having to lower himself to speak to me.

Can't say I was sorry to see him leave. Gave me a chance to take stock of the situation.

"Are you all right?" I asked Christy.

She finally looked up. "I'll make it."

"You sure, because you look..."

"I'm fine," she replied with a tone that said I really should reconsider that line of questioning.

"Tom?"

"He wasn't there."

That was worrisome. "Was there any sign of a struggle?"

"No," she replied. "It was all quiet. I think he may have left to come find us."

"Not the brightest strategy."

"This is Tom we're talking about," Ed said from beside her.

"Let me guess. You ran right into François's waiting arms?"

"Bingo. Talk about a small but unpleasant world."

"Sorry. Should have warned you he was around, but I thought he'd have hightailed it full speed out of the area."

"You should have seen the look on his face when he saw me. Would have thought the fucker had woken up on Christmas morning."

"Well," I replied, "maybe it was just the sight of you running out of the woods wearing a loincloth. Tell me, did you entice him with a 'me Tarzan, you Jane' line?"

Ed flipped me off, but then said, "You're one to talk. What the fuck happened to you two?"

Oh crap. I almost forgot that Sally and I looked like we'd just been sent back in time in a Terminator movie and only had a moment to divide one hobo's clothes between the two of us. "It was a rough fight with Turd."

"Rough enough that he tore your pants off?"

"Guess not even Turd can resist the allure of Freewill junk."

"Please tell me you didn't skull-fuck him to death."

"Nope, he choked on my massive..."

"Oh enough of this shit," Sally cried. "We're living out a worst case scenario and all you can talk about is your dick. Newsflash. It wasn't all that impressive."

Uh yeah. All at once, the other non-compelled eyes were on me. Well, okay, that was just Christy and Ed, but even so, I felt like I was under the glaring heat of a spotlight.

I glanced back at Sally, my eyes wide.

She just shrugged. "Sorry, bucko, you're on your own."

Bitch!

I tried to laugh off Sally's comment as a joke as I explained the battle with Turd to my friends. As for my missing pants, describing my clothes ripping as I transformed helped back up that – with maybe an editorial or two about my massive Dr. Death wang refusing to be denied freedom. Sally was even good enough to keep her trap shut for most of it, outside of maybe the occasional guffaw.

Yeah, that didn't quite explain her state of undress, but I sort of glossed over that part of the story. Although I got the sense that Ed definitely had a few questions of his own, the implications of my tale seemed to take priority at the moment, thank goodness.

"So your inner self lied," Christy stated.

"I'm not even sure he's my inner self."

"What do you mean by that?" she asked, a curious eyebrow raised.

"I don't know," I admitted. "Something he said. That he was never a part of me to begin with, that my turning had made him possible."

"Could be more lies."

"Maybe. I'm pretty sure that cock-knocker wouldn't know the truth if you shoved it up his ass and lit the fuse."

"Way to go on the split personality, Bill," Ed said.

"Tell me about it. I mean, I have my quirks, but I never had myself pegged for being a fucking nutcase."

"You might not be," Christy replied.

"A part of my mind goes rogue and hijacks the whole ship? Yeah, that pretty much counts in my book."

"Most people who suffer from split personalities don't physically transform into monsters."

"He wasn't really a monster," Sally added. "I mean, claws and fangs yes, but that's par for the course with vampires. The rest of him, though..."

She let the statement hang in the air, and Ed threw me a stink-eye that made his body smell like roses in comparison. Oh boy, was this turning out to be an uncomfortable death march or what?

"Christy has a point," I said, trying to steer us back on track. "Shit like that is just not normal."

"Maybe it's a Freewill thing," Ed replied.

"I was thinking that too." I shrugged as best I could with my hands cuffed in front of me. Oh well, at least they weren't in back. I could still scratch my nose, or other parts, if need be. "Problem is, that in itself is fucking terrifying."

"You really don't need to tell us that."

"It's even more so. Don't forget, Vehron is a Freewill too. What if he has his own rage beast inside of him? I mean, the guy is halfway to Superman as it is. We're talking *World War Hulk* here if he decides to fly off the handle. How the fuck do we beat something like that?"

No answer was forthcoming from my companions. Not too surprising.

"Maybe we'll get lucky and his split personality is a good guy," Ed offered.

"Somehow I doubt that. Ugh, I thought being a Freewill had potential to be kind of cool, but if I'd known it came with a side dish of crazy, I'd have..."

"It might not be that," Christy said.

"Huh?"

She glanced at me, then over my shoulder at Sally real quickly. "I'm not sure yet. Just a thought really. I need some time to mull it over."

I glanced at her and sighed. "Take all you need. We have plenty."

The blue morning sky could be seen above. This was one time when I found myself glad of the Sasquatches' sorcery. The heavy canopy kept us from frying like bugs under a magnifying glass. Sadly, it meant we could continue our trek southwest, even if the going was slow.

Eventually, the sounds of battle began to fade behind us. After a time, quiet reigned again. I wasn't sure if that was a good thing or not. What I did know was that no Mongolian assassins swooped out of the trees for another miraculous save. Then again, maybe that was for the best.

As powerful as Gan was, she and her entire entourage would have been easy fodder for François to ensnare. How fucking marvelous would that be? We'd come up here to kill Vehron, and instead would be served on a silver platter with substantial reinforcements for him to add to his growing fan base. Yeah, great fucking plan this was turning out to be.

"Halt!" François called out from somewhere ahead of us. I glanced up, trying to see past our guards – Adam and Dave were still about as mind-fucked as one could get – and saw what I thought to be a clearing up ahead.

Wait, no, that wasn't right. I saw a street sign, then beyond it a traffic light.

"I think we're back in civilization," Sally said. She was right. What I thought was a clearing was in actuality the edge of this unnatural forest.

From the look of things, it wasn't much different up here than in New York. The scene looked disturbingly normal beyond the tree line. Apparently, while the sun was out, human society still held onto its grip.

That definitely put a damper on our trek. I had a feeling that regular people – no doubt paranoid at, oh I don't know, a phantom forest growing overnight – would likely not take kindly to a bunch of armed weirdos stepping from the forest. What a flipping pity that would be.

There was also the tiny little fact of many of us being vampires. It's not like we could get very far without turning into a fine ashen powder. With any luck, we'd all need to wait until nightfall. That wasn't great, but it would give us several hours to maybe figure our way out of this.

Fuck it, if I could get François yammering again, maybe I could get close enough to put the bite on him. He'd still have the edge in experience, but I could at least cancel out his compulsions. One of the Draculas or not, I had a feeling Salem coven would be none too pleased at the prospect of him selling them out for fun and profit.

I made my way forward to see if I could get a better view. It was only when I got a little too pushy that I heard guns being cocked. I backed off a bit, but still positioned myself in a spot where I could spy on François.

Sure enough, the asshole was maybe a dozen yards ahead – standing right at the edge of the clearing, sunlight just inches shy of his feet. Ah, what I wouldn't give for his shoelaces to be tied together right now. Pity there were no otherworldly beings that owed me a favor – probably because I'd managed to piss off most that I'd met.

Maybe I didn't need divine help, though.

Flashing lights appeared from beyond the edge of the forest – cop cars, two of them from the look and sound of it. Though I didn't relish the thought of being smack dab in the middle of a potential shootout, I wouldn't mind it as much if François took the brunt of the lead fired our way.

The cars stopped just short of the forest, and four officers got out. They quickly spotted François and approached.

Come on, guys, a little paranoia goes a long way. At least tell the fucker to drop to his knees or something!

"Shit," Sally said.

"What?"

"Just listen."

I tried to focus in. François's conversation with the police was fairly low in volume – making it difficult to pick out from a distance, especially with a group of compelled mouth breathers between us and them.

However, maybe I didn't need to hear the details of their discussion. One of the cops turned to the others and nodded. Those three turned and walked back to their cruisers while the fourth cried, "Hail Ib!" and stepped forward into François's waiting arms.

## 44

## DOCTOR'S NOTE

"What the hell?" I asked to no one in particular as François pulled the cop in and immediately tore into his throat. His fellow boys in blue reacted by turning their cars around and driving off as if nothing interesting had occurred.

"Fucking thralls," Sally spat.

"Smart," Ed replied.

"Not for us."

Ed had a point, though. Perhaps Boston's daylight existence wasn't as normal as I had assumed. It was too early to make guesses, but I hadn't given much credence to Vehron's reputation as a battlefield commander up until now. I mean, when you're an uber-powerful killing machine, it doesn't seem like you need to put much finesse into things. But this new development said different. "Think it's all of them?"

"Just the ones in power," Sally said. "Authority figures, to keep the rest of the cattle in line and report in to home base if anything interesting happens."

"Damn. Any way to sniff them out?"

"Nope. They smell just like any other human."

"Maybe they're wearing nametags."

"Wishful thinking."

Ugh. "So that means his spies could be anywhere."

"And likely are."

I thought of Sheila and her contingent. "With any luck, the Templar will figure this out. Hopefully sooner rather than later."

"If they don't, my sisters will," Christy replied, then quietly added, "I hope."

"Anyone got their cell phone still on them?" I asked.

"Of course," Ed replied. "Got mine shoved up my ass. Been chafing a bit for the last couple of miles."

"I'm gonna say a silent prayer that you're joking." I turned toward Christy. "Any chance of one of them having a blood mark, like you gave me?"

"Sadly, no. Besides, I'm not sure what good it would do. I used mine to try to warn you and..."

"Yeah yeah, we all know how that worked out." Boy Scouts we definitely weren't.

"If we can get free, though, I can do a sending to my sisters, assuming..." She trailed off. There was no reason to voice the worst-case scenario.

Oh yeah, this mission was definitely turning into an epic clusterfuck.

Speaking of which, the head fuck-meister himself was marching back toward us, that same arrogant grin on his face. God, how I wanted to punch his lights out, smash the bulbs, and rub his face in the broken glass.

François stepped past the guards and stopped just short of my group. He pulled out a handkerchief and nattily wiped a few stray drops of blood from his chin before addressing us. "You will be pleased to learn that this day, which started out so poorly for me, has increasingly become more fortuitous."

"Find a few puppies to step on?" Ed asked.

I thought François might hurt him for the outburst – most vamps didn't like getting lip from humans – but he merely grinned instead.

"Ah, my prize. By all means, feel free to flap your tongue now. For later, well, who can say if you will even have one?" He glanced around us. "***REMAIN ALERT!! WE SHALL BE HERE A WHILE YET!!***"

The compulsion washed over Ed like nothing. You'd have thought François hadn't even spoken. Christy gritted her teeth, but otherwise, it appeared that her shields held. Good for her. Sally and I might as well have been punched in the teeth by it. Getting hit by a compulsion from a vamp of François's age was kind of like someone throwing a bowling ball directly at your brain.

Hah! Go figure. Thanks to Alex's mucking around in her mind, Sally was temporarily able to experience what they were like from my perspective. All around unpleasant, but without the side effect of being robbed of your personal freedom. Guess Alex didn't like anyone else playing with his toys. All things considered, I'd count my victories where I could.

I stuck a finger in my ear to shake out the ringing, for all the good I knew it wouldn't do. François, for his part, seemed to enjoy the fact that he'd caused me discomfort.

"Ah yes. I am still curious to see how many compulsions it would take to outright liquefy that pedestrian brain of yours."

"Better vamps than you have tried ... Umph!"

Like lightning, François's hand had lashed out. He could have decked me, but instead opted for a somewhat less devastating, but oh so more humiliating, bitch-slap. Even so, it almost spun my head completely around. I really needed to remember to stop mouthing off around this cock.

"You would be hard pressed to find a vampire better than

me," he said, anger coloring his otherwise pale cheeks. "On the other hand, I doubt I could throw a rock and fail to hit one better than yourself."

My friends all made to take steps toward the dick, even Christy. Nevertheless, their assistance would have resulted in nothing more than people getting their brains splattered out in a hail of bullets, so I quickly held up a hand to let them know I was all right – even if I was pretty sure my jaw was dislocated.

François, for his part, took a deep breath and smoothed the lapels of the tattered suit jacket he still wore. At least I could take some solace in knowing I'd discombobulated him a bit. I had that habit with the older vamps. Call it a talent.

"I have arranged for transportation to be provided for us," he said, speaking as if our little verbal ping-pong match hadn't occurred. "It will take some time, but I dare say it will be more pleasant than marching through this disgustingly bright day."

"Nice to see you care." There I went again, speaking before thinking. Oh well, maybe François would be good enough to belt me with his other hand – give me a matching set of bruises. I oh so hated being unsymmetrical.

"Believe me when I say, Freewill, that I would take great pleasure in watching you march naked into the daylight."

I glanced sidelong at Ed, a barely concealed smirk on my face. He gave his head a single shake. Yeah, he was probably right. Some jokes were too easy.

"But," François continued, "I will take greater pleasure in presenting you to The Destroyer myself and receiving the accolades due my effort - and those accolades shall be great indeed." He stared into my eyes. "The only other Freewill in existence handed to him, practically giftwrapped. Alexander puts great stock in you for some reason that escapes me.

Though I consider his judgment to be worthless, I think the embarrassment caused by your removal from the game board will be more than enough."

He stepped past me and addressed Christy. "Your kind are wildcards. Neutral in theory, but we all know such lofty ideals are often cast to the side when convenient. More importantly," he reached out a hand toward Christy's stomach, causing her to flinch back, "you are both the Freewill's friend and in a vulnerable physical state. If nothing else, you shall make for excellent leverage to ensure his cooperation."

Apparently, this was the part of the plot where the evil asshole told everyone the devious fate he had in store for them. Gah! As lethal as this guy could be, his attitude went a long way toward dispelling his threat and making him little more than a pathetic caricature.

"The strumpet," he continued, stepping in front of Sally. "Fear not, my dear. Vehron's power is more than sufficient to remove the meddling Alexander has done in your head."

Wait, he was?

"You will be given the choice that many others have been given. Pray that you choose wisely."

Point one, Sally's cure was potentially at hand. Counterpoint: she'd either be forced into a life of slavery or be dusted. Either way, she was smart enough to keep any of her opinions on the matter to herself.

"And you, the anomaly." I didn't need to turn to know he spoke to Ed. "I am not sure what your purpose is in this, but I do know that Vehron wants you very badly."

"So badly he tried to kill my ass with extreme prejudice last time he saw me?" Ed replied, no doubt counting on the old "your boss wants me in one piece" conceit to keep him from being splattered against the trees.

"Did he now?" François asked, raising an eyebrow. "That is interesting. Perhaps, much like your Freewill friend, you simply make a lasting first impression on others." I had to suppress a chuckle at that. Me and my roommates did seem to invoke more reaction than indifference in those we met. "Or perhaps it has to do with these."

François reached into his jacket and produced a notepad – Dave's. What the...? He casually flipped through a few pages, his eyes scanning them greedily. After a moment, he glanced back in my direction. "Were you aware of this? No, don't answer. Your expression tells me everything I need to know. I am afraid a future in high stakes gambling is simply not in the cards for you, boy."

He again turned to the pages in his hand. "Do you have any idea how much trouble you would be in if this got out? I was denied my rightful place among the First for almost seven decades because I dared sate my curiosity. Those who assisted me were not nearly so lucky. They lacked my experience, my political clout. The First had them executed without a second thought and all of my notes burned."

"Your poor notes," I commented.

"Yes, indeed. Years of research by some of the finest minds in Europe."

Yeah, the finest minds conscripted by the Nazis, he meant. "I'm sure they were all a swell bunch."

"Your friend here isn't nearly at their level of intellect. I can tell that much by his banal scribbles, but what he lacks in genius, he has made up for in breadth." He once again resumed flipping through the notes, his eyes opening wide. "A Freewill, an anomaly, and even a Shining One. How ever did you manage that?"

"Dave's a persistent kind of guy."

"He must be indeed. Pity the fool obviously lacks the insight to form even the most base conclusions."

"Oh? Like?"

"Like a very important fact about your friend here."

I turned to Ed. "See? I told you that haircut really didn't work on you."

François ignored me as he faced my roommate. "Congratulations are in order. It would seem that you are a vampire after all."

What?!

## 45

# PANDEMONIUM

"I will be the first to admit," François said, circling Ed like some sort of smarmy French shark, "I too found this surprising. You don't smell like one of us, you can somehow completely ignore compulsions in a way that not even the Freewill can, and, if rumors are to be believed, your blood is lethal to our kind."

"Why don't you try him and find out? It's the only way to know for sure."

Rather than zip on over and rearrange my face, a predatory smile appeared on François's. "That is a most excellent suggestion, Freewill. However, since you came up with it, perhaps it is only fair that you are the one to sup on your friend."

"Um, no thanks. I'm already full."

"He had some Turd earlier," Sally added. Bitch.

"I could insist, you know." François snapped his fingers. Both Adam and Dave immediately raised their weapons and pointed them at Christy's head.

"No need for that," I quickly said. "Besides, didn't you say Vehron wanted us all in one piece?"

"I said nothing of the sort," he snapped, his eyes flashing black. "You need only take a sip. I'm sure that will leave you alive enough for The Destroyer's uses."

"And if it doesn't?"

François shrugged. "One does not make an omelet without the risk of breaking some eggs. While we are considering tests, perhaps we should also test your resolve for the Magi. Which is greater? Your fear for her life or your own? I will be generous and give you until the count of three to decide."

"Listen, I was just..."

"One."

"Okay, okay!" I said, holding up my still shackled hands. I'd seen this shit play out in too many movies. François was enough of a psycho to happily show up at the Boston complex with our bodies and a whole pile of excuses. "No need to play the two and a half card." I took a step toward Ed.

"Good." He snapped his fingers again. "Should the fool take a less than adequate sip, kill the witch and his whore friend too. One cannot skimp on science, after all."

I put a hand on my roommate's shoulder. "Sorry about this."

"I have a feeling we're both going to be. Just do me a favor."

"Anything, man."

"No tongue, please."

"You should be so lucky."

François cleared his throat. "I am about to commence counting again. This time, I shall not stop. Do not test my..."

"The master is displeased with you!" an unfamiliar voice called out.

What the...?

All our heads spun toward the direction it had come

from, back where the forest ended and the suburbs began. Standing just beyond the trees was a figure clad in a cloak and hood.

In the chaos that had just occurred, none of us had heard him approach.

I took a sniff of the air to determine if our visitor was human or vampire and came up blank. Whoever it was, they smelled as if they weren't there at all.

"We shall resume this momentarily." François turned and stomped away toward where the newcomer waited.

Ed and I locked eyes. That was too close.

I turned my attention to Adam and Dave, still holding their weapons on us. "Come on, guys. Snap out of it."

Their response was to stand there and continue to give us the most lethal thousand-yard stare on the planet. Shit! There was no fucking way I could break them free, at least not without all the other vamps around us filling me with silver-jacketed bullets first.

"I'm open for suggestions," I said at last.

"How fast can you get out of here if we break those manacles?" Sally whispered to Christy.

"A couple of seconds, but it'll take longer to bring the rest of you..."

"Don't worry about us."

"They'll shoot you."

"Yeah, but we'll heal ... eventually, anyway. You won't."

"I probably won't either," Ed pointed out.

"You're special. The guest of honor," I replied, hoping I understood what Sally was getting at. "If Vehron wants you that badly, even François isn't stupid enough to piss him off."

"Exactly. There's no time to argue." Sally turned again to Christy. "As soon as he's distracted."

Christy nodded. "I'll find my sisters and the others. We'll come for you."

"Sooner rather than later, I'd hope." I glanced over to see François stalking to the very edge of the tree line where the figure awaited him. "Any second now. Get ready."

"What is it?" François asked, obviously annoyed to be interrupted.

The three of us converged around Christy, pretending to pay attention to the altercation going on, but in reality trying to provide enough cover so that Sally might snap the magic-dampening cuffs without being immediately noticed.

"Your tone is insolent," the newcomer replied, his voice deep – a little too deep. He sounded like someone doing a bad Batman impersonation.

"I do not answer to you. Tell me The Destroyer's message and be gone while I still allow you to walk away."

"On the count of three," Sally whispered.

The hooded figure approached to where François stood, stopping barely a foot away from him. "I said the master, not Vehron."

"One."

"What are you talking about, fool?"

"Two."

"Bill's master, actually," the figure replied, his voice dropping an octave to a familiar cadence. "At least the little tyke thinks she is."

"Thr..."

"Wait!" I hissed, just as the figure threw back his hood, revealing himself to be Tom. How in the name of fuck?

"I know you," François said with a snarl.

"Yes, but have you met my little friend?" Tom replied in a bad Cuban accent. "If not, say hello to him."

With that, Tom took a swing at François. It was hard to tell from this angle, but it looked like he had something attached to his hand. Whatever the case, he'd clearly gone insane. Because there was no way...

...That François's head would burst into flame as the blow connected?

The asshole screamed and backed up a step. Tom took the occasion to throw his cloak off, revealing his *armor* – a collection of stolen toys duct-taped to his body. Yep, we'd definitely taken a detour to Crazy Town.

"Don't be sad. Come here and give Daddy a big hug." Tom leapt forward onto the stunned François and gave him the least friendly greeting one could give a vampire.

Up in Canada, François had proven himself pretty tough when it came to resisting a faith-magic imbued object. However, my roommate's entire body was covered in them. That upped the ante by several hundred percent.

I didn't dare fool myself that he'd win, though. Even if he got supremely lucky, there was still François's compelled minions to take into account.

Speaking of which, I grabbed Christy and dragged her to the ground. Just in time too, as the compelled vampires brought guns to bear from all sides. Considering François's orders had included ventilating her head if anything happened, I didn't like her chances just standing there in the crossfire.

Sally and Ed, no idiots, joined us ... which, on second thought, might not have been a great plan as all the rest had to do was aim downward.

Thankfully, that didn't become an issue as, just then, a burst of light caught my attention from ahead of us. One of the Salem vamps had been dusted. The reason became clear less than a second later as a crossbow bolt struck another right in the forehead.

The cavalry had arrived.

Oh shit! Remembering that I had friends among the compelled, I kicked Dave's legs out from under him. Sally saw what I was doing and then did the same to Adam, socking him in the jaw on the way down – for good measure, I guess.

It was a good thing we'd acted when we had, because barely a moment later the area around us descended into pure unadulterated chaos.

Gunfire erupted as the compelled vamps began opening fire seemingly in every direction. The problem was, they were poor schmucks recruited against their will to fight. Gan's people – because who the fuck else would be out in the woods with crossbows? – were heavily trained warriors fighting for the honor of their psychotic princess.

It was only a matter of moments before more flashes of light joined the first, as the Salem coven was exterminated one by one. I didn't have time to worry about them, though.

"Stay here!"

"Where are you..."

"I have a friend and you have a fiancé that needs some help right now." Yeah, I'd just committed Tom's ass to marriage without his say so. Fuck it. It wasn't like he had much choice in the matter anyway.

I jumped to my feet, praying Gan's people had it drilled into their heads that her *beloved* was on the do-not-pepper-with-arrows list. When I didn't immediately die like a redshirt on Star Trek, I bolted forward toward where Tom still struggled with François. A red-hot lance of pain seared through my leg, but I ignored it and continued on.

I was just in time too. François, though looking like Freddy Krueger served up well done, was still an ancient vampire with a scary shit ton of power. He finally managed to mount a defense and, in doing so, threw Tom off. My roommate went flying through the air, out of the tree line, and landed hard on the asphalt of the street, rolling until he came to a halt. He lay there unmoving, but I couldn't stop to check on him, not with a major asshole in the way who was gonna be mighty pissed just as soon as he regrew about ninety percent of his skin.

"You dare touch me? I am François of the First!"

"And it's about time you came in dead last!" I plowed into him from behind, savoring the cheap shot karma had been saving up for this motherfucker for centuries. "This is for Mike!"

His feet left the ground, but, more importantly, his body left the protection afforded by the trees – on more or less the same trajectory as he'd sent my friend. His clothes in tatters and his body already burnt nearly beyond recognition, he had nothing to shield himself from the rays of the sun that shone down upon him.

I managed to catch hold of a tree limb to stop my forward momentum, and stopped to watch the show.

François screamed, loud and high pitched – sounding like a teenaged girl in a horror movie. An asshole in life, a bitch in the end. Worked for me.

He tried to stand, make one last effort to reach cover even as his body began to immolate, but Tom – scraped the hell up from the fall – still had enough sense to kick out and hit the back of François's knee.

The elder vampire stumbled and that was all she wrote. His body was consumed by fire and I watched as his asshole features melted away seconds before there came the telltale flash that rendered him little more than dust in the wind.

Couldn't have happened to a nicer guy.

46

# OUT OF THE FRYING PAN

With François dead, his hold over both the vampires of Salem Coven and my other friends had ended.

Sadly, that didn't mean shit to Gan's troops. I yelled for them to cease firing, but that still didn't stop many Salem vamps from dying with confused looks upon their faces. By the time an order was barked out and the hail of medieval weaponry stopped, there were maybe a handful of the poor Salem schmucks left.

Tom had gotten back to his feet and joined me in the tree line by then. "You okay, man?" I asked.

"I think I lost a Furby in the fight."

"Fuck you."

"Nice to see you too," he replied with a smile as we walked back to take stock of the carnage.

"Everyone okay?" I called out.

"What's going on?" one of the Salem vamps asked. He saw me and immediately raised his weapon again. "You're that Freewill guy. What the hell did you do to me and my friends?"

397

"I wouldn't do that if I were…"

One more bolt zinged in from somewhere beyond us, catching the vamp square in the chest and ending him then and there.

Oh for Christ's sake! "Will you fucking knock it off already?!" I screamed to the surrounding trees.

Silence reigned once again — for about two seconds anyway. Then there came a cry of joy as Christy nearly knocked Tom off his feet.

He tried to mumble "hi," in that idiotically nonchalant way he had, but her mouth was too busy crushing his to let out any sound.

Her public displays of affection rapidly approaching uncomfortable levels, I decided to leave them to their own devices for the moment as I went to check on the others.

Sally was already back on her feet and giving Ed a helping hand.

"Anything hurt?"

"Do egos count?" Ed asked.

"Only if you're wearing pants."

"Look who's talking."

Oh crap. He was right. In all the excitement, my makeshift kilt had almost slipped off. Not quite what I wanted to happen, especially with Gan in the vicinity. Thankfully, Sally was there to help snap my cuffs off so I could re-secure my meager coverings properly. When I was finished, I turned my attention to my other friends. "How are you guys doing?"

"What the fuck happened?" Adam asked, looking about as dazed as expected.

"That vampire from the pit, François, he took over your mind."

"Huh. Everyone always thinks they're gonna be the Jedi and not the weak-minded fool," he replied. "Guess we won't be training with Yoda anytime soon. Did we do anything stupid?"

"Stupid is such a subjective concept," Sally said with a snicker.

"Where the hell are my notes?" Dave asked, standing up and searching his pockets. Yep, good to know he had his priorities straight.

"Sorry, man," I replied. "François took them."

"Well, where is he?"

I hooked a thumb over my shoulder where the still smoldering pile of ash could be seen through the trees.

"Shit! Please tell me he didn't..."

"In his jacket when he went poof, I'm afraid."

"Goddamnit! I'm gonna have to start all over again with my samples."

"Yeah," Ed interrupted. "Speaking of your notes, when were you going to tell me that I..."

"Beloved!" a disturbingly familiar voice called to me.

"Oh shit."

"Have fun, Bill," Ed said, clapping me on the shoulder. "That's now two you owe her in the last day alone. Good luck living that one down."

"I could always join François," I whispered back.

He gave me an unsympathetic smile and backed away as Gan came striding over with two burly guards flanking her.

I glanced around, and more of her people stepped out of the forest. There didn't seem to be nearly as many as earlier, but then again, that any remained at all was surprising considering the force they'd gone up against.

Oh well, no point in delaying the inevitable. "Thanks, Gan. That's another I owe you."

Gan bowed deeply before me and, when she stood, I saw a serious look upon her face. She pointed to the guard on her left. "This pitiful excuse of a warrior disobeyed my orders and fired his weapon after I had commanded him to cease." She then indicated the other. "And this is the dog who dared wound you."

"Huh?" That's when I remembered the pain in my leg when I'd run to help Tom. I glanced down and, sure enough, there was a smear of blood on my calf. Must've been a glancing blow because it was already healed over. Sometimes, adrenaline was an awesome thing. "Okay. Just be more careful next time, guys. I mean those vamps from Salem Coven were..."

Gan snapped her fingers and both men drew their swords.

"Whoa!" I held up my hands. "There's no need to take offense. I didn't even know them."

She nodded and both of her men turned their blades inward and impaled themselves through the chest with them. Both burst aflame. Their weapons and fur-lined armor clattered to the ground as the clouds of dust that had been them settled on top – not even a speck so much as touching Gan.

"Honor has been satisfied, my love," she said. "I beg your forgiveness and pray you are too."

"What, satisfied? Why the fuck would I be satisfied with *that?*"

"You wish for more of my men to atone? Very well. They shall happily lay down their lives for you."

"No! Not what I meant!" I realized I was shouting and that every vamp in the vicinity was watching. Hell, any nearby humans dumb enough to approach the woods probably were too. I didn't give a fuck, though. "What, don't your people have any words for 'I'm sorry?' That would have been fine. I'm a simple guy to please."

Gan appeared puzzled by this. "I am aware that in many things you are simple." It wasn't too late. I could grab one of their swords and follow them. "However, you should not be in this matter. A disciplined soldier follows his commander's orders to the letter, never deviating unless given the authority to do so. A proper commander never lets a slight go unpunished. It serves as a reminder of the consequences to the rest."

"You were a horrible squad commander in your ROTC group, weren't you?"

"R ... O...?"

"Never mind. Yes, I'm satisfied. Honor is restored. My ancestors can rest easy and stop spitting upon me from beyond the grave."

*Had I still lips I would gladly take over for them.*

The voice was muffled, but unmistakable – Decker.

I turned toward Tom, from whom the insult had seemingly originated.

"Almost forgot," he said, pulling away from Christy for a moment. "I brought your friend." He unshouldered the backpack he'd been wearing, unzipped it, and pulled out Decker's skull – still spewing purple light, and definitely still an asshole.

"The vestige of the maapamba I killed, beloved?" Gan asked, sounding far less surprised than any sane person should. "I am impressed. Such defilement of an enemy to make a fortune totem is admirable."

*I am no totem, you murderous filth! I have seen things...*

"That's enough, Harry," Christy said, taking him from Tom. She danced her fingers across the top of the skull, yellow sparks escaping, and it momentarily stopped yammering.

"Thanks, babe," Tom said.

I was tempted to second that, but I didn't want to get back on Christy's bad side. Instead, I waved everyone in – well, everyone except Gan's people, who took to the trees to form a defensive perimeter. That was fine. I hadn't known her servants to be the best conversationalists anyway.

"So what the hell happened to you?" I asked Tom.

"I could ask the same. You guys join a nudist colony or something?"

"Never mind that. Let's just say we had a couple of major wardrobe malfunctions and leave it at that." I could feel Ed glance towards me, but I quickly shunted us back to my original question. "You do know we were captured by the Feet, right?"

"I eventually figured it out," Tom replied. "I mean, I heard you all thumping around upstairs, but I thought maybe Sally was on the rag..."

"What?" she snapped.

"Or something," he quickly amended. "Anyway, I came up about an hour later and was like, 'What the fuck happened here?' So I stuffed all my shit into a bag and..."

"You mean you took the time to finish robbing that place?"

"Fuck yeah. I mean, that's not how Indiana Jones would have played it, but that's why he was still teaching for a living."

"Whatever, meatsack," Sally prodded. "Get to the point."

"Well, the Feet's footprints weren't hard to find. So I tried following them, but then I got all confused. They were all over the fucking place, leading this way and that. So, after a while, I decided to head back to the house. That's when I found this." He reached into his pocket and produced the vial of de-scenting agent that Gan had loaned us. "Oh, and the note you left too. Thanks, babe."

I glanced at Christy.

"I only said that I wasn't going to use it," she replied defensively. "When we got to the house and didn't see him there, I left it along with instructions just in case he came back. If we missed him, I didn't want him wandering around without at least some sort of protection."

I nodded. Smart, actually, and probably required her to swallow a good deal of pride to make use of something from Gan.

"So anyway," he continued, "I doused myself with that shit and waited around. Was kind of boring, so I started putting my outfit together – in case any vamps stopped by."

I gave him the once over. He'd basically made brass ... err ... plastic knuckles from some action figures and tape. He'd then fashioned himself a makeshift bandolier from which the most valuable figures hung. Well, most of them anyway.

"I see Max Adventure got the starring role in this action flick."

He looked down at the big-mustached figure in the center of his chest. "Yeah, I decided it was to honor my dad."

"Your dad is still alive."

"I know, but I always felt bad blowing the shit out of his."

"This is all remarkably fascinating," Ed said. "But how the hell did all of *this* happen?" He waved his arms to indicate the chaos that had just transpired.

"I believe I can answer that, and much more concisely than the human," Gan said, stepping up to my side. "After the battle, we were able to track your back-scent to the domicile in question. There we found this human. At first, my men wished to kill him. The fight left them thirsty and they wished to pass him about until he was drained."

"I assume you put an end to that," I replied.

"In actuality, I was going to allow them to do as they wished. They had fought bravely and deserved it, but then I remembered your edict, my love."

"My edict?"

"Yes, that I was not to harm your friends. That doing so would potentially cause you mild displeasure."

Sally, Ed, and Christy all turned to stare at me.

"I'm pretty sure I put it a little more adamantly than that."

"If you say so, beloved," Gan continued. "Thus, I offered to spare his life so long as he didn't become a burden. After that, it was a minor matter to catch wind of François. The coven he compelled to his bidding were no warriors, so my people were able to track them with ease – all but invisible to you. Once it became obvious where they were headed, I summoned the human and we devised a trap."

Although I wasn't particularly pleased that Gan's idea of a trap was to pit my friend against a vampire so far out of our league that it was almost bad comedy, I found myself impressed with her foresight.

"How'd you figure out that François had betrayed the Draculas to go work for Vehron?"

She cocked her head to the side, for a moment looking like a confused, albeit lethal, puppy. "He had?"

"Yeah. He was going to hand us over to the asshole and then join up."

"I was unaware of that. I thought he might barter you for safe passage, but I had no inkling that he had betrayed the trust of the First."

"Wait," Sally said. "Then why did you attack him? You did know he'd been promoted, right?"

"Of course, whore," she replied dismissively. "I make it a point to keep up with the politics at play."

Sally gritted her teeth. "Then why did you do it?"

Gan turned to me and smiled. "My beloved is aware of my motivations."

I was? Then I remembered. Gan's ambition extended far beyond just marrying me. No, she wanted to off the current regime and take over. Her as empress and me as, I guess, her concubine. "This was all part of that fucking insane plan of yours?"

"Is it not obvious? I knew François to be both treacherous and incompetent. Neither are traits I wish to foster among my ranks. I likewise knew I could not persuade him to join me nor did I wish him to. This was a perfect opportunity. One of the thirteen has fallen and in enemy territory too. None shall be the wiser and we will soon see to the rest."

Holy shit. I thought Alexander and his crew were the dark side. Compared to Gan, they were just standing in some minor shade.

"Whoa," Adam said. "This chick is hardcore."

"Chick?" Gan asked. "Are you comparing me to a hatchling?"

Oh shit. "No!" I said, jumping in front of my friend. "Nothing of the sort. It's a term of endearment in my society. Right, guys?"

Sally shrugged and found something interesting on her nails to look at. "You're on your own with this one."

I muttered a few unkind things under my breath, then quickly added, "Yes, it's a good thing, Gan. It indicates a fondness."

She smiled. "Very well. I apologize for my lack of understanding. Know then, Dr. Death, that I consider you to be my favorite chick."

I waited for the asshole laughter to die down before steering us back to more serious matters.

"You don't happen to have any spare clothes we could borrow?" What? I didn't have a build like Vehron's. I wasn't about to face down anyone dressed like an extra from *Planet of the Apes*. I mean, shit, Sally made her torn dress look good, but I didn't fool myself for a second thinking I, or Ed's skinny ass for that matter, did the same.

There were scraps around from the vamps that had been killed, but most had been badly burned when they went up in flames. Thankfully, Gan was able to cobble together – and by that I mean order some of her people to strip – enough clothing for us to ensure no nip slips occurred.

While this was going on, Christy walked off to try to make magical contact with her sisters. That was good since it seemed we didn't have a working cell phone among the bunch. Well, Tom still had his, but the idiot hadn't charged it before we'd left. With any luck, the witches and Sheila had met smooth sailing on their end of the journey. Wishful thinking, I'm sure.

Once my ass was properly covered again, Gan turned her creepy little eyes back to my face and said, "We should go now, beloved."

"Go? As in together?"

"All of us."

"Oh, yeah. Sorry. Just got a little..."

"Excited? I know. I, too, have ... what is the saying ... butterflies in my stomach when I am around you."

"Good to know. But you do have a point. Any element of surprise we had is probably lost."

"Undoubtedly. Though necessary to ensure François's death, doing so outside of the protection the forest affords us has no doubt alerted Vehron's vassals to our presence."

"It's worse than that," Sally said. "François talked to a few of the thralls here. They went to fetch some cars to drive us to the Boston complex. Safe to say that since they were expecting prisoners, there's going to be an armed escort."

Gan nodded. "Your whore is correct. We..."

"That's it!" The claws on Sally's right hand extended and she stepped forward to point a talon right at Gan's face. "If you call me 'whore' one more time, I'm gonna..."

"Suck it up," I hastily interrupted, "and get on with your life because sticks and stones and all that shit."

"What?" She glanced back at me, doubtlessly noticing at least half a dozen of Gan's people were pointing crossbows armed with silver-tipped bolts in her direction.

"You were saying?" Gan asked conversationally, having not so much as even flinched.

A vein popped on Sally's forehead, but she somehow managed to restrain herself. "I ... was about to ask what you thought might be best as a course of action."

"As both the most seasoned warrior here as well as holding the rank of prefect, I would expect no less," Gan replied.

She gave the barest of dismissive waves with her hand and I saw weapons being lowered in my periphery. A part of me wondered if she'd have actually done it, but then I realized that was stupid. This was Gan. Of course, she'd have done it.

"The Alma's magic extends east of here for several kilometers," she continued. "I would suggest we use that to our advantage." Gan drew her sword and began to scribble in the dirt like this was some old-timey World War Two prison break movie. "We will march east, staying at least three hundred meters inside the tree line. Should we encounter additional Alma resistance, it will be dealt with quickly. Vampires sent by The Destroyer will be compelled to forget our passing. Humans will be divided up amongst our ranks."

"Wait," I interrupted. "Did you just say we were going to eat any people we came across?"

"Works for me," Adam said.

I promptly slapped him upside the head. "Mind your manners, junior. Mom and Pop are talking." I turned back to Gan. "Why not just compel them too?"

"Compelling humans requires extra effort. It is effort I

care not to expend. Besides, it makes sense to utilize them as nourishment."

"Yeah, but these are the same people we're trying to help."

Gan looked up from her makeshift battle plans and cocked an eyebrow. "I am not following."

"The humans under Vehron's rule."

"What of them?

"We're here to help them."

"I am not. I am here to help you, beloved. In addition, the Wanderer has expressed concern for the existing prefect of Boston."

"Calibra."

"Yes. As a favor to him for his years of service to my father, I wish to ascertain her fate, learn what she has divulged to our enemy, and then dispatch her if necessary."

"Dispatch her? I thought you said you were doing James a favor."

"If she has been compromised, then I *will* be."

I decided to not argue the point. The thing was, compromised or not, if we managed to take down the big bad asshole, the rest wouldn't really matter.

No. If she was still alive, we'd try to save her along with the rest of Village Coven and any others that had been abducted. If we failed, well, we probably wouldn't be in much position to worry about what happened next.

Sadly, failure seemed more an option than ever now. I had been counting on gaining access to Dr. Death's power or cooperation. Now it seemed as if that was one avenue that had been closed off – with any luck, for good.

We discussed things for a bit more, knowing that time wasn't on our side. It was decided that, assuming Christy reported the all clear, we'd double back and join up with our backup team. Though we'd have certainly lost the element of surprise, Gan's forces would hopefully reinforce our own enough to make up for it. That her people were all trained killers was a gift horse I didn't care to look in the mouth, even if it meant having to deal with her a little longer.

I hated to admit it, but Gan's presence might also serve as a buffer to any weirdness that was lingering between me and Sheila. The creepy little munchkin had a way of saying the worst things at the worst times, which at least kept the conversation from getting too deep. Now to just hope she kept her fucking mouth shut around the Templar about kidnapping their brothers.

I looked up to find Tom walking over.

"How's it going with Christy?"

"She made momentary contact, so that's a good sign."

"Momentary?"

"Sounds like they were kinda busy."

"Just so long as they're okay," I said with a sigh of relief. "With any luck, most of the eyes in Boston are still preoccupied looking north toward where Turd and company were coming from."

*... life.*

"Huh? What was that?"

"I didn't say anything," he replied.

"Sorry. Thought I heard you mumble something under your breath."

*The s... er ... mar s ... fall ... die!*

We glanced at each other for a moment before realization hit. "Hold on a sec." Tom pulled off his backpack and opened it up. "Forgot I stuffed him back in there." He yanked out Decker's skull; apparently all charged up and ready to yammer nonsense again.

"What was that, Harry?" I asked without much enthusiasm.

*I said the power of prophecy is still mine to command, fool, so you would do well to listen.*

"It didn't sound like that's what you said."

*Then allow me to repeat, simpleton. The Sun Strider marches. Tears will fall for those about to die, drowned in the flow of false life.*

What the...? "Translation please, asshole. I'm not Gollum. I don't like riddles."

"The Sun Strider?" Gan asked. "The totem speaks of Vehron."

"Huh? Oh yeah. Didn't Colin say something about that?"

"Yeah," Tom replied. "That was one of Chuck's many nicknames, I think."

"Chuck?"

"Inside joke, Gan. Either way, Decker's crap makes no sense. Hell, for all we know, the guy is just marching to the bathroom to take a shit. I..." Whoa! I felt the back of my head tingle just a moment before the mass compulsion washed over us.

**"BROTHER, I HAVE COME FOR YOU!!"**

Okay. So much for that theory.

# 47

# THE BIG BAD

Though there was no command given – the compulsion having been sent out to catch our attention only – the power behind it still caused the leaves in the trees to quiver.

Where in the name of Flash Gordon's used condoms had that come from?

"There!" Sally said, pointing.

No fucking way. He stood facing our direction, standing beyond the tree line in the middle of the fucking street – not too far from where Tom had approached just a short while ago.

Vehron was dressed in a much more contemporary fashion than when last I'd seen him. He wore boots, jeans, and actually had on a shirt for a change. Sure, it was just a t-shirt – doing little to hide his hulking frame – but it was better than the Conan the Barbarian look he'd been trying to cultivate during our previous encounter. Hell, his hair was even in a ponytail. If he'd had a guitar, he wouldn't have looked out of place in a Bruce Springsteen tribute band.

It wasn't his outfit or that he'd seemingly come alone,

though, that really caused my eyes to bug out. It was the fact that he was standing out in the daylight with no cover. Small wisps of smoke rose from his bare arms, but that was it.

"Dude must have some killer sunscreen back home."

"Do not be foolish, human," Gan said to Tom.

That's when realization hit. This wasn't the first time he'd done something like this. Back in New York, I'd sent him out a window on a hundred-foot freefall into a bright New York day, and he'd shrugged it off like it was nothing. Then, it finally hit me. "Wait, Sun Strider? Holy crap, you mean this fucker can walk around in the daylight?"

"In a sense. However, I believe that is self-evident, beloved," she replied.

"But how?"

She glanced at me, a mix of love in her eye mixed with something else. Oh, never mind, I recognized it – pity. "We shall discuss this later. After we have dispatched him."

"We?"

"I, of course, mean my men."

She made the barest of movements, and all at once, over a dozen crossbows were leveled in Vehron's direction. I heard the clack of metal and turned to see some of her people doing one better, aiming high-powered sniper rifles. Gan was a lot of things, but stupid wasn't one of them.

***"BE AT PEACE, MY FRIENDS!!"***

I winced, as if someone had just stabbed my frontal lobe with an ice pick. Unlike the last one, this compulsion had some meat behind it. It wasn't full strength, I could tell that since I hadn't been knocked on my ass, but it was more than enough.

All around me, vampires lowered their weapons. Hell, even Gan appeared under his spell. Although their eyes didn't completely glaze over, he'd eliminated the threat – basically tossing the equivalent of a Calm Emotions spell over the crowd, something Carl's cleric used to do when he was in the mood to fuck with us.

Holy crap, even Sally – who'd been in the middle of grabbing one of the weapons discarded by the Salem Coven vamps – ceased what she was doing.

Aside from myself, Ed and Christy seemed to be the only ones not in the process of getting ready to sing Kumbaya. On that latter front, she quickly scrambled over to Tom, no doubt trying to snap him out of it. Good luck there.

Vehron was no idiot. Forcing someone to do something that went against their nature, something they'd fight tooth and nail against, was difficult. But it had been Jeff himself who'd taught me that a neutral compulsion, something that did little more than ask someone to chill out, required much less effort because it didn't give much impetus to resist.

I glanced back. Vehron still stood where he was, his hands in his pockets, looking quite relaxed. The smoke rising from his arms appeared thicker now, but he paid it no heed.

***"MUCH BETTER!! COME OUT AND SPEAK, LITTLE BROTHER!! WE HAVE MUCH TO TALK ABOUT!!"***

I turned to Ed, but he just shrugged and mimed handing me a phone. "Looks like it's for you."

Great. One of the few times I would have welcomed a telemarketer.

"Stay back," I said to Ed.

"How's that gonna help?"

"I don't know. Maybe he doesn't know you're here."

"Great plan, Mussolini."

"Sue me. I'm making it up as I go."

I walked past the small legion of oddly calm warriors. I

hadn't seen anyone so mellow since the last time Tom and I had passed a couple of blunts around. Hell, even Sally was just sitting on the ground, looking like she was at a picnic.

"Snap out of it!" Christy's voice, and the yellow flash that accompanied it, caught my attention.

I glanced over to find her hands around Tom's head. He was reaching up to pull her off. "Okay, okay. You don't have to set my fucking hair on fire."

She glanced my way, and I tried my best to mouth to her, "If this goes bad, get out of here."

"What was that?" Tom asked, but Christy merely nodded in my direction. Thank goodness I had one member on my team with her wits about her. I only had to hope she had enough left in her to take Sally and Ed too.

Vehron continued to stand where he was, patiently waiting for me. He could have covered the distance between us and probably snapped everyone's neck in the process before I could so much as spit. Thus, I found his current level of inaction to be far creepier.

I walked to the edge of the trees and faced him. A grin broke out on his dumb fucking face as I did.

Oh well, time to break out the compulsions if this was going to be any sort of meaningful conversation. "***WHAT DO YOU WANT?!***"

Probably not the best opening line of all time, but he'd caught me by surprise.

Speaking of which, I was caught even more off guard when he replied, "There is no need for that, brother." His voice was heavily accented, but he was understandable.

"You speak English?"

"This is a new world for me. It would be unwise to not learn its ways. Do you not agree?"

"Well, um, yeah."

"I have no wish for us to be enemies, brother," he said, taking a casual step in my direction.

I tensed in order to bolt the opposite way, but then I remembered this guy could have caught me without breaking a sweat. I forced myself to remain where I was, even leaning against a tree as if we were doing little more than discussing who was the keynote at Comic Con this year. "Oh? So I guess I just imagined you turning one of my friends, killing another, chasing me halfway across Manhattan, enslaving my coven, oh, and let's not forget when you decided one of my other friends was a filthy abomination who needed to be erased from existence."

Okay, perhaps that was a bit overkill for someone I was trying not to provoke.

If he took offense, he didn't show it. He simply lifted his arms as if to say "What are you gonna do? Shit happens." I noticed blisters beginning to form on his flesh, his arms taking on a badly sunburned look. "Put yourself in my place, brother," he said. "Imprisoned for centuries, having no body but being unable to die. Then to be freed, yet driven mad by thirst. When at last I came to my senses, I was alone in a place I knew not. I merely did what comes natural – waged war against any who attacked me."

Maybe he did have a point. There was definitely a chance that, if our positions had been reversed, I might have also acted out a bit. I can't say for certain that a thousand years spent on Alex's bookshelf wouldn't drive me batshit crazy too. Still, this guy's reputation preceded him.

"So, you're ready to talk sense, then?" I asked. "Okay, let's start by you surrendering the Boston complex and letting everyone go."

"It is not that simple, brother."

Ugh, that was gonna get old real quick. Not quite as bad as Gan calling me "beloved," but definitely annoying.

"My people are dead, hunted to extinction by your so-called First Coven. Do you think the Macedonian would show mercy to me? Would he allow me to live in peace and sing the praises of the true First?"

"Ib?"

"Many names have been claimed by our progenitor. That is but one of them."

"Seems to be a lot of that going on."

"The Macedonian fears our ways. He always has. Sadly, we were fools. None of us suspected his ambitions. By the time we did, it was too late."

"You talking about your fellow cultists?"

"I speak of them, yes, but I also speak of us, brother, our kind."

"Freewills."

"Yes, the Night Spawn. Once, we were legion. Now we are but two."

"And a whole bunch of heads overlooking Alex's private bath."

He smiled as if sharing some secret with me. If I was hoping for enlightenment, though, it was not to be. "Yes, all that remains of a once great people. For now."

"Whatever. Anyway, they told me about your cult. Said that you were all a bunch of fucking psychos." Oh yeah. Once again, I proved to the universe why I wasn't cut out for hostage negotiations.

"I follow a different path from the Macedonian. Is that so great a crime?"

Considering what a dick-nugget Alex was, there was something to be said about his words, but then I remembered what happened when last I'd been up here. "You killed Starlight."

"Starlight?"

"My friend."

"She was yours?"

"Yes ... no. She was in my coven."

"I know not this name. I only know that all who come before me are given the choice. All choose their path."

"And if it's not the path you like, they get dusted."

For a moment, his calm demeanor fell away and raw, naked annoyance showed on his face. Of course, it might have been the fact that the blisters on his arms were now becoming full-on third-degree burns. Ouch. What the hell was up with this guy? At this rate, maybe if I kept him talking he'd eventually incinerate. That would be awfully convenient.

"Tell me, brother, do you enjoy life under his reign?"

"Enough of this crap. My name is Bill. I'm an only child, so I sure as shit ain't your brother."

"I call you brother because that is what you are. You are both a brother in darkness and one who is able to resist the call."

"The call?"

"The will of others."

"Oh, compulsion."

"The word itself is meaningless." He waved his hand dismissively, the skin on it starting to look mighty crispy. "What I speak of is the brotherhood I feel for all who walk the path. Tell me, *Bill*, does the Macedonian consider you a brother?"

"Heh. I'm more like a punching bag mated with a scapegoat."

He looked confused. I guess he'd just recently passed English 101 and hadn't had time to catch up with the colloquialisms. "I will take that as a no. What of the rest, his so-called First Coven?"

"Well, he calls them brothers and sisters, but I'm not entirely convinced he means it."

"I meant, how do they treat you?"

They mostly treated me like a pile of dogshit on the side-walk, but that didn't mean I cared to let this guy play Dr. Phil with me. "James treats me well."

He raised an eyebrow.

"The Wanderer. The one whose arm you tore off."

"I know of whom you speak. I have learned much since being freed."

That didn't sound good. It meant that Calibra had most likely been compromised. If so, I'd need to keep Gan on a short leash around her.

"Very well. That is one," he continued. "Once the time comes, he will be given the choice as well – in deference to the favor he shows you. As for the rest..."

"Let me guess – heads in jars?"

"And give them a chance to be freed as I was? No. I will not make the same mistake the Macedonian made."

Yeah, that sounded far more practical than what I suggested.

"I can sense the uncertainty in you."

"Beats sensing the dark side, Palpatine."

I was certain he had no fucking idea what I was talking about, but he continued as if I hadn't interrupted. "They called us chaotic, dangerous. The truth was, we were not beholden to their rules. They could not control us, so they hunted us down. I seek to return the old ways. I seek to free us from our servitude. I wish for us to roam free, to do as we please, to blanket this world with our seed and let it sprout."

"Saw that movie last week. Gave it three stars. Not enough tits." I realized I was rambling, going off on tangents with a nutcase. That wasn't going to help things. I also sensed a zero percent chance of convincing him to change his mind. The problem here was, one wrong word from me and he could snap me in half, shit in my torso, and then sew me back together without any real effort. I needed to use a little strategy. "Say I believe you. What then?"

"Then you will come with me. I will show you the future."

"And we'll rule the empire together as father and son?"

"No. Our kind shall only bow to the true First. But it will take time. There is need for us to lead for now, until our influence is wide, but then no more. Then we shall all be truly free. Does that not sound ideal to you?"

"Peachy. And if I say no?"

"Then you will still come with me."

There was the kicker. I knew it was coming. It was like being asked if I wanted what was behind door number one or number two, only there was only one to choose from.

"My friends?"

"I do not wish to fight you, brother, so I shall offer you another choice."

"Oh?"

"You and the other I seek will come with me. If you do this, I will let your friends leave in peace."

"The other?"

"The pure one."

I knew it! The Jahabich had called Ed that too. Personally, I didn't get it. What the fuck was so pure about him? It sure as shit wasn't his language, his thoughts, or even the way he left his room most days. "You mean the one you were trying to kill? The one you called ... what was that word, oh yes – abominatio? I believe that means abomination, does it not?"

He nodded, a solemn look upon his face. "That was unfortunate on my part. I did not realize what he was then."

"So what is he?"

"The future. *Our* future."

That was a wee bit ominous, but at the same time, didn't really make any fucking sense. Ed had some weirdness in him, that much was obvious, but as far as I knew, there was only one person here with a prophecy hanging over their head – unless maybe this was some weird-ass fan theory bullshit in which Neville was actually the chosen one instead of Harry.

"What if we won't come with you?" I asked.

"Then you will still come with me and your friends will be given the choice."

"You can't have Ed ... the pure one."

"You think yourself his protector?"

"Yes, and I also think myself his roommate. He isn't getting out of his share of the rent that easily."

He appeared to consider this for a moment. "Face me, then."

"What?"

"Out here, now." Vehron raised his arms, now charred and blackened under the blistering gaze of the sun. He looked at me and smiled. Just as he did, his hair caught ablaze. Dude was seriously fucked in the head. "Face me, show me you have the mettle of our brothers in your veins. If you do, I will let your friends go."

"All of my friends?"

"All of them. I give you my word upon the blood of Kala."

Wait, blood of Kala? Wasn't that...?

"Die!"

I spun to find Christy a few steps behind me. I'd been so caught up in Mr. Crazy's loony rants that I hadn't been paying attention to much else. Alas, I'd never been a particularly good multitasker. Her presence itself wasn't the issue, although what she'd just shouted was a wee bit worrisome. Oh, and the fact that she was glowing bright red was definitely a minor cause for alarm.

"Christy, don't..."

Yeah, that worked about as well as expected.

I'm not sure what would have happened next otherwise. Facing Vehron out in the open sunlight was pretty much a death sentence, but if it would have saved my friends, it was definitely worth considering. Of course, I'd seen enough movies to know that the bad guy's word was typically worth a steaming pile of horseshit. All he needed to do was watch me vaporize and then waltz in and say, "Fooled you!"

However, that was all meaningless conjecture now as a bolt of red-hot death magic lanced out from Christy's outstretched arms and...

...and created a smoldering crater where Vehron had been standing just a second earlier.

Shouting out your intended attack might be cool as all hell on Dragonball Z, but doing so in real life was just plain old dumb – not that I was going to tell that to the hormonal witch with murderous intent.

Besides, I had bigger fish to fry, such as the musclebound weirdo who was now standing about a foot away, looking down upon me with a grin on his face as if this was how he wanted things to play out all along.

"So be it," he said.

And with those three words, I knew we were royally fucked.

# 48

# ONE SHALL FALL

I'll give myself credit, mostly because almost nobody else ever does, but at least I didn't hesitate to act.

No one-liners, no snappy puns. Hell, no shitting my pants either. That last one was a definite plus in my favor. Nope, all I did was raise my knee into his crotch in the cheapest of cheap shots.

It worked about as well as it did last time I tried it.

Removed from direct sunlight, Vehron's burns healed right before my eyes. I had to assume the damage dealt by my blow, more than enough to have cracked a two-by-four in half, was being handled in a likewise manner. He barely winced from the shot. Instead, he actually smiled.

"You are not entirely ignorant of the paths to victory, brother. Perhaps there is hope for you yet. But for now ... *TAKE THEM!!*"

I was just about to question whether Vehron was talking to himself in third person when the ground around us started to rumble.

Was this the most convenient earthquake in the history of the planet? Somehow, I didn't think so. The trees and houses beyond the forest didn't show any signs of getting all shaken to shit.

I heard a sound off to my left and turned to find that Christy, still alight with pissed off mage fire, had fallen to her butt. Maybe that was for the best, as I wasn't entirely sure she'd have hesitated to blast me if it meant sending Vehron to that big dustpan in the sky. I also wasn't sure if his mention of the White Mother's name was coincidence or not. Hell, for all I knew, it was as common as Joe back in the day, but I had a feeling it wasn't. The bigger question was why was he invoking her name at all?

Alas, such speculation needed to wait. The rumbling grew worse, to the point where I needed to grab hold of something – preferably not Vehron – to keep from teetering over. All at once, I heard a tremendous crash and spun to see a copse of trees collapse in on themselves, quite literally disappearing into the ground. The resulting sinkhole took one of Gan's men – a look of dopey peace still on his face – with it.

Oh crap. Not now.

To which fate pretty much replied, "Of course now, stupid!"

A rocky head appeared out of the hole a few moments later, its orange lantern eyes glowing malevolently in the shade provided by the forest. And it wasn't alone, not by a long shot.

Seems that the ambush during our trial, in which Ib's name was invoked, hadn't been some sort of ruse to misplace blame after all. The Jahabich were somehow working with – or for; it wasn't quite clear yet – Vehron. Talk about being double, triple, and probably even quadruple fucked.

I'd known there was a chance of this happening, but hoped it wouldn't. Sadly, hope is the last holdout of the truly screwed.

If that didn't describe us right then and there, I didn't know what would.

The Jahabich swarmed out of the ground, over a dozen strong. Outside of Ed, Christy, and Tom, the rest of the group – Gan included – looked like they were a bunch of stoned hippies waiting for Hendrix to perform at Woodstock. Shit! They didn't stand a chance.

Unfortunately, that left me in quite the pickle. Stay and try to hold off Vehron, or go fight the Jahabich? Neither seemed a winning gambit. Hell, between the two sides, they could make one heck of an asshole sandwich, with me as the meat.

"Go, brother," Vehron said. "I will not interfere." I turned to find the grin wider than ever on his face. Fucking dick-weasel. "Should you win, I will consider reinstating my offer."

"You're too kind."

Apparently, he hadn't reached the part in his English lessons covering sarcasm, because he replied, "In my day, I was known to be quite merciful. Behold, as I shall give you even greater quarter to impress me."

What was he...?

I heard a screech behind me back in our camp. No, more of a battle cry. I spun to find Gan back on her feet, having just delivered a spin kick that nearly decapitated a Jahabich who'd been advancing upon her position. It wasn't just her either. All around, vampires got back to their feet and retrieved their weapons. Vehron had released them all from his compulsion.

What was his game? Was this little more than amusement to him?

Well, okay, that probably was the case. Hell, when you're Caesar, what better fun than to watch the gladiators battle it out for your entertainment while you sipped wine and placed bets?

Out of the corner of my eye, I saw Christy waddling back to her feet. Fuck it. I didn't see much choice in playing along for now. We might still find our way out of this, but it wasn't going to happen if she kept kicking the hornet's nest.

I gave Vehron the stink eye, then turned and stepped away from him. For a moment, I was certain it was all a ploy and the next – and last – sensation I'd feel would be his fist punching though the back of my skull. However, that didn't happen – thank whatever gods there are. Good thing too, because it would have sucked royally.

"Come on," I said, grabbing hold of Christy's arm and steering her back toward our friends.

"Did you hear him?" she asked angrily. "Did you hear him swear upon her name?" Tears were now streaming down her face. "He..."

"He's going to kill us all if you take another potshot at him, that is, if his friends don't kill us first." I pointed toward where our group was engaging the Jahabich.

Sally saw me as she dodged a blow from one. "Any time now, jackass."

"Be there in a minute," I called back. Jeez, impatient little minx, wasn't she? I turned back to Christy. "He said he'd let my friends go if we win."

"You can't trust him."

"I know, but maybe this will buy us some time. Give us a chance to – you know, *apparate*." I was counting on the fact that Vehron's current lexicon didn't include Harry Potter terminology. Christy's eyes narrowed at my use of the term, but thankfully, she was more than smart enough to get the hint. She didn't bother to correct me this time.

So instead, together, we turned to meet our fate.

Decisions, decisions. There were so many potential enemies to go after. Ah, yes. Thankfully, Tom and Ed were around to make this much easier, being that they were both, more or less, tits on a bull in a fight against these rock monsters.

Tom might have been decked out in the latest in zealot-wear, but we'd both seen Sheila fight against these things and knew that faith magic wasn't particularly effective on them. As for Ed, despite whatever François might have ranted during his last few minutes, as far as I could tell, his main power in a fight was still to bleed all over his enemies.

Sadly, it looked like that was definitely an option as one of the Jahabich got past Sally and charged him.

"I don't have a clear shot," Christy said.

"No worries, I got this," I shouted back, already halfway there.

I raced past my friends and shoulder-tackled the beast, nearly breaking my arm in the process. Fuck me! It was like fighting a pile of granite. Nevertheless, vampire strength is nothing if not formidable. I managed to knock the creature off its trajectory. It stumbled to the side, where two of Gan's soldiers took over. With their advantage in age over me, they were able to rend the creature in two – the strange orange goop that made up its blood spraying out in an arc.

That gave Christy the opening she needed. Rather than shoot red death into an already confused battlefield, she muttered something unintelligible in the chaos, made a few gestures, and a shimmering purple dome of energy appeared around my roommates.

She advanced on our position and told them, "Stay inside; it'll protect you."

"Maybe you should get in there too," I said. Hell, she already looked winded from the effort. Surely she was putting more strain on herself than her body needed right now.

"No chance," she replied.

"Listen, babe," Tom said from inside, "Bill has a point. Maybe you should..." She turned and glared at him, to which he put up his hands and added, "Or, I could just hang out in here with Ed. All's good."

Poor guy. Forget cats or ravens. I had a feeling he was in for a lifetime of being little more than her familiar. Oh well. I'm sure there were worse fates ... like getting our heads caved in by rock monsters.

Speaking of which, I needed to make sure that didn't happen. Another of the creatures stepped in, and I raised my hands just in time to hold it off. Though my hands were torn to shreds as I wrestled with it, it sure beat the alternative.

As we fought, its strange orange eyes glowed greedily and it opened its jack-o-lantern mouth. *"Mother will be pleased. You will join us and the pure one will be hers."*

"Sorry, but Mommy says it's nap time first." Sally stepped up to where I was trying to fend off the creature and shoved the barrel of a gun in its eye socket. It wasn't quite her old Desert Eagle, but any port in a storm.

She pulled the trigger, and I ducked to make sure I didn't get hit with any ricochets.

The creature screamed as she continued to fire, the light in its one eye flickering several times before finally going out.

She used the distraction to get behind the beast, grab it by the eye socket she'd just peppered with gunfire, and begin to pull. "Make a wish!"

"Fine," I replied, reversing course and pulling the Jahabich toward me. "I wish for a pony for Christmas."

"What about living through this?" she asked, continuing to put on the pressure.

"I ... think ... I have ... a better shot at the pony." The creature's head snapped at the jawline and its rocky hide crumbled as half its face was pulled back over its body.

"That's one," I said, breathing hard from the effort. Damn, these things were tough.

"Rest break's over, lover," Sally said. "There's more coming."

I glanced up at her use of the L-word. She immediately realized her slip of the tongue because she rolled her eyes and said, "Not now, genius."

Just like a woman to send mixed signals when in the middle of an apocalyptic battle with rock monsters from the center of the Earth. It figures.

I took a moment to gather my bearings, to see where I was needed most.

Vehron was still standing at the periphery of the fight, his eyes glued to me – oh great, a voyeuristic asshole to boot.

Christy was hitting the creatures hard, whenever she could get a clean shot in – fusing them solid with lances of magical fire.

Dave was playing it smart – and cowardly – strategically keeping a few of Gan's men between him and the Jahabich. Vampire or not, he knew his limitations as a warrior.

Not so much Adam. He was fighting alongside the Mongolian assassins, still acting like this was one big game – failing to realize that where they were knocking chunks of rock away with each blow, all he was doing was getting in the way.

Ugh. I had a feeling that by the time this was all over and done with, I'd need a completely new gaming group.

I turned to check on Tom and Ed and saw they were ... oof!

I'd forgotten the Jahabich might look like piles of shit-colored bricks, but they moved with a surprising amount of stealth when they wanted to.

The creature hit me from behind in a glancing blow that just caused me to stagger. When I turned around to face it, though, I found myself right in the path of a sweeping haymaker from one of its club-like arms.

My ribs snapped like matchsticks, and I found myself airborne. At least dirt made for a somewhat softer landing than asphalt. Of course, that didn't mean it hurt any less.

I tried to sit up and immediately screamed in pain. Two of my ribs had splintered and were now poking out of my abdomen. It was just as pleasant to see as it was to feel.

The funny part was, as the creature advanced upon me, raising its arms to pound me into pudding, the only thing I could think about was how disappointed Vehron probably was in my performance. Story of my life. On the upside, I didn't have to worry about anyone labeling me an over-achiever.

"Hold on, Bill, I'm coming!"

I glanced past the creature and saw Tom rushing my way, having left the safety of his fiancée's force bubble. Idiot. What the fuck was he going to do, hope the Jahabich wanted to trade Pokémon cards with him?

I'd have yelled for him to not be an idiot, but my insides were currently disallowing any vocalizations outside of bloody gurgles.

"Hey, asshole!" Tom yelled, gaining the Jahabich's attention for a moment. "Pick on someone your own size. I am the jalapeño in Satan's cheese dip, fucker!"

Huh?

Just then, something else entered my periphery. Gan appeared on the opposite side of the creature. While its head was swiveled toward Tom, she attacked it with the heavy mace she'd been carrying. I'd always been a sword guy in our weekly game, but suddenly, I could understand the appeal of the ungainly, but far heavier weapon. The Jahabich's head exploded from the impact as it were a water balloon.

Rubble and orange goo sprayed out, most of it catching Tom straight on.

"Oh gross!" he cried as the remains of the creature fell over and landed with a heavy thud in the dirt.

Gan dropped to her knees by my side. "There is no time to argue, my love, so do not try."

"Why?" I gurgled, my healing finally starting to kick in a little.

Gan simply reached over, raked her hand over the razor-sharp skin of the dead Jahabich, and then shoved it into my mouth.

Oh gross. Who the hell knew what shit piles that thing had walked through? I tried to spit it out, but she was far stronger than me – especially right now. When I tried to protest, she just shoved her hand further in, nearly triggering my gag reflex.

Instead, my mouth filled with her blood. I'd been there before, so I knew the drill. I swallowed, and her crazy puberty-ridden vampire blood, blood that somehow gave her the speed of a vamp twice her age, hit my stomach like a bundle of dynamite.

Yep, that was another one I was gonna owe her.

Gan's warriors did their damnedest to keep the creatures off us as my healing gladly accepted the boost and I watched, wide-eyed, as my ribs shifted and pulled back into my body. Gross to see, but pretty fucking magnificent to experience.

Not a moment too soon either. With Gan's blood in me, I stood a chance against these things.

After several more seconds, I sat up, feeling the rest of my internal organs shift back into place where they belonged.

"Are you okay, beloved?"

"Fine." I swallowed my pride and added, "Thank you, Gan."

"It is always a pleasure to share my fluids with you, my love."

Well, if that didn't creep me the fuck out, I didn't know what would. Speaking of fluids, though, Tom also stepped to my side – still looking like someone had dumped a mega-sized Orange Julius over his head.

"How you feeling?" he asked.

"Better. You?"

"Nothing a long shower won't cure."

"Hah. You look like the guest of honor at a radioactive bukakke festival."

"I am not familiar with those, my love," Gan said. "Perhaps one day you shall take me."

Tom spewed laughter, spraying some Jahabich gunk on me. Asshole. I reached up a hand toward him, then seeing the slime-covered one he went to offer, pulled back. "Never mind. I think I can do this on my own. Oh, you might want to get some wet wipes for those."

He glanced down at his bandolier of toys and sighed. "These fuckers better hope this shit cleans off easily because if not, I'm gonna kill every single one of them."

"That is unlikely," Gan replied, turning to see if any more of the creatures were advancing upon us.

"What the hell was with that cheese dip line?" I asked him.

"Oh, we're always spouting someone else's one-liner. Thought I'd give it a shot and try something of my own."

"Keep trying." I stood up and glanced around. About half the Jahabich were dead or fused into statues. Unfortunately, there were just as many clouds of dust settling to the forest floor.

Through it all, Vehron continued to watch me – bemusement on his face. Fucking asshole. It was time to wipe that grin right off.

"Gan," I said as quietly as I could.

"Yes, beloved."

"I need your help."

"Anything. I would climb any mountain. Fight any enemy. Slay half the world if you so..."

"Yeah, yeah, yeah, that's all fascinating. I need to bite all of your people."

"Oh?"

"I don't have time to explain," I whispered. "I just need you to trust me, and send them in one at a time."

"You need not explain, Dr. Death. You wish to see if their cumulative power will be enough to engage The Destroyer."

"You know about that?"

"Of course. I am a student of our history. How could I not?"

"Well, I didn't know until recently and ... anyway, never mind that. Will you help me out?"

The insane gleam in her eye told me all I needed to know. Hell, if I'd asked, she'd have ordered her men to line up and slice off their own balls for my amusement. Needless to say, I was really glad I didn't work for her.

I sincerely doubted any of her warriors were under a century in age. Most of them were probably a great deal older. The only question was whether there were enough of them.

I didn't just need to match Vehron – I needed to blow

him out of the water. The guy was an experienced warrior. Equal power meant shit if he took me apart with a bunch of ancient vampire Jujitsu moves.

"Get back to Ed," I told Tom.

"I can..."

"I can't do this if I'm worrying about you."

For a moment, he looked like he was about to argue, but then he nodded and turned back toward...

"Where the fuck is he?"

"Huh?" I glanced past him. Christy's purple force shield was down. But how?

"There!" Tom pointed.

Christy was on her knees, obviously exhausted. Sally was the only one with her, trying to fend off two of the creatures and paying the price for it.

"Oh crap."

"Double crap!" Tom said. Sure enough, he was right. One of the Jahabich was walking toward where Vehron stood, Ed's unconscious form draped over its shoulder.

"I will help the witch and your whore," Gan said, stepping to my side.

"But I thought you hated Christy."

"Indeed I do, but I dislike earning your ire more. She is, after all, your friend."

Holy crap. I was touched. Maybe the psychotic little hobbit understood a bit of what I'd been trying to tell her after all. "I could kiss you," I said, before realizing what a stupid thing that was to say.

"When this is over with, my love, I shall hold you to your pledge." Without another word, she was off – covering the distance to Sally in a heartbeat.

Then I remembered I could do the same. I had her power. I didn't intend to waste the opportunity.

"Stay put," I said to Tom, then I felt everything around

me seemingly slow down as I sped up far past my normal limits. Gan might be the fate worse than death waiting for me at the end of all this, but she could sure as shit be handy in a pinch.

The Jahabich was only steps from its master, partner, or whatever Vehron was to it. Thankfully, those were steps it was never going to take. I overtook it easily, extending the claws of my left hand and driving them into its back.

The creature didn't particularly appreciate that and spun to face me, flinging Ed away in the process. Oh well, at least I didn't have to worry about accidentally decking my roommate.

The enraged Jahabich threw itself at me, a mass of swinging clubs and a big honking mouth full of granite teeth. Too bad for it, that I'd just eaten my Wheaties.

I leapt inside its defenses, its massive arms closing around my midsection. Before it could lay the bite down on me, though, I shoved both my fists deep into its glowing eye sockets. I wasn't too keen on touching Jahabich brain, or whatever passed for it, so I immediately spread my arms wide, putting everything I had into it until my fists exploded out of opposite sides of the creature's head.

Needless to say, that took the fight out of it.

I kicked it to the side and looked up to find Vehron standing over Ed.

"Don't touch him," I said.

"I have not, have I?"

"You said you'd make good on our bargain."

"I said I would consider it, if you won. Your friends fight bravely and you..." He hesitated, as if trying to find the right words. "You have a style all your own. As of yet, though, you have won nothing. I am simply ready to claim what is mine when the inevitable occurs."

"Why do you want him?"

"I do not."

"I don't suppose you could maybe give me a straight answer, y'know, without the fucking riddles."

"And my reason for this? I have called you brother, yet you insist upon calling me enemy."

He had a point there. I supposed telling me his nefarious plan was entirely optional on his part.

Gah! I didn't have time for these games, standing around and talking while my friends fought for their very lives.

I glanced over and saw Gan making good on her word, helping Sally defend Christy. Unfortunately, more of those things appeared to be swarming out of the hole and heading their way. Looking back at Vehron's smug grin, I got the impression this was purposeful. He wanted me to choose.

"I'm taking Ed with me."

"No. He shall stay here if you choose to help your other friends. He will be safe."

There was no way I could win this. I could help my friends and lose Ed, because don't think for one second I trusted this guy to not pick him up and walk off. Or I could fight him, which would kinda be like me deciding to try and punch out a mountain.

At least in the one scenario, I could do some good, make a difference. If we managed to win, we could still maybe get away, join up with Sheila, and storm this guy's fortress together.

Yeah, that made the most sense.

So, of course, rather than do that, I made the decision to do the craziest thing possible.

It's just who I am.

I turned and took a few steps toward my friends, keeping an eye on Vehron, who just kept grinning that asshole grin of his. God, how I hated smug douche-bags.

Then, using Gan's speed to my advantage, I bent down, grabbed the Jahabich I'd just killed, and whipped its body at the fucker.

Having nearly a half ton of rock thrown your way is nothing to sneeze at, for normal folks anyway. Vehron merely backhanded the beast, the sound making a crack like thunder throughout the forest. It practically exploded from the impact, rocks and orange sludge flying in every direction.

That was the part I'd been counting on.

No matter how strong you are, how good you can see, or how well you can smell – a distraction is still that. He'd smacked the creature, no doubt aiming to send a message of just how powerful he was. He had, don't get me wrong, but he'd also created a cloud of debris that masked me as I rushed in.

I went low, grabbed Ed's arm and dragged him toward me. I was sure when he woke up, he wouldn't appreciate being given the sack of potatoes treatment, but for now, he didn't get a vote.

Before I could make any headway, though, a pair of powerful hands grabbed me from behind and dragged me off. Guess I wasn't as distracting as I'd hoped. Fast as I was, this asshole was even faster. I was pulled to my feet as Vehron locked an arm around my neck.

Without giving it any thought, I bent low and twisted my shoulder – throwing him over me and onto the ground below. Woo! Once Sally got her memories back, I'd have to solemnly thank her for those grueling Judo lessons.

Just for good measure, I drove a punch into Vehron's face before he could get back up. I might as well have been trying to sink a battleship with my fist, but it still felt good to hear a crunch from his nose as my knuckles hit home.

"Bill, catch!"

Huh? I turned and Sally, maybe a dozen yards away, threw her gun my way. I watched it sail right past me, clattering to the ground several feet away. Damnit! Probably should have told her that games of catch with my dad often ended the same way.

Sadly, my momentary respite was over. Vehron did a kip-up back to a standing position, then spun to face me. Fuckers always gotta show off. I had a feeling I wasn't going to get a second chance. So much for my plans of sucking on all of Gan's men – which would hopefully have been far less fruity in practice than it sounded.

"You get Ed. I've got this motherfucker!"

What?!

In the chaos of battle, neither of us had noticed Tom come running our way. Well, okay, I hadn't. Vehron probably paid him about as much mind as a flea.

"Get back, you crazy..."

But I was too late with my warning. Tom jumped onto Vehron piggyback style, like he was a kid asking for a horsey ride. However, this cowboy had spurs.

A small pantheon of faith-empowered toys touched home against the elder vamp, and their wrath was terrible to behold. White flame erupted from Vehron's back like he was being doggy-styled with a magnesium flare.

Gone was the smug grin and in its place a roar of surprise and anguish. Ah, it was music to my ears.

"Feel free to just keep fucking standing there," Tom cried, barely holding on.

Oh yeah. That spurred me to action, especially since painful didn't necessarily equal lethal where a guy like this was concerned. We'd hit him hard before and it had barely left a dent.

I glanced to my left where Sally's gun had fallen. With any luck, it was full of silver bullets, a skull-full of which would definitely fuck up this guy's shit.

It was the space of only a few steps to retrieve it, barely a blip of time with Gan's speed at my disposal, but it was still too long. I spun back, bringing the gun level with his face, only to find he'd reached back and managed to snag a handful of Tom's jacket.

Vehron's hand immediately ignited as Tom was quite literally covered in collectibles, but that didn't seem to matter to him as he dragged my roommate off.

Aflame or not, he backhanded my friend, sending teeth flying. Shit!

"Tom!" Christy's voice rang out from somewhere outside of my periphery, but I was already on the move.

Claws extended, I raked them down the asshole's face, digging deep furrows in his cheek as I raised the gun with my other hand and prepared to ventilate this fucker's skull up close and personal ... UGH!

Something hard collided with my jaw, and it was only as I was knocked away that I realized it was my roommate's skull.

I landed and immediately rolled back to my feet, but I was too late.

***crack***

"NO!"

I wasn't sure whether it was me, Christy, or both of us screaming in unison as Vehron twisted Tom's head a hundred and eighty degrees, but in the end, it really didn't matter.

The surprised look on my friend's face quickly faded as his eyes clouded over.

Vehron let go and dropped him like he was little more than useless meat.

Just like that, my roommate, my best friend in this whole world, was dead. I had failed him more completely than words could describe.

**49**

# GREASY KID STUFF

I t was as if time stopped for a moment. I was stuck in that awful place – the split second between when Tom ceased being my friend and became just a lifeless pile of flesh and bones.

I'm certain that plenty was going on. We were in the middle of a battle, after all, but the only thing that registered was the sound of Tom's heart. My enhanced vampire ears, normally an advantage, were now my curse as I was forced to listen to it slow, stutter, and then finally fade away into silence.

We'd been through so much in our lives. He'd been the first friend I'd made in kindergarten. We'd shared toys, games, dreams, everything. Hell, our friendship had even survived my own death. It was funny, but as much as I tried to keep my friends from harm, a part of me was convinced of our invincibility.

We'd survived Jeff, Turd, Remington, even Alexander the Great. As much as I liked to bemoan my own fate, I was certain that it smiled upon my group as a whole.

We'd survive this. The end of the world was nothing

compared to us.

Until now.

This was reality. Fate was neither cruel nor kind. It didn't care either way, and it was now showing me this in a way that I would never forget.

Screams began to filter in, but once again, I wasn't sure if they were coming from me or Christy. Hell, it was probably a safe bet that we were both expressing our anguish. The only question was which of us would be the first to turn our grief into lethal action.

No, that one was easy. It was going to be me.

I raised the gun again, intent on emptying it into my grinning foe. I'd wipe that smile off his face, maybe make him eat it afterwards. That wouldn't bring my friend back, but maybe it could avenge him. However, squeezing the trigger produced nothing – no explosion of sound or satisfying buck of a bullet being ejected toward my enemy.

I then realized why. In my anger, I'd crushed it. The mechanism of my revenge was now little more than a useless heap of metal and plastic in my grasp. I hadn't even realized I was utilizing my vampiric ... wait!

Vampire! I was a vampire. What a fucking idiot I was.

Maybe I could still save Tom.

Fuck revenge. Getting him back was far more important.

Ignoring everything else, I bared my fangs and leapt toward my friend. Even knowing that I was on my knees in front of perhaps the most lethal foe I'd ever faced didn't deter me from my task. Let Vehron kill me if he needed to. So long as I could bring my friend bac ... "ARGH!"

My hands burst into flame as I touched Tom's body. The goddamned toys he was wearing were still charged with his power. Much like Sheila's sword, they'd absorbed the faith magic and still radiated with it.

No!

It couldn't end like this. I fought through the pain, pushed closer to my friend. I just needed one bite. Hell, I'd happily succumb to the fire at that point. Just one little...

A boot to the face ended what little chance I had.

It wasn't much. Had Vehron hit me with his full force, I'd have surely been decapitated from the blow. But it was more than enough to send my burning form tumbling away.

Removing me from the source – as well as an impromptu stop, drop, and roll session – caused the flames of faith to quickly die down. I looked up to see Vehron step over Tom's corpse, blocking my way to it.

"I think not, brother," he said, the humor gone from his voice. "It is time to teach you your place in life."

I gritted my teeth as I looked up at him. All the anger I had in my heart coalesced into a fine point aimed directly at him.

My fangs extended along with my claws as a red haze descended upon my vision. I stood to face him, my injuries already healing – although whether from Gan's blood or the power that dwelled inside of me, I wasn't sure. I prayed it was that second option, though.

Whatever his evil, whatever he sought to do to the world, Dr. Death seemed the lesser of my devils right now. Fuck it, if it meant avenging my friend, then I'd gladly let him raze the countryside to the ground if he wanted.

I gave in, opened myself up to it. Never had I wanted something as much as I did at that moment. Sheila, Sally, to live a normal life – all of it paled in comparison to making Vehron suffer.

"Let's do this," I muttered, my tongue grazing the edges of my razor-sharp fangs. "This body is yours to do with as you please, Dr. Death."

I mentally handed him the keys, throwing my own out the window of the imaginary apartment we shared. So long as the fucker in front of me met a death that made Turd's seem pleasant in comparison, I'd happily lock myself away for all of eternity.

*Fuck you.*

What?!

That was it. Those two words and nothing more. There was no change. My clothes didn't rip. I didn't retreat back into myself. Nothing happened, save my opponent stepping forward and wrapping one impossibly strong hand around my throat.

"You will not meet your friend's fate, brother," Vehron whispered, "but you may wish you had. You should not have challenged me."

I couldn't have responded had I wanted to. My air was completely cut off. Even with Gan's power at my disposal, I might as well have been a toddler trying to pry open a vise grip.

Out of the corner of my eye, Christy approached. Sally and Gan were still covering her, but she was running as if Hell itself were on her heels. She was screaming something, but I couldn't hear anything beyond the pressure building up in my head. Much more, and I was sure my eyes would pop out like party favors.

Christy started glowing and, for a moment, I thought she might be planning to go nuclear and just flat out vaporize Vehron and anything in his vicinity – including me. Oddly enough, I was okay with that. I wasn't sure I deserved to live, not after failing my friend so utterly. Dying was fine so long as this fucker came along for the ride.

It wasn't to be, though. She dropped to her knees at Tom's side and began pouring whatever power she'd been gathering into his body. The look on her face screamed of desperation. Whatever she was doing, it was some last-ditch effort to bring him back. I didn't know if there was a God or not in this fucked-up universe we lived in, but if there was, I said a silent prayer to give the poor girl a break for a change.

All at once, though, my view of them was obscured by the asshole who was busy squeezing the life out of me. "I am speaking to you, brother. Pay them no mind. They are of no consequence. There is only you and I, a reality I will make you painfully aware of when..."

"*Mother demands the pure one.*"

The look on Vehron's face turned from one of mild interest in my fate to outright annoyance. I couldn't see who'd spoken, but the gravelly voice was that of the Jahabich. Judging from where it came from, I'd say the creature had approached from my blind side and stood directly behind me.

C'mon, Christy! Do it now. Three for the price of one. That's not a bad deal.

"I am busy. I will bring the abomination momentarily."

"*She has waited long enough. She wishes the pure one now.*" Almost as if to emphasize the point, it repeated, "*Now.*"

I was certain Vehron would tell the stony asshole to take a flying fuck off the nearest cliff face. That or maybe beat it to rubble, using my body as a club.

Thus, my amazement when he simply nodded was such that I almost forgot my neck was being pulverized. According to what I'd heard, this guy had once been the vampire nation's premier general. That and he was a fucking Freewill too, a pretty goddamned badass one, if I did say so myself. Yet he was being told what to do and accepting it like he was a little kid being called in for dinner.

What the fuck was going on?

Sadly, any answers would have to wait. Vehron flung me

to the side as if I were little more than trash. I landed hard, maybe twenty feet away. Damn, this guy was tough.

Even with Gan's blood bolstering me, it was still several long seconds before I could so much as draw a breath.

***"STEP ASIDE!! DO NOT HINDER ME!!"***

There wasn't a lot behind it. He could have easily ordered all the combatants on my side to be good lads and slit their own fucking throats. Instead, he'd given little more than the vampire equivalent of "excuse me, coming through."

I sat up in time to see him grab Ed and sling his unconscious form over his shoulder. All of the vampires in the area were dazed from his command, and Christy was still pouring energy into Tom's unmoving form. There was nobody left to stop him.

Even the Jahabich were still for the moment, as if waiting to see what would happen.

I was still pulling myself to my feet when he passed the rock monster who I assumed was the one who'd given him the order. He turned to it and said, "I leave the rest to you. Bring them when you are finished – should you prove victorious."

Although I couldn't be certain, I got the impression that his passive aggressive compulsion had been a not-so-subtle "fuck you" to the Jahabich for daring to tell him what to do. Either way, he walked past the creature and kept going until he passed the tree line and stepped into the daylight beyond.

I was tempted to catch up to him. With Gan's speed, it would have been child's play. But then what? Burst into flames under the sun? Facing him now was a losing strategy. He'd already proven that. He'd beaten me with no effort at all and would do so again. I, quite literally, had nothing in my arsenal that could touch him.

What I did have, though, was a fallen friend and his grieving fiancée. Whatever Vehron's plans for Ed, they seemed to want him alive. That meant a chance to rescue him. But to do that, I'd need the help of my friends.

Before I could ask for that help, though, I needed to be there for them.

Some things were more important than revenge.

Once Vehron was out of sight, his compulsion evaporated. Gan's forces reengaged the Jahabich, who were only too happy to continue the fight. As I numbly walked toward them, Gan gave some order in Chinese. No idea what it meant, but her men began to pull back and form a defensive ring around where Christy and Sally knelt by Tom's side.

Gan joined her men in their assault. I thought she might say something to me as I passed her, but she simply nodded. I immediately understood. As much as she might have disliked Christy, Tom had died honorably. That demanded some respect. Or at least, I thought that's what she was doing. Getting inside her head wasn't something I tried to do on too many occasions.

Regardless, I joined my friends, kneeling beside Tom just as Christy ceased whatever she was doing. The glow faded from her, but nothing seemed to have changed.

"I tried," she sobbed, looking up at me. Tears freely streamed down her face. "Dark magic, an abomination to my people, but I didn't care so long as it might save him. It didn't work, though."

"Maybe we're not finished yet," Sally said. I knew exactly what she meant. She was talking about what I'd been about to try before Vehron tauntingly stopped me.

I expected Christy's staunch denial. No matter how chummy she and I had become, there was always that feeling that she considered the undead to be a lesser species. Thus, I was surprised when she simply nodded at Sally before burying her face in her hands.

Sally looked at me expectantly, and I mouthed, "Do it." She was far more experienced at this anyway. I'd never turned someone before, at least not that I was aware of. Sally, on the other hand, knew what she was doing.

As Gan's forces kept the Jahabich at bay, Sally ripped swatches of cloth from the outfit Gan had given her to wear and wrapped them around her hands. Thus protected, she tore off the bandolier of blessed toys and tossed it to the side. I wrinkled my nose as she did so. The combination of holy fire and Jahabich juice left an odor in the air reminiscent of burning tires.

Without further ado, she bit into Tom's neck – his head still turned at an unnatural angle.

Christy closed her eyes and put her hands to her ears. I couldn't blame her. This wasn't something she wanted to either see or hear. If it worked, though, it would be worth it. We might have to corral him a bit, wait for the bloodlust to abate, but it could be done. I just had to hope he wouldn't turn out to be like my gaming group.

Speaking of which, I looked around and didn't see any sign of either Adam or Dave. A part of me was sure they'd perished in battle, easily the weakest links in this fight. Oddly enough, though, that thought brought with it only a cold numbness. Seeing my best friend in the world laid low had drained me. My broken heart seemingly had no more room left in it.

That was unfair to them and I made myself a promise to make good on things.

For now, though, I could only wait expectantly.

After what seemed an eternity, but in reality was just a few seconds, Sally raised her head. She wiped some of Tom's blood from her lips and looked me in the eye.

"Well?" I asked.

"He's gone."

"What?"

"I don't understand it either. It only happened a few minutes ago. I should be able to bring him back."

"How do you know?"

She just shook her head. "It's hard to explain. Once you ... practice ... enough, you just do."

"It's my fault," Christy said.

"Huh?" I turned to her. "How is this your fault?"

"The magic. It must have backfired. Ruined him for ... your kind."

"Don't be so hard on him, babe. Bill might be a dick, but he's not a total cockmeat sandwich."

The voice caught my attention and I immediately glanced around at our little circle. "What was that?"

"Wasn't me," Sally said, the confusion on her face echoing mine.

I knew it wasn't Christy. She'd just been speaking. Besides, that had been a male voice. It had been ... Tom's?!

"You heard that, right?"

Both of them nodded, and we all simultaneously looked down at my roommate. It was all for naught, though. Nothing had changed with him – no smiling face, no movement. Hell, not even a mouthful of fangs. His eyes were still glazed over, lifeless.

"Um, guys, could I get a hand?"

Again his voice. What the fuck?

Sally raised her hands and shook her head.

Even Christy looked perplexed.

"Um, is his ghost haunting us?"

"It will be if you don't fucking help me," the voice replied. "My face is stuck in the dirt – oh God, let this be dirt – and I can't fucking move."

Sally pointed off to my left. "It's coming from over there."

"There isn't anything over there except those toys you yanked off of him. What the fuck?"

I quickly scampered over there anyway, not waiting for the others to catch up. There was no time to waste. Gan's people were still holding back the Jahabich, but more had climbed out of their sinkhole. It was rapidly becoming not an issue of if but *when* they'd overrun us.

Remembering what I was about to touch, I pulled my hands into the sleeves of the fur-lined jacket I wore and used them as makeshift gloves. I quickly sorted through the pile of discarded action figures – dirty and broken Star Wars toys, He-Man, and even a Transformer or two. "There's nothing here," I said.

I picked up the last piece, Tom's Max Adventure doll. It had been lying face down. I was about to toss it to the side too, when out of nowhere, Tom's voice asked, "Jesus Christ, Bill, when did you get so fucking big?"

Needless to say, it was at that point that I promptly freaked the fuck out.

## 50

## A SMALL PROBLEM

"Holy fucking shit!" I dropped the doll like it was covered in spiders. It hit the ground, where it bounced once and landed face up.

For a moment, there was nothing to hear save the battle raging around us. I began to wonder if maybe I'd imagined it. Hell, for all I knew, Dr. Death was fucking around inside my brain – rewiring everything for shits and giggles. Of course, then Christy started screaming, which may have clued me in ever so slightly that if this was some sort of illusion then it had graduated to mass hysteria.

"What the fuck, guys?" Tom asked, his voice coming from the Max Adventure figure lying in the dirt. He didn't sound overly pleased. "I get crippled and you all turn into assholes? Seriously, could someone please help me?"

Sally, easily the least nonplussed among our trio, stepped past me and gingerly reached down toward Max ... or Tom. She touched it with one outstretched finger, then, when nothing happened, she picked it up. She looked down upon it, glanced back at us quickly – one brow raised, and then said, "You're not crippled. You're a doll."

"Thanks. You aren't bad looking yourself."

"Not like that, stupid!"

"Huh. I never noticed how wide your nostrils flare when you're angry."

She turned back and shoved the cursed toy into my hands. "Here. Because otherwise, I'm going to do what my sister used to do to all of my dolls."

"Which was?"

"You probably don't want to know."

"Bill?" Tom asked.

"Yes?" I replied tentatively, being that I was totally creeped out.

"Is there a reason why I suddenly seem to be so small?"

"Well..."

"And can't move?"

"Um..."

"And everyone keeps making doll jokes?"

"I did this," Christy said from behind me. I turned and found her back on her feet, tears streaming freely from her eyes.

"You meant to do this?" I asked. Christ! What the hell had my friend done to piss her off that much?

"No!"

"Then how?"

"I don't know!"

"Not really following here," Tom added.

"This isn't even remotely normal."

"I think we can all agree on that," Sally said.

"The only way for something like this to happen is through magic," Christy explained, taking a moment to wipe her eyes. Though obviously still upset, the weirdness of the whole scenario was a bit too much to allow for the grief we should've been experiencing.

"Yeah, fine, magic," Tom said, sounding a bit exasperated. "But can maybe someone tell me what the fuck is going on?"

Considering the circumstance we were in, I didn't see much point in sugarcoating things. "You died."

"Really? I find it hard to believe that..." I held him up and pointed him toward where his body lay. "Holy fuck! That's me! How the fuck can I be over there?"

"You're in one of the toys you stole from that house."

"Which one? Anything good?"

"Max Adventure."

"Oh Jesus Christ! I couldn't be goddamned Darth Vader?"

"Hey, at least nobody's going to throw your ass onto eBay and then stuff you into a glass cabinet somewhere."

"True. I could see how ending up like the Prospector in *Toy Story 2* could drive someone crazy."

It was only then that I realized the absurdity of the conversation I was having. Glancing back over at my other friends, I saw it wasn't lost on them either.

"So, what happened to me?" he finally asked.

Before any of us could answer, though, a low muffled chuckling caught my ears. Sally and I both glanced over to Tom's corpse. The laughter was coming from him. No, make that from *on* him. From the sound of things, his backpack, to be precise.

It was Harry Decker.

The three of us marched back over to Tom's body. A part of me was tempted to kick it over and then tear open the pack to see what that asshole had done. However, giving in to my emotions might not be the best thing to do, especially since Christy might take offense to that. Instead, I gently turned him over and stripped the backpack off.

"Shouldn't you say a few words?" Tom asked.

"Huh?"

"I thought it was customary. I mean, shit, you're robbing my corpse. The least you can do is tell everyone what an awesome guy I was."

"It's not like I'm going through your pockets for spare change."

"Yeah, well, I'm watching in case you do. Damn, why didn't anyone tell me my bald spot was that wide?"

I held him out to Christy while I fumbled with the backpack. However, she shrank away as if it were a rattlesnake. Poor girl was probably holding on by the barest of threads. It didn't help that she couldn't even properly grieve without Tom making some asshole comment about it.

I handed him to Sally instead, who seemed to be taking this weirdness in stride – one of the benefits of having been around the supernatural longer than the rest of us, I suppose.

Once I unzipped the pack, I saw the sickly purplish light that continued to glow from within. I grabbed Decker's skull and pulled it out.

"What did you do?" I demanded of it.

*Me? I did nothing, fool. I simply gave a warning and it was ignored.*

I couldn't help but notice one difference between the two disembodied ... err ... entities. Decker sounded like a radio broadcast, almost distant, whereas Tom's voice was pretty much normal – except maybe a bit more diminutive.

That's when it hit me.

Crap! We'd been so caught up in the part of his prophecy about Vehron that we'd ignored the rest. "Tears will fall for those who die..." I repeated.

*Just as I proclaimed.*

"Wait," Christy snapped. "You knew? You knew it was talking about Tom?"

Again, Decker's skull did nothing but chuckle – a fucking douche to the very end.

"Why?"

*Because, my child, he was your undoing. You were always such a good pupil, such a devout witch. You were meant to follow in my footsteps, but then you met him. He was only supposed to be a tool, a means for us to get to the Freewill, but instead, he swayed you. He confounded you, turned you away from your path – from me. Because of him, I died. Because of him, your sisters died. And because of him, you have doomed all Magi to die!*

Decker might have had more to say, but in that moment, Gan's forces faltered.

What had happened to Tom had so consumed us that we'd neither helped nor noticed that the Jahabich continued to reinforce their ranks while continuing to thin ours.

We'd been so distracted by Decker's grinning skull, that we didn't notice the soulless orange eyes surrounding us until it was too late.

# 51

# INFILTRATION

The Jahabich were like fire ants. Tough enough for a younger vampire, but individually, not much of a challenge to either an older vamp or me after I'd gotten a power boost. Their real strength lay in a hive mentality that dictated overall victory trumped any individual needs.

Strategically, I could see how that could be their downfall given sufficient resistance. Against a small group with no hope of reinforcements, though, it was a pretty damn effective shock and awe tactic.

Had Gan's people been at full strength, they might have held off our attackers indefinitely. However, she was coming off a brutal campaign against the Feet, followed by tracking our asses through the forest, and then having Vehron playing compulsion-pong with their brains.

I half expected her to order her troops to fight to the death for her glory, which I would have done my best to ixnay. Surprisingly, though, once it became painfully obvious this fight was unwinnable, she told her troops to lay down their arms. Even she, nutty as a fruitcake, understood the logic of surviving to fight another day.

The Jahabich, thankfully, had been ordered to bring us in, as opposed to pounding our skulls to mush. We were forced to leave our weapons; no surprise there. I was afraid they'd make us abandon the talking skull and possessed toy that happened to be in our possession too. However, curios such as those were apparently rare, even for monstrosities from a hellish cavern deep beneath the Earth, so in the end, they confiscated both and brought them with us.

Well, okay, after hearing Decker's bullshit, we really just wanted to make sure Tom didn't get left behind, but it seemed to be all or nothing. Alas, Tom's body wasn't a part of the deal. It was left where it lay, along with the other discarded treasures he'd brought with him. I could only hope we'd have a chance to retrieve it later and put him to proper rest.

Thankfully, we weren't sent back the same way Vehron had gone, as the sun was still shining. No idea how that dude did it, but none of the vamps in our current group would have made it twelve paces, much less all the way back to the Boston complex. The Jahabich solved that problem, though, by forcing us to use the underground passage they'd dug to ambush us.

Once down below, they lined us up and marched us forward. Much like when Sally and I had been taken prisoner far below the streets of Vegas, the Jahabich showed little interest in us so long as we kept moving and didn't try to escape. Thus we were able to at least converse.

Sadly, any additional info that we might have pried out of Decker went unanswered. He fell silent in the grasp of the Jahabich who carried him. It had assumed a human form so as to have fingers to hold our disembodied comrades.

Whereas Decker seemed content to let his words from

earlier stand, Tom wasn't nearly so inclined to the silent treatment. "So anyone have a clue why I can't fucking move? I mean, I'm not looking to pull a Child's Play or anything, but what if my nose gets itchy? What if I need to take a shit?"

"Off the top of my head," I answered, continuing to march along, "I'd say it's because dolls don't have muscles."

"Action figure, asshole."

"Whatever the fuck. Oh, and since you don't have an asshole either, chances are you're safe when it comes to number two."

"Yeah, thanks for explaining the mechanics of plastic, Bill. You're forgetting something, though. My mouth is just a line of molded plastic, yet I can still talk. Oh, and I'm pretty sure these painted-on eyes don't really have retinas, yet I can see your ass trudging along in front of me just fine."

"Enjoy the view. As for the rest ... honestly, I have no fucking idea."

"He's a golem," Christy said. She'd been silent ever since we entered the tunnel. I was afraid she might've finally snapped, but her voice was surprisingly steady.

I considered that for a moment. "Aren't those usually big honking monsters?"

"That's just a modern conceit. Legend has it that golems could be made of anything, large or small, so long as they were a representation of the original soul."

"Hey, I don't have a porno-stache!"

I ignored Tom's outburst and asked, "Legend?"

She took a deep breath. I realized she was trying to stay strong, analyze the situation, but it was taking a toll on her. "It's ... it's because that's all it is – legend. Artificial life; it goes against our beliefs." She paused for a moment. "Most of our beliefs anyway. No Magi, true to our ways, has dabbled in such things in recorded history. As far as I was aware, the concept of golems was little more than a fairy tale – at least up until recently."

"Seems to be a lot of that going on in my life," I muttered, before raising my voice again. "But what about Decker? Isn't that what he is?"

"That's different. His remains were still tethered to his spirit, even if only by a thread. All we did was strengthen that thread and use it as a sort of fishing line to bring the rest of his soul back."

"But isn't that the same idea?"

"No! It's temporary, only because we thought it was a necessary evil. When the spell ends, he'll return back to where he belongs. The tether will be broken. He'll be at peace."

I sincerely doubted an asshole like Decker would ever be at peace, but I kept that opinion to myself. "So, you didn't try to do the same thing with Tom?"

She turned at once to glare at me, her eyes momentarily glowing red. Yeah, not a great color for her – or me, for that matter. "I was using healing magic on him at first. When that didn't work..." She faltered for a moment, the words she was trying to say obviously distasteful to her. "...I switched to stronger stuff – meant to reshape a broken body, fill it with vitality from another source ... nature, the plants around us in this case. Besides, what we did with Harry, it wouldn't have worked. Tom isn't a Magi. Our life force isn't the same as a normal human's. The magic that infuses us goes much deeper than just our bodies."

"So then how did *that* happen?" I hooked a thumb back toward the Jahabich who held Tom.

"I don't know," she snapped. "I've never seen anything like it."

"What else did Decker say?" Sally asked suddenly.

"He's been pretty much yammering about all sorts of shit," I replied offhandedly.

"No, in that crackpot prophecy of his. When I had him on my desk in Vegas, he used to spout them all the time. They were cryptic, but concise – not a lot of wasted words. Once things came to pass, it was usually pretty easy to figure out everything in hindsight."

"He spoke of being drowned in the flow of false life," Gan said, nearly causing me to jump into the arms of the Jahabich marching silently on my other side. She'd somehow sidled up next to me without me noticing.

"The only thing I was drowned in was rock monster jizz," Tom said. "And, no, you are never to quote me on that."

"Like hell," I replied. "When we get home, I'm updating your Twitter profile with that. I'm..." I trailed off as realization hit. Holy crap. Was that it? "I am a fucking idiot!"

"It's about time you accepted yourself for who you are."

"Not that, moron." I turned to Sally. "When we were underground, in the Jahabich's lair."

As I said that, I couldn't help but notice our silent guards all turned their pumpkin-sized heads in my direction. A few in the front pulled a complete one-eighty with their necks to do so. Apparently, I was finally saying something of interest to them. Shit! If so, I'd already spilled the beans. If they really wanted me to continue, it's not like they couldn't just beat the truth out of me.

Ignoring their creepy gaze, I turned back to Sally. "Yeah, I know, you don't remember, but I do. The pool, that glowing orange pool of gunk. These fuckers submerged the remains of their enemies in it. That's how they made new baby Jahabich, sorta."

That caught Christy's attention. "The power the White Mother used to trap captured souls in these false bodies. That's it, isn't it?"

"*Mother*," all of the Jahabich present repeated, the sound echoing in the tunnel. Yeah, definitely a bunch of creeps. After a couple more seconds of their dead-eyed staring, they all turned away, apparently having concluded we'd finished the interesting part of the story.

"Uh yeah," I replied. "The stuff the white ... chick did, I guess. Anyway, my point is that goo is basically the Jahabich's blood. Tom got absolutely drenched with the shit."

"Don't remind me," he said.

Christy held up a hand to her mouth. "Oh God!"

I turned to her and nodded. "Yeah. That's what I'm thinking. Maybe that blood somehow acted as a catalyst."

"But we all got it on us during the battle," Sally said.

"Yeah, we did. Same thing back in NORAD, but the main difference is none of us died."

"That is not entirely true, beloved," Gan replied. "Following your trial, many died covered in the remains of these creatures. None, so far that I am aware, rose again."

"It was me," Christy said, her voice low. "The power I poured into him, the dark magic. The blood *was* the catalyst, but it needed a power source to activate it."

"That doesn't make any sense," Sally replied. "These things are walking, talking monstrosities. The meatsack is just an immobile piece of cheap plastic."

"You do know I can hear you, right?"

"They're golems too," Christy said, certainty filling her voice. She turned to me, her eyes gleaming, but thankfully this time, it wasn't with anger. "This pit you mentioned; it's full of this stuff, right?"

"Yeah," I replied. "An Olympic-sized swimming pool of it at least. No idea how deep, but it's pretty much in a pit of rock..." I trailed off, realizing the rock surrounding it wasn't all too different-looking from the things marching us forward to our doom right now.

"To infuse life where there is none would require a lot of power to sustain, far more than I could generate myself," Christy continued. "All I did was make a spark by comparison."

"But it was enough," I concluded.

*Indeed it was,* Decker said, breaking his silence with a chuckle. *Congratulations, my dear. No one can say how this power was first found. That is lost to the mists of time. Even I cannot peer through them. But I can hazard a guess that perhaps it was an accident – maybe not much different than today. They say those who fail to learn the lessons of history are doomed to repeat it. It would seem ignorance of those lessons leads to the same result.*

"Shut up," Christy hissed.

*In turning your back upon our ways, spitting upon the glory of the White Mother, you have become her. All hail the new White Mother.*

Unsurprisingly, the Jahabich were right there to once more add their voices to the chorus. "*Mother.*"

I could only echo their sentiment, but added my own twist for our current predicament.

"Motherfucker."

We marched in silence for a while. There wasn't much else that needed to be said.

Okay, maybe not total silence. Tom kept up with his bitching. Oddly enough, though, I found his voice comforting. Despite all that had happened, at least he was still with us – in a manner of speaking.

At one point, maybe an hour after we'd started our trek, the tunnel ahead forked. As we neared the split, we found a few more Jahabich waiting for us. They weren't alone.

"You guys okay?" I asked Dave and Adam after reining in the whoop of joy I wanted to let out. Now was not the time to celebrate. Also, it would have probably just gotten us pummeled.

"Aside from getting the fuck beaten out of us, sure," Dave replied bitterly.

"What happened to you two?"

"What the fuck do you think? We ran."

"Our heroes," Sally commented as they were integrated into our group.

"Nothing wrong with a tactical retreat," Adam said.

"Exactly," Dave replied. "Remember those beholders you guys pussed out on a few years back?"

"Who the fuck throws beholders at a first level party?" I snapped.

"The whole concept of a random monster encounter is that it neither need be fair nor level appropriate." Dave glanced around, taking in our group. "Your roommates get away?"

"Nope, I'm still here," Tom replied.

"Vehron captured Ed," I added.

Dave spun around, no doubt looking for Tom, until his eyes settled on Max Adventure. One of our Jahabich captors, not particularly appreciative of having their forced march interrupted, clubbed him in the chest and shoved him forward.

"Whoa, hold on for a second there," Dave sputtered once he had caught his footing again. "What the fuck is going on? You didn't tell me you lived with Doll Man."

"Maybe it would be best if you stopped talking now," Christy said.

"No, seriously. What the hell happened? Did his mom fuck a voodoo doll or something, because that is some fucked-up shit right there."

All at once, Christy turned toward him, a bright red glow enveloping her. "I said it would be best if you stopped talking."

Oh crap.

I stepped between the angry, grief-stricken witch and my tactless DM. That was a mistake, as it brought me into contact with the boiling hot power flowing off of Christy's body.

"Fuck!" It was like putting my hand onto a hot stove. I jumped back instinctively, only to feel my backside bump into razor-sharp stone.

I turned, just in time to learn that the Jahabich's first warning against Dave had been their last.

A club-like arm of solid stone smashed against my skull a split-second later, and I was mercifully carried away into darkness.

**52**

## UNDEAD ALIVE

"C'mon, Bill, wake up."

"Let me sleep a little longer, Mom. It's Saturday."

A hand grabbed my shoulder and gave it a shake. It was gentle at first, but then gradually got stronger – far stronger than my mother had ever been, even when I'd been a child. Hell, if she'd used half the strength being used on me right then, she'd have dislocated my arm.

I'm sure I'd done things as a kid to deserve it, but I wasn't a kid anymore. My eyes popped open to find a beautiful face smiling down at me – light brown skin and dark eyes surrounded by a cascade of dark brown hair.

"Oh good, you're awake."

"Hey, Star," I said, giving my head a shake. It was a good thing vampires healed so quickly, because otherwise, I'd need a CAT scan to go along with all the times I'd been knocked out as of ... wait a second. "Starlight?"

"It's nice to see you too, Bill."

My brain immediately went from fuzzy to "what the fuck?" I sat up and instinctively scooted back a bit until my

464

hands felt nothing but air and I tumbled backward, landing clumsily on the floor. I glanced around and saw I was in a room. It was Spartan in appearance, and first I thought it might be a holding cell, but then I saw the whiteboard hanging on the wall above me. I looked up at the table I'd been lying on. It appeared I was in a conference room.

Had I died? After all, spending eternity as a cog in corporate America sure as shit fit my definition of Hell. Starlight's presence didn't help to quell that fear either. Don't get me wrong. As far as ghosts went, her shapely form was a metric shit-ton more welcoming than some old dude wearing chains and moaning about Christmas past.

Then I noticed the sub-standard lighting. Where normally overly-bright fluorescents would be shining from the ceiling – their artificial glow burning away all semblance of motivation for most – the lighting instead had a soft flickering quality as if little more than a nightlight illuminated the place.

I was in the Boston complex.

"What happened?"

"They carried you in a little while ago. I thought it might be easier if you had a chance to wake up in a quiet place. The halls can be a bit chaotic."

The pounding in my head was still noticeable, but starting to subside. My healing was taking care of any blunt head trauma. After a couple of seconds, I pulled myself up and regained my footing.

All the while, Star stood close by, concern on her face. She'd always been an odd duck amongst vamps; a gentle soul within the wolf pack. The problem there was the past tense part of it. When last I'd seen her, she'd just been newly promoted to master of Village Coven – the position having been vacated by Sally when she moved to Vegas. Unfortunately, our reunion had been short-lived as I'd brought baggage with me in the form of a two-thousand-year-old killing machine.

"Don't take this the wrong way, Star, but if you're fucking with me, I'm going to be mighty pissed."

"You didn't know I was still here?"

"That's one way of putting it. They told us you were dead." She smiled at that, to which I added, "For real, as in dusted."

"They?"

"Firebird."

"Oh, *her*." Star's tone implied she didn't find that all too surprising. "She definitely didn't waste any time falling in line. Guess she was still angry that Sally chose me to take over. No offense, but I wouldn't expect her to say anything other than whatever she thought would make her look better."

"Or piss off Sally?"

"Or that. I don't know what you've heard, but they have history."

"I gathered that," I replied. "Just not sure how much of that history she remembers."

"Excuse me?"

"Never mind. So you're saying that Firebird lied?"

"I'm standing here, aren't I?"

That she was, in all her hotness. Even so, I wasn't quite ready to concede the tearful reunion yet. "Speaking of Sally, where is she?"

"With the others."

"My friends?"

She nodded. That was a good sign, but I thought it best to play it coy before demanding to be brought to them.

"Any other survivors beside you?"

"The rest of Village Coven are here. The new recruits, anyway. Although we're not called that anymore."

I'd been turning toward the door, curious to see what lay beyond, but her words caught me. "What do you mean by that?"

"At first, nobody was happy. Firebird sold us out. We were prisoners, forced to do as we were told."

"What changed?"

"Everything. I can see why the Draculas forbid the Cult of Ib. There are no covens under their teachings, no strict code of control. We work toward the common good, but there are no quotas to meet, shadow treaties with the humans, that sort of thing. If someone wants to go out and hunt, they hunt. There's freedom here that I haven't known since before Night Razor turned me."

"Freedom, huh? And yet you're still here."

"What was there to come back to?"

"Your friends."

She let out a musical laugh. "Somehow, I knew you and Sally would make your way back here."

"Oh? Do you know why we're here?"

"I can guess."

"So then the question is, where will you stand?"

"Just hear him out. Please."

Ah, and here was the sales pitch. As much as my heart had leapt for joy upon seeing Starlight, I knew it was too good to be true. That Firebird had been lying about her death didn't seem too much of a stretch. At the time, it had seemed she'd been way too into putting the screws to Sally, knowing that she and Starlight were friends of a sort. Those two had a history I really needed to ask about one of these days.

For now, though, it was probably wise to keep my emotions in check and not be distracted by the one piece of potentially good news I'd seen in some time. "I already heard him out," I replied, bitterness creeping into my voice. "When he was done feeding me his bullshit, he killed my best friend."

I expected her to fall in line like a good thrall, tell me that it wasn't Vehron's fault or that maybe one couldn't make a world domination omelet without breaking a few human eggs. Thus, I was caught off guard when she stepped up to me and put a hand on my arm.

"I'm so sorry, Bill."

"So am I. So is Christy."

"The witch? So the baby is his?"

"Yeah."

She appeared to think about it for a moment. "I don't know if that can ever be made right with you. I imagine not, but I'm telling you things are not as you think they are here."

"So again, I ask why haven't you just left?"

A sardonic smile spread across her face. "And again, I ask you, what would we return to? I know how things work. It would be endless compulsions to pry the truth out of us, even more to bend our wills to theirs, ensure our loyalty to the Draculas. Then what?"

I knew what would happen then. They'd be given tasks to prove that loyalty, more of Alexander's dirty work. However, that had come back to bite him in the ass. Somehow, a young vampire schmuck by the name of Farley had been insulated against not only Alex's compulsion ability – something that was terrifyingly powerful in itself – but also that of other members of the Draculas.

Starlight had a point. Who knew what paranoia the Dracs would adopt now that they knew their power wasn't absolute? Hell, might they not just take a scorched earth policy and dust any vamps they couldn't be entirely sure about? It's not like they couldn't just make more to replace them.

Damnit, I hated when logic that ran counter to my

beliefs made sense. Still, it didn't do much to dissuade me either. I knew Vehron was an animal. I'd seen him in action, seen what he'd done, and would have to live with the fact that I was the one who'd unleashed him onto the world.

"Fine," I replied, looking deep into her brown eyes. No trace of glazed compulsion stared back at me, but that didn't mean anything. That look was usually only present when a vamp's full will was being subjugated. Who was to say whether Vehron's mind-messings weren't of a more subtle nature? "I can understand why you might not want to leave, but don't forget, he's the one who kidnapped you to begin with."

"I know," she said, heading to the door. "Believe me, I've thought long and hard on that one. The vampires from Village Coven were my responsibility. Any decision I made had to be with them in mind. The thing is, once the choice was made, it was surprisingly easy to live with it."

Had any other vampire said those words, I'd have laughed my ass off. Most of the undead were nothing if not self-absorbed douche canoes. The only thought most coven masters would give to their charges was how many to use as cannon fodder. But not Starlight. Though older than me by a fair bit, she managed to retain her compassion for others. I'd often been mocked for keeping in touch with my humanity, but, if anything, Starlight might have been the one vamp even more human than I tried to be.

*Which makes you both fools.*

Oh, *now* he wanted to talk to me again? "Shut up."

"What?" Star asked, turning back from the door.

"Sorry. Talking to myself." And if that wasn't the truth, I didn't know what was.

I half expected Star to tell me to stay put, followed by her stepping out the door and multiple heavy locks engaging. Instead, she waved me on.

"Where are we going?"

"I'm going to bring you to your friends."

"All of them?"

A guilty look crossed her face. "Not all."

"What did you do with..."

"That Chinese girl, Gansetseg – her and her men have been separated from the rest. They're down in holding being guarded. Sorry, but it was felt they were too unpredictable, potentially dangerous."

"Oh," I replied, surprised. "I didn't really mean her."

"Then the others should be waiting for you."

"Have you seen them yet?" I asked as we stepped out of the door. I'd been right; this was a conference room. Beyond it lay little more than a sea of cubicles. Things didn't appear to be quite the same as I remembered it, though. They weren't all filled, and those that were seemed to have maps and other tactical information in them. No dreary paperwork in sight.

"No. I wanted to make sure you were okay. Also, I heard that Sally is acting a little weird."

I thought back to what Star had said about the Draculas compelling the shit out of anyone who tried to leave this place, and I found a streak of anger worming its way through me. Hell, hadn't I seen it firsthand, the way Alex casually wiped Sally of her memories? Who knew what else he did to her, all in the name of proving that I was nothing to him but a Freewill guinea pig – a gun to be aimed and fired at his discretion. "You don't know the half of it."

Starlight led me through the cubes. I couldn't help but notice another change – the place definitely had more security than before. Vamps with silver stakes and other riot gear stood guard at every entrance and intersection. Although whether they were protecting against outside intrusion or keeping an eye on the vamps working the cubes, I couldn't say.

Still, things didn't look as drastically different as I had thought. Hell, one could have almost confused this place now with how it had been run under James if not for the lack of...

"Hey, Star, where are the zombies?"

"Huh?" she grunted as she continued to lead the way.

"Zombies. Before things got all clusterfucked, there were zombies all over the place doing paperwork, running errands, dripping bodily fluids everywhere."

"They were dismissed."

"Dismissed?"

"Yeah. They aren't allowed by Ib. It's a vamps-only club here now."

That's when I remembered James's warning about the cult – how they were purists, not allowing those who were different. That had accounted for Vehron's initial hostility toward Ed, even beyond my roommate's normally surly personality. It was something to remember. That freedom that Star kept talking about came with a price – marching under the equivalent of a vampire Gestapo flag.

Thoughts of Ed brought me back to the present. "What about my other roommate?"

"Other roommate?"

We were walking through a set of double doors now, heading through another section filled with office drones. Awe-inspiring terror this was not.

"Yeah, Ed. They keep calling him 'the pure one' for some stupid reason."

"No idea."

"Really?" I asked, my tone dubious.

"Yes, really. Sorry, Bill, but I'm not exactly a general here. I just do my job and help out where I can. Outside of that, I don't really ask a lot of questions. Unlike some others, I don't have a place by the big guy's side, or on his lap."

There was a trace of bitterness in that last part that would have almost caused me to chuckle had Firebird not completely fucked us over last time we were here. "So what have you been up to all this time?"

"Helping to organize the city."

"Organize Boston? How?"

"Much like in New York, there were a lot of back alley treaties here, agreements with the local authorities. Heck, there's more because this place was such a big hub for us."

"Yeah, I kinda figured that would be the case."

"Well, those are all with the old regime. We've had to tear down those alliances, put new people in power, reorganize the police force; those sorts of things. Boston isn't a small place. Those things take time and manpower. Believe it or not, working for Sally really gave me a good handle on administrative tasks. If you can manage the office of Village Coven, you can herd cats. So that's where they've put me to work."

What she was saying made a lot of sense. The old treaties were all under the Draculas' power structure. That gave them a potential network of spies and allies once the time came to strike. That's why Boston hadn't been retaken yet. Vehron was fortifying his base of power, even as he expanded his sphere of influence.

It was smart. I was almost embarrassed to admit I probably wouldn't have thought of it.

It was also disturbing. We'd come up here to stop Vehron, to free all of those conscripted into his service. However, if Starlight was to be believed – and I still wasn't convinced there wasn't some mind-fuckery going on – a lot of the vamps here were perfectly cool with his old world order. Why wouldn't they be? On paper, it sounded pretty good, but then, so did Communism.

But Starlight had a point. Even if one wanted to escape, what was waiting for them outside: interrogations, compulsions, suicide missions to prove their loyalty?

Fighting a legion of compelled vampires and their Jahabich allies had sounded difficult enough, but if those vampires weren't compelled – were actually true believers in this cause – then our mission had just taken a downturn from really fucking hard to downright impossible.

**53**

# CLASS REUNION

y tour of the Boston facility didn't turn up too many new or useful details. In many ways, it wasn't much different from how I remembered it – a bustling place where stuff got done. As much as Starlight might have expounded upon the freedom of the new management, empires required plenty of bureaucracy, no matter who was in charge.

The main differences I saw were in the heightened security, albeit I hadn't been to this place during wartime, so perhaps that wasn't such a major change. The zombies were gone – that much seemed to be obvious. I remembered seeing some loose on the street when last I'd been here. Were the rest now wandering around feral, attacking people like a scene straight out of *The Walking Dead*?

And what of the Jahabich? Had they merely shown up to be Vehron's delivery boys? Did they drop me off, get a tip, and then leave? It would have seemed so, but it was hard to tell. The Jahabich had an earthy scent to them, but the majority of the Boston complex was underground. That didn't help.

Likewise not helping were the various perfumes, deodorants, and aftershaves worn by the masses inhabiting this place. Don't get me wrong, it was a fuck-load better than hundreds of unwashed bodies all congregating in one enclosed space, but it all mixed together into a fairly confusing stew of aromas. I mean, fuck, several of the cubicles even had air fresheners in them.

The problem was, I had no idea what Vehron's motivation was with regards to those monsters. Was it an alliance? Had he subjugated them? Were a few of them poker playing buddies from millennia past? Without knowing that, there was no chance of ascertaining their place, if any, on the game board.

Starlight led me to a door labeled "Sparkle." Two guards in full body armor stood outside, but it was more the name that caught my eye. "What the hell?"

"Yeah. All the lounges have names here. Don't look at me. I didn't choose it."

"I'll assume it was there pre-Vehron." Or maybe not. For all I knew, Firebird was bringing Mr. Muscles up to speed on the modern age by having him sit through chick flicks. Now, there was an image. Maybe the way to beat him wasn't through strength, but in forcing him to watch *The Hunger Games* over and over again.

Movie night would have to wait, though. Star opened the door and stepped inside. I followed, my fingers crossed that nothing more had befallen my friends.

All talk ceased the moment we entered. It was quite the interesting scene. The doll that housed Tom's soul was sitting propped up on the edge of a table. Dave and Adam were standing in front of it, obviously engaged in some conversation.

Christy sat off on a couch against the back wall. Her eyes were red rimmed and had circles beneath them. Sally was seated next to her, her head propped on one hand, looking quite bored.

The room itself looked like a typical office lounge: comfortable, with places to sit or hang out. There was a Keurig machine on one counter. Vending machines for snacks and drinks lined one wall – and me without my wallet. The only thing that set it apart from the mundane were the odd sigils painted onto the walls. Although Christy didn't look as if she had any interest in zapping anywhere at the moment, it was a safe bet those were in place in case she changed her mind.

A frown creased my face as I noticed that was it. I hadn't been expecting to find Ed here, but sometimes hope is all we have when we're deep in enemy territory surrounded by creatures that would gladly kick our asses if given minimal cause.

"S'up, Bill," Tom said. I had to admit, his voice coming from the unmoving, perpetually sneering face of the toy had potential to get creepy. "How you doing?"

"Nothing not getting punched in the head anytime soon won't cure. How are..."

"Star?" Sally asked, getting to her feet. For a moment, a big grin lit up her face, but then she composed herself back to her normal nonplussed look. I decided to be nice and not mention it.

"Hi, Sally," Starlight replied.

Sally turned to me. "I thought you said she was killed." She'd been there when Firebird had broken the news, but that fell under yet another memory buried deep within her skull.

"Firebird lied."

"Wait, you mean she's the one who told you ... fucking cunt." All things considered, that about summed it up. "Why would she do that? You know what? It doesn't matter. This entire operation has gone tits up. What about the rest of Village Coven, Star?"

"They're here."

"Good. I want you to gather them up. We need to find a way out of this place."

"I'm not leaving."

"What?"

"This is where I belong. This is where *we* belong."

Sally's eyes narrowed. "Goddamned compulsions."

"I'm not compelled."

"The hell you're not."

To my surprise, Starlight didn't back down. It was probably the first time I'd seen her stand her ground with Sally. "I'm serious. That's not the way things run here. Compelling others to do their bidding is frowned upon."

"Oh really? That's not what I saw just a few hours ago."

"You were a hostile invading force. *Of course* it's going to be used in that case. But the choice is always made with a free mind. You'll see."

"I don't know what choice you're talking about, but I don't care to see anything except this place getting smaller in a rearview mirror."

"Second that," Dave said.

"Can we stop and grab my body on the way out?" Tom asked. "I'm kinda partial to making sure I get a nice funeral."

"Not funny," I replied. "Besides, we can't leave without Ed."

"Sorry," Adam said, "but watch me. I don't know what you had in mind when you set up this quest, but shit isn't turning out like either of us hoped. I just want to get back to Newark and the guys."

"The guys are dead!" I snapped. Silence descended on the room at my outburst. "There're not in Newark. That's just a stupid game rule so DMs can fuck over their players. In real life, you get dusted, you stay dusted."

"But that means..."

"Mike and Carl are gone. I'm sorry."

"Wait, you lied to us?"

"Seems to be a lot of that going on," Sally muttered under her breath.

I felt all the frustration of the last few days – hell, months – bubble up inside of me. I stepped across the room and grabbed Adam by the shirt, lifting him to his tippy toes. "Yes, I lied. You guys were acting like animals and I saw a chance to kill two birds with one stone – save people from you and recruit some extra muscle for my mission."

"Heh. Just like the Baron of Stormgaard did to you guys last year."

"Fuck off, Dave." It was a good thing there was little chance of our game continuing after this, because I had a feeling I'd just doomed Kelvin to a most ignoble death ... *again*. Oh well, fuck it. I didn't have time for games right now. "Like I said, we don't leave without Ed."

"No!" The lights in the room seemed to dim, replaced by a swirling torrent of colors. The runes on the walls glowed brightly in response to Christy's power, but did little to contain the raw fury emanating from her. "We came here to kill Vehron, and we're not leaving until he's dead."

For all the prophecies written about me or Sheila, I was forced to concede that, as far as I was concerned, Christy was the scariest person in our group when she wanted to be.

"Vehron isn't your enemy," Star said, seemingly unimpressed with the display of power. "He doesn't wish you any..."

"He killed the father of my child."

A slight tremor shook the room. Oh boy.

"I'm right here," Tom said.

"You're not!" she screamed. "What you are is ... is *wrong*."

With that, the light died down in the room and Christy once more sank back onto the couch, putting her face in her hands and quietly sobbing.

Sally and I looked at each other, then at her, then back at each other. I gave a single shake of my head. Finally, she rolled her eyes at me and walked over to put an arm around the distraught witch. Sorry, but providing comfort wasn't really my thing.

"Harsh," Tom said after a few moments. "I mean, sure, I'm not exactly a vintage Han Solo, but I still have a kung-fu grip. You just don't find that shit on toys today."

I walked over and picked him up off the table. "Here's an idea. Why don't you try not to help for a while?"

"Wait, what are you...?"

The rest was muffled as I shoved him deep into a pocket of the Mongolian fur coat I still wore. Oddly enough, it was quite the satisfying act to perform. Would have saved me and Ed a lot of grief in the past had Tom just been a shitty action figure from the get go.

Still, that was a temporary balm at best, a little amusement to cover the grim reality of the situation. The bottom line was that we weren't going anywhere until this was finished, one way or the other.

"I'm gonna kick your ass when I get out of here," came Tom's tinny voice. "What the hell is this? There's a..." I cut him off by shutting the flap over the pocket.

Wait, speaking of disembodied voices that had gone oddly quiet. "Where's Decker?"

"Oh, the demi-lich?" Dave asked. "They took him."

"Who?"

"I didn't get a chance to ask for names. Once those rock monsters marched us in to this place, one of them made off with the skull."

"Star?"

"Like I said, Bill, they don't really make me privy to all their plans. What's so important about this skull?"

"Oh, nothing. Just a disembodied wizard noggin with an attitude problem." I purposely left out the part about him being able to see the future. Despite my joy at learning Starlight had survived, I found myself not quite willing to fully trust her so long as she wore her Team Vehron hat – even if her reasoning for doing so made pretty good sense.

"Oh, *that* skull," Starlight said, recognition filling her eyes. "Is it still spouting off those creepy predictions?"

"You know about that?"

"I'm the one who went up and got it," she replied. "Sally sent me up to Westchester for it. Had to boil it for hours to get rid of..."

"Never mind that," I quickly said, glancing out of the corner of my eye toward Christy. "The skull's not important. Vehron's probably just using it as a wine goblet or something." Okay, that probably wasn't helping either. "Let's get back to Ed. We need to find him. Any chance you can help us with that much, Star?"

She appeared to consider this. Behind her, I could see Sally raise an eyebrow. After a moment, she opened her mouth and I felt a tingling at the base of my skull. She was about to throw a compulsion at Star. While I had little doubt it was a practical course of action, I didn't like the thought of mucking with the head of a friend. Also, there was every chance the guards standing outside would notice.

I quickly shook my head, which caused Starlight to turn hers.

"What are you doing, Sally?"

"You know me, Star – whatever it takes."

"It's not going to work. You should know that."

"Can't blame a girl for wanting to try."

Starlight put her hands on her hips, once more refusing to back down. "They'll know if you do, and their response won't be a friendly one. I'll help you find your friend, but not if you're going to play games with me. As I told you, they don't allow that here."

"Who is this *they* you're talking about?" Sally asked. "Isn't Vehron calling the shots?"

"It's ... more complicated than that."

"How?"

Starlight held up a hand. "You'll see soon enough." She turned toward me. "I'll ask about your friend. In the meantime, try to keep everyone from doing anything stupid."

She turned and walked out the door. Although there was no click of a lock engaging, I didn't fool myself into thinking we were free to explore.

As for her warning, I quietly muttered to the closed door in front of me, "We're already here, so it's far too late for that."

# 54

# THAT SINKING FEELING

"Yeah, how'd you like that, fucker?"

I stood before my vanquished foe, enjoying the spoils of battle. It would not sate me for long, but for now, I would savor the taste of victory – for a sweet taste it was indeed.

"Are you finished punching out the vending machine?"

I turned to Sally and held up my spoils. "Twix? They're even better when they're free."

She sighed disgustedly, but took the candy anyway before she stepped away.

Trying to escape might've been suicidal, but I would be damned if I wasn't going to show my captors some form of passive protest. Also, I didn't have any change on me.

I glanced over to where Christy lay. The poor girl was out cold on the couch. Dave had groused about her not leaving room for anyone else to sit, but Sally had immediately thrown a chair at his head. That pretty much ended the argument.

I had wanted to spend some time with Christy, discussing what happened with Dr. Death and how to maybe salvage things, but after Starlight left us, she pretty much zonked out. There was only so much stress one could dump on a person in a single day, and she'd surely passed her limit long ago. If blissful unconsciousness could give her a modicum of peace, then so be it.

Speaking of the cause of that stress. I'd almost forgotten about Tom in the few hours since we'd been left to stew in our own juices. Not that I'd forgotten about what happened to him. No, I'd just forgotten he was still in my pocket. I walked over to a corner, opened the flap, and pulled him out.

"Still with us, buddy?"

"It's about fucking time. It smells like someone jacked off an ox in there. And what's with the wires..."

"Sorry," I interrupted. "I think Christy needed some space."

"I'm the one trapped in Ken doll Hell here."

"I know. It's just weird – even weirder than normal."

"You're telling me. I mean, I think I actually remember dying."

"You do?"

"Yeah. It was fuzzy at first – guess the whole Max Adventure thing was a bit of a shock to my system – but it's getting clearer in my head. I remember Chuck twisting my neck, feeling something pop like my head had just turned into a champagne cork."

"Then what?"

"It all went black, but I could still feel things. I know when I hit the ground, but all at once, I felt disconnected, like a stranger crashing in someone else's apartment."

I considered how things were in my own head and nodded.

"Then there was light. I know, fucking cliché as shit, but I swear there was a light at the end of a tunnel."

"Was your Aunt Gracie waiting for you in it?"

"I fucking hope not. She was a bitch. But I never got there. It was like I took one step, and then the world exploded around me in orange light. Suddenly, I was spinning in it, like being sucked down a giant toilet. The next thing I knew, I was face down in a pile of dirt."

"Christy thinks that maybe the same thing happened to you as what happens to the Jahabich, except obviously on a smaller scale."

"You're a fucking laugh riot, you know that?"

"I try," I replied, staring down at his unmoving plastic face.

"Think she can fix me?"

"I won't lie, man. I have no fucking idea."

"This sucks. I mean, if I was one of those asshole rock monsters, I could at least turn back into me."

"Yeah, somehow I don't think that would be an ideal situation."

"I wonder if every part of them is human when they're like that. I mean, would my dick still work?"

"*That's* what you're concerned with?"

"Fuck yeah. What's the point otherwise? I gotta take care of my lady. She has needs, if you know what I mean."

I thought back to how Christy appeared when we were in my head, but decided to keep that to myself. "I can't help but think there are more important things to worry about."

"Hey, you worry about saving the world. I'll worry whether my dick works. To each their own."

"Yeah, well, I have news for you, buddy." I yanked down his camo pants, revealing the smooth plastic between his legs. "You ain't exactly anatomically correct."

"What the fuck, dude?!"

"Bill," Adam called over from where he sat with Dave. He'd apparently been watching us. "I bat for that team, and even I have to admit that was one of the most fucking gay things I have ever seen."

"Mind your own business." I quickly pulled the action figure's pants back up and addressed Tom again. "I was trying to illustrate a point."

"Yeah, the point of why you aren't getting any from a female."

"That's not true."

"Oh really? Lack of pussy has you delusional now?"

"Fuck you, ass." I lowered my voice to a whisper and brought my lips to Tom's ear. "I'll have you know I got some more recently than you. As in a few hours ago."

"A few hours? We left Sheila over a day ago."

"Trust me, I'm well aware, but I'm not talking about her. It was right after I killed Turd."

"Wait. You were with ... no fucking way. Ed? Really?"

"No, not Ed, shithead!"

"Well, the only other person with you was..." He trailed off as realization finally hit his dull plastic orb of a brain.

Yep," I replied, my voice lower so she didn't hear. "Tapped it real good."

"Holy shit! You fucked Sally?!"

Goddamn it! I immediately felt all eyes in the room turn toward me. The thing was, there was only one pair that counted, and I could feel them boring a hole into the back of my skull.

"Thanks," I grumbled to Tom.

"Don't mention it."

I lowered my voice to a bare whisper. "I swear to God when this is over with, I'm gonna tear your fucking arms off and tell Christy to use you as a dildo."

Thankfully, fate was kind that day, and by that I mean Starlight walked back in before Sally could pummel the snot out of me. Sure, I had no idea what her presence meant for us, but right at that moment, I would have welcomed being escorted to the torture chamber. I had a feeling it would be preferable to seeing how Sally reacted to being slut-shamed.

I stuffed Tom back into my pocket, ignoring his protests lest he cause any more chaos on my behalf. I said a silent prayer to whatever gods were listening that we could fix him somehow, then added in a personal vow to punch him in the face once we did.

Glancing over my shoulder, I saw Sally turn to give Christy a gentle nudge awake. Even with her memories wiped, she seemed to have a soft spot for the witch. Of course, that might just have been because Christy was currently her best bet to get those memories back. Either way, it gave her something to do aside from kicking me in the nuts.

Dave and Adam both retreated to the far corner, as if that would help. Oh well, guess this was my show to MC after all.

"What's the word, Star?"

"You want the good news or bad news first?"

"I imagine there's a lot more of the latter, so why don't we get the first bit out of the way."

She gave me a sad smile and nodded. "I found your friend. Would have been pretty hard to miss him. Apparently, there's a whole big hullaballoo about him."

"Why?"

"I don't know, but I do know he's in the main hall outside of the prefect's office."

That made sense. Last time I was here, that's where Vehron had set up shop – usurping the area and turning it into some sort of throne room for himself.

Hold on; the prefect's office. Holy crap, in all the excitement, I'd forgotten about James's request.

"Calibra, the current – former, whatever prefect, is she still alive?"

"Of course," Star replied, her tone indicating that I'd asked a particularly stupid question.

"James will be happy to hear that, or maybe not. Is she being held against her will?"

"I already told you, none of us are here against our will. It's funny in a way. Everyone calls you the Freewill because you can't be controlled, but in a sense, we all have it here for the first time."

"You're still serving someone."

"Yes, but we are happy to serve the greater good. Maybe you just don't get it, but our eyes have been opened. To us, the ways of the Draculas are the abomination."

"Pretty sure Anakin Skywalker said something similar right before being dropped into lava."

"Excuse me?"

"Never mind. Was a stupid scene anyway." What she was saying wasn't promising. I remembered what Gan had told me about neutralizing Calibra if she'd been compromised. Well, if she was here willingly as was claimed – and I still wasn't quite sure I bought into that – then she'd sure as shit been compromised. In that case, the damage was done. If she had secrets to spill, they'd most likely long since been spilled. I was pretty sure that was unforgivable to a bunch of cocks like the Dracs. Either way you looked at it, she was doomed. Amazingly enough, letting Gan take care of her might be the kinder option.

Oh crap – Gan!

"My other ... friends, Star. Gan and her people. You said they were being held elsewhere."

"That's part of the bad news."

"Oh no. Don't tell me they've been..."

"They are to be given the choice."

"Huh?"

"In the main hall, where your friend is being held. Everyone who comes here is given it."

I remembered back to last time. Vehron had been marching vamps before him and pretty much giving them the option to serve or die. Not much of a choice, especially since the latter was carried out immediately. Hell, that's what I had been told happened to Star, that her loyalty to Sally and me had won out and ultimately cost her everything. I saw now that wasn't the case. I tried not to be insulted by it. Fuck it; if given the choice between serving an asshole versus instant death, I knew which one I'd take. Still, something didn't quite jibe.

"So they either pledge their loyalty or get killed?" I asked accusingly.

"It's not as black and white as that. There is no dictate to serve. The choice is to listen. That's all – to be willing to hear out what the teachings of Ib have to offer. I already told you, nobody is here against their will. Only those who are so locked in to the existing dogma that they can't fathom another path choose differently."

"But the end result is still the same," I pointed out. Arguing with her was useless. I still considered Star a friend, but something had changed in her way of thinking. I could try to argue my point, but I imagined that would be about as fruitful as arguing online about whether Windows, Mac OS, or Linux was superior.

Also, there was still the little issue of not being sure what I was really trying to change her mind to. Vehron needed to die. There was no doubt about that, but trying to argue that the ways of Alexander and his merry band of assholes was superior was like trying to claim that one should get gonorrhea because syphilis was so overrated.

"So what's the rest of the bad news?" I asked.

"That's why I'm here. I'm bringing all of you there too."

# 55

# THE CHOICE

"Why? Are we going to be given *the choice* too?"

"Honestly, I'm not sure. I hear they're pretty angry at you."

"'They' again. Is Vehron talking about himself in third person?"

"It's not important. All I've been told is they want you there."

I stepped in close to Star and lowered my voice. "Not Christy."

"Sorry, she comes too."

"Seriously, Star? She's over six months pregnant and just had a front row seat to watch your great savior shatter her fiancé's spine."

"It was my neck, genius!" Tom's muffled voice yelled from my pocket. I slapped the side of my coat to shut him up.

"She's suffered enough. I know you, Star. You care. You're not a heartless motherfucker like the rest of them. Most vampires couldn't give two shits about witches, but she's got a kid on the way. Let her go."

Star's gaze wavered between looking at me and over my shoulder toward where Christy sat. Her eyes met mine and I saw indecision in them. Her mouth creased into a frown. The Starlight I remembered was still in there.

"She's not a part of this," I said, keeping my gaze level with hers.

All at once, the understanding was gone from her eyes, replaced with something else – something colder. "You're wrong. She is."

"How can you..."

"You'll learn soon enough." She backed up to the door and knocked once. Several armed guards entered, one of them holding magic-neutralizing manacles. Judging by the sounds my ears were picking up, there were more of them just beyond the door. This wasn't a fight we were going to win.

"What happened to you?" I asked Star.

"I made my choice. Soon you will too."

The place was how I remembered it – the one area of the complex that actually felt like a vampire lair and not some corporate park that had forgotten to pay their electric bill. The walls were carved from the surrounding rock, giving it the feel of an unholy underground cathedral.

At the far end lay a set of foreboding double doors, which, during better times, led to the prefect's office. Not too long ago, the ominous illusion would have been broken by a desk right outside the office, upon which sat a modern Macintosh desktop. When I'd first come here, Colin had manned it. A small part of me almost wished for his smarmy face again, but then I realized no, I really didn't.

The office beyond used to be a pleasant surprise. Under

James, the black stonework gave way to a comfortable office full of curios; more something you'd expect to belong to an archaeology professor than a six-hundred-year-old vampire. I had no idea what, if any, changes Calibra had made during her brief tenure, but considering the throne that sat right in front of her doors, I had a feeling I wasn't going to be given a chance to find out.

Okay, so it was more of a really nice office chair than a proper throne, but it served the same purpose. Upon it sat Vehron. Between him and us were dozens, perhaps hundreds, of vampires packed in tight as their lord and master held court.

Guards stood in a semi-circle before him, although they were probably ceremonial at best. Seriously, who here was even remotely a threat to this guy? I sure as shit knew I wasn't.

*But you could have been.*

"Fuck off and die."

Multiple sets of eyes turned my way at the outburst, but I paid them no heed. I set my gaze straight ahead, taking in the scene.

Our gracious host wasn't alone in his place of power. Standing immediately behind him, one hand perched lovingly upon his meaty shoulder, was Firebird. She wore a strapless mini-dress that spoke volumes of her place in this hierarchy. What good was being in charge if you didn't have a hot piece of ass to tap on command?

"Remind me to claw her eyes out of her head," Sally commented from my side.

"Glad to," I replied, happy to see her anger directed else-where. I glanced to my other side where Christy stood – the only one of us in chains. "How are you holding up?"

Though still looking haggard, the brief nap she'd had seemed to have recharged her a bit. Her eyes were hard as stone, despite the bags beneath them. "Get these cuffs off of me and I'll show you."

I had little doubt what she meant, but I merely gave a single nod. If the opportunity presented itself, I'd be happy as a clam to let her flash fry everyone up front.

Wait! Scratch that. Make that everyone minus one, I amended internally as a couple of guards shifted position.

Ed stood several steps off to Vehron's right. If anything, he actually looked better than last I'd seen him. He was cleaned up and had been given a change of clothes. Had he not been flanked by a trio of vampire guards, I'd have almost thought he was a willing guest.

His eyes searched the crowd until they met mine and he mimed a sigh. I couldn't help but grin. He did seem to be developing a habit of being my personal damsel in distress, although maybe I could cut him some slack since none of us were really in a great spot at that moment.

The only positive aspect of our current dilemma was our location. This was one of the few spots in the massive complex I was familiar with. Most importantly, I knew where we were relative to an exit that would let us out aboveground.

Sure, there was bound to be *a bit* of resistance and, unlike last time, we didn't have James to back us up, but it was an escape plan in progress. Hell, it was hope, however dim. One couldn't blame me for grasping at straws.

I was about to tell Sally to keep an eye out for anything that might present an opening, laughable as the suggestion might be, when I felt a familiar tingle in the back of my head.

A compulsion was incoming.

My head tingled for a split second, then something akin to a gentle wave passed over me. The thing was, nothing had physically touched me. Also, I hadn't heard any orders or anything. I was about to dismiss it as maybe me losing my mind, when I realized the room had fallen silent.

Where before there had been some quiet chatter, now all the vamps in the room faced forward intently.

"Did you feel that?" Sally whispered, sounding very loud in the now quiet chamber.

I glanced forward, past our guards, and saw Vehron grin in our direction.

Starlight turned around toward us and said, "Silent compulsion."

"That's a thing?"

There was no answer to my rhetorical question, nor did there need to be. Compulsions were partially telepathic in nature, or so I'd been told. What I'd felt was pretty weak. All it did was catch the audience's attention, a sort of clearing of the throat in compulsion form. If anything, I had a feeling he was showing off. If so, good job. Color me impressed.

Vehron finally stood. "May the glory of Ib alight upon us as a sunrise."

Having attended my fair share of Catholic masses as a kid, I was half tempted to reply, "And also with you."

There was no response from the crowd. That struck me as odd, considering this was known as the Cult of Ib – cult being the operative word. You'd think there'd be people throwing themselves to the ground as the spirit invested itself in them, or whatever it was cults did. But there was nothing of the sort.

A small worm of doubt began to weasel its way into my thoughts. Could maybe what Starlight had been trying to tell me been true?

"W ... ut's ... goi ... on?"

The muffled voice from my pocket reminded me that it really didn't matter. Vehron had killed my friend. Because of him, Christy's child would grow up not knowing their father.

*And whose fault is that?*

I was about to tell Dr. Death to shut the fuck up again, but then I remembered what Starlight had said about us being the aggressors. I heard the faintest echo of laughter in my head as I replayed things in my mind. We'd fired the first shot. Hell, our mission was about as far from benign as you got. This wasn't a diplomatic envoy gone bad. We were assassins, a fucking suicide squad sent to do the Draculas' dirty work all because I'd...

"Now is the time of the choice," Vehron continued, thankfully interrupting my disturbing flash of insight. He turned and reached out a hand toward Firebird. She accepted, and he led her out from behind his leather throne.

She stepped in front of him, looking more the hostess of a trashy game show than anything. I found myself curious as to what her role in this would be. Was there an offer of a last blowjob for the condemned? I mean, I wasn't ready to check out quite yet, but that definitely beat a last meal of meatloaf and mashed potatoes.

She stepped forward and raised her hands. "Invaders stand among us, seeking to return you to the shackles of slavery." She paused for a moment to look directly our way. "When they glance at you, they see not the lords of this world, but mere fodder to be used and cast aside."

"She's his mouthpiece," Sally whispered to me. "Among other pieces, I'd gather."

I had to stifle a chuckle. She was the Vanna White to his Pat Sajak ... except perhaps with more sucking involved.

"But we bear them no ill will," Firebird continued, sounding more eloquent than I remembered. I wouldn't have doubted someone had written this speech for her. "Instead, we shall offer them what we offer all who come before us: the choice. Step forward."

I expected us to be shoved toward the front, but my entourage remained unmoved. Instead, a procession of warriors was led in from a side entrance. At the forefront was a vampire half the size of the next smallest, but probably twice as dangerous – Gan.

They were obviously unarmed, but they otherwise appeared the same as when last I'd seen them. Gan, at least, didn't look as if she'd learned any lessons in humility.

The group stopped in front of Firebird while Vehron resumed his place in his seat, sending out the obvious signal of who was in charge.

"The choice is a simple one," Firebird said, addressing the group as a whole – something that I'm sure ruffled Gan's feathers to no end. "Open yourself to the teachings of Ib. Live among us for a time. Learn our ways. Should you find it not to your liking, you will be free to follow your own path. The alternative is to remain blinded by what you think you know, to hold on to the dogma that has been drilled into you time and again. If so, know that the glory of Ib has no use for those who refuse to think for themselves."

Gan looked up – mainly because she was the shortest person in the room – and replied, "I would answer to the Sun Strider, not his whore."

A murmur rose up among the crowd, including a small chuckle from Sally.

I glanced over at Christy, who merely shrugged in my direction – the meaning obvious: it had been nice knowing her.

Firebird appeared livid, but Vehron merely said, "None, save my soldiers, answer to me. The wisdom of Ib drives us all."

I expected Gan to tell him to go drive his ass off a cliff if that were the case, but to my surprise, she replied, "Very well. I speak for my people when I say we shall learn your ways and then decide accordingly."

"You speak only for yourself here, child," Vehron replied.

I couldn't see Gan's face well from my vantage point, but from her posture, I got the impression she didn't like that much at all. Before she could reply, though, Vehron once more waved a hand to Firebird.

"That is a conceit of those who falsely claim title to the First. Their laws hold no sway here. Your people must make the choice themselves; for here, they are beholden to none but themselves."

"I've never known her to sound so ... not stupid," Sally whispered again to me.

After a moment, Christy leaned in. "That's because it's not her."

"What do you mean?"

"Can't you see it?"

"See what?"

"The aura around her head."

"All I see is a shitty perm," Sally replied, "and a face used to sucking a lot of cock."

"Thanks. That helps," I muttered.

Christy ignored us and said, "I think it's a glamour of sorts. Regardless, there's definitely something else at play here."

"Magic?"

"Yes. I'm just not sure whether she's being fed lines or someone is talking through her."

"Who would be doing that?"

Christy held up her manacled hands. "I'm not really in a position to find out."

Point taken.

So things weren't as they seemed. Starlight had kept referring to a "they." Now it seemed that perhaps there was someone else behind the scenes; a man behind the curtain, if you will.

Great! Because things had obviously been far too easy up to this point.

56

# THE SACRIFICES WE MAKE

As we discussed things quietly among ourselves, knowing full well there was little chance of not being overheard, the scene before us continued to play out in a somewhat anticlimactic manner.

Gan's answer to the choice was accepted and she was allowed to step into the crowd unmolested. Talk about extremes. It was like a game show where the only two ways to leave were either with a million bucks or getting shoved into a wood chipper.

Despite Firebird's instruction that each person here was master of their own fate – ironic, considering she apparently had a magical earworm – Gan's men followed her lead to the letter.

All in all, I didn't find her decision too surprising. Gan was far from stupid. An opportunity to live was an opportunity to escape. I also didn't think for one second she'd buy into any dogma but her own. Ego was a hell of a motivator.

Speaking of the little narcissistic midget, she spotted me and immediately headed my way – apparently free to mingle.

499

Ugh! All of a sudden, choice number two didn't sound so bad.

The rest of the crowd was still mostly silent as the ritual played out up front. Gan, however, seemed to not give two shits from a rat's ass.

"Greetings, beloved," she said at a conversational volume as if we were alone. "It pleases me to see you have done nothing to give them cause to kill you."

As far as welcomes went, it ranked only slightly higher than my Aunt Gerty's sloppy kisses on Christmas day. "Yeah, you too, Gan."

"A most peculiar circumstance we find ourselves in," she replied as if we were discussing tomorrow's weather forecast. "I can see why the Cult of Ib grew so powerful in centuries past."

I continued to keep my voice low, even if she didn't. "I will admit, there is some appeal to the concept."

"Academically speaking, yes. However, by its very nature, such chaos is ultimately doomed. Even in nature, apex predators are in a state of constant check. Without that, ecosystems fail and species go extinct."

Wow, I didn't expect Gan to go all Jane Goodall on me. I glanced up front to where her men continued to accept the terms of their release. I expected them to flock to their mistress, figuring maybe that was her plan. Once enough of them were around us, that might give us a fighting chance. Albeit, that chance would still be so infinitesimally small as to be suicidal. As trained as her people were, they were still disarmed, clad only in the fur-lined coats and – I dunno – probably yak skin clothes they walked in with. Badly outnumbered as we were, that wouldn't end well.

However, much to my surprise, they fanned out – each picking a different direction to head. Maybe, having been told they were masters of their own destiny now, they all came to the same conclusion – their boss was a spoiled megalomaniacal bitch. As far as employers went, one could choose better.

"As much a fool as Alexander is," Gan continued, "he is wise enough to know that we need order to both thrive and maintain a balance. He is too obsessed with control, though, and that breeds resentment. It is through this resentment that a long dead cult such as this can gain a toehold."

"That and a resurrected super warrior."

"And whomever controls him."

"Somehow, I don't think you're gonna be able to recruit him, Gan."

"I speak not of myself. I speak of another. Did you not smell the magic in the air?"

I so hated when she asked things like that. One could almost hear the "you idiot" tacked on at the end. Add condescending to her list of character traits. Yeah, I could understand why her people would enjoy a breath of fresh air without her constantly being up their asses. "I must have missed it."

"Regardless, it is unimportant for now."

"Oh, no doubt."

"Especially since they will soon be dead."

"What?"

"By your hand, of course." As I said, Gan wasn't even trying to keep her voice down. Thus, her proclamation of my inevitable murder-fest caused dozens of eyes to turn in our direction. "I look forward to seeing it, my love."

Damn, that was a lot of vamps glaring daggers at me. I glanced quickly over at Sally, but she held up her hands. "You're on your own, *Loverboy*."

I started swatting at nonexistent bugs flying around my head. "Yeah," I replied loudly. "All these damn mosquitos will soon be dead by my hand."

Vehron chuckled from up ahead. His ears were sensitive enough to hear a fly taking a shit two blocks away, so I had little doubt he'd caught the entirety of what my group had just discussed.

"Ah, little brother," he said, rising from his chair. "There is fire in you yet. But what to do with you? You have come here on a mission of hate." The angry glares around me got even angrier. Oh yeah, this was going swimmingly. "You slew a key recruit of mine, spat upon my entreaties for peace, and dared attack me with the white flame."

Now murmurs were rising up in the crowd, whispers of, "The false Freewill," "Alexander's puppet," and, of course, "Death to the enemies of Ib."

Yeah, not a lot of warm fuzzies headed my way.

"Yet, you make me laugh," Vehron continued. "You show spirit for one so young."

Hmm, why did I have a feeling a jester hat was in my future?

"More importantly, you protected us, even if you did not mean to."

I did?

"You faced the Grendel leader and crushed him, ending their crusade against us."

"I didn't do it for y ... oof!" Sally caught me in the ribs with an elbow. Probably smart too, as I'd just been ready to talk without thinking again. "Um..." I coughed. "Never mind. You're welcome."

"You are a walking..." He paused, speaking some word that sounded Latin. After a second, he leaned over to Firebird, and she whispered something in his ear. He gave her a peck on the cheek in return, to which she turned to my group and gave a triumphant smile. Yeah, we get it; you found yourself the sweetest of sugar-daddies, you gold-digging bitch.

"You are a walking contradiction," Vehron continued, now armed with more words. "Most here would see you struck down, but I think perhaps I would see you given the choice."

More murmurs came from the crowd. I was half-amazed to hear that not everyone was in agreement. Had that happened during one of Alex's rallies, it would have been followed by a lot of industrial strength vacuuming. However, Vehron appeared not to give it a second thought. "Eventually," he added. "For now, you will watch and learn."

The meaning was clear. We were prisoners. What a surprise. He'd probably try to use me as a bargaining chip too, but I had a feeling Alex wouldn't trade a pair of his dirty underwear for me, much less anything of importance.

Fuck it. Vehron held all the cards, but I had to try anyway. "Let my friend go and I'll play along."

"Ooh," Gan said, entwining an arm with mine, "your bravery sets my loins afire, my love."

Oh God! I yanked myself away, wishing I had some brain-bleach to remove that image from my mind.

"Your friend?" Vehron asked from across the expanse.

"I don't mean her," I quickly amended.

Apparently, I didn't need to clarify, as Vehron turned his head in Ed's direction and smiled.

More whisperings rose up from the crowd.

"The abomination."

"The pure one."

"What is he?"

Jeez. Why was it I got the death threats and he was just called a few names?

"Come forth," Vehron said to him.

Ed appeared to consider the command. "If it's all the same, I'd rather you go fuck yourself."

"Your friend does not wish to continue living, does he?" Gan asked me.

I looked down at her. "At some point, every guy needs to decide if he wants to live like a man or die like an hors d'oeuvre."

"Your insightfulness fills me with..."

"Oh, just shut up," I replied as I turned my attention back toward Vehron.

On the upside, Ed's refusal wasn't met with his body being snapped in half. On the other, Vehron's statement obviously hadn't been a request. He nodded and two vamps grabbed Ed by either arm and dragged him forward. Once he was in front of Vehron, the guards backed off a step. It wasn't like my friend had anywhere to go. Hell, even with a straight line to the door, he had no chance of outrunning even the slowest vamp in the place.

"What do you think they're gonna do to him?" Sally asked from my other side.

"You're watching the same movie I am."

Despite my attitude, I felt like a fucking helpless failure. I'd let down Tom, and Ed was next. But for what purpose? They could have killed him and been done with it several times over by now. I mean, I sincerely doubted they were gonna clap him on the back, declare him an honorary vampire, and let him go.

I tried to rack my brain for some insight. "Star?" I asked, but she didn't respond. She just stood in front of us, watching raptly.

Vehron lifted a hand and caressed it gently down my roommate's cheek. Okay, that was weird. Hopefully, he wasn't going to snap his fingers and summon a gimp mask. "You are pure, but you are not whole."

"If you're taking requests," Ed replied, "you know what would make me feel whole? Seeing my friends kill you."

Gotta love when people wrote checks with their mouths that my body couldn't cash.

Almost as if reading my mind, Vehron turned toward where I stood and barked out a quick laugh. He held out his hand and Firebird stepped to his side, placing a wicked-looking dagger into his palm.

Suddenly, it all made sense. Vehron was a known fanatic of the Cult of Ib and there was one thing that crazed zealots throughout history were known for.

He was going to sacrifice my friend.

"Shit! We need to do something."

"Why?" Gan asked.

"Why?! Isn't it fucking obvious? Oh, fuck this. Christy, if I can break..."

"Who's that?" Sally asked, interrupting my panic attack.

I followed her gaze to the front again. Another pair of vamp guards had marched up. A woman stood between them. At first, all I saw was jet-black hair, making me think it was maybe Calibra being brought in for some reason, but then I saw her face and realized I was mistaken.

Vehron turned and approached the woman, who I now saw was holding what looked to be a plastic bowl. What? Was she bringing him some leftover potato salad from this morning's cultist picnic?

Gan stood on her tiptoes next to me for a better look. "Hmm, a thrall."

"How do you know?"

"Is it not obvious from the way she moves?"

I was tempted to shove her away from me, but then I saw Vehron smile lovingly at the woman. He lifted his free hand to her chin and tilted her head up to face him.

"I have a feeling this is gonna get messy," Sally said.

All at once, I understood.

The woman gazed into Vehron's eyes and said, "Praise Ib" just as he brought the dagger up and slit her throat in one fluid motion. The guards grabbed hold to keep her upright as Vehron, quick as a snake, caught the bowl and held it under her gushing throat.

There'd been a sacrifice, all right. I'd just been wrong about the victim. Whoever she was, she'd seemed willing enough, but that was pretty much how it went with thralls – their freedom scrubbed away over time and replaced with a litany of compulsions. And all for what? A quick snack for the big man? Hell, and a cheap bowl too. Jeez. The guy couldn't find one ceremonial chalice or even a fucking pimp cup in all of Boston?

I was half expecting Vehron to take a sloppy sip, maybe drool some blood down his muscular chest so Firebird could rush in and lap it up with her tongue. Not that I fantasized about such things, mind you, but it seemed to fit the whole vampire ceremonial vibe.

Instead, he held out the hand with the dagger. Firebird, like a good little plaything, was right there to take it from him as he turned toward Ed.

My roommate tried to back up, but there was a wall of militant vamps waiting right behind him.

"Drink and be made whole," Vehron said, holding out the bowl.

"I'm not really one for a liquid diet," Ed replied.

What the fuck? I quickly looked around and spied Dave and Adam standing behind us, pretty much doing everything they could to not be noticed. I reached out, grabbed Dave by the collar, and dragged him over to me. "What the hell is he doing?"

"How the shit should I know?"

"Your notes."

"What about them?"

"They said Ed was a vampire. What did you mean by that?"

"They were just notes about his blood composition. I didn't have time to come to any conclusions before your buddy burnt them to ash. That French guy was just making shit up."

I glanced back and saw Vehron continue to hold out the bowl to Ed. I had a feeling he was gonna skip the "nummy nummy, for your tummy" bit and go straight to pouring it down my friend's throat like they were Mola Ram and Indiana Jones.

I turned back to Dave. "Come to a conclusion now. What's that going to do to him?"

"Less filling, tastes great? I don't fucking know. I'm figuring this shit out as I go."

"Seriously?"

"Sorry, man. I have..." He averted his gaze from mine. "...nothing. Never had."

"What?"

Dave's guilty look said it all. For all the samples he'd taken and promises he'd made, and now to hear this. I couldn't believe it.

Fuck. I let the useless asshole go.

"Hold him," Vehron commanded.

Shit! I made to step forward when Sally grabbed my arm. "What are you doing?"

"Probably something stupid, but I'm not going to let him hurt another friend."

"You will fail," Gan said.

"Thanks for the vote of confidence."

"Unless I help you."

"Huh?"

"I had wished to save this for a more opportune time, but for you, my love, I would change any plan under the heavens."

"What are you...?"

Gan opened her mouth and let loose the battle screech I'd come to hear in my nightmares. Just for the record, it was even less pleasant up close. I had a feeling it would be ringing in my ears for a long time to come.

All eyes in the room turned toward us. Even Vehron, who had been in the process of lifting the bowl to Ed's horrified face, looked our way.

Then, just like that, she stopped and smiled.

"Okay, so what the fuck did that accomplish?"

And that's when the world seemingly exploded around us.

# 57

# ALL HELL BREAKS LOOSE

In the space of a second, the underground cathedral — for that was certainly what it had been repurposed into — turned into a living Hell of sound, heat, and flying debris.

And it wasn't over yet.

More explosions rang out in the crowded space, drowning out the screams of pain that came after the first.

Instinct took over and I plowed into Christy — knocking her down and shielding her with my body. She was the most vulnerable among us, but maybe not for long.

She'd been caught by surprise, just like I had been. Fortunately, she was aware enough that I caught the glimpse of a predatory smile on her face. She didn't need to say a word. I used the distraction to snap one of her manacles off.

Oof! Someone stepped on me in the panic, followed by another. Okay, so maybe getting trampled wasn't a great way to start things off. Thankfully, a pair of hands from above dragged me back to my feet. I grabbed hold of Christy and pulled her with me.

I found Gan standing there, grinning from ear to ear, looking quite pleased with herself.

"What did you do?" I screamed at her, the only way to make my voice heard above the chaos.

Another explosion rang out from off to the left, sending vampire parts flying. Dust and pebbles rained down from the ceiling, reminding me that we were far underground.

I turned to Christy and pointed toward the exit, but she gave her head a single shake before her eyes lit up with red fire.

I caught her mouthing "duck," but she needn't have bothered. I dropped to my knees as an aura of power collected in her upraised hands.

Before she could fire, movement registered in my periphery. Gan spun and swept the legs out from under a vampire guard who wandered too close. He hit the floor, but before he could respond in any other way, Gan used her claws to tear his windpipe out. *Fuck!*

She smiled a psychotic little grin at me and shoved his bleeding form in my direction. I normally wasn't one to kick a guy when he was down, but then I mentally slapped myself. This was a gift horse, but it wasn't his mouth I needed to focus on.

I leaned in and got myself a mouthful of the red stuff, letting it pour down my throat and enjoying the rush of power it offered.

I had no idea what a bowl of blood would do to Ed, but I sure as shit knew what it did to me, especially if it was from another vamp – and, lucky me, this one was at least a couple of centuries old.

Thankfully, my other friends weren't the type to stop and gawk ... well, mostly. Seeing what Christy was about to do, Sally likewise hit the deck. I glanced back and saw Adam and Dave were also on the floor, albeit they appeared to be more cowering than reacting. Whatever the case, Christy picked that moment to blow, and a wave of energy exploded out from her in a circle.

The magic acted like a red-hot scalpel, bisecting flesh where it hit home. I looked up and saw three surprised vamps get their heads taken neatly off. Light flashed all around us, and a host of disintegrated vampires joined the thick dust already in the air.

Before I could rejoice, a panicked voice cried, "Star!" Sally bolted to her feet once the destructive wave of magic had passed.

"How come my mage can't do that?" Adam asked from somewhere behind as I too scrambled to my feet.

Starlight stood wobbling a few steps in front of us. It wasn't her legs that were the problem, though. She'd apparently tried to duck when Christy unleashed her power, but had been a tad too slow. The top of her head right above her eyes had been seared clean off, the ruins of her skull still smoking from the blast.

Sally stepped forward, and I made to join her when I realized something. Such a hit should have been fatal. Why then had Starlight not joined the vamps who'd just been dusted?

A moment later, that question was answered as her head began to expand outward.

"Oh God, Star, no!" Sally gasped as her friend's body followed suit.

Starlight's skin took on the tone of granite and her eyes sank into her head, the soulless orange orbs of a Jahabich replacing them.

But how? I'd seen her teeth, smelled her scent. Those were all telltale signs of the Jahabich. Unfortunately, as she completed her metamorphosis, I sensed there were no answers forthcoming, only a grim understanding.

Firebird hadn't lied to us after all. It was the choice that was the lie. One could serve the cult willingly, or one could die – only to come back as a rocky abomination.

Either way, there was no escape.

Starlight wasn't alone either. Although the smoke was still thick from whatever the fuck had blown up, I could see more lantern-like eyes, their freaky orange glow made even creepier by the destruction that surrounded us.

"That fucking bitch," Sally said from somewhere beside me.

I paid it no heed. Christy was charging up for another disintegrate spell, but she wasn't going to make it. The Jahabich that had been Starlight was advancing on her quickly.

Sally's voice rang out louder than before. "Goddamn that cunt!" I couldn't spare her the cycles right now, though, in whatever rage she felt against Starlight's betrayal.

I raced forward, using the strength stolen from the vampire guard, and engaged my former friend before she could reach Christy. With my added power, I knew it wouldn't be much of a fight. Even with her razor-sharp skin cutting rivulets into my hands, I overpowered her quickly, ready to tear her head off her fucking shoulders.

But then I remembered the nature of the Jahabich. They were creatures created from the remains – the souls – of the fallen, shape-shifters who could assume the guise of their former selves. Therein lay the problem. As Sally's ex had shown, when they were in their original forms, they possessed the memories, personality, and even a degree of the free will of their former selves. According to Christy, that made them abominations of nature. But weren't they also victims?

And what if there was a way to free them?

"You goddamned bitch!" Sally snarled from close by, but I positioned my body between where I thought she was and Starlight.

Fuck me for being a softy, but I just couldn't do it. Not to one of the few vampires I gave a shit about in this world. She'd just wanted to do right by Village Coven and had paid the price, all because I couldn't leave one fucking severed head lying where I'd found it.

*You're weak. You deserve this.*

I ignored the voice in my head. Fucking asshole. "If there's anything left of you in there, Star," I said as I struggled with her, finally lifting her from the floor, "then run!"

I spun, once, twice, and then let go – sending Starlight flying off into the smoke and debris.

"You fucking whore!" Sally screamed.

I turned to explain myself, and that's when I realized I'd been wrong in assuming Starlight had been the focus of her outrage.

"I swear by everything that is unholy, Firebird, I will make you hurt before I fucking kill you ... GAH!"

Sally collapsed onto the floor, convulsing as if she'd just touched a live wire. I dropped to my knees by her side, trying to do what I could, but powerless to help.

I'd seen this before. I knew what was happening. She was remembering.

I thought she'd been pissed at Starlight, but I now saw my mistake. The true betrayal had been made by Firebird, and it had cost Sally someone she considered a friend, someone she actually cared about. Though that loss had been buried by Alexander's compulsion, it was now resurfacing –

perhaps with other memories, judging by the violent reaction.

"We do not have time for this, beloved."

Goddamnit, but Gan was right. This was our one chance. I doubted we'd get another.

"Christy..."

"Don't think about it for a second," she snapped. "I'm in this until the end."

Goddamned stubborn witch. Fine, then. Adam and Dave were slinking away a few feet behind us, heading toward what they probably hoped was the exit. It was the work of a mere second to catch them and drag them back.

"You two stay with Sally."

"But..."

"*STAY WITH SALLY!!*"

I hated to compel them, but I didn't have time to argue. They immediately froze in place. Ugh, that was no good. Robots weren't going to get the job done. I snapped my fingers in front of them, hoping to snap them out of it.

Once they blinked their eyes a bit, I said, "Stay with her, watch over her. *Please!*"

"The witch is already on the move, my love."

"Of course she is."

Within the space of another second, so were we.

"I need you to gather your men," I said as I tore the arm off a Jahabich that had tried to flank me. "Have them give us some cover."

"My men are no more."

"What? How do you know?"

"Who do you think was responsible for this destruction?"

She punched straight through the stomach of a vampire who'd gotten too close – one of the civilians. Oh well, fuck it. He'd chosen the wrong side.

Gan spun and shoved the wounded vamp my way. I gladly caught him and sank my teeth into his neck – adding to the stolen power already racing through me. Oh yeah, I could dig this!

Wait, her men had been prisoners like the rest of us. "How'd they do it?"

"Pardon?"

I raised my voice. "How did your men do all this?"

"Their clothing had explosives sewn into the seams. When I gave my signal, they detonated. Why else would they have dispersed into the crowd, if not to cause maximum consternation for our enemies?"

Whoa. Vampire suicide bombers. "But how? All they had were knives and..."

"Do not be naïve, Dr. Death," Gan chided as she pointed in a direction – probably the one Christy had taken. A flash of red fire through the smoke in front of us seemed to confirm that. "I believe in tradition, but am not so ignorant as to ignore modern strategy."

"Well, okay then." I really needed to stop underestimating her and remember she'd been raised by one of the great military minds of history. Maybe then I could ... hold on. "Sewn into their clothing? You mean like the stuff I'm wearing?"

"Indeed."

"Are you fucking saying I'm wired to blow and you didn't tell me?!"

"Yes, my love."

"What the fuck am I supposed to do now?"

She turned to continue fighting, but before doing so

glanced over her shoulder and smiled. "I would suggest you fight most carefully. It would indeed be a shame were you to be immolated before you could fulfill your destiny."

## 58

# TO DESTROY THE DESTROYER

"Hey, where are you going?"

The voice from up ahead caught my attention. It was very familiar to me. "Ed?"

In the ensuing chaos, Gan and I managed to fight our way through more of the Jahabich. They'd seemingly survived the explosions in far better shape than any vamps caught at ground zero.

Even so, with my little helper, I managed to suck on two more of the undead as we fought our way onward. Gan was a whirlwind of lethal action, her fighting skills making her look like a miniature Bruce Lee in a wig. I may not have had her black belt in Whateverthefuckfu, but what I did have on my side was increasing power from every vamp I managed to take a sip from.

Whoa, we were like Bizarro versions of Power Man and Iron Fist ... if maybe Iron Fist had a crazy-ass crush on Luke Cage.

Oh well, that was fanfic to consider for another day. For now, I plunged ahead, hoping to hear my roommate's voice again.

517

Instead, fate delivered one better. A shape stepped forth from the smoke and haze. I reached out, grabbed it by the collar, and pulled it in – ready to knock its freaking head off. Thus, I was glad I took a moment before letting fly since I found Ed's surprised face staring back at me.

Sadly, he wasn't the only one who ended up being surprised.

"Oh fuck!" The hand holding on to him immediately flared up in white flame. I hadn't noticed he'd been bleeding from a split lip. It was just a few drops of blood, but more than enough to turn my left hand into a fucking bonfire.

"Shit, Bill! I'm sorry. I'm..."

My roommate's eyes opened wide as I pulled back my flaming fist then shot it out again, turning at the last second to let it fly past him.

"HADOUKEN!!" I screamed as it hit home against a vampire guard who'd decided to pursue my friend. It hurt like a motherfucker, but goddamn, was it satisfying.

"Are you finished, Ken?" he asked.

"Fuck you. I'm more a Ryu guy anyway," I replied as I tried beating the flames out against my jacket.

"I would not do that, Dr. Death," Gan said.

Oh yeah, that whole exploding business. I quickly stopped. Thankfully, the flames were already dying down of their own accord.

"What they hell happened?" I asked Ed as Gan circled us, fighting off anyone who came close.

"What do you think? Shit blew up and I ran."

"No, I mean with the bowl of blood."

"Fucked if I know. I leave anything that has to do with eating clotted shit to you."

"Fine. We'll figure it out later. Get your ass back to the rest. I need to find Christy."

"She's that way. I ran into her in the smoke and she

pretty much just barreled through me. I would've tried to stop her, but she sorta looked a bit angry."

"Understood. There's a lot of that going on now. Adam and Dave are back the way we came, watching over Sally. Don't worry; she's fine."

"Okay, just as long as I don't get kidnapped *again*."

"It's nice to be loved."

"Fuck you." He turned away, then hesitated. "Tom?"

"Huh?"

"Where is he? I didn't see him with you guys in the crowd."

"Don't worry about him," I replied, plunging forward once again. "He's in my pocket."

Ed's cries of "What the fuck does that mean?" followed me into the smoke and fire. That wasn't going to be a fun conversation later on.

"***ENOUGH!!***"

Fuck me with a sandpaper-covered hamster! The compulsion exploded out of nowhere, its sheer power blowing a wave of smoke and dust in my face, which would have been bad enough had it not also hit me like a cinderblock to the head.

I doubled over as a wave of nausea passed over me. The sheer power of Vehron's compulsion totally knocked my equilibrium out of whack for a moment. I hadn't felt anything like that since the time my dad took me on a bunch of spinning rides at the Fireman's Fair right after I'd just downed a funnel cake and three fried Twinkies. Needless to say, I struggled not to puke like I'd done that night. Spewing up a stomach-full of vampire blood would be gross enough, but it would go a long way toward ensuring my boost was short-lived indeed.

Thankfully, it passed after what felt like three or four hours, but was probably just a second or two. Unfortunately, I wasn't the only one affected. As powerful as Gan was, the compulsion had completely smashed through her defenses. She stood there unmoving, like a creepy little lawn gnome.

More figures in the gloom stood still as statues – all vampires. Unfortunately, what movement I *did* see was topped off by orange lantern eyes. The Jahabich were immune to Vehron's spell. Though he'd done me the favor of taking out some foes, that still left more than enough to deal with. I needed help.

I glanced down at Gan, then sighed. "Please don't take this the wrong way."

Who the fuck was I kidding? If she remembered it, of course she was going to take it the wrong way.

Oh fuck it! I grabbed her hand and sank my teeth into her wrist. She might've been out of the fight, but she could still be of use to me.

Just then, a klaxon alarm went off, deafening to ears that had already been abused by a series of explosions. At first, I thought reinforcements were being summoned, but then a torrent of water began to rain down from the ceiling, drenching me to the bone almost immediately.

Go figure. Vampires believed in sprinkler systems.

There I was, sucking on Gan's wrist in a downpour. Thank goodness I hadn't gone for her neck, because that would've been far too close to a romantic scene from a chick flick for my own personal comfort.

Regardless, I got what I needed – feeling my body strengthening even more. Best of all, I knew Gan's freakish speed was now at my disposal.

"Thank you," I said to her glazed, unblinking stare as I prepared to take this war to the enemy.

"Oh." I turned back for a moment. "And just in case you're wondering, this does *not* mean we're engaged."

Steam replaced smoke as fires were extinguished. Still, it was definitely an improvement. The cascading water served to wash the dust and debris out of the air, leaving the floor slippery with gunk. At least I could see better. Oh, and now all the Jahabich in the room had a much clearer line of sight to me too.

So maybe not much of an improvement after all.

Sadly, the vampires enthralled by Vehron's spell, of which there were still plenty standing, didn't seem to have been given passes against the violence. In their attempt to get to me, the Jahabich clubbed aside or outright trampled many. I didn't feel too bad. I mean, these assholes had made their bed. Now it was time to lie in it. At the same time, I could see how Vehron's bullshit could have appealed to the naïve.

Oh well. There'd be time to take stock later of anyone who wanted to switch sides. For now, I grabbed two of the monsters who'd managed to close the gap between us and slammed them together with enough force to make sure someone would need a jackhammer to separate them.

There was no time to celebrate, though. I needed to clear a path.

The floor was thick with muck, most of it probably what happened when you introduced dusted vampires to water. Although I'd never stolen a base in my life, I had spent many a summer flopping across my lawn on a Slip N Slide. This wasn't much different, albeit a bit grosser. I got a running start in the direction I needed to head and slid between the legs of a Jahabich standing in my way. I popped up behind it and slammed a fist through the back of its rocky skull, exposing the creamy center within.

There! A hiss of steam and a flash of red from up ahead caught my eye. It was Christy. Thank God she was still alive. Even better, she hadn't brought this entire fucking place down on our heads. As powerful as I currently was, I didn't care to test if I could survive being crushed under a hundred tons of rock.

It was time to stop playing with the appetizers and get to the main course before Christy ended up becoming dessert. I grabbed one more compelled vamp from the crowd and dug my teeth unsportingly into his neck before throwing him into another Jahabich that came at me. I didn't have any delusions that I was on par with Vehron yet, but I was a shit-load closer than I'd been at the start of this mess.

Maybe between me and Christy we'd have enough to finish this fight.

If not ... well, then I had a feeling neither of us would live to rue the day.

## 59

# FREEWILL VERSUS FREEWILL

A booming laugh caught my ear as I tore the arms off one last Jahabich standing in my way. I shoved it to the side and finally had a clear view to where Vehron and Christy faced off.

Maybe facing off was putting it too nicely. Vehron stood there laughing. Steaming craters lay all around him, but he himself appeared to be untouched. Christy, on the other hand, was leaning against the far wall to the right of the prefect's office. She was still aglow, but her power was fluctuating and she was breathing hard. If I had to guess, she'd fired maybe five of the bullets in her six-shooter.

I wanted to glance back, see if Sally was on her feet yet and, hopefully, rushing to help, but I didn't dare. Vehron had already noticed me standing in the torrent of the fire suppression system. He smiled and waved a hand, indicating that I was welcome to join the party.

Unsurprisingly, I found myself hesitating. Insanely enough, it wasn't so much that I was vastly outclassed. Hell, that was pretty much par for the course. It was because for maybe the first time, I felt truly naked. Without Sally by my side, brains scrambled or not, it just felt wrong – as if I had no hope of victory without her.

I glanced again at Christy, reminding myself of the life growing inside her.

No!

Sally was awesome. She'd had my back through the worst of it, but we weren't conjoined twins. To think she'd be there to help me clean up every mess that occurred between now and the end of time was both foolish and selfish.

All throughout this ordeal, I'd been pretending to take a different attitude, to act tough in the face of adversity – all in the hope that this fate could be avoided. Obviously, that hadn't quite worked out in my favor. However, I'd been right about one part of it all.

It was time to man up.

"I did not wish for this, little brother," Vehron said, his voice betraying no hint of the regret he claimed. "Time and again, I offered you my hand. It is still not too late, even now."

I stepped to Christy's side and instead offered my hand to her. She smiled at me, took it, and together, we turned to face our enemy. "I know my friends and I know my family. You aren't either."

"So be it, slave to the Macedonian."

"Better to be a slave in heaven than to … um … never mind. That saying doesn't really apply here. Let's just get this over with."

Vehron tore his sopping wet shirt off and tossed it to the side, revealing the black tattoos adorning his muscular shoulders. I guess it was meant to be intimidating. That, or he'd spent his few months of freedom in the modern world watching too many hours of professional wrestling.

Noting that he seemed to be waiting for me to make the first move, I asked Christy, "Are you okay?"

"Far from it. I don't have a lot left."

"Then make what you do have left count. For Tom?"

A sad smile graced her face. "For Tom."

"You know, I can hear you. I'm still in your fucking pocket!" Though muffled, my ears – boosted by vampire blood – easily picked up his words.

Oh yeah. Well, it was a little late for me to find a shelf to put him on.

"Sorry," I said sheepishly as I stepped away from Christy so as to not present our foe with two targets for the price of one.

"Face the Sun Strider if you dare," Vehron said. "I am the tamer of Mirros the Brave, the slayer of Kyra the Pious, he who broke the walls and sacked the city of Acanthus. I am the Destroyer."

"Let me guess: choose and perish, right?"

"What?"

"I'm imagining J. Edgar Hoover in a dress, if that helps."

"Your words make no sense, little Night Spawn. Has fear so clouded your mind?"

I saw his game. Apparently, we were supposed to list out our resume before fighting, like some sort of pregame pissing match. I guess it beat three episodes of powering up before a fight on Dragonball Z.

"My name is Bill. They call me Dr. Death. I may not have sacked any cities, but I once managed to piss off an entire guild in World of Warcraft. Beat that, motherfucker."

A loud sigh escaped Christy's lips from off to my right. Yeah, one of these days I really needed to learn to just keep my mouth shut.

Movement out of the corner of my eye caught my attention, and I turned to see the Jahabich closing in. For a second, I thought Vehron's idea of a fair fight would include me being buried under ten tons of rock monster, but to my surprise, they started to line up next to each other. Their soulless orange eyes cast an eerie glow through the water that continued to cascade down on us. Jeez, was nobody going to shut the damn fire extinguishers off?

Just then, all of the Jahabich turned to face away from us. After a couple of seconds, I realized what they were doing. They were forming a living wall, similar to the cage Sally and I had been trapped in while deep underground. Except they weren't just penning me and Christy in. They were forming a wide semicircle against the back wall with the three of us inside.

This wasn't a jail cell. They were forming an arena – a makeshift Thunderdome where there would be no outside interference and only one side would leave.

"Are we supposed to wait for the bell to rin..."

Before I could even finish the sentence, Vehron was on the move. He was frighteningly swift, crossing the distance between us faster than a person could blink.

Much to my amazement, though, I saw him coming. He was still disturbingly quick, don't get me wrong, but Gan's speed allowed my reflexes to react before I consciously knew what I was doing. Vehron stopped his movement right in front of where I stood, just in time to place his face in the exact spot I'd aimed the uppercut.

The dude's jaw felt like it was made of titanium, but I had just enough firepower at my disposal to make a dent.

His head snapped up and he backed away several steps.

Christy, probably hoping for a quick kill, picked that moment to let loose with a beam of vampire-killing goodness.

As quick as he'd been to charge me, though, he was even faster to sidestep her attack. The ray missed him by several inches and struck one of the Jahabich walling us in on the far side, fusing the creature into place and sending up another billow of steam.

"Impressive, brother," he said, rubbing his chin. "But I will not grant victory so easily."

"One can hope," I replied.

He held out his hands to his sides as if to say "come at me, bro." I glanced at Christy and gave my head a single shake. She didn't look so hot, and I'm sure standing in an indoor monsoon wasn't helping. While I loved the idea of her turning him into a crispy critter, the only way it would work was if I managed to slow him down a bit. As it was, his age gave him speed and reflexes that made even Gan seem like a slowpoke.

*Yo, Dr. Death*, I said in my head, *don't suppose we could work something out – just this once?*

My inner hell-beast responded with nothing but silence. Wonderful; he was a psychotic murderer, a rapist, and a petulant child all rolled into one. Oh well, it had been a long shot anyway.

Fuck you, then, I'll do it myself.

I rushed forward, putting my own speed to use but holding back ever so slightly just in case I needed it. I thought I was gonna come up blank with regard to possible strategies, then remembered an old issue of *The Hulk* where Doc Samson had managed to knock the big ape out. It hadn't been because he was more powerful. It had been through sheer tenacity – and a nonstop pummeling before the Hulk could recover.

It was better than nothing.

Vehron continued to stand there, unmoving. The guy was the epitome of an arrogant prick. I decided to make sure he paid for it.

I threw a punch right at his smug face, missing as he

tilted his head to the side at the last second. Another came at his gut. His hand was a blur of action, blocking me easily.

A roundhouse punch ... nope.

Another uppercut ... blocked.

A straight jab to the nose ... missed.

Fuck this shit!

I threw another punch at him, but this one was a ruse to cover up a solid kick to the fuckhead's shin.

Score!

I don't care how tough you think you are, there are some places where all the muscle in the world doesn't mean shit. Vehron howled in anger as my strike hit home.

Sadly, it was about as far from being a fatal blow as one could get with a guy like this. The next thing I knew, I was eating a backhand to the face – hard enough to almost spin my head around.

I landed on the wet floor with a splash and slid back, stunned.

Even with the stolen healing at my disposal, it still felt like my jaw had been completely rearranged. Pity that I'd been fired from my previous job. Their dental plan had been pretty good. I had a feeling I might need it by the time this was over.

I looked up and saw Vehron advancing, taking his sweet time. His posture said it all. I wasn't a threat and he knew it.

Fortunately for me, though, Christy didn't. She let loose again, but this time changed tactics. A fast-moving target was way too difficult to hit. A stationary one, however, not so much. The floor, for example, was pretty darn hard to miss.

Christy's blast exploded at Vehron's feet, forming a crater large enough that even he couldn't sidestep it in time. He went down, showered by debris.

The distraction was enough to allow me to get to my feet,

grab a fist-sized rock, and chuck it at the fucker's head at what I hoped would be terminal velocity.

And miss, of course. Like I said, not a baseball prodigy. Guess there was a reason Dad didn't play catch with me much as a kid.

I glanced over at Christy and found her on one knee, her reserves no doubt rapidly draining. Before I could convey my concern, though, a sickly black glow surrounded her. I wondered what she was planning to throw at Vehron next, but he wasn't the target.

Either her head was scrambled or I'd done something else to piss her off, because this time, when she released her energy, it came screaming straight at me.

**60**

# FACE OFF

I was certain the next sensation I'd feel would be that of my body melting into goo.

With my speed, I could have avoided the blast, but Christy had caught me off guard. As it enveloped me, though, I was pleasantly surprised to find that all I felt was the barest of tingles. It was actually kinda pleasant in a Magic Fingers sort of way.

Still, perhaps now wasn't the time for a metaphysical handjob. I glanced back and saw her face strained as if in concentration. What was she...?

"Where have you fled to, brother?"

Huh? Vehron had managed to pick himself up, the cascade from above washing any debris from his muscular torso. Fucker looked like he belonged in a shampoo commercial. He stood not ten feet away, but instead of advancing to continue his beat-down, he was looking out past where the Jahabich stood guard.

"Where did he go?" he asked nobody in particular.

"*None have passed,*" the freaky voices of the Jahabich answered in unison.

530

What the hell? Had the dipshit gone all Ravenous Bugblatter Beast of Traal on me?

Wait a second. Was it possible?

I glanced back at Christy, and saw her body shaking with effort. That's when it hit me. The spell she'd zapped me with was a glamour. She'd done it to herself when hiding from the Feet and now she'd covered me in one. Holy motherfucking hot dogs, I was invisible!

That wasn't all. I could see Vehron's nostrils working – no doubt trying to sniff me out. Whatever Christy was doing was blocking me entirely – sight, smell; hell even my movement in the downpour didn't seem to attract his attention.

Vehron raised his voice as he turned in a slow circle. "You have left your friend, little brother. The teachings of Ib dictate that we should not suffer lesser Magi to live." He took a tentative step, a look of annoyance crossing his face. "Very well. The choice is made. She will ... ARGH!"

I didn't quite know how one did an "argh," but I did know how to walk up behind someone and raise a boot up between their legs. Oh yeah! That felt good, especially since I finally had enough firepower behind me to make this asshole feel the pain. He doubled over, and I grabbed him from behind around the waist – kinda glad that nobody could see me to snap a picture.

I then fell back, launching him over my body as hard as I could. The satisfying crunch that came a split second later was music to my ears.

Even better was the blood. I'd tossed the asshole right into the back of one of the Jahabich. The rock-encrusted fuckhead hadn't stood a chance in the collision, but at least it got to tear the shit out of my foe with its obsidian-laced skin before being smashed into rubble.

Sadly, that small victory was short lived. Vehron's freaky

fast healing took care of the worst by the time I closed the distance between us. That was okay, though.

There was a lot more where that came from.

I could see how Kevin Bacon's character could go all punch drunk with power in *Hollow Man*. Being able to attack, sight unseen, was pretty fucking awesome as far as powers went. However, it also paid to not be stupid. I wasn't about to just stand there playing a life-sized game of Punch-Out with the asshole that time forgot.

It was all hit and run – a constant game of moving and punching, trying not to become repetitive lest he figure out a pattern and shit-stomp me.

And it was working too, especially after I brought my claws out. The beauty of the indoor flooding – and damn, the puddles were definitely starting to build up now – was any gore that landed on me from my attacks got washed away before he could draw a bead on me.

We danced like that for a couple of minutes, but I was rapidly beginning to see that it was like spitting into the wind. I'd cut a furrow across his stomach and by the time I sidestepped to take a chunk out of his arm, he'd already begun to heal. Still, I persevered. He had to have a limit. There had to be a point where he'd lose enough blood where his body just couldn't keep up.

I'd find that point or die trying.

Emphasis on that last part, sadly.

I hit him hard, then leapt over him, only to land in one of the aforementioned puddles, making a big enough splash that even Christy's glamour couldn't completely cover it up.

Unfortunately, that was the signal that player two was up. Vehron's eyes flashed black in an instant – rage enveloping his face – as he lashed out. The blow was a glancing one – I'd been in enough scraps to know when to get out of Dodge as fast as possible, but it was at his full power and I just wasn't fast enough.

Holy Jesus! My left shoulder shattered as what felt like a fist-sized bus plowed into it. Any defensive posture I might have had was rendered moot as my arm became a useless bag of meat attached to my body.

The only upside, and believe me, I perfectly understood the irony of calling it that, was the hit sent me flying head over heels. Up was down, and then back up again as the off-center strike sent me pinwheeling.

I landed face down, a good fifteen feet away – leaving a trail on the grimy floor as I skidded along its slick surface. Hidden though I might be, it practically painted an arrow that said, "Here I am!"

The scream of pain I let out as I rolled to my feet in a desperate bid to hide myself again didn't help. Yeah, I'd definitely fumbled that dice roll.

"You okay, Bill?" Tom's tinny little voice asked from my pocket. "Getting kind of bumpy in here."

"Not now," I sputtered, feeling my injuries begin to knit themselves back together. Bones shifted around back to where they belonged, a not altogether pleasant experience.

"You need to watch out with the flipping around because I almost hit…"

"Not now!" I snapped, slapping my palm against the flap of the pocket.

I quickly sidestepped a few more times, trying my damnedest to avoid making too many splashes. Good timing too, because Vehron was right there, his eyes following the trail of muck, searching for any sign of me. But I was already elsewhere.

Oh yeah, cocksucker.

I felt just like Kelvin Lightblade this one time I rolled a natural twenty while trying to hide from a pack of angry wyverns. Fuckers couldn't spot me for shit and I made it out with the treasure of... "URK!"

Quick as lightning, Vehron spun and grabbed me by the throat. How the fuck had he known where I was? Was he able to read minds too?

I glanced over toward Christy, hoping maybe she had enough juice left in her to knock muscle-boy for a loop. That's when I realized exactly how Vehron had caught me so easily.

Christy's spell was no longer in effect. She'd finally reached her limit and passed out from the effort.

By my estimates, I had over a thousand years' worth of vampire blood coursing through my veins. Yet it still wasn't enough to even budge him. I felt like a toddler trying to pull his hand out of his parent's grasp on a trip to the toy store.

"Enough," Vehron said softly. "Accept your fate with dignity."

Oh yeah? Well, you know what? Fuck dignity.

If it came down to it, I couldn't have cared less if my final moments were spent screaming and crying. The phrase "take it like a man" wasn't in my vocabulary ... sorta anyway. Needless to say, I chose to ignore his request – extending my claws so as to try to sever his tendons.

***crack***

An openhanded slap got my attention, ringing my bell real good. I swear, I felt like an average Joe trying to fight off the mighty Hercules, and that's saying a lot, considering right at that moment I had enough strength in me to force even James to his knees.

*Are you ready to stop fighting me?*

"What?" I gurgled, it taking a moment to register that the question came from within my head.

*I can help you. I can even the odds.*

Dr. Death wanted to have a meaningful conversation *now*?!

Vehron stared hard at me. "I said you will accept your fate with dignity."

He eased up ever so slightly on his grip, enough to let me speak.

"Not you, stupid. How can you even the odds?"

*You know how.*

"We already tried that."

"Tried what?" Vehron asked, his head cocked slightly to the side. His voice took on a hard tone and he tightened his grip again. "Tried to befriend you? Tried to convey my brotherhood upon you?"

*Yes,* Dr. Death replied, ignoring Vehron, *but this time, you need to stop fighting. You need to let go of everything and give yourself wholly to me. You need to stop caring.*

Caring? About what? That was an odd request.

Wait a second. Did that have something to do with how I broke free last time? I mean, according to Sally, I became me again when he crossed the line and decided to kill her.

*Make no mistake; I let you go.*

Oh, really? Somehow, I was finding myself doubting that.

*I simply grew bored with your whore, nothing more.*

His excuses reeked worse than Turd's ass, and that was saying a lot. Yeah, well, fuck that shit. There was nothing that could be done to me to make me want to willingly give up control again.

A moment later, Vehron decided to test that resolve as he raked his claws across my midsection, pretty much gutting me like a fish. Oh, so *that's* what my intestines looked like.

One more item to cross off my bucket list. And also ... OH GOD, IT HURT!

*He will make you drown in your own blood.*

I had a feeling that drowning was the least of my worries, although maybe the asshole in my head had a point about blood. Last time I'd had the *pleasure* of dining on Vehron, I'd ended up puking my guts out. I still wasn't sure why. Maybe Freewills weren't compatible with each other, or maybe it had been all the silver bullets in his body at the time. Either way, I'd gotten about a five-minute boost from him before I'd felt the need to upchuck everything. Still, a few minutes was better than nothing. Battles could be won in that time.

Once the pain had subsided a bit, I slammed a fist down into the crook of the arm holding me. The blow didn't cause him to release me, but it did bend his arm at the elbow, allowing me to push off with my legs and force myself in closer.

Fangs extended, I bit into his shoulder.

Or tried to.

My teeth had barely scratched the surface of his skin when his free hand grabbed me by the hair and yanked me away.

"You are not worthy of my blood," he whispered into my face, slathering me in his death breath. Guess Firebird hadn't exposed him to the modern miracle of mouthwash yet.

Vehron shifted his grip from my throat to my lower jaw, squeezing until my mouth was forced open. I found my gag reflex tested as he shoved his other hand in. Ugh, the indignities I was forced to suffer. Oh well, at least he didn't shove any other appendages into my mouth. Things could definitely be worse.

Or not as he pulled back, ripping a handful of my teeth out with him.

"You are not a true Night Spawn. You are barely a vampire. You have no need of these."

He held up a handful of bloody teeth, including at least one canine, and crushed them to dust before my eyes.

Vehron wasn't finished with me yet, though, not by a long shot. Apparently, I'd done pissed him off real good.

Again grabbing a fistful of hair, he dragged me over to the wall of Jahabich and shoved me face first into one's back. Imagine trying to French kiss a drawer full of steak knives. Yeah, well, it was a lot worse than that.

He shoved me hard into the creature, shattering my nose in the process. I opened my mouth to scream, and my lips were shredded against the monster's rocky hide.

Vehron pulled back for a moment and then slammed me into the Jahabich again, twice as hard. My glasses shattered, and everything turned first blood red and then black as the shards ground into my eyes.

*I can make this stop. I can hurt him back.*

Sadly, the part of my brain that was still mine was in no position to do anything other than scream in agony. Vehron began to grind me against the rock monster's hide as if my face were a hunk of cheese in need of grating.

I braced myself against the Jahabich, trying to push off, but only succeeded in shredding my hands – further adding to my torment

To even begin to describe what it felt like is to give words to something which can't be described in any sane way. I never thought that I would beg for death, but then I never thought I would ever experience my face being sanded off. In that moment, I wanted nothing more than the sweet release of oblivion.

Sadly, that wasn't to be. As horrific as my wounds were, I didn't think them fatal – at least for a vampire. They'd probably heal completely within minutes at most with the blood-boost I'd gotten.

But therein lay a new horror. That meant he could do it over and over again, as many times until he got bored. Worse, soon my power would wane as the blood wore off. As I grew weaker, so would my suffering increase, as it would take hours, maybe more, for the damage to sort itself out. I had no idea what Vehron went through, losing his body for over a thousand years, but I couldn't fathom this torture lasting even an hour.

*Give yourself to me and end this now.*

I wanted to end it all right, but not his way. I wanted to die. I didn't want my friends to see me like this, broken and pathetic. I didn't want to hear them as they realized I'd let them down. I didn't want to live with the knowledge that they were next.

Most of all, though, I wanted it to stop hurting.

# 61

## STING LIKE A BEE

I was right. Between Gan and the other vamps I'd bitten, my wounds healed at a pace that would have made Wolverine proud. That didn't really make it pleasant, mind you. The sensation of my eyeballs reforming was not something I cared to experience again.

Nevertheless, I could have cried with joy once I realized I could see again. Sadly, most of the room was now a blur around me with the only thing in focus being the one person I really didn't want to see.

The look on Vehron's face was pure evil itself – a mix of crazed triumph, disgust, and anger. Pity that Gan hadn't set her sights on him. They might have made a cute couple.

"What's going on out there? Are you kicking his ass yet?"

My roommate's tiny voice caused Vehron to laugh. I guess from his perspective, it probably *was* kind of funny. Hell, having gotten a taste of his strength, I actually found the whole prospect pretty goddamned hilarious too. I'd have joined him in a good chuckle, but my jawline was still knitting itself back together.

"All those who come before Ib are given the choice,"

Vehron said, holding me by the collar of my coat so as to keep me upright. "You have made yours, brother."

He lifted a hand, claws extended, and placed it against my chest. Slowly, he applied pressure. The tips of his talons, sharper than any dagger, began to sink into me. Red-hot pain lanced through my body as they parted skin and began to work their way into muscle.

"Save some of that asshole for me, Bill!" Tom said from his fur-lined prison near my hip.

This time, I did laugh. I couldn't help it. As much as I hurt, the thought of smacking Vehron around with a plastic toy was too good to let go of in these last few moments.

My mirth wasn't shared. Vehron twisted his hand ever so slightly, shutting me the fuck up. "The love of Ib is such that even those who fail her are still allowed to serve. You will learn to accept this fate."

Oh crap. I was gonna end up like Starlight. Dusted, then thrown into a pit of orange spooge – my will subverted for the greater good. Welcome to the Borg, resistance is still futile.

"Your friends will also be given the choice," he continued. "No matter their answer, though, they too have already made their decision."

Thoughts of Sally, Christy, and Ed floated through my mind.

*Now, before it's too late.*

Then I saw Sheila's face. I had no idea where she was or what had happened to her, but I had faith she'd make her way here eventually. It was her destiny. Vehron was the Freewill of legend, after all.

My body shuddered in pain as his claws began to saw through my sternum. I could only pray he didn't use me and my friends against her when the time came, but I knew that was a fool's hope.

He would use every advantage he had. As powerful as she was, it would be too much. The last defender of humanity would fall and, with her, all hope for any future that wasn't a living Hell.

*It need not end like this!*

"C'mon, man. Throw me a bone. I want to see what's going on out there."

The warring voices of Dr. Death and my roommate both competed for my attention. Too bad for them, Vehron's claws were nearing my heart. That was a hard argument to ignore.

As I accepted my death, I turned my thoughts inward. I envisioned the bedroom threesome that I'd accidentally shown Christy, figuring my last thoughts could at least be pleasant ones.

Something went wrong, though. Maybe the pain was too great or my failure too complete, but even that glimmer of happiness was denied me. When I mentally pulled back the covers of the massive bed, all I found waiting for me was Gan. Oh, for Christ's sake!

She popped up, wearing her furry armor, and admonished me for trying to escape my fate. Somewhere in my head, Dr. Death laughed, and I knew it was him fucking with me.

*Stop this foolishness and accept what you must do.*

I mentally stared at Gan's image for another second as a thought hit me. I realized that maybe Dr. Death's words had merit – just not quite how he intended.

As Vehron's hand worked to end me, mine worked its way up and into my pocket. I immediately felt the plastic form Tom inhabited. I tried pulling him out, but he was caught on something.

Fuck, it's always shit like that when you least need it.

I finally yanked him free, just as I opened my mouth and coughed out a wad of blood. I could feel Vehron's hand inside my body and knew he was seconds away from squeezing the life out of me. Hell, he could have done it already, but the fucker was teasing it out – making sure my final moments hurt.

It was time to repay the favor.

I spat up more blood, but this time, made it a point to hock it right in the fucker's face. He closed his eyes against the spray, giving me the opening I needed.

Now, I'm not stupid. I know full well that jabbing a nearly indestructible super-warrior with a plastic toy was a laughable tactic at best.

Unless you rammed that toy's outstretched arm right into his eye-socket.

You can probably see where this was going, but sadly, Vehron didn't – at least not until he opened his eyes again, at which point it was too late.

I slammed Tom home, driving him as deep as I could while at the same time pushing off with my free hand. As hoped, a hunk of cheap plastic to the optic nerve was enough distraction for him to release me.

Vehron's claws slipped out of me and although I was grievously wounded, with the mother of all sucking chest wounds, I could already feel a millennium's worth of healing powers kicking in to take care of it.

"Oh yeah!" Tom screamed in triumph. "I got your cornea in my motherfucking kung-fu grip, bitch!"

It didn't take Vehron more than a second or two to rip the doll from his head and drop it to the floor where it landed with a splash. That's all I needed, though. I side-stepped the big ape, ripped off the coat I was wearing, and threw it over his head – holding on for dear life as he struggled.

I turned my head and squinted, praying that Christy was awake again, but no dice. The poor girl had given everything she had to give. I'd been hoping for one last fireball from her, but it was not to be. Fuck!

Sadly, with the sprinklers going full blast, all the fires from the first series of explosions were long since extinguished.

"Anyone got a match?" I yelled out in vain.

Shit! How the fuck did Gan's people trigger themselves to go boom?

Sadly, my time was running short. Vehron screamed with rage, his voice muffled by the fur-lined jacket over his face while I desperately searched for something on the inside lining – a trigger or...

"Be careful, Bill!" Tom shouted. "There was some kind of button in the pocket with me. I think it was wired to something."

Bingo! "Thanks, buddy!"

I leapt onto Vehron's back, wrapping my legs around him. I'm sure to an observer we looked like we were shooting some bizarre fetish video, but the stakes were far higher.

I pulled back on the coat wrapped around his head, using it sort of like reins on a horse. It wasn't quite as elegant, but it shifted Vehron's center of balance enough so we stumbled away from where Christy lay.

That was good. I didn't want to be anywhere near her as I clumsily fumbled for the pocket where Tom had spent the greater part of the past hour. Needless to say, it was a wee bit more difficult when the whole thing was tangled around an angry motherfucker's noggin.

Vehron's hand closed over my right ankle and he squeezed, all pretense of playing gone. The bone shattered like glass and I cried out, wanting nothing better than to curl up in a corner and cry.

But I had other plans. I finally managed to stuff my hand into the deep pocket where I began to root around for something vaguely button-like. Now my only concern was to figure out how to hobble away before...

*"I WILL KILL YOU!!"*

The compulsion hit me in the face like a bowling ball, almost knocking me loose. Goddamn it!

*"THEN I WILL KILL YOUR FRIENDS!!"*

Holy shit. It felt like my head was going to pop right off. François was right. Immune to control I might be, but enough high-powered compulsions could scramble my brain like an egg.

I'm sure my vision doubled, but since my glasses were shot to shit, it really didn't make much of a difference.

*"STARTING WITH THE MAGI!! I WILL CUT THE CHILD FROM HER BELLY AND FEAST UPON IT BEFORE HER DYING EYES!!"*

Blood burst from my nose as the compulsion slammed into my head. It was so powerful, the room itself shuddered and debris began to rain down from the high ceiling. I didn't think I could stand another and remain conscious, but then his words registered with me and I realized what I needed to do.

Escape was secondary to stopping him. A few short minutes ago, I had been ready to beg for death. Doing so was freeing in a way. When you wanted something so badly, it was hard to be afraid of it. That acceptance was still there, but in a different way. I had been prepared to die like a dog, but now I knew I had it in me to die like a man.

*What are you doing?*

"Living up to our name, my man! Dr. Death all the way!"

*Don't do this. Give me control and we can finish this my way.*

"Not gonna happen, fuck-face. You're not getting a shot at them either."

My hand closed around something hard and metallic. There! I had it.

Vehron reached up and began to tear the fabric away.

**"*DIE, FALSE NIGHT SPAWN!!*"**

*I don't want to die!*

Both of them cried out at the same time, and it felt as if something ruptured in my head. My vision began to fade, but they were both too late.

I pushed the button.

*Nooooooo!*

For a moment, it seemed as if nothing was going to happen, but then my world erupted in an explosion of light, sound, and fire that consumed me whole.

**62**

## THE CLEANUP CREW

Being dead – really dead – was kinda weird. I mean, I never bought into the whole heaven concept – fluffy white clouds, harps, and shit like that. Hell, even if it existed, I doubted my pedigree would gain me entrance anyway.

I figured being reincarnated as a cat could be cool, or maybe haunting a house would work, especially if it was a sorority house.

No such luck, though. Instead, I found death to be rather uncomfortable. Cold, wet, and hard, like I was lying on a slab.

Ugh. I hoped that wasn't the case. But then, how could it be? Vamps turned to ash when they died, and I was pretty sure I wasn't a pile of...

My eyes popped open and I blinked as rain fell into them. No, not rain. It was still the motherfucking sprinkler system. Did nobody know where the goddamned shutoff valve was?

Wait a second.

I sat up and looked down at myself, noticing the horrific

546

burnt tissue covering my now exposed upper body. But then, right before my eyes, my flesh began to mold itself back into shape – healing at an incredible rate.

As my skin returned to its normal color, I realized something still wasn't right. I'd never had abs before – at least none that I could see.

I placed my hands on my rock hard stomach and was amazed to see the size of the talons attached to them.

What the...?

Movement caught my attention from the periphery of my vision and I turned to see ... what the fuck was that?!

It was like something out of a nightmare - legs and a torso stumbling drunkenly about, but above chest level, there was nothing but charred skin, exposed bone, and gristle. For a second, I thought my eyes were playing tricks on me, but then I realized everything I was seeing was in crystal clear focus, my lack of glasses be damned.

I caught a glimpse of the ragged bottom of a tattoo – a black sun. It was Vehron, or what was left of him. As I watched this bizarre spectacle, his flesh and bone started to regrow. A cold pit of fear appeared in my stomach and began to spread. He was still able to regenerate?! But how?

No fucking way. How the hell was I supposed to kill this...?

And that's when his body exploded in a shower of ash.

For a second, I sat there, my eyes wide and staring – waiting for the other shoe to drop. Surely it was a joke. Maybe he somehow had the power to disintegrate at will and then reform. What a mind-fuck that would be.

Nothing happened, though, save the dust rapidly settling to the floor where it mixed with the falling water to become a thick sludge – indistinguishable from the rest of the muck.

Holy crap, I killed him. I actually killed him!

Unable to help myself, I did the only sensible thing I could think of.

I laughed.

It took me a few moments to notice the sound escaping from my lips was much deeper than normal. Then realization hit – the abs, the claws, and now the manly voice. I'd somehow become Dr. Death again.

Panic immediately gripped me and I scrambled to my feet, ready to bolt.

Hold on. I'd meant to get to my feet. I looked down at my hands and willed the claws to retract. They did without hesitation, leaving large, but otherwise human-looking hands. I closed my fist, then opened it again. It obeyed, just like it normally did.

"I'm still me."

"Yo, Bill, you still alive? I can't see shit."

Tom's voice was muffled, but I heard it clear as day. Hell, I could hear a lot of things – his voice, every drop of water as it hit the ground, Christy's breathing ... hell, the respiration of every being in the room.

It was almost too much to take in. Talk about sensory overload, and that wasn't even counting the smells – oh God, even down to a little patch of mold off in one corner. I sensed it all.

I forced myself to focus. There'd be plenty of time to play Name that Stench later. For now, I needed to find my friend.

Thankfully, it didn't take long. He was maybe twenty feet away, covered in grime and lying face down in a puddle.

I picked him up and cleaned him off as best I could.

"I did it, man. I killed that asshole," I said.

"Who the fuck are you?"

"It's me."

"Newsflash, cock-face, that doesn't narrow it down since I have no idea who you are."

"It's Bill, dipshit!"

"Bill? No way."

"Yep. Somehow, I became ... well, my monster."

"Prove you're him. What was I doing when...?"

"Probably jerking off to hentai."

"Wow. Good guess. Damn, bro. You look ripped."

"Thanks. I work out."

"Liar."

"Fuck you, you dildo with..." I trailed off as I suddenly sensed movement from all around us. "Shit!"

"What?"

"Hold that thought."

Even without my newfound ocular acuity, it would have been hard to miss the glow of orange eyes as the Jahabich broke formation and turned to face me.

"What happened?" a voice asked from beyond them.

"Where is The Destroyer?"

"Who is that?"

"What did you do with the Sun Strider?"

More voices began to speak – some questioning, but others starting to put two and two together. With Vehron dead, his compulsion had died with him. The whole room was waking back up.

Ripped though they might be, at least I was still wearing pants this time. I stuffed Tom into my back pocket and turned to face the group.

"Vehron is dead!" I shouted.

"Dead?"

"Impossible!"

"Who will lead us now?"

"Kill the murderer!"

Huh? That wasn't quite the response I had hoped for.

I'd been betting on them maybe thanking me for freeing them or, at worst, just disbanding like Thulsa Doom's followers after Conan gave him the last close shave of his life.

Regardless, the Jahabich didn't need the coaxing of an angry crowd. Almost as one, they started to march toward me.

Seeing a living wall of angry rock advancing was a bit unnerving, even for someone who'd just stopped a guy who was all but unstoppable.

I took a step back as a shriek rent the air. The head of one of the Jahabich exploded in a mass of orange goo as a tiny fist erupted from it.

Its body dropped to the floor, revealing Gan, also now free from Vehron's spell. She nimbly leapt over the creatures and raced to stand by my side, seeming – if anything – even smaller than normal.

She glanced up at me and smiled broadly. "You look ravishing, my love." Aw gross! Talk about ruining my victory dance. "We shall fight together to the end."

All of a sudden, I realized maybe I wasn't as big on self-sacrifice as I'd been a few short minutes ago. I mean, how much of a downer would it be to finally kill Sauron, only to be finished off by some orcs?

Even so, the odds were against us. Gan's suicide squad had killed many, but there was still a small army of Jahabich and vampires facing us – and many of those vamps looked to be both armed and well trained.

But maybe the odds didn't need to be as stacked as they looked. After all, if it had worked for Vehron...

Of course, I made it a point to be a wee bit more specific. ***"FOLLOWERS OF IB, STAND DOWN!!"***

Whoa! I couldn't believe the power that seemed to flow out of me. It felt like I could've compelled anyone to do anything. For a brief moment, I understood why the older vamps found it so appealing, so intoxicating.

And that's why I realized how dangerous it was for me to ever acquire a taste for it.

Regardless, it worked – mostly. Once again, all the vampires in the room – save my friends this time – stopped what they were doing and became as statues. Sadly, the actual living statues lining up to attack us weren't affected by it. However, their forces cut down by at least two-thirds and with Gan by my side, the odds seemed much more palatable.

There was still the question of what to do with the vamps once we were done pulverizing some gravel, but hopefully, inspiration would hit before then. For now, though, we had plenty of other things to hit.

"Follow me," I said.

"Even to the gates of Hell, my darling."

Ugh! I so needed to watch what I said to the little freak. First things first, though. Right now, it was too easy for us to be dogpiled. More space was the answer, especially if I could lead them away from where Christy still lay unconscious.

Thus, I ran straight at the orange-eyed devils and took a flying leap over their heads – way over their heads, as a matter of fact. Good thing the ceiling of this place was nice and high, otherwise, I'd have cold-cocked myself.

I landed and almost lost my footing on the slick floor. But just as I was about to fall, my toenails elongated into talons and caught hold. Neat trick. I'd have to remember that.

"What the fuck's going on now?"

"Sorry, man," I said to Tom. Fuck this. It was too dangerous for him to be there with me. All a Jahabich needed to do was take a swipe at my ass. "Make that double sorry." I pulled him out of my pocket and tossed him toward a far corner of the room where there didn't seem to be any fighting or bedazzled vamps standing around.

"Fucking asshole!" he yelled, sailing off into the distance.

I turned to face the monsters just as Gan made a similar, if much more nimble, leap over them. She landed as gracefully as a gazelle – fucking little show off.

"Let's do this."

Just as the words left my mouth, the water from the sprinkler system began to slake – turning from a torrent to a drizzle and then just a few residual drops.

It was about fucking time. Now who...?

"Dr. Death, your whore." Gan pointed in the direction of the double doors leading to the rest of the complex.

In the chaos of battle, I hadn't given much thought to my friends – save to hope they'd managed to find a quiet corner to ride things out in. With Vehron's compulsion in place and everyone on a time out, it had seemed safe enough, but now I needed to remember that had all changed.

Amazingly enough, Sally was stepping back in. Had she been the one to shut off the fire system? How the fuck would she even have known where it was?

Oh well, no matter. Hopefully, the others weren't far behind. I doubted she'd forget about them in the middle of...

Hold on. *Forget?* Holy shit, some days, I am so fucking stupid I'm surprised I remember to breathe. The Jahabich were almost upon us, but I needed to try. I didn't know when or if I'd get another chance.

Besides, she was worth it.

**"SALLY, REMEMBER EVERYTHING!! PLEASE!!"**

My last compulsion had been frightfully powerful, but had been widely dispersed. This one, with its laser-like focus, made me feel like I was the Death Star and she Alderaan. It was hard to explain, but I could sense the wave of power as it traversed the room and hit her straight on.

Sally screamed as her head snapped back from the force of it. She went down like a ton of bricks.

Sadly, I wasn't afforded the luxury of checking on her right then, as our enemy was upon us. A massive clubbed arm swung at me as I was still distracted, slamming into my face.

Hmm, it split my lip, but that was all. Such a blow would have taken me out of the battle before, but now – now it felt like being in a schoolyard slap-fight.

I returned the favor, taking the creature's head right off its wide shoulders.

Hah! If that was how this fight was going to be, then I probably should've tied one arm behind my back to make it almost fair.

Nah!

As Gan bounded around, looking like an extra from *Crouching Tiger, Hidden Dragon*, I waded into the brunt of the monsters, let them surround me, and then tore the fuckers to pieces. Limbs, teeth, bits of things that I couldn't identify – they all went flying in every direction. So this was what being a human sledgehammer felt like.

Each time I took one down, I got splattered with more of their gooey insides. Gross, but harmless as long as they didn't kill me and, sadly for them, I'd already decided that maybe I wanted to live after all.

I was gonna tear these fuckers apart one at a...

"Bill?"

I turned my head, slapping aside a Jahabich who I heard step in to take advantage of my distraction. Oh yeah, eat your heart out, Daredevil.

It was Sally, and she was awake. She was still a bit dazed, looking like she'd just taken a baseball bat upside the head, but she was back on her feet.

I didn't care to leave Gan alone against these monsters,

but she appeared to be more than holding her own against their dwindling numbers. Fuck it. My partner needed me.

Time appeared to slow down for a second, but I knew it was just me accelerating across the room at a speed that would have normally been impossible. Sally's eyes opened wide in surprise as I stopped in front of her, probably appearing as if I'd just teleported.

She looked up at me, more so than usual, and took a step back – uncertainty and a little fear showing on her face.

"It's okay, it's me," I said.

"How do I know that?"

"Want to take another tumble and I'll show you how much better things are when I'm in the driver's seat?"

I fully expected to be decked for the comment, but instead, she remained serious. Had my compulsion failed? The old Sally wouldn't have hesitated to make some crack about...

"I remember." She looked into my eyes. "I remember everything."

"How we met? Jeff? The Woods of Mourning..."

"Yeah, yeah, all of it," she said, averting her gaze and looking down at the floor.

I'd done it. Holy shit, I'd actually done it!

A wave of euphoria spread inside me – happiness that I hadn't known in what felt like forever. Everything else seemed secondary in that moment. The only thing that mattered right then was that Sally was back.

I raised my head and let loose with a whoop of joy, probably sounding like a total idiot, but not giving a single fuck.

So enthralled was I, that it took me by surprise when she looked up again and gasped. I was about to ask what was the matter when I realized something had changed.

It took me a moment to figure it out, but then it hit me.

She looked normal again – well, not her so much as the height she typically was compared to me.

That's when a feeling of – I don't know how else to describe it – *deflating* hit me. It was like exhaling an impossibly long breath, except that it wasn't coming from my lungs.

After a moment or two, I looked down at myself. Where there had been abs, now there was flab. I watched in amazement as my hands shrunk – turning from big-ass enemy clubbing mitts back to stubby fingers meant more for programming SQL subroutines.

That was weird enough, but then I realized my pants – stretched out from my abrupt growth spurt – were now in danger of falling off. Crap! I quickly grabbed hold and hitched them back up, lest I end up celebrating our triumph with my ass on display for all to see.

There was no denying what had happened. I was me again.

I glanced back at Sally and grinned sheepishly. At least she was still in focus – apparently a welcome side effect of my transformation. I didn't know how long it would last, but it was nice to be able to see her without the benefit of lenses.

She met my gaze, but where I expected an eye-roll or perhaps a snarky comment on my appearance, I was instead surprised when she simply said, "I'm so sorry, Bill."

Before I could question what she meant, the doors burst open and a sea of armed soldiers charged in, guns ablaze.

## 63

# UNEXPECTED COMPANY

While I stood there gaping like an idiot, Sally grabbed me and threw me to the side. At first, I thought she was attacking me, but then I realized it was only to move me out of the way.

The newcomers immediately opened fire on the vampires standing about, still under the spell of my compulsion.

The poor schmucks never stood a chance. Heads and chests exploded in sprays of blood, followed by streaks of light as their owners exploded into ash.

"What the fuck?" I cried as the carnage played out before me. I stood and took it all in, appalled at the utter lack of mercy on display.

That's when I saw them. Off to the side, not far from where I'd told Adam and Dave to keep an eye on Sally, lay my friends. Ed and Dave were both sprawled on the floor, unmoving. Adam was – crap – nowhere to be seen. In the chaos following Vehron's death, I hadn't noticed what happened.

I turned back to Sally, grabbed her shoulders, and shook her like a rag doll. "What did you do?!"

"She did as commanded, Freewill."

The voice was barely audible over the gunshots ringing out, even to my ears, but somehow, it still managed to convey a sense of authority.

I turned toward its source, finding Alexander – leader of the First Coven – standing just inside the doorway. He was wearing similar body armor to the goons busy mowing down Vehron's minions, except, of course, much more regal in appearance. Gold highlights were apparently still the fashion for dickheads in power looking to distinguish themselves from the rabble.

He stepped in and two other members of the Draculas joined him – Vargas, who I'd met briefly during my trial, and another whose face was much more familiar.

"James?"

"The Wanderer did warn you not to trust her, did he not?" Alex asked, raising his voice so it was discernible above the gunfire. James's eyes opened wide at the statement. "Oh please, Wanderer. One does not live as long as I without developing some skill in foreseeing the actions of others."

Shit!

I wanted to pummel the smile right off his fucking face, but could sense the weariness in my body. I was back to normal – the boost from both Dr. Death and all the stolen blood was gone. There was no way I could do anything against him ... unless.

For the briefest of moments, I'd been in possession of Dr. Death's power – the hidden strength within me. Then I stupidly let it go somehow – probably the elation at seeing Sally back to her old self.

Go figure. Just my luck to pick the exact worst moment to do so. If I'd held onto it for even a minute longer, I could be feeding Alex chunks of his own asshole right now.

The question was – how did I get it back?

Was it even possible to?

I hadn't heard a peep from Dr. Death since almost blowing myself to bits, and I had a feeling he wasn't going to be particularly helpful, even if he did deem me worthy of a mental conference bridge.

I was on my own, but maybe that was enough.

The very sight of Alex filled me with rage. His casual words of how he'd used my friends against me did nothing but add to the disgust I felt toward his continued existence.

I let those feelings take me, just as he'd taken Sally from me. He'd manipulated her, filled her with a hidden agenda, and now was nonchalantly enjoying the fruits of his labors – his men blowing others to bits as if this was a shooting gallery.

And yet, as the anger filled me, I was still just me, and me I remained.

"Destroy the Jahabich," Alex commanded, his tone no more emotional than if asking someone to change the channel. "Cleanse this place of their presence."

Oh crap! I spun back to where Gan had been fighting, but saw that she'd leapt clear of the fray as some of Alex's men began to engage the creatures, switching from guns to melee combat.

She strolled in our direction, seemingly unfazed by the slaughter going on around her. One of Alex's men turned toward her for a moment, but a quick sidelong glance from her sent him back to his task.

And a slaughter it was. The vamps I'd unwittingly ordered to act like statues were starting to snap out of it, but it was too late. Many had already been exterminated like bugs, and still Alex's men continued their advance.

The thing was, considering everything that had happened here, I wasn't sure I wanted them to stop. For all his bluster,

Alex had been right about the Cult of Ib being a blight upon this world.

I turned away, disgusted with myself as much as anyone else here, and glanced back to where my friends still lay. Thankfully, they'd been untouched by the newcomers. I aimed to keep it that way.

I stalked up to Alex, ignoring every self-preservation instinct I had. "If your people harm my..."

He merely waved a dismissive hand. "Spare me your impotent rage, Freewill. Had I wished this facility fully cleansed, we would not be having this conversation. You and your friends have fulfilled the terms of your sentence. Regardless of what you might think of me, I honor my bargains." I couldn't help but notice a note of annoyance in his voice as he said it.

"Oh?" I asked before common sense could take over. "Is that why you're here now? Is that why you ordered Sally to ... um ... do whatever she did?" I glanced back and saw her slumped against the wall, her knees drawn up and her head down in them. A wave of pity washed over me at seeing her like that, used like a pawn in a game of chess.

"That is precisely why I gave her the orders I did," Alex said, drawing my attention back to him. "I knew you would try to fulfill your end of the arrangement. She was to be my contingency once you failed."

"Wait?" I replied. "When I failed?"

"Indeed. Facilities such as these are heavily modernized, but even modern security measures are a fickle thing. They can be beaten, circumvented. Unsurprisingly, passwords were changed and remote access cut off not long after Boston fell. However, each of our strongholds has an override as well —

known only to the eldest of the First – hardwired at the very deepest layer."

"What's that got to do with...?"

"If you had been paying the slightest attention," he interrupted, "you would have noticed what I said about remote access being severed. The override could only be triggered from inside the facility. Your dear Sally was given that override along with orders to use it at the first available opportunity, letting nothing stand in her way. Doing so shut down all security protocols, allowing my strike team access."

"So why are you here with them?"

"I am not some armchair general who commands from afar. I am a born leader of men." He stepped past me and watched as the Jahabich resistance continued to be whittled down. "I am also quite aware of Vehron's power." He glanced back at James, a mixture of pity and disgust on his face. "As well as the fact that I alone possess the strength to defeat him."

"Yeah, but you didn't. I did."

Alex turned to face me, the brow over his blue eye raised ever so slightly. "As I can see. Imagine my surprise. Sorry to say, but you, the Icon, and your friends were all expected to perish at The Destroyer's hands. You were merely a means to an end to gain access, carrying a payload that you were not aware of."

"So this was a suicide mission all along."

"Oh, I don't think Yehoshua meant it as such, but have no doubt that I am every bit as amazed as I sound. I suppose I owe you some modicum of gratitude. Though I am not certain how you managed to pull it off, I am nevertheless impressed that you saved me the effort. You will forgive me, though, if I do not shower you with praise. This was, after all, meant to be a death sentence for your betrayal."

"Sorry to not oblige." I glanced back at Sally again. Free

of Alex's compulsion, she thankfully hadn't blabbed about walking in to find me in control of Dr. Death's skin. I had little doubt Alex would have found that too interesting to let pass and possibly far too dangerous to let me live.

"How did you defeat him?" Vargas asked.

"The beast inside of him raged out of control," Gan said, joining us. "It proved too much for even The Destroyer."

Alex acknowledged her with a slight nod. "Prefect Gansetseg."

"Lord Alexander," she replied, bowing.

"I will admit to some trepidation in risking you on this mission," Alex said to her. "However, I see that those fears were unfounded." She merely smiled as if there was no doubt in her mind. "As I do not sense his presence, is it safe to assume that my dear brother François is in need of having his seat on the First Coven filled?"

"Wait," I replied, "how did you know that?"

"As I said, child, one does not live as long as I and not understand the workings of lesser men. François harbored deep resentment toward me. Coupled with his ambition and an exaggerated opinion of his own intelligence, I had little doubt of his betrayal. It is almost a pity, though. The misinformation he'd been given access to would have wreaked havoc with The Destroyer's plans in the short term."

"Lord François fell," Gan stated neutrally, "in a manner most ignoble."

"Of that, I have no doubt, but such knowledge will be expunged from the official record. He was of the First, after all."

Gan nodded again, her expression all but unreadable.

"You were able to tap into your hidden power once more?" James asked me. "Fortunate."

"Yeah," I replied, trying to keep my tone conversational. "Even more fortunate that Vehron didn't do the same. I don't remember much, but I doubt we'd be talking now if he'd gone all apeshit on me. Not sure why he didn't."

"Is it not obvious, Dr. Death?" Gan asked. Before I could deck her, she added, "He could not."

"What? Why not?"

"Freewills throughout history have manifested their powers in myriad ways," Alex said, continuing to watch the fight going on. The final handful of Jahabich were in retreat, forced back nearly to the prefect's office doors.

Oh crap!

I almost had a major panic attack, but then I saw two of Alex's men helping Christy away from the fight. She was back on her feet, but they were both supporting her on either side. The poor girl still looked out of it, which was probably why the vamps hadn't been disintegrated yet.

I turned back to the discussion at hand. "What do you mean by that?"

Alex, obviously deciding this topic was beneath him, simply nodded toward Gan, who said, "Any student of our history knows this."

"I must've missed that class."

"That is not surprising," she replied. "Most who are young do not care for such things. All Freewills shared some abilities in common – their ability to resist compulsion and their capability to feed upon our kind. It is recorded in our archives, however, that some exhibited talents above even that. Wang Leng, for example, was said to be able to defy gravity. In tenth century Byzantium, there was a Freewill known only as the Grey Fox who could blend invisibly into shadows. In..."

"That's fascinating, really it is. So you're telling me Vehron couldn't do what I do?"

"Of course not," Alex said. "He was known as the Sun Strider. He was unique in that he was able to resist the rays of the sun for up to an hour. It made him singularly dangerous amongst our kind."

"I'll bet. Wait, so why didn't anyone tell me this?"

"I would think you would have asked," Gan replied matter-of-factly.

I took a deep breath, concentrating on ignoring her. "So that means my ability to turn into a rage beast..."

"Is unprecedented," Alex said. "Even I must admit it is among the more interesting manifestations I have seen. Such a pity it is uncontrollable. However, now that you have reawakened it..."

"Lord Alexander," James said, stepping forward just as Alex was about to broach a dangerous subject for me. "Perhaps we should concentrate on securing the facility first. There are no doubt more zealots about and likely even more kept prisoner here against their will. With The Destroyer dead, perhaps we need not purge the entirety of the population."

"Still holding out hope for your protégé, Wanderer?"

James turned his head toward me, his brows raised questioningly.

"Sorry," I replied. "I haven't seen Calibra anywhere. Although, to be fair, I haven't exactly had time to look for her. Assuming there are no more surprises here, maybe we can find out what happened..."

A creaking sound at the far end of the room caught our attention. It was the double doors to the prefect's office being pushed opened from within.

As usual, I'd spoken too soon.

**64**

## FIRST BASE

Two figures emerged from the room beyond as a contingent of Alex's men broke off from the Jahabich and raised their guns toward the newcomers.

Firebird was the first, which explained where she'd disappeared to during the fight. Though I wasn't at all comfortable with how Alex had dealt with the compelled vampires in the room, a small part of me wouldn't have minded seeing that traitorous bitch eat a bullet or three.

"Oh, you fucking whore," a voice behind me growled. I didn't need to turn to know that Sally was back on her feet. Whatever guilt she'd been feeling was obviously superseded by her anger. That was fine by me. I didn't blame her for what happened. Hell, I was just glad to have her back, even if it meant I had to watch a prolonged session of her tearing Firebird's entrails out. Ah, the sacrifices we make.

It took me a moment to recognize the other person. Calibra looked much different than when I'd last seen her. Gone was her tight bun and prim business suit. Her hair was down, long and black with a bit of waviness to it, and she

564

wore a flowing white dress. Think Lily Munster, minus all the eye makeup.

The way she moved was also different. When last we'd met, the best way I could describe her was as having a massive stick up her ass – both in attitude and presentation. Now, she moved with an easy gait. Maybe it was the new attire, but she almost seemed to float toward us.

"At ease!" James said, striding past me. The guards, who looked like they were just waiting for Alex's signal to start blowing more holes in things, lowered their weapons and stood at attention.

I risked a glance over and saw that while a small handful of Jahabich remained, they appeared to have given up. They stood still as, well, statues, while Alex's men surrounded them.

Seeing that the chances of eating a stray bullet were significantly lower now, I started toward my other friends. Dave was awake, albeit looking spooked out of his fucking mind. Go figure. Ed was still down, but appeared to be stirring.

Halfway to them, I stopped and turned back – seeing Sally still standing there, glaring in Firebird's direction. She noticed me and I waved her over. For a moment, I thought she might turn away, but then she shrugged and started in my direction.

"There'll be time for her later," I said as she caught up to me.

"Oh, believe me, there will be lots of it. I'm gonna make it so fucking slow, she'll think it lasts forever."

"If you're expecting me to talk you out of it, don't bother."

She glanced sidelong at me, but then once more averted her eyes. Oh fuck this. I stepped up and put an arm around her shoulders. "Hell, I might even help you, partner."

I expected some retort, or maybe an elbow in my gut, but all she said was, "I'm sorry, Bill. I really am."

I lowered my voice to a bare whisper. "There are lots of people who deserve to be sorry. You're not one of them."

A look of gratitude crossed her face for a single moment, then it was replaced by something I would have given my left testicle to see – her familiar arrogant smirk. "Let's go check on the meatsack," she said, striding forward. "But be warned. If he bleeds on me, I'm kicking his ass."

"I think you already did that," Ed said, finally sitting up.

"Sorry." She offered him a hand. "I didn't mean to hit you so hard."

"What happened?" I asked.

"Bad timing all around," she said. "After I realized what that red-headed bitch had done to Starlight, I sort of lost it."

"You remembered things?"

"Yeah, but nothing good. All it did was put me in the mood for murder. Right about then, Alexander's orders kicked in. Let's just say it was like mixing whiskey with a blowtorch."

"I can see that." I turned to Dave. "You all right?"

"Define all right," he replied.

I faced Sally again. "Adam?"

Sally gave her head a single shake. "Like I said, I'm sorry."

Fucking Alex! That was yet one more life I owed that fucker. This whole thing had been his deal, his setup. I'd been little more than a pawn to him – we all had.

Well, this was one pawn who wasn't going to forgive and forget.

"It's okay. It wasn't your fault." Oh, the hell with this. I turned and grabbed her, pulling her in and hugging her hard. For a moment, she stiffened against me, but then she let her guard down and returned it. I could have sworn I heard the softest of sobs come from her, but maybe it was just my imagination.

"Eh hem."

I turned to Ed. "Get the fuck over here too." He narrowed his eyes, my affection toward Sally perhaps a bit too out in the open, but then he sighed and jumped in, grabbing both of us.

I glanced quickly at Dave, but he just held up his hands and mouthed, "No." Oh well.

The missing member of our quartet weighed heavily upon me and I gripped my friends all the tighter for it. Ed must've sensed this because he asked, "Tom?"

"He's a twelve-inch plastic doll."

"What?"

"I tossed him into that corner over there."

"You're not making any sense, Bill."

No, I most certainly wasn't.

Nor would I be given a chance to, because right then, the screaming started.

My friends and I broke contact to see what the commotion was all about.

It was Christy.

She'd broken free of the vampires helping her along and was pointing an accusing finger toward where Alex and the other elder vamps were converging with Calibra and Firebird in the center of the room.

"What are you?" she snarled.

Alex looked at her as if he'd noticed a gnat on his arm. "Restrain the Magi. She is clearly ... overstressed."

The two vamps managed to take a single step before

Christy's power flared up around her. They were flash-fried from the waist up, turning to dust in the next moment.

Okay, that was unexpected. Had the poor girl finally gone round the bend?

Alex raised the barest of eyebrows. "I would highly suggest you stand down, witch."

"Oh crap. Let's go." I didn't wait for my friends to start moving. Christy was tired and stressed, but apparently still dangerous as all hell. That was a bad combination when facing the most powerful vampire on the planet. I sincerely doubted Alex would tolerate even the slightest hostility from her.

Thankfully, James stepped forward, hands raised in a placating manner. "You have nothing to fear from us, Christine. I promise you that."

"Not you," Christy shrieked. "Her!"

Who? Firebird?

"I can assure you..." James began.

"Oh, it's quite all right, James. This charade has truly gone on for long enough," Calibra said.

I skidded to a halt just short of Christy, partially to avoid ending up like the last two guys and also because of what Calibra had just said. What the hell?

James turned toward the former prefect, his expression still disarming. "I beg your pardon, my dear. I know you have had to endure quite the ordeal, but I must insist you remain silent for the time being. Until we can assess what damage The Destroyer did to your mind, I cannot guarantee your safety."

Calibra raised what looked to be a bemused eyebrow at that. "I've been silent for over three thousand years. You have no idea how sick of it I am." She turned to Christy. "How did you know?"

I jumped back a step, almost bowling over Sally and Ed,

as Christy began to power up again. The strain must've been incredible for her, but she was somehow managing it nevertheless. "I sensed it earlier," she said. "You were using the redhead as your puppet, your mouthpiece. And now it's stronger than ever. I can feel the connection between you and those things."

Calibra let out a musical laugh, far different than the stuck-up bitch attitude she'd used when last we'd met. "I'm impressed. As for my children, call it a necessity. I'm afraid they've always been a rowdy bunch, very much in need of a mother's touch."

At that, the remaining Jahabich simultaneously replied, "*Mother.*"

Oh, I didn't have a good feeling where this was going. Not good at all.

"Silence them," Alex said to his troops before turning back to the unexpectedly mouthy vampiress.

**"*YOU'LL DO NO SUCH THING!!*"**

The compulsion that erupted from Calibra was like nothing I'd ever felt before – subtle, painless, but seemingly attached to the world's biggest bass, one that just happened to be vibrating beneath our feet.

"Did you feel that?" Sally asked.

"Kind of hard to miss."

Alex's soldiers definitely didn't because they all went slack – doing the very worst thing a vampire could do: ignoring his orders.

As for Alex, the only sign from him that anything was amiss was a slight frown creasing his face. "So, it would seem you were compromised after all. A pity. The Wanderer spoke highly of you. In time, you might have even made a fine contender for the First."

The next thing I knew, Alex was flung clear across the chamber. He slammed into the wall, and slid down to land in a heap. Calibra stood where he'd been just a moment earlier, her arm outstretched as if she'd just backhanded him, but I hadn't seen any blow – not even a blur of motion. Yet the scene spoke volumes.

Holy crap. She'd just punched out Alexander the Great. A part of me would have been tempted to applaud had I not been scared shitless.

Vargas was quick as a snake to respond to James's wayward protégé. He shoved Firebird aside like she was nothing – which she probably was to him – and then advanced upon Calibra. "Die, slave of Ib!"

Sadly, he ended up following his own advice as a second later, he turned to ash around Calibra's arm – plunged through his chest at nearly the same blazing speed she'd struck Alex with.

This shouldn't have been happening. I mean, we'd won, for Christ's sake. Why was everything falling apart?

For a second, I was sure it was Dr. Death doing all of this and that I was stuck in my freaking head again.

Unfortunately, if it was all just a delusion, it was a damned good one. Just then, Christy began to pulse with dazzling energy, hot enough to singe my eyebrows even from several paces back.

Gan saw what was coming and dove into James, knocking him out of the potential path of the spell.

She needn't have bothered.

Just as Christy let loose, Calibra held out a hand palm up, and a skull shimmered into existence in it. I wasn't a phrenologist by any stretch, but the sickly purple glow from within gave me a clue as to who it had once belonged to.

"No!" Christy shrieked. The energy wave dissipated instantly, leaving not even a single scorch mark on Calibra's stark white dress. As this transpired, Decker's spectral laugh emanated from his noggin – an asshole to the end and beyond.

"You asked what I was, child," Calibra said. "It is not what, but who. I believe you know, though. Your friend here certainly recognized me."

Christy dropped her hands to her sides and her knees buckled. Fuck the danger. I immediately stepped in to catch her, hoping she didn't decide to go nuclear in my arms. "Kala the White," she whispered. "The White Mother."

How the fuck was that possible? "Why didn't you tell me witches were immortal?" I asked Christy.

"That's because they're not, Freewill," Calibra replied.

"Then how..."

"A bargain, no doubt." I turned and saw Alex was back on his feet. If he'd been injured by the blow, he didn't show anything beyond a theatrical wiping of his lips for a non-existent bloodstain. "Tell me, Magi, to what entity did you barter your soul so as to serve the abomination of Ib?" He began to casually saunter her way, but I had little doubt he was ready to strike. You didn't deck someone like Alex and hope they were gonna let you get away with it unscathed.

"Alexander of Macedon, for all your vaunted wisdom, you truly are as blind as those fools you keep in your cave." She smiled, revealing a set of fangs.

"Impossible," James said, picking himself up off the ground, Gan by his side. "Magi cannot be turned."

"Um, is that true?" I whispered to Christy.

She elbowed me in the ribs. Okay, probably not a great time for Q&A. By then, Sally and Ed had stepped in, standing on either side of us. Now where was...

I glanced back and saw Dave making a beeline for the door. I really needed to kick his ass when this was over.

"Magi cannot be turned, this is true," Calibra replied.

"Then how..."

"Unless they are the very first to be turned."

What the fuck?

Holy shit! That's when it hit me. Vehron had said it in passing, referring to his so-called master as a her. I just hadn't paid it any attention at the time.

The room seemed to grow dim, the light condensing in on itself until it seemed a spotlight shone on Calibra, her white dress nearly glowing in the illumination.

"I'm surprised none ever figured it out. I even made it a point to hide both of my names in plain sight. I was once Kala the White, but I am now and will forever be Ib. I am The First, your lord and master. And my time has finally come."

**65**

# THE END DAYS

I waited a moment to see if any other shoes were going to drop – like maybe she'd turn out to be Colin in a wig – then took a tentative step forward. "Um, excuse me."

"This is not your concern, Freewill," Alexander replied conversationally, continuing to approach Calibra, who, for her part, appeared unworried.

Risking a pounding by multiple beings that outclassed me several times over, I ignored him. "What do you mean, your time has come?"

"Is it not obvious, boy?" Calibra asked. Oh God, I could see where the others got it from. "I am…"

"No, it is *not* fucking obvious!" I snapped. "Would everyone please stop fucking saying that?"

All heads in the room, including the Jahabich, turned in my direction. I really needed to watch my mouth. Still, when one has a captive audience, one must make the best of it.

"I have not known you long, boy," Calibra replied. If she was irked by my outburst, she didn't show it. "But in that time, you have managed to impress me as a seemingly inex-

573

haustible fount of stupidity. The mantle of Freewill chose poorly this time. Listen well, for I will not repeat myself. The time of Ib has come. My influence, once buried and forgotten, is again fertile, and I have you to thank."

"You're welcome, but I think you might have missed the memo on that one. In case you didn't notice, your boy Vehron is now waiting to be mopped up whenever the janitorial staff clocks in."

"The Destroyer was a loyal servant. His passing is quite regrettable. Once I heard he'd returned from his long exile, however, I knew it was time. The portents did not lie. My position as the Wanderer's protégé, chosen so carefully after millennia in hiding, proved fruitful indeed. For when Vehron rose, I was near enough to quickly join him."

"Yeah, thinking that didn't turn out so hot."

"Quite the contrary. Little did I know that fate would be so kind. My salvation indeed lay with a Freewill, just a different one than expected. You, boy. Somehow, despite your mediocrity, you helped facilitate the birth of the pure one."

"Ed?" I glanced back at my roommate. "No offense."

"None taken, man. I am the epitome of innocence lost."

"In your dreams," I replied before turning to face Calibra again. The look on her face was one of mild amusement.

Before I could say another word, though, she let loose with a compulsion. ***"ALEXANDER, BE A GOOD DOG AND STAY!!"***

To my surprise, and a good deal of horror, Alex's forward progress halted immediately. Oh boy, this wasn't looking good.

James's legs tensed, but Calibra held up a finger toward him and gave it a single shake.

"Okay, excuse me for calling bullshit," I resumed, hoping to buy time ... for something. I wasn't sure what. Maybe we'd get lucky and a random meteor strike would hit. "But for all your crap about pure ones, your boy toy tried his best to kill Ed when they first met. Also, if I recall correctly, you were with us when we were trying to track down Mr. Muscle Dick. You saw Ed fry at least one vamp with his blood. You could have grabbed him at any time if he was so fucking important to you."

To my surprise, Calibra's mask of composure dropped ever so slightly, replaced for a moment by one of annoyance and maybe even slight embarrassment. "Very simply put, I did not realize his significance at the time."

"And you're the all-powerful progenitor of our race? You'll excuse me if I'm less than impress... URK!"

All at once, it felt like my body was shoved into a giant vise grip. I was dragged away from Christy and lifted into the air by seemingly nothing. Oh yeah, I almost forgot – this chick was queen of the witches too. That was gonna prove a bad combo for me when it came to mouthing off.

"I am tolerant to a degree, but your insolence grows tiresome."

"Yeah ... I get that ... a lot."

"The pure one is the first of his kind – *ever*. I have peered into worlds your feeble mind could not fathom. Yet not even my divinations foresaw his coming. He is simply, so it would seem, a byproduct of the chaos you cause wherever you step."

I felt like an orange about to be juiced, but still managed to spew out, "So he's just ... dumb luck?"

"In a sense, yes. Albeit, fortuitous luck for my cause."

"Let him go!" Christy snarled. She began mumbling something under her breath. I had a feeling it wasn't just a few insulting names.

"What counter-spell do you hope to use against *me*, child?" Calibra's tone was one of contempt. "Have you not spent your entire life mired in my teachings? I am power incarnate, able to tap into the very essence of creation itself."

"You create abominations."

"Speak not of my children. They may be unruly, but they are loyal, unlike some ... ***THAT WILL BE ENOUGH!!***"

James and Gan had picked that moment to rush her. Smart; always pimp-slap the bad guy when they're monologuing. Sadly, she'd been ready for them. Quick as they were, they barely managed to cover half the short distance before being stopped dead in their tracks. All the while, the pressure around me kept increasing.

"Stop it," Ed said, stepping in front of us.

"Don't..." I spat out, right before my lungs collapsed. Ugh!

"You want me. I'll go with you peacefully."

I wanted to scream out, to tell him he was fucking insane, but I had no ability whatsoever to draw air. My vision was starting to turn black around the edges. Hell, it felt like someone had tied a rock to my feet and dropped me into the Marianas Trench.

"What are you doing?" Sally hissed.

"Mind your tongue, girl," Calibra replied to her. "I have not forgotten your insolence either – that you dared point a weapon in my face, however pointless it would have been." She then addressed Ed. "You will come with me regardless, but I am intrigued. Such loyalty is rare. You would truly choose to surrender yourself to save your friend?"

"No fucking way," Ed replied, "but it makes for one hell of a distraction."

And that's when Christy unleashed her spell.

I'd thought maybe she'd planned to launch another death ray or something similar. The problem was, shit like that was expected. When fighting a foe this powerful, this ancient, one needed to be smart about it.

Fortunately, Christy was quite smart.

Rather than some display of pyrotechnic awesomeness, calling forth the spirits of the damned or whatever the fuck witches liked to do, what happened was simplicity itself.

Harry Decker's noggin leapt up out of Calibra's hand, seemingly of its own volition, and slammed into her stupid face.

Simple, but highly effective, as the top of the human skull is pretty darn hard indeed.

Calibra's head snapped back. Blood spurted from her smashed nose, ruining the perfect whiteness of her dress. Served her right. She might've been a lot of things, but pure as the driven snow wasn't one of them.

Decker cried out, whether in surprise or pain I didn't know – although I knew which I hoped for. His head hit the ground with a solid *thonk* and rolled away.

At that same moment, the spell holding me was broken and I dropped to the floor, sucking in a delicious breath of air and enjoying the sensation of not being crushed.

Unfortunately, the problem of what to do still remained. It was stupid to think one good hit was going to do anything more than piss Calibra off.

Much to my amazement, though, someone else had that covered. Alex sprang back to life. One second he was a statue, the next he'd slashed Calibra across the stomach with his claws. Bitch was gonna need a gallon of Tide when this shit was finished.

"You think me your puppet?" he spat, scorn etching his voice even as he etched more out of her body. "I am Alexander. I call no one master!"

Whatever the cause, none of the other vamps under Calibra's spell moved a muscle – not even James. Sadly, the same couldn't be said for the Jahabich. The second Alex attacked their mommy dearest, they were on the move again. Most of them transformed back into their vampire guises – no doubt to take advantage of the extra speed afforded them. I was horrified to see Starlight among their number.

I turned to Sally. "You up for cracking some skulls?"

"I'd be insulted if you didn't ask. You'll excuse me, though, if I decide I want to get some red on my hands."

I looked over and saw what she meant. Firebird was busy backing away from where Alex continued to tear into Calibra.

"Be my guest," I replied with a smile. "Ed, stay..."

"You don't have to tell me," he replied to my back. "No way do I want a piece of this shit."

"Good boy," I said before heading out to engage the enemy once more.

The Jahabich were closing in on Alex. Normally, I would have made myself some popcorn and enjoyed the show, but today, that seemed a poor strategy. What we needed was some extra firepower. Thankfully, both Gan and James were close to where Alex continued to engage Calibra.

I just needed to wake them both up somehow.

Screw this shit. Back when Night Razor had compelled Sally to play statue, during our final battle, a good slap to the face had brought her out of it. I might have to hit a lot harder with these two, but it seemed as good a strategy as any.

The Jahabich would be upon us in seconds, so I needed to make it count. Of course, that meant slugging Gan first.

Who said I couldn't enjoy a moment in the midst of soul-searing terror?

I passed Alex just as he delivered a haymaker to Calibra – the sound echoing like thunder in the chamber. Hopefully, it hurt. Now it was my turn to do the same.

I reared back and prepared to try to wake my two friends – well, okay, one friend and a personal stalker – but before I could deliver the blow, a hand caught me at the wrist.

I was spun around and found myself face to face with Alex. Though still composed, he had a wild look in his eye. Calibra lay maybe thirty feet away, although she didn't look like she was gonna stay down.

"Though I am loath to do so, I must admit to a tactical error," Alex said quickly. "She will be healed before I can reach her again."

"Well then, let me wake up…"

He pushed his hand into my face, shoving it between my lips. "They cannot help us, but *you* can. Now, before I change my mind or it is too late, drink."

I didn't have time to debate him. Though his blood had the potential to bring out the beast inside of me, the white witch in the room – an ironic title if ever there was one – could presumably do far worse.

Also, fuck this guy. My fangs extended and I sank them into the webbing of his hand between his thumb and forefinger – putting a little extra bite into my bite.

It had been a while since I'd had human blood, so I had a feeling that when this was all over and done with, a serious crash was in my future, but for now, I sucked down on Alex and swallowed – trying real hard to pretend I had mentally envisioned some different way of putting that.

The effect was immediate. A small nuclear bomb went off in my stomach as I ascended to heights few vampires had ever known.

My ears reacted to the slightest of sounds, one of which was Calibra regaining her feet. Although her dress was covered in gore, she appeared whole again. If she was truly as old as she claimed, then injuring her with anything short of a killing blow would be pointless. But hey, if I was going to have any chance of making that happen, it was n ... URK!

Fuck! I'd hoped that perhaps I'd grown accustomed to Alex's blood, but no such luck. His power exploded inside of me. Last time, I'd been lucky and Dr. Death had been asleep. Now, though, whatever happened was anyone's guess.

All I knew for certain was that I was changing. I dropped to my knees as my body began to expand.

The only question that remained now was who would be in charge once I rose back to my feet?

"You surprise me, Alexander. I should have guessed that were anyone able to resist my commands, it would be you. It will do you little good, though."

I looked up from where I struggled to maintain my sense of self to see Calibra with her hands on her hips, looking smug as a bug.

Alex contemptuously backhanded a Jahabich who'd gotten too close, nearly bisecting it. "You are wrong, Ib, false god to our kind. I toppled your empire once. I shall do so again."

"Oh? And you propose to do that alone?"

"If I must. However, I am not alone, for the Freewill has dined well this evening."

Calibra glanced in my direction. I probably looked about

as much a threat as someone trying to not shit their pants. The look on her face said as much.

The momentary distraction cost her, though, as just then, a blast of energy lanced out from somewhere off to the side. Calibra lifted a hand and warded it off, but a look akin to worry finally appeared on her mug. Christy was back in the battle.

I turned my head, sweat breaking out on my brow as I continued to fight the change, and saw her. She didn't look great, but she was still with us. Now, if I could only get my shit in gear, we could make this a fight.

Calibra seemed to realize this too and backed up a step, baring her fangs at us all.

I mean, hell, the Cylons didn't give a shit about fighting one Battlestar, but once two were in the mix, it was a whole different ballgame. Maybe the same rule applied here – except we had three.

Apparently so, because the next words out of her mouth were a doozy. ***"TO ME, MY FAITHFUL!! WE HAVE THE KEY TO OUR FUTURE!! LET THESE FOOLS DIE BURIED BENEATH THEIR FAILURE!!"***

The words themselves were ominous enough, but it was their delivery that was the real killer – a full-blown compulsion, possibly the most powerful ever heard on this planet.

The entire room shook from its power. Had I not been full of Alex's blood, I had a feeling I'd be waking up a week later craving a case of aspirin. As it was, it still felt like an icepick to the brain. Migraine, take me away.

Unfortunately, that wasn't a luxury I had. Calibra's compulsion had gone wide and every vampire in the room, save me and Alex, responded to it.

Gan and James plowed into Alex from behind, knocking him off balance as they made their way to their new master. The Jahabich broke off from their advance and joined Alex's strike team in marching her way as she backed up toward the doors leading to her former office. I couldn't quite call it a retreat, because she laughed all the way.

All at once, it was like Calibra had a sea of bodies between her and us – one that she could order to do whatever she pleased.

Oh no! In both the chaos and my continued struggles to control my body, I hadn't realized the blonde-haired vamp amongst their number. Sally! With Alex's compulsion undone, she was just as susceptible to control as the rest.

No.

No fucking way was I losing her again.

Feeling like my guts were trying to squirm their way out of me, I struggled to my feet. With my level of power, it should have been child's play to overtake her, but my body was trying to rewire itself. That made moving just a wee bit difficult.

As I stumbled, my partner continued to walk away – ironically enough, side by side with the redheaded traitor she'd set out to kill. Firebird must have sensed my eyes on her backside, because she turned and flashed me a saucy little smile before doubling her pace to catch up to her master.

And still Sally marched onward.

I gritted my teeth and bit down on my lip, drawing blood. Not on my watch.

Pushing myself forward, willing myself to stay me, I hobbled after her – slowly at first, then with more confidence.

Calibra stopped before the entrance of her office and held up her hands. Sadly, it wasn't in surrender. Myriad colors ignited from her body. She was apparently going the Saruman route. As dangerous as Christy looked when she was pissed, she was a firecracker next to the walking fusion reactor that was Calibra. The entire cavern lit up as power coalesced around her.

"Do not let her escape!" Alex shouted.

I silently told him to go fuck himself as I reached Sally and spun her around. Her eyes were so completely glazed over as to appear white. There was no recognition in them whatsoever, no sense that she was in there fighting back. The only reaction from her was to try pulling away so as to resume walking toward her new master.

I glared Calibra's way, hatred in my eyes, and she smiled back, mouthing a single word – "fool." The power she'd been gathering lanced out from her in an upward arc, where it spread out over the granite ceiling above us. The room immediately began to shake, but not like before. We're talking the difference between one of those tiny New York quakes and something that could tear California apart.

Despite my strength, I lost my footing and went down. Sally almost slipped away, but I grabbed her by the ankle and dragged her back to me.

"Sorry about this." Before she could escape again, I turned her over and decked her in the mouth.

She went limp as the ceiling began to crumble from above. Huge chunks of rock fell all around us. I immediately scrambled to cover her body with my own, barely noticing that, in the chaos to save her, the change had receded. I was still me.

Of course, that would be small comfort if I ended up crushed like a bug.

The room continued to shake itself apart, but I dared risk a glance up anyway. By now, Calibra had retreated into her office – which didn't strike me as a particularly safe place if this whole cavern collapsed. The vampires under her thrall were busy marching in after her.

I was about to duck my head again when movement

caught my eye. Still more compelled vamps walked in that direction, heedless of the destruction raining down upon them.

I remembered how vast the Boston complex was. There were surely more vamps present in this place and Calibra had seemingly summoned them all to her. Talk about power. How many could that be in total?

"Let me go, cocksucker!"

Turns out I only needed to care about two.

I glanced to my left, still shielding Sally from the falling debris, and saw Dave. His escape attempt had apparently been cut short by Calibra's power. That in itself was bad, but what made it far worse was who he was dragging along with him – Ed.

Fuck!

By now, it was getting hard to see. Boulders – some as big as a car – fell from the ceiling and smashed into the floor, kicking up a storm of dust. Still, Dave continued his onward trek toward the doors Calibra had disappeared into, while Ed struggled ineffectually against his vampiric strength.

I was stuck between the proverbial rock and a hard place – in more ways than one. Continue to shield Sally or save Ed?

Sally was helpless, but for some reason, Calibra – a being from the dawn of time itself – wanted my roommate. I had to think it wasn't to invite him over for a tea party.

Sadly, right then, my choice was made for me as a particularly heavy slab of stone landed on my back, pinning me. More and more debris rained down around me until my friends were finally hidden from sight.

"Ed!" I screamed, choking on dust as the place shook itself apart.

It was the last thing I was able to utter before everything went dark under the crushing weight of oblivion.

# 66

# THE SPINE CRUSHING EPILOGUE

"There he is!"

"Well, get him out."

"It's not that easy. You want to do it?"

"Sorry, babe. Those who can't do, teach."

"That's not funny."

Ugh! Waking up from a bender was never fun, and this felt like one of the worst of them. My head was pounding. It was dark. There was a near crushing weight on top of me – that was new. Oh, and something soft was beneath me.

Wait, it felt like ... holy crap, was that a boob?

Did I say "worst"? Fuck that shit. Any night when one could wake up to the feel of tits beneath them was epic indeed.

"Ow!"

Something hot seared into my back. What the fuck?

After another moment, my head started to clear. College was years ago, yet I kept dreaming of it like it was yesterday. I really needed to move on with my life at some point.

Wait a second. I *had* moved on ... quite literally, as in to the other side. It all came back to me as I continued to feel something red-hot grind into my back – Vehron, Calibra, Alex ... Sally! That's who was beneath me. I'd been shielding her as what seemed like the entire Boston complex dropped on our heads. Hopefully, taking that into account, she wouldn't begrudge me the quick feel I'd copped upon regaining consciousness.

Holy crap, we were alive. Or at least I was. I assumed Sally was too, since most piles of dust didn't have a set of awesome funbags to play with.

"Fuuuck!" The heat reached a temperature that I was pretty sure no person, alive or otherwise, cared to experience and then – right as I was certain I'd be burnt to a crisp – a good chunk of weight fell away from atop me.

I pushed myself off of Sally and was happy to find that I was able to move. Rocks, dust, and other assorted debris fell to the side and I forced my way up.

"All right, you did it!"

"Tom?" I asked, recognizing the voice.

I glanced around and immediately caught sight of Christy, a red glow fading from her fingertips. She was bruised and battered. Dark circles ringed her eyes, making her look like a tired raccoon. She was alive, though. Same with the bad seventies action figure she had tucked into the crook of one arm – sorta anyway.

"Are you okay?" she asked wearily.

"I'll live. You?"

"I sensed what she was doing. Managed to get a kinetic shield up around myself in time. Just don't ask me to do anything else. Getting you out really was the last I had. I doubt I could even light a candle right now."

"Don't sell yourself short, babe."

Tom appeared unhurt – for a toy anyway. At least I didn't see any busted pieces. I shifted my gaze between him and

Christy, then raised an eyebrow. Mindful of the potentially fragile state of things, I asked, "Are you both okay?"

"I'm still not sure," she replied. "But I do know that once everything started to fall apart, he was all I could think of. No offense, Bill."

"None taken. We vamps can take a licking. Speaking of which..."

I reached down and grabbed hold of Sally to drag her out of the rubble. She groaned as I pulled her free, and her eyelids fluttered before opening a crack. I was happy to see that although they appeared dazed, they didn't have the vacant look of being under compulsion anymore.

She sat up and began to rub her jaw. "What hit me?"

"Um, a rock. Yep, fell right off the ceiling onto your head."

"Then why does it feel like somebody socked me one?"

"It bounced?"

She narrowed her eyes at me for a moment, but then smiled. "I'll buy that for now. What happened?"

I gave her a brief rundown, then turned to Christy. "Did you see anything after things went boom? Any sign of Ed?"

She shook her head. "I was too busy trying not to die, but it seemed like everyone was headed that way."

The whole place was a mess. It was a miracle the entire thing hadn't collapsed. Torn wires hung from the ceiling, still sparking. Dust and smoke hung heavy, obscuring even my vampire vision. Still, I didn't need to see to know what was in the direction she indicated – the doors to the prefect's office.

I pulled Sally to her feet, noting that I could feel her weight – however slight. Whatever power I'd gained from Alex's blood was rapidly wearing off. No surprise there. I'd felt what hit me. No doubt my body had been working overtime to heal from the crushing weight that had been busy trying to squish me like a roach. "Come on," I said. "We need to check and see if they're still…"

"I can assure you, they are not," a voice answered from somewhere off in the gloom. Of course. It was too much to hope that a little thing like tons of falling rock would take out the leader of the Draculas. A few moments later, Alex stepped into view. He looked like a bus had been dropped onto him, but despite his disheveled appearance, he still carried himself with an air of arrogance. Goddamn, what a walking fuck nozzle.

As he approached, my friends all huddled closer. Can't say that I blamed them.

"There is no one here but us," he said.

"How?"

"I believe we have our friends the Jahabich to thank. A tunnel was cut into the back wall. Even amidst the destruction, it is easy enough to make out. They collapsed it behind them, though. I get the impression they did not wish to be followed."

"Where'd they go?" Tom asked.

Alex raised an eyebrow, noticing that an action figure was addressing him. However, that was the extent of his surprise. He'd been around the block once or twice in his day. I had little doubt he'd seen his fair share of shit. "Elsewhere. That is all I can say for certain."

"Great. No forwarding address," I groused.

"The caverns," Sally said, gripping my arm. "The one with the cave painting."

I glanced at her questioningly.

"It's all back." She tapped her forehead. "Nice to remember the little things. I'd have hated to forget my tour of the Vegas sewers."

"Maybe," I said. "That statue down there. It was her, wasn't it?"

"What are you talking about, Freewill?" Alex asked.

"Just idle chitchat," I replied blithely.

"I am not in the habit of tolerating insolence. Now would be a particularly bad time to test my resolve. I would highly suggest you..." Alex trailed off and his head whipped toward the opposite end of the room. "Impossible."

"What are you talking about?"

There came a sharp squeal of metal against rock. We all spun toward the direction of the doors leading out of here. It sounded like they'd been damaged in the fallout, but someone or something was forcing them open.

Beams of multiple flashlights began to cut through the gloom from that end of the chamber, headed our way. A moment later, though, a far more brilliant light shone through the darkness – an aura of pure white.

A look of unadulterated irritation passed over Alex's face as Sheila approached us, flanked on either side by a contingent of armed Templar. She looked around, whistled in appreciation of the destruction, and then smiled once she saw me and my friends.

"How did you get in here?" Alex asked.

"Someone left the front door open," she replied, her sword held at the ready.

I glanced over at Sally, who shrugged. "There wasn't anything in my orders about locking back up afterwards."

I stifled a chuckle at Alex's expense, but just barely.

"Looks like a hell of a party," Sheila said. "Sorry we're late. We ran into zombies, a lot of them ... and a few other things. Anyway, Sister Bernadette insisted they all be laid to rest before we moved on."

"Sounds like something she'd do," I replied.

"Oh yeah. Last rites and everything." She turned toward Alex and pointed her sword his way. "This guy giving you any trouble?"

Alex crossed his arms over his chest. "If you think I am intimidated by you, you are sadly mistaken."

"What about us?"

"Sisters!" Christy whooped in joy as the three witches stepped out from behind the Templar. Each began to glow with power, adding to the light show already on display.

After a few moments of letting the tension grow – enjoying it ever so slightly – I decided that things had escalated far enough. Outmanned and outgunned as he was, Alex was still incredibly dangerous, especially if he decided to start throwing compulsions around. Considering all that had transpired, it was foolish to let this devolve into another royal rumble.

I stepped forward and held out my hands, one toward Alex and the other toward our reinforcements. "I believe what we have here is an impasse."

"Oh?" Alex replied, his tone dangerous.

"Yeah, exactly what I said. I know how powerful you are."

"You have no idea what I can..."

"I have a good imagination. But at the same time, you're facing both the Freewill and the Icon – not to mention a bunch of guests who brought party favors. Would it be too much to presume that no matter the outcome, it would be hard won and costly?"

Alex appeared to consider this, eyeing the newly arrived forces as he did. "I will allow this presumption."

That would have to be good enough. "Thank you," I replied as diplomatically as I could.

"Yeah, you tell him, Bill!"

Why oh why?

Christy hastily stuffed Tom into a pocket of her maternity outfit before he could say anything else to fuck things up. "Sorry," she said. "He can be a bit ... over-enthusiastic."

I took a moment to massage the bridge of my nose. "As I was saying, we've all suffered losses today. Vehron may be dead..." I allowed myself a quick glance in Sheila's direction. A look of surprise crossed her face, but then she smiled and nodded back to me. "...but we have uncovered an enemy potentially far more dangerous. To make matters worse, she has hostages – including a member of the First Coven and..."

"That is not knowledge I wish shared beyond this room," Alex stated.

"Understood. I was simply emphasizing the stakes at play. Calibra also has..."

At my mention of her name, the Templar broke out in murmurs. I heard things like "The first demon," and "Lilith" spoken. I made it a point to ask about that, but decided it could wait until later.

"Calibra also has my friend Ed and..."

"You think a human carries as much importance as my brother?" Alex asked.

So much for being allowed to finish a thought. "She wanted him for something. I have no idea what that is, but I plan to find out. Regardless, I think it's fair to assume it isn't for anything good."

"Perhaps there is logic in your words. The Cult of Ib once sought to grind this world beneath their heel, subjugate all who opposed them. I dare say, I would be almost disappointed to learn their current plans involved any less."

"I wouldn't, but I sorta get what you're saying."

Alex lowered his head for a moment, as if pondering something. Finally, he looked up. "You continue to surprise me, Freewill. I accept your terms."

"Terms? I haven't gotten to any..."

"I propose an alliance," he said, raising his voice. "A fellowship of sorts. A great evil has awoken, one that threatens us all. Until such time as this cancer is put down, sent fleeing back to the myths of the past where it belongs, I say that there shall be no quarrel between my people, the Magi, the Templar ... and the Icon. You will be treated as equals under the condition that you aid me in stopping whatever machinations have been set in motion this day. Once this task is complete, I will allow for a one-month grace period so that none may fear immediate reprisal."

"How do we know we can trust you?" one of the Templar asked. Oh great. Just what we needed – a Jesus freak to fuck it all up. "You speak of evil, yet reek of it."

"What you call evil, I call order," Alex retorted. "Nevertheless, the word of Alexander of Macedon is law. Any of my people who dare break it shall know my wrath."

Alex's word was law, but that didn't mean he couldn't or wouldn't twist it to meet his needs. Working with him was like hashing out a contract with a legion of opposing lawyers while trying to make a wish in D&D that couldn't backfire on you.

"In return," Alex continued, turning to face me. Ah, here was the rub. "I expect there to be full disclosure of all information concerning this matter. Do we have an accord?"

"Full disclosure in due time," I amended, hoping to buy us a bit of breathing room – especially since we were still sorting through the pieces ourselves.

Alex's eyes narrowed for a moment, but he said, "Agreed. Know that time is short, though. I will not allow us to perish simply because you do not think the time is right to share."

Alex departed shortly after, presumably to meet with the remaining Draculas. There were reinforcements to gather, plans to make, intelligence to ... err ... not be dumb about. In short, all the things one would expect of a commander.

As for us, Sheila sent the Templar topside to guard the place. No point in being lax just in case there were still zealots, thralls, or more zombies about. I'd had enough surprises for one day.

Christy's sisters set up a scrying circle on one of the upper levels to track where Calibra had gone – just on the off chance we were wrong about her intended destination. I didn't have a lot of faith that they'd succeed. After all, we were dealing with the witch who'd pretty much written the book on magic. Still, it didn't hurt to try, and it gave them something to do.

Since this place was a fully stocked complex, complete with living quarters, I managed to snag some new clothes to wear – ones that weren't lined with explosives, hopefully.

Once that was done, I decided to help my friends sift through the rubble. Maybe there was something still there that might give us more of a clue as to what was going on.

On the way down, I ran into Sheila – thankfully not in any way that would have ended with me being blasted through a wall.

"Hey," I said.

"Hey yourself."

"That was some awesome timing you guys had back there."

"Funny how that worked out," she said with a smile. "Believe me, it wasn't planned."

"I can live with the occasional happy coincidence."

"I'm not sure it was."

"What do you mean?"

"Seems we've had an awful lot of coincidences lately, happy or otherwise."

"Yeah, I've noticed that too."

"It's almost like fate has..."

I held up a hand. "Let's not get started with the F word again."

She nodded and, for a moment, we stood there in uncomfortable silence before she said, "I'm sorry about your friend."

"Which one?"

"All of them. We'll save them. I promise you that."

"Hopefully," I replied, leaning against the wall. "So far, I've been batting zero in that dugout. I mean, my D&D group and I weren't what I'd call close, but they deserved better."

"It sounds to me like you tried."

"Not hard enough." I sighed. "There's nothing else I can do for them, but we can still save Ed. As for Tom..."

"That's just a *little* weird, no pun intended."

"You can say that again."

"Do you think we can ... fix him?"

She, the girl with the freaky healing powers, was asking *me?* That somehow didn't instill much confidence. Rather than voice that, though, I just shrugged my shoulders.

After a couple of seconds, she reached out and put a hand on my arm. As usual, I felt a slight tingle at her touch. I had to assume it was just her power reacting with mine, because right at that moment, I was too drained to do the puppy-dog thing. In some ways, that was a sobering thought.

"We'll find a way," she said.

Though I knew she was talking about Tom, I nevertheless asked, "Will we?"

Again, she hesitated. When she finally answered, it was guarded. "For now, let's just concentrate on the task at hand. How's that sound?"

"Probably a smart idea."

She nodded and started to walk past me.

"But what about when it's over?" I asked, the words slipping out of my mouth.

She stopped, but didn't turn to face me. "I don't know, Bill. We might have bigger problems than our powers."

"What?"

"Fate."

"I told you not to use the..."

"I know, but I can't help myself."

"Okay, fine. So what's the issue?"

"The Destroyer is dead."

"Trust me, I'm aware. I was there."

She paused for a moment, then glanced back at me. "What was it like, facing him?"

I couldn't help but let out a bark of laughter. "You really don't want to know."

"Fair enough. You did good, though. I'm proud of you."

"Thanks, but I can't help but hear the *but* in your voice."

She once more turned away and this time didn't stop. "You're the last Freewill again, and I think we both know how that's supposed to end between us."

Sheila's little pep talk certainly hadn't done any wonders for my morale as I entered the ruined chamber where, during better days, James had once held court. Ah, fate. It seemed no matter what I did, it just didn't want to leave me be.

A conversation from up ahead caught my ear, and I gladly turned my attention toward the participants. Christy wasn't resting like she should have been, but at least she wasn't doing any heavy lifting. She was sitting on a boulder holding Tom, while Sally shoved aside some debris.

"So how come nobody told me my sister was a vampire?" Tom asked as I approached.

"We didn't want to worry you," Christy replied.

"Oh sure, because that's no big fucking deal. When the hell did this happen anyway?"

"Remember when I took that trip to Vegas?"

"You said that was just business."

"It was," Sally added, "and maybe a little gambling too."

"With my sister as the all-you-can-eat buffet?"

"Yeah, sorry about that. If it helps, though, she's doing pretty well."

"My parents are going to fucking flip when they hear this!"

"Oh?" Sally asked, turning over a slab of broken rock. "And they're not gonna freak when they find out you're a GI Joe doll?"

"For starters, I'm an action figure. Secondly, do I look like General Hawk to y...?"

"How's it going?" I interrupted, walking up to them.

"Pretty pointless so far," Sally replied.

"I was hoping to find some notes in her office," Christy said, "but there's nothing left – at least nothing that hasn't been burnt beyond recognition."

"If we had scared her off, maybe," I said. "Unfortunately, she had time to cover her tracks."

Sally stood up and wiped her hands on the seat of her pants. "Yeah, and if she's been hiding right under the Draculas' noses for all this time, then that means she's become damn good at covering them."

"So that means all we have to go on is the Jahabich's lair."

"Which, if you recall," Sally said, "we sort of blew up the entrance to."

"There were other tunnels leading out from it."

"Oh yeah. Those should be a breeze to find. We'll just spelunk down every cave on Earth until we find the right one. I somehow think Alex is gonna expect just a bit more of a detailed plan than that."

"Probably," I conceded. "Too bad I can't sniff out Gan like she seems to be able to do to me."

"Would you really want to?" Christy asked.

"Not really," I joked, but there wasn't a lot behind it. The truth was Gan had helped us out big time. We ... *I* owed her. It was a debt I didn't take lightly, even if I had no intention of repaying her in the way I knew she wanted.

I looked around with a heavy sigh. We were just spinning our wheels in this place. "Oh well, if there's nothing else here, let's bug out. I don't know about the rest of you, but I really don't want to use this place as our temporary HQ."

Sally nodded. "I think it's safe to say that Alex can probably find us no matter where we are. Let's just make sure wherever that is, it has a shower and hot water."

"Amen." I helped Christy down and we turned toward the exit.

*...ease me.*

I stopped in my tracks. "Did you hear that?"

Whatever it was, it had been faint, barely audible. Maybe sound carrying through the pipes from another part of the complex.

*e ... had a ar ... gain.*

No, I was wrong. It hadn't been barely audible to my ears, but in my mind. One glance at Christy confirmed she'd *heard* it too.

"No way."

"That's Harry," Christy declared, turning back. "We need to find him."

"Do we really?" Sally asked. Christy fixed her with a glare, and she held up her hands in mock surrender. "Relax. I'm just kidding."

It was the work of two more hours. Decker kept calling during the entire time – all of it faint and hard to understand. Unfortunately, unlike a person trapped under rubble, it was really hard to home in on a psychic cry for help. Thus, it was all trial and error, with a lot of digging on my and Sally's part.

By the time we shoved aside a heavy pile of rocks and caught a glimpse of skull – dirty and almost imperceptible from the debris around it – we were covered in grime.

A sickly purple glow, just barely visible beneath a layer of dust, though, told us we'd hit pay dirt. I reached down and lifted him out.

"Ugh. He's seen better days."

Indeed he had, and that was saying something. His lower jaw was missing, and there was a wide crack across the side of his skull from which that purplish light appeared to be leaking out of.

Christy snatched it out of my hands without any preamble.

*My child, you came for me*, it weakly said.

"What's wrong with it?" Sally asked.

"The binding is starting to wear off," Christy replied. "I need to fortify it."

"Um, is that safe?"

"Not really, but most of the strain is in creating the link. I should only need a little bit of power to strengthen the tether."

Before we could stop her, she placed a hand on either side of the broken skull and started muttering words.

"Don't do anything stupid," Tom said, having been propped up where Christy had been sitting.

"Hush," she snapped. "I'm concentrating."

A few moments went by and Christy's hands began to glow. Whatever she was doing was seemingly absorbed into the former desk toy – like water flowing down a drain. It all lasted less than a minute, but when she was done, the glow of power from Decker's noggin appeared to be back to normal.

Christy, however, needed to sit down again. Though her body was exhausted, when she spoke, her tone was iron. "Give me one good reason why I shouldn't leave you down here to rot."

*I raised you. I...*

"Cut the shit, Harry," she snapped. "I heard you laughing as she held you."

*As you wish. Think of the honor – to meet the one you have spent your whole life revering. To have a chance to speak with her, to listen to her wisdom. It was marvelous. All I could ever hope for and more.*

"Yeah, I'm sure it was an emotional asshole to asshole chat," I said.

*A fool such as you could not hope to appreciate the glory of Kala the White.*

Christy rapped the top of the skull with her knuckles. "Back to the point, Harry. Like I said, tell me why I shouldn't leave you, and you'd better make it good."

The light inside Decker's skull pulsed. I knew I shouldn't attribute human emotions to the equivalent of a sentient lava lamp, but I could have sworn he was thinking it over.

"I'm waiting."

*I will admit I was led astray. Her grandiose plans were hard to deny.*

"Not really convincing me."

*She was to take me with her, show me the glorious works she had performed. To be able to assist her in even the most base incantation would have been glorious.*

"I assume there's a point here," Sally said.

*But then the Freewill goaded her to battle...*

"What?! No I didn't."

"Shhh. Let him finish," Christy said.

*The White Mother, she dropped me. I assumed she would come back. I cried out to her, begging her to do so, to take me — her loyal devotee — with her.*

"But instead, she abandoned you like a rat from a ship," I surmised.

*Betrayed!*

"This is pointless," Christy said, pushing herself up again. "Sally, find me a nice spot to bury him, please."

*I know where's she's going,* he quickly added.

"So do we," I said.

*In the basest sense, fool. But do you know how to get there?*

"Be nice, Harry," Christy warned. "I'm this close to picking up a shovel and making sure nobody finds you again."

*The flow of false life. I know what it is!* He sounded kinda desperate now. Guess he knew she wasn't fucking around.

"I'm listening."

*It is from whence they come, the Jahabich.*

Sally and I shared a glance. "This wouldn't happen to be a glowing pool of orange monster jizz, would it?"

"Hey, I got splashed with that shit," Tom protested.

*You have no idea what it is! But I do.*

"Go on," Christy said.

*You alone among this rabble can appreciate what I am about to tell you. It is The Source.*

"Impossible," she said.

"Wait, what?" I asked.

*All of the remaining ley lines on the planet, they draw from it. It is the last of its kind. It is the well from which all magic flows into this world. It is the last gateway to the realm of spirits.*

"Okay, that sounds pretty heavy," I said. "What does that have to do with Ed?"

*The pure one? I don't know.*

Sally picked up a fist-sized rock, which she began to toss back and forth. "If you're holding out on us..."

*I swear, I don't. But I do know it can be used to imbue life.*

"Those things aren't life!" Christy snapped. "They're abominations. They're..."

*I am not talking about them. They are a perversion of the flow's true power. I am talking about true life. It can be used to restore your lover.*

"Whoa," Tom said. "That's kinda cool."

I glanced at Christy and saw that her eyes were misting over at the thought of it. "Be careful," I warned. "He might just be saying what he wants you to hear."

*That is not all,* Decker continued, *The spell, the one from the cave wall. I have been studying it, divining its meaning. It created the Jahabich and is the key to stopping them.*

"We kind of figured that. But how?"

*The spell is incomplete, but I believe it can also be used to close the doorway to seal The Source. If done, those creatures will never darken your lives again. They...*

Decker went silent as Christy touched the top of his skull with her fingers, producing a yellow flash.

"Wait. He wasn't finished."

"I've heard enough," she said, rising.

"Was he telling the truth?" I asked dubiously.

"I'm not sure. Maybe."

"So what do you think?" Sally asked.

Christy turned to face us. Though I could tell her body was weary beyond belief, the strain of the past few days lining her face, her eyes shone brilliantly, alight as if with some internal flame. Whoa, talk about a chick with crazy eyes.

"You heard him. If what he says is true about the pool..."

"I don't know what the fuck Sally and I saw down there, but it was definitely big and powerful."

Christy nodded. "It would have to be. Harry mentioned closing the door. He was just talking about the Jahabich. But, if he was right, if it is as powerful as we think, then maybe we can do more than that. Maybe we can stop it."

"Stop what?"

"Everything," she said. "Think about it. What happens if we manage to kill Kala?"

"We earn our impossible odds survival badges?"

Sally slugged me in the arm. "The war continues. The vamps and the Feet will keep battling it out until civilization is ground into paste."

"True," I said, forcing myself to be serious, "but there's more. If we team up with Alex and win, then he'll potentially end up with a piece of prime real estate at the center of the Earth, complete with its own built-in hot tub. Probably safe to assume he won't be happy just using it as a vacation home."

"That can't be allowed," Christy replied. "But either way, Sally is right. Kala the White needs to be stopped. There is no question in any part of my soul about that, but ending her evil won't fix anything else. We need to do more."

I began to see what she was getting at. "It might help if a certain party were to, perhaps, meet a gruesome end along with her."

"Alex," Sally said bitterly.

"Yep. He's the one who wanted this war, the one who's been forcing the others to keep it going, and the one who will probably fuck us over if we somehow gain the upper hand down below. As long as he's alive, he won't stop until he gets what he wants."

"What about the rest of your leaders?" Christy asked.

"I got the impression they were pretty happy with the status quo before things went to hell. No way to tell for sure, but I think if Alex were out of the picture, we might have a shot of pulling things back from the edge."

"Hopefully," Sally said. "We'll have to cross that bridge when we come to it. For now, let's worry about killing two assholes with one stone. Oh, make that three. No way does Firebird walk away from this."

I wasn't about to argue with that. I turned back to Christy. "So what do we need to do?"

She smiled grimly. "Surviving will be difficult enough. The White Mother's power is immense. I don't think I need to tell that to either of you."

"Hadn't noticed," I joked.

"If we make it through, though, remember what I said. Magic is just energy. Introduce the right catalyst to an energy source and you can use it. That's what I'm hoping to do. Of course, introduce the wrong thing and..."

"Kaboom?"

"Exactly."

"How big of a boom are we talking about?" I asked, just for argument's sake.

"I honestly don't know. We're talking about perhaps the most potent source of that power anywhere. I have no reference to base anything on."

"Take a guess."

"If I'm lucky, I'll be able to tap into it to create a localized *disturbance*."

"And if you're not?"

"It could collapse the entire cave system, maybe worse."

"Worse?"

Christy merely shrugged.

"Um yeah. But if that happens..." I glanced down at her pregnant stomach.

She looked down at herself for a moment, but when she raised her head again, her eyes were hard. "If events continue the way they are, this world may not be worth living in for any of us, my baby included."

"Harsh," Tom commented.

"Seriously, we've seen what's happening," she said. "Things are getting worse, not better. We need to end this. Gods forgive me, but it's worth the risk."

"What are our chances?" I asked.

Christy spread her hands wide, indicating she had no idea what to expect.

I turned to Sally. "What do you think?"

She fixed me with a glare. "What do I think? I *think* this is insane and you're even crazier for asking me. In fact, I think you are the single most infuriating person I have ever met. You break all the rules, fuck up everything you touch, and drive me batshit constantly."

Okay, then.

"Be that as it may, though," she continued, "I *know* I would face the fires of Hell if you were by my side."

"Which it seems is what we're planning on doing," Tom interjected.

"Thanks for ruining the moment, meatwad." She knocked him over with a flick of her finger.

"I'd do the same," I said, ignoring my roommate.

"Of course you would," she replied with an infuriatingly cocky smile.

"Partners?"

Sally held out her hand to me. "To the end."

"To the end," I repeated, taking it.

"Hey, if you guys are doing the whole hands in the middle thing, count me in."

Christy laughed and picked up her plastic fiancé. She

lifted one of his hands to ours, and then topped us off with her own.

For too long, fate had manipulated us, set us up as pawns in some giant chess game. Whether it was Alex, Turd, Vehron, or now Calibra, there was always someone trying to manipulate us.

Well, maybe now it was finally our turn.

I had no idea what the coming days would hold. There were plans to make, strategies to discuss, and probably a few personal issues to sort out. Regardless, in the end, I'd do everything I could to protect the friends around me, restore the friend who'd fallen, and save the friends who were missing.

And then, when that was done, I'd shove a giant middle finger at the powers that be and let all Hell break loose.

As for what happened after ... screw it. Maybe just this once, I'd let fate decide that.

**THE END**

Sheila will return in:
**Shining Fury** (A Tome of Bill Adventure)

Bill Ryder will return in:
**The Last Coven** (The Tome of Bill - 8)

If you enjoyed this story, I invite you to sign up for my newsletter at www.rickgualtieri.com.

# BONUS CHAPTER
## SHINING FURY

### A Tome of Bill Adventure

"Go away!" he screamed at me.

"I'm so sorry! I didn't mean to. It just happened."

The stench rising off the mulch pile assaulted my nostrils. The acrid smoke made my eyes water. Considering this was all my fault, though, it seemed a small price to pay. Deep down, I knew it could be far worse, that I *deserved* far worse.

After all, I wasn't the one on fire.

All I'd wanted was to drop the charade of my existence, to be myself for a change, and end the impasse between us. I wanted to finally make a move to show that, despite everything, I believed we had a chance. That I, ironically enough, had faith in *us*. I'd tried to tap into the confidence that had made me what I am, the same confidence I was supposed to feel when facing every damned obstacle set before me, of which there were no shortage as of late.

It hadn't worked out quite like I'd planned.

I quickly stepped forward to offer what aid I could. The flames were already dying down, thank goodness, helped by the damp ground upon which he lay. As I reached out, though, a white glow illuminated my outstretched hand, causing me to pull back quickly lest I make things even worse. I gritted my teeth, forcing the power back inside of me, willing it to not strike out again unbidden. At times like this it could be like a snake, struggling to be set free, lashing out at that which it deemed an enemy despite my conscious insistence to the contrary.

"Please, let me make it right," I said more to myself than anyone, but I knew he'd hear me nevertheless. His kind had senses far beyond that of a normal person.

"Leave me alone!"

I couldn't blame him for being angry. Time and again this had happened. We'd come into close contact, some of our encounters closer than others, and the white fire inside of me would lash out.

Each time it had happened in the past, he'd laughed it off, pretended it didn't hurt despite the painful obviousness of it. I'd always known, though, that eventually even he would reach his limit. That the jokes would end and, with them, whatever he'd felt toward me. I'd hoped – prayed, even – that I would find the control I needed before that happened.

I'd done it before, so I knew it was possible, but that had been before Remington.

A growl, disturbingly inhuman in pitch, escaped from him, reminding me that he'd been affected by that incident, too, in many ways worse than I had. I didn't know if the sound he made now was due to pain or fury, but it didn't matter. He needed my help.

I reached down and grabbed hold of his still-smoking shoulder to turn him over. I needed to know he was all right, and he needed to know how sorry I was.

Under different circumstances, that first concern

wouldn't be a question – his kind healed at an exaggerated pace. Anything short of a fatal wound would be gone in minutes. There were exceptions, though, and I was one of them.

I'd been told my power was a gift, the blessing of light, God's way of balancing the scales against the darkness. I never really bought into that, despite how often such dogma was repeated. There was no denying, however, that the white hot fury inside me was capable of consuming his kind whole. Considering the vast majority of the undead hated me with a passion – wouldn't have hesitated to kill me if given the opportunity – this wasn't necessarily a bad thing. Most that I'd met had been little more than monsters given human form anyway; wolves in sheep's clothing.

He was different, though. He was kind where they were cruel, self-deprecating where they were arrogant. He'd told me he didn't want to hurt anyone, and I believed him. That he was one of them, a vampire, wasn't his fault. He hadn't asked to be turned, to be dragged into their world. Despite our powers being polar opposites, we had that much in common. I hadn't asked for any of this either.

I pushed that thought away, although a bitter aftertaste remained as always. A part of me blamed him for that, and I hated that part of me for doing so. It was stupid and selfish of me to dwell upon it now, especially when I'd just hurt the man I...

His eyes opened – inhuman black orbs that seemed to contain no trace of the gentle soul within. I knew better, though.

"It's okay, it's me." I dropped to one knee by his side. "I won't hurt you again."

The promise was a lie. I had no way of knowing if I might lose control of the surging torrent of power inside of me. No matter how much I tried, it was almost as if it had a life all its own at times.

He seemed to sense the untruth in my words, but where I expected scorn and rejection, he instead sprung from the ground and tackled me with savage strength. His fingernails became talons that dug into my arms, pinning me in place. He opened his mouth, revealing his fangs.

With a snarl, Bill Ryder – a man I called friend and had hoped to call more – was upon me, forcing my head to the side and digging his teeth into my neck.

I wanted to lash out, to call upon the power within me. It was what the Templar had trained me to do, told me was my destiny – to destroy the Night Spawn and, in doing so, save the world.

But I instead forced it back down, took control of it at last, even as the life blood flowed from my wounds. This was what I had brought upon myself.

It was what I deserved.

◄———— ◄◄◄ ————►

**Shining Fury**
Available in ebook, paperback, and audio.

# AUTHOR'S NOTE

I sit here typing this as the last of the leaves are falling off the trees outside my office window. Mind you, most of those leaves are now sitting atop my pool cover. Note to self: clean that crap out before it freezes solid.

Anyway, dear reader, the end is near. You've just finished the penultimate book in this chapter of The Tome of Bill — what started as little more than the goofy exploits of a dorky vampire trying to survive in the world of the undead and which is now the goofy exploits of a dorky vampire trying to stave off the apocalypse. It's been quite the journey and now he stands at the precipice of either victory or an eternity of darkness.

I sincerely hope this series has been an enjoyable experience for you. I know it has for me. This story in particular was quite the surprise. Some tales practically write themselves, while others fight the author kicking and screaming all the way. This was one of those latter efforts on many different levels, all the way to me having to step away from the story for several weeks after feeling I was spinning my wheels on multiple difficult chapters.

I never gave up, though, and I'm glad I didn't because after going back and reading the complete story for the first time I found myself smiling. Was it perfect? Hell no. My first drafts are a lot of things, but perfect isn't one of them. However, the foundation had been laid for this roller coaster of a tale and I, for one, found it to be a heck of a ride. I hope you did too.

The ride isn't over yet, though. Bill Ryder still has a ways to go before his story is finished. We've gone through twists, turns, hills, valleys, and even a few loops and it's all leading up to the big showdown. I've brought you this far, I hope you'll stick with me for the rest.

Until then...

**Rick G.**

# ABOUT THE AUTHOR

Rick Gualtieri lives alone in central New Jersey with only his wife, three kids, and countless pets to both keep him company and constantly plot against him. When he's not busy monkey-clicking words, he can typically be found jealously guarding his collection of vintage Transformers from all who would seek to defile them.

*Defilers beware!*

Also by Rick Gualtieri
**THE TOME OF BILL**
*Bill the Vampire*
*Scary Dead Things*
*The Mourning Woods*
*Holier Than Thou*
*Sunset Strip*
*Goddamned Freaky Monsters*
*Half A Prayer*
*The Wicked Dead*
*Shining Fury*
*The Last Coven*
**BILL OF THE DEAD SAGA**
*Strange Days*
*Everyday Horrors*
*Carnage À Trois*
*The Liching Hour*

**FALSE ICONS**
*Second String Savior*
*Wannabe Wizard*
*Halfhearted Hunter*
*Deviant Dark Dryads*

**HIGH MOON**
*The Girl Who Punches Werewolves*
*The Girl Who Fights Witches*
*The Girl Who Hunts Fairies*
*The Girl Who Defies Fate*